And All of Us Were Actors

A Century of Light and Shadow

By Gustavo Gac-Artigas

Translated by Andrea G. Labinger

Ediciones Nuevo Espacio

And All of Us Were Actors: A Century of Light and Shadow
Gustavo Gac-Artigas
© 2017
English Edition, March 2017
Translated by Andrea G. Labinger
Paperback:
ISBN: 1-93087972-5
ISBN: 978-1-9308-7972-0
E-Book:
ISBN: 1-93087973-3
ISBN: 978-1-9308-7973-7

Y todos éramos actores, un siglo de luz y sombra
Gustavo Gac-Artigas
© 2015
Spanish Edition, December 2015
ISBN: 1-930879-64-4
        978-1-9308-7964-5
ISBN: 1-930879-63-6
        978-1-9308-7963-8

www.editorial-ene.com

Cover Picture: Las Cruces, Chile
Ediciones Nuevo Espacio

For information about permission to reproduce selections from this book you may write to:
academicpressene@gmail.com

Printed in the United States of America

For Priscilla,

in whose eyes I was shipwrecked.

For our children,

Melina and Alejandro,

whose smiles led me back to shore.

G. G-A

At the peak of the mountain, at the edge
of the abyss,
my mind stripped of all adornment,
I hold out my arms to embrace you,
Oh, Bella entre las Bellas!
first curve of the spiral
of life and death.

I, the naked
the actor
the witness.

I,
the wound
the balm
he who dies to give life.

I,
I invoke Changó and Yemayá,
I invoke the savage wind,
I invoke the calm before the storm,
I invoke the void before the word,
I invoke love to drive away fear,
I invoke the stone and the sand.

I,
I invoke all of you
to guide me on this journey.

And you, spectator,
I invoke you, too.

In the spiral of death,
fall and die with me,
brother.

In the spiral of life,
rise up brother, be born with me.

And, treading the final step,
disappear along with me,
brother,
for in this story
there are no spectators,
only actors.

O gods,
have mercy on me,
give me the strength I need
to go up in flames
and be reborn in the word!

Portrait of a Teenage Actor

She prays now, she says, that I may learn in
my own life and away from home and friends
what the heart is and what it feels.
Amen.
So be it. Welcome, O life, I go to encounter
for the millionth time the reality of experience
and to forge in the smithy of my soul the
uncreated conscience of my race.

James Joyce

I. Of how our hero scrambled down from the rock to plunge into turbulent waters and begin his voyage

The first time I stepped onto a stage I was three years and three months old. With great difficulty I managed to clamber up and conquer the peak of a rock in order to look over the first wall in my life, the one that defined my universe and the garden of my parents' house.

I was able to see the roads that led to the *cordillera* as they faded into the distance; looking all around, I was able to see, behind me, the swimming pool where soon I would nearly drown.

Head down, exhaling the last bubbles that gleefully rose to the surface to announce my death, I faced my spirals for the first time: the spiral of life and that of death. Between them, the maelstrom, the infinite whirlpool in which my story would unfold.

A hand snatched me by the seat of the pants and brought me back to face my destiny.

I had returned to my lookout in an attempt to get over the wall, if not with my body, then with my mind, when a cold, bony hand, covered in wrinkles and age spots, abruptly yanked me down from the stage, tossing me into the shadows. The talons of this bird of prey showed me that my life would play out on my stairways and that mounting a single step was not the same as ascending, much less escaping my destiny.

I, the combatant, stumbled through the garden, grabbed a broomstick, walked over to the talons' owner, and, with all my strength, smacked my great-grandma María in the head. I didn't manage to free myself from the wall or the obstacle – she was still alive! Nearly 100 years old, and she was still alive!

That was the first battle I ever lost.

From that point on, my life would develop in a labyrinth filled with paths and doubts, on the one hand trying to eliminate obstacles while knowing I didn't have the power to do so, and on the other, hurtling myself between the two spirals, knowing there was no way out.

I leaped over my first wall.

And so it was that I climbed down the first step, passed through the doors that led me back into the world, and once again ran freely through the forests of my childhood, the forests of my imagination, which, when converted into pulp, gave me the pages on which to write my last book, the first one, and thereby abandon the last of my stages, my shelters.

On the slopes of Ñielol Hill in Temuco, on the border, the last outpost of civilization, defensive walls, and gateway to the un-known, I learned to run along the ground, keeping my balance on the edge of a path made of air, above pine trees that led to the road of Aguas Santas, the one that flowed, unfettered, freely, among vines and hundred-year-old araucarias.

It was the hill that taught me to discover life behind the false, but beautiful, cardboard scenery, to understand the language of birds and of insects, to appreciate the caresses of hairy spiders on my skin, to practice my lines in an attempt to draw tears from the sacred *coligüe* plant, the moon beetle, and the *madre de la serpiente* beetle, and to make the *dihüeñes,* those parasitical mushrooms, sing as they made love to the *maqui* plants.

I told them stories of frustrated loves, my own; whenever they looked sad, I invented the image of La Bella entre las Bellas, the beauty among beauties; I told them of her hips, her eyes, her infinite constellations, and the spiders danced for joy. I told them of the petals that sprang from her fingertips, and the moon beetle, the loveliest one, with its rainbow of colors, grew pale with envy.

When night fell, each of them returned alone to their caves, awaiting another speech that would draw them back to the surface to dream, or perhaps bury them forever in the depths of the *cordillera* and of oblivion.

I slid along the slopes, descended along secret pathways, began my life on the stairways.

In the distance, the *coligües* shook their hips, saying: Don't forget the way we move.

"Or the beauty of the rainbow," added the moon beetle coquettishly, "or the pleasure our bodies offer as they pass over the bodies of your characters and your mind" – the hairy spiders piped up, adding, "Remember, only pleasure brings pleasure."

15

Only the *dihüeñes* remained silent; they were busy making love to the *maqui* plants.

The ring of the *cordillera* disappeared behind me. I descended another step and found myself before my audience and my destiny. Years later I would see my spiders again at an art cinema in Paris. They smiled at me from the screen.

"Pleasure, do you remember?"

I squeezed the hand of La Bella entre las Bellas.

"I remember."

I placed my other hand on her sex to block the entrance to the cave: you never can tell with spiders.

II. Of how he learned to confront loneliness

I became a militant because I was a lover: because I was a lover and because I'm terrified of being alone. The image of the hairy spider crawling back into its cave, all alone and trembling over the *coligües'* tears, pursued me.

I got involved in it as one gets involved in a sect, not out of conviction, since the sect is unknown and the unknown attracts us, nor out of ambition or the desire for power.

Some powers are different: the theatrical director's is the power to transform, the power to listen, to understand, to propose and be proposed to, the power to decide in a single moment what will work and what won't, the power to be wrong and to rise and be cremated in the bonfire of the sorcerers.

The other power is that of humiliating, of judging, the power over life and death, the power to decide who can or cannot repeat the dogma, kneel down, conceal his thoughts so as to be accepted and break through the loneliness, and, once admitted, become part of the sect. Absolute power, the even more awful power of expelling you from the sect, of erasing you from history, of throwing you over the wall to the other side and sending you to travel through eternity, directionless and alone.

Thank you, almighty ones!

Those were times of dreaming, of believing, times when you could hear the pitiless cry of empty stomachs, their music slipping in between the violin strings, the rage and impotence of parents trapped between the strings of a double bass, the explosion of repressed anger that made the kettledrums roar.

Those were times when the orchestra conductor rescued even the smallest pain.

They were times when a new, wild, chaotic symphony arose from the audience, escaped from the score, and took over the stage.

I got involved in it through all of the above and none of the above.

I got involved in it because I was a lover, a flirt, because it was chic, fashionable, to adorn my skinny, impoverished student's body with an aura of heroism at a time when social activism was accompanied by heroism.

It was my way of fighting loneliness; the alternative would have been to accept it, but unlike my spiders, I am a coward.

The aura and the accompanying romantic image conveyed by a slender body and an incipient beard managed to cover up my fear of rejection, the fear that frightened the beauties away.

It worked: the beauties who had never noticed him stopped for a moment to take a look at him, fascinated by his sad smile and imagining it was the key to an unknown universe filled with unknown adventures and pleasures, not knowing that those adventures and pleasures were unknown to him as well, and that his new world and conscience would come later, only when his hunger became unbearable.

It works still, albeit without the slenderness or the sect, but always bearing my loneliness on my back; and the beauties approach to break through that loneliness, unaware that they will tumble into the abyss of a shared solitude.

From that moment on, he devoted himself to wandering through history. He had the dubious fortune of standing where no one should ever have been, a watchful observer of reality, recording stories to be told after his death, naïvely thinking he was a part of history without realizing that history had passed over him without giving him a second glance.

I wandered through history, thinking I belonged; she passed over me in order to forget me, to make me disappear from history, aided by the sorcerers of the sect. History taught me that in order to possess her you have to agree to disappear. The alternative? The alternative is to repeat other people's history without ever possessing her.

Those who know say that only he who possesses her will succeed in bringing her onto stage, throbbing; he who controls her by force brings a corpse.

Before my eyes, the Cau Cau, Las Cruces and Valdivia rivers brutally spread their legs, giving birth to Isla Teja; from the juncture of their labia there emerged a wooden staircase that expelled students into the meadow, those who dared defy the waters to be the first to reach the first beauty.

I got in line.

Everything about her tempted me to press her in my arms and protect her: fragile, her black hair tossed by the wind – a narrow ribbon clearing her forehead – her childlike body – spindly, sparrow legs – her smile lighting up her face and the meadows. No makeup: it would have been a crime to cover up her face.

A goddess emerging from the waters, a female conceived among the railroad ties, she emitted perfumes of desire and scented fliers, inviting us to a meeting of the Communist Youth.

I accepted the invitation.

"You became a militant for her sake, for her, the first woman to succumb to the web of your aura, the woman desired by all and truly possessed by none; for her sake you set out for the World Youth Festival in Bulgaria armed with a plane ticket and two visas: the official one and the unofficial one, the kind that isn't examined in airports. You set out thinking she would go with you, she, the one who succumbed to the poet's sad verses and gave him her seat on that journey. Your journey."

"I have to learn to write poetry," I said to myself.

"It would have been wiser if you had learned how to operate underground. The guy who stamped your unofficial visa was from military intelligence, as Lieutenant Medina would tell you years later in the Rancagua jail, brandishing a well-used rubber stamp with refined cruelty and a triumphant air.

One week earlier I had traveled to Santiago, leaving behind the turbulent waters surrounding Isla Teja, and she was with me. When we arrived at the Hotel España, on the corner of Avenida Brasil and La Alameda, the clerk at the reception desk asked sardonically, "A room with a double bed, right?"

To punish the faithlessness of someone who had no reason to be faithful to me, I said, "No, two rooms."

And that night I was left alone with my desire, alone and filled with desire, with that unpleasant, reheated odor that always accompanied me in the sad rooms of exile, from Stockholm to Paris.

"To teach her a lesson," I said with a huff.

"No, 'huff' isn't the right word. And it's "in," not "with.""

III. Of how he was transformed from spectator to actor and found his vocation

When we arrived in Paris, it was the month of May, and the year was 1968.

On the Morris columns, a poster: *Les Misérables*, and a drawing of Gavroche waving a flag over a barricade. Escaping from the posters, a forest of banners, thousands of Gavroches picking up the lovely cobblestones of the Latin Quarter streets in order to restore to them a more noble function than being trampled on by the boots of uniformed soldiers, because there's nothing lovelier and more noble for a cobblestone than to feel, through a pair of delicate sandals, the caress of the beautiful coeds who traverse the neighborhood in search of knowledge.

Thanks to the democratic spirit that roused the students, the flagstones could choose either to be a barricade or to be hurled at the helmets and shields of the Republican Guard, the CERES. The liveliest cobblestones exercised both functions, first as a barricade, though not for long; more like those brief Cervantes *entremeses*, only to fly afterward over the roofs of Paris, falling like arrows upon the police squadron.

The Latin Quarter was burning; my heart was aflame. They handed me a cobblestone, I threw it. I went from being a spectator to being an actor. I had found my vocation.

The poet threw a verse; his aim was true. He knocked down a CERES guard. I missed my mark and found my destiny.

We turned our backs on the Jardins de Luxembourg, descended the steps of La Sorbonne, crossed both arms of the Seine that caressed the Île de la Cité, and continued along Boulevard de Sebastopol. As we passed by Les Halles, we were bathed in the aroma of onion soup. We turned left on Rue Saint Denis, where those girls with aching souls can be found, leaving them alone to sell their bodies along the pavement. Singing, we headed for the newspaper *L'Humanité*, the French Communist Party daily, to bring them the good tidings, *"Nous sommes un groupuscule."* I had no idea what it meant, but I was sure it was the right password: there are texts and contexts that transcend language. Besides, we were a microgroup of hundreds of thousands.

I was there and I can prove it. If you look at photos of the period, you'll see on the corner, in front of Théâtre Rex, amid the throng, five little blank spaces. Four of them belong to *The Three Musketeers*, the film they were showing. The fifth and smallest, the spare wheel — that's me. It was the first time that history had erased us from history: them, for showing the wrong play (you don't get down off the stage with impunity), me, because it was my destiny.

When we arrived at the Opéra, we abandoned the *groupuscule*, or maybe the *groupuscule* abandoned us, headed for the Comédie Française, greeted Molière before dumping him, guided by the unmistakable fragrance of . . .

"La Bella."

"No, onion soup."

Dawn was breaking.

The automobile workers – Renault, Citröen, Peugeot – turned off their machines and joined the students; the Opéra displayed a new décor: an enormous red banner; theaters changed their official programs; stages refused to follow the rules. Everything was thrown open for discussion.

Prohibiting is prohibited – a slogan that marked a break with the establishment and the birth of a new art.

De Gaulle had moved the government to the provinces. Paris was burning "They're going to take over," shouted *les précieuses ridicules*. Tartuffe rubbed his hands together; Danton and Robespierre walked along Rue Saint Antoine; the Bastille prepared to fling open the doors of its cells. Things had gotten red hot: the military was growing uneasy; the barracks were in turmoil. If Paris was worth a Mass, democracy was worth a retreat, people said to one another in Place Colonel Fabien, site of the building designed by Niemeyer to house the central committee of the French Communist Party.

The workers returned to the factories, De Gaulle to Paris, and Daniel Cohn-Bendit, known to all as Danny the Red, was expelled from the country on De Gaulle's orders.

They called for elections.

Whistling *La Marseillaise*, we headed for the Gare de l'Est to catch the Orient Express. Behind us lay the lovely, uncobblestoned streets of Paris. We were on our way to Bulgaria.

The smoke from the locomotives surrounded the passengers, those who were coming, those who were going, those in transit, those who had chosen the wrong era to travel, those who belonged to May of 1968.

An old, faded photo shows a happy group of three at the station: the reporter from the newspaper *El Siglo*, the Chilean Communist Party daily, the poet (that wretch had no doubt slipped into La Bella's room), and me: short, neatly combed hair, in a tie and a yellow suede jacket, a gift from my father, a man of experience who told me, "Wear it, it's brought me luck. It helps hide loneliness."

For the first time, I saw reflected in his big eyes the portrait of a woman who wasn't my mother. And I was right: the poet had slipped into La Bella's room.

Behind us lay Paris, though Paris never lies behind. Perhaps, without being the most important thing about it — for me, it was — Paris is shaped like a snail: those were my spirals.

Behind me, on Isla Teja, was La Bella, though a beauty, if truly beautiful, never remains behind.

"I wanted just one room, and the size of the bed didn't matter," her memory whispered in my ear from afar.

When I returned, I answered her with my thoughts.

I saw her again seven years later, in Paris, at a huge party that would change my life forever.

When we recognized one another, we approached each other slowly to offer the long-postponed embrace, and she whispered in my ear, "I got El Guatón Romo," and that was enough for me to imagine the wounds that crossed her abused body, while my tears attempted to heal them.

That night we went to a little hotel in Rue des Écoles, and when we asked for a room we smiled at the memories. "Just one, and the bed doesn't matter," she said to me sweetly. "I can't yet."

We spent a sleepless night recounting our loneliness.

When we arrived in Rome, they shooed us off the train. We'd taken the wrong one: ours was part of a different story.

"Perhaps that was what raised your consciousness. Not having taken the wrong train, but rather moving from second to third class. Besides, you'd left your tie on the Orient Express, and that makes a difference."

After three days of traveling, they were greeted by a forest of red banners, revolutionary songs from around the world, blending their notes in Russian, in Italian, in Spanish, in French, and in Vietnamese, creating an enormous anthem of hope.

When we left the station, our arms filled with embraces and bouquets of red carnations, we were blinded by the brilliance of the golden cupolas of the Bulgarian capital's churches.

Paris had resumed its normal programming and the *les misérables* had been removed from the posters.

Sofia opened her heart to them and lit the way with her golden cupolas. And yet he had the feeling it was all part of some shopworn, cheap, and repetitious scenery, and that the libretto would soon show its flaws. It wasn't until many years later that he realized the gold wasn't really gold: the gold had been stolen many years before and the cheap paint had flaked off.

While the crowd plunged into the forest of banners and dreams, for the first time I felt uncomfortable without knowing why, but I quickly cast off all negative thoughts. To tell the truth, it's always easier to plunge into a forest of banners and the echo of drums than to spoil the party.

Furtively I tried to match my steps to the marchers' rhythm. Luckily I've got no rhythm.

IV. Of what happened to him when he faced the sorcerers of the sect

"Society is divided into two classes," said Nikitin's manual. "The problem arises when one doesn't know which class one belongs to because both classes are based on the same interests."

I know, everyone is quite aware of the class they belong to, or else they hide by identifying with the one that suits them best, almost like the incipient beard that lends you a romantic air that makes the beauties fall for you, a beard that can be shaved off in a flash after plucking the desired fruit.

Ideology is pretty much like trains, the Orient Express and its extravagant *luxe*, or the humble, ordinary train that stops at every station with its precious, sad cargo of dispossessed: dispossessed of goods, but not of hopes, real hopes, not those dreams of pyrrhic victories when the hour of lies arrived at the huge, dusty halls stretching from Stockholm to Paris, from Québec to West Berlin, or the shiny, golden, imperial halls stretching from Moscow to Sofia.

Both kinds of trains ran on steel tracks to avoid being derailed, but in both of them there were first class, as well as third class, cars.

"To La Piojera, the flea-bag neighborhood," they said, despite the fact that in the flyer I was given in Valdivia it said "hotel." The only thing they hadn't clarified was whether it was a room with a double bed, as I had requested when I still thought La Bella would come with me.

It didn't matter to him: quite the contrary, he made himself comfortable in the narrow bed, got used to the narrow balcony, and especially to the bubbly commotion that drifted upstairs every night when the flea-bag neighborhood was transformed into a cosmopolitan, fraternal, and collective brothel.

People were fucking in French, in Italian (the noisiest), in Vietnamese (sweeter, as if it was the last act of love before being embraced by napalm), in Russian, or in Polish. The most boring fucks, in Chilean, were the most exaggerated, as if they were preparing for the hour of lies.

But first, that same night, the first one we spent in La Piojera, the charming neighborhood, not the lively restaurant in Santiago, they brought us together to listen to the head of the delegation, a student leader from the State Technical University. At his side, his secretary, Anita, not to be confused with Martita, the secretary of the Communist Youth organization, the glorious JJCC, gloriously beautiful Martita, kind Martita, always ready to show off those lovely, long legs sticking out of her tight miniskirt.

A beauty, that Martita, the first Bella entre las Bellas, but not as beautiful as my Bella, a beauty who years later would be reincarnated in yet another beauty, this time a student leader who would sadly be torn between her lively, independent way of speaking, her hair floating in the wind at the podium, and the rigid, aging patriarchs who wanted to starch her hair and her ideas and wizen her speeches by offering to exchange her bravery for a place in the first-class car.

But let's not get ahead of ourselves in the story. I might make a mistake, but not get ahead of myself – now *that's* something really unforgivable, and yes, she did hop aboard some first-class cars. I tried to justify it: her beauty was fading.

That night, as I was saying, the first one, they read us the commandments.

"You were beginning to learn: every sect has its tracks and its own rules. And the nights aren't the same, either. It depends on whether you belong to the first class or the third."

In brief, clipped words, they explained to us that the enemy was infiltrating, that they had even introduced a clandestine printing press to produce false documents about the socialist reality, that the Chilean guy they had seen us talking to, a scholarship student from Poland, the land of Grotowski – the maestro of the Poor Theater – a student who had enjoyed the beneficence of the system thanks to the fact that his father, a miner, was a brave militant, lacked his father's strength, had allowed himself to become corrupted, and almost certainly had been expressing ideas that could contribute to our eternal enemies' campaign, since he was unable to explain where he'd gotten the fifty-dollar bill that he'd tried to exchange for three times its value in Bulgarian levas on the black market. They had consulted with the comrade in charge in Poland, they said, and, in fact, the Chilean had dangerous ideas about the development of democracy and individual liberties, ideas that neglected to keep in mind the fundamental principle, the collective interest over the individual. Out of respect for his father's proletarian origin, his scholarship wasn't revoked, but he was sent back to Poland under guard, without even being afforded the possibility of self-criticism before us. He had "promised to send it in writing" so that the comrade secretary of the comrade in charge could read it to us aloud.

I thought to myself: the truck I'd noticed at one point (the reflection of the golden rooftops hadn't blinded me, as I'd believed), filled with men and women who weren't singing or laughing, weren't carrying banners like the others and were escorted by two guards from the Narodnia Militzia – the Bulgarian police – were surely corrupt and infiltrators. Otherwise how could one explain the sadness in their eyes?

For the first time he looked around and not behind the set, with the terrible and annoying sensation that he was deliberately looking at the faded theater curtain to avoid seeing reality.

One week later, a dejected crowd left Sofia amid oaths of eternal love and promises to reconnect in battle or in bed; the songs coming through the loudspeakers sounded tired, and a horde of plump women, their heads covered with gray kerchiefs, began to sweep the streets littered with condoms and memories.

The committee, with the approval of the Komité, to reward me for not asking questions, deemed me worthy of being shown another jewel of the system, and this time, with a reduced delegation – possibly harder to contaminate, or apparently easier to manipulate – they sent me off to Czechoslovakia. In beautiful Prague a secretary general was attempting to reform the regime from within.

"The difference from Sofia was that in this case, happiness came from those on the inside, and you people simply joined in; evidently you had forgotten about *nous sommes un groupuscule,* and, don't forget, you hadn't even passed through the halls of Berlin, and don't ask which one. Remember that the Committee keeps a close eye on things and that your father's not a worker."

This time, without being among the first class crowd, I was treated as though I were. Apparently Alexander Dubcek had more confidence in those in third class than those in first. He welcomed us with a hotel and all, but the most important part could be found in the pubs bursting with young people who never stopped talking, as if someone had greased their tongues.

The joyous atmosphere was contagious: even the reporter from *El Siglo* managed to flex his fingers and change his style; the poet forgot to put on his living dead face, which had brought him such great results in Chile; and I explored the Black Light Theater to see what was backstage. It concealed nothing: it was a mixture of cinema and theater that allowed movie characters to leap up

onto the stage before my astonished eyes, transformed into actors. It was as if life had been reborn, like being assaulted by life. It
was ideas in motion, barriers destroyed. It was the dream that allowed me to run free and uncensored along the paths of my mind;
it was the pleasure that they – unsuccessfully – wanted to take
away from me.

"That was why, every time you opened your mouth, you
ended up sitting on the glass shard-covered crate, while your
stern-faced judges pressured you, some to make a self-criticism,
others to give the names of your *compañeros*. How close one
group was to the other!"

To tell the truth, as people say, when those groups are in
power they differ only in the color of their shirts or uniforms; in both
of them the need to cling to power, to reproduce, to destroy the
enemy, is the same. With more or less uniformity, they march to
the same drumbeat.

I know, you can't compare them: in one case you have the
possibility of being the hangman, without realizing it, to perform a
balancing act in the car of the speeding train, moving from third
class to first.

In the other case you'll always be the guy dangling from the
rope.

If you're lucky, in both cases you'll be the victim.

And when the bars come down, both uniforms turn olive
green.

Lovely, the avenue along which the three escapees from

the old photo of the Gare de l'Est directed their steps toward the castle that overlooks Prague: wide, pleasant, luminous, open to the grand avenue. As they crossed the bridge, the water sang love songs, not marches, and I even felt like forgiving that son-of-a-bitch poet for using the ticket that wasn't meant for him. But, of course, no matter how beautiful Prague – and the movement – might be, it wasn't enough.

Before heading for the palace we wandered through the little district where Calle Neruda can be found. In his honor, the reporter recited "Poem 20," though if it was in homage to the Czech writer or the Chilean one, we'll never know. The poet muttered: Rise up, brother, be born with me . . . and I declaimed: I like it when you're silent . . . a poem I adored, but never practiced with my *compañeros* despite knowing what doing that implied. We crossed Golden Lane, the street of the alchemists, where Kafka's house is, a narrow, little cobblestone lane with charming, brightly colored houses no more than two stories high, still redolent of the chemical mixtures with which they sought, not the philosopher's stone, but gold, the gold they never found, but which scintillated around its walls at nightfall by the light of the lanterns and the moon.

Near the bridge, in a little square, balancing precariously atop a column was a small tank, the first Russian tank to enter Prague to liberate it from the brown plague on September 21, 1944.

"The first, and, we hope, the last," said the official translator, only to point out later, with an imperious gesture, a window of the palace that towers over the lovely Prague, adding, "Through this window we tossed the representatives of the Hapsburgs and any other invaders that tried to impose a king, emperor, or other type of government on us, and if another Thirty Years' War becomes necessary, we will fight for thirty years more."

One week later Alexander Dubcek received us; strangely, the joy in the streets hadn't crossed the threshold of the beautiful wooden door. Standing beside him was the bold defenestrator himself, and heading our reduced delegation, a student leader of the Pedagogical Institute, who years later would stray from the path – "A part of life," as Volodia would say, adding *sotto voce,* "and a literary necessity."

Kind Volodia, a kind writer, a kind fan of good movies and long conversations on Parisian nights, so kind of him to wait till the day he died for his kindness to be repaid. And yet, his son – who wasn't really his son – the Party's best-kept secret – changed his surname to that of his real father, a well-known choreographer and habitué of first-class cars, and didn't show up at his putative father's deathbed, let alone accompany the tears and floral offerings that saw Volodia off at the main cemetery. It seems he was lied to before the advent of the hour of lies.

But that morning, the 19th of August of 1968, fifty years after the declaration of the independence of the Republic of Czechoslovakia, a day when people crowded St. Wenceslas' Square, laughing, singing, weeping with joy for the first time, Dubcek explained to us in a passionate speech how he wanted to prove to the world that under socialism one could be free and smile and build one's own destiny, that socialism could wear a human face, and that criticism was not a sin and was permissible, and that one could be just as democratic – or more so – under socialism than in the democracies on the other side; that the citizenry must have the right to free assembly, to express itself without fear, and to enjoy freedom of thought, "new rights added to those already guaranteed by our system, like social welfare, the protection of life, and the right to good health."

And looking us directly in the eye, he added, "The right to elect one's governors freely and change them if necessary, for if not, confidence in our institutions and in the Party is lost . . ."

And . . . before he could go on, an ex-*compañero* and friend, who still hadn't strayed from the path, interrupted him in a firm voice, the reflection of firm convictions:

"What liberty and what rights is our *compañero* talking about? I feel like I'm listening to the enemy's speech, a capitalist speech disguised as social democracy. You forget – and here the *compañero* disappeared from that story in order to discuss past history – that true democracy is that which is under the mandate of the dictatorship of the proletariat, and any deviation is a crime against the people, and you know what happens to the enemies of the people," he concluded, smiling to cover up the threat.

The night of August 20, 1968 was approaching: the dream had lasted seven months and two weeks. The first liberation tanks were nearing the border. They emerged from the forests surrounding Potsdam (370 km. from the heart of Prague), from Rumania (530 km. from the heart of Prague), from Poland (394 km. from the heart of Prague), and from Hungary (444 km. from the heart of

Prague): gray, serious – I can't imagine a smiling piece of war machinery – intimidating, but with a red star that symbolized hope.

At least that's what I was told.

The tanks that emerged from their hiding place in the GDR crossed over near the hospitals where 50,000 patients had been used as guinea pigs by western pharmacies, with Ulbricht's permission and Honecker's blessing, to test new, experimental drugs, prepaying $750,000 for each of the approximately 600 experiments carried out on a large scale. The moans of the sick and of consciences were muffled by the clamor of the tanks as they crossed the bridges, some of them built by political prisoners, the same ones who worked as cheap labor for western furniture factories in order to be re-educated, in order to learn what it means to work for capitalism. They also used Cuban political prisoners, but not for long.

"Whew, what a relief!"

The hallucinations of the poor alcoholics treated with those drugs went from a dream of love with La Bella to the march of a column of tanks which, flaunting the red star of hope, would squash that dream, a hallucination so apparently real that they swore by what was most holy that it was true. And although they reported what had happened – they were on their way to Prague and they were Russians, they stubbornly repeated – no one believed them.

"Please," repeated the little drunk, "don't be confused. It has nothing to do with other experiments or other patients under other circumstances. Those came from Joseph, the Angel of Death."

The multinationals respected the norms that govern these types of experiments.

"Whew, what a relief!"

Of the experiments, not of the individuals.

"Ooh, how sad!"

But I didn't know it.

"Whew, what a relief!"

Maybe that explains the walls or the iron curtain: they're not to prevent enemies from attacking, they're to hide secrets, so that people can say:

"I didn't know," and so we can all look the other way.

"Ooh, my stiff neck!"

I wonder what they would think, those who waited for them, armed with hope, clutching flowers in their hands instead of rifles, in sad Wenceslas Square, and what might have happened to those who were on their way to their re-education camps in Sofia, far from the sea of banners and the sound of the loudspeakers.

I left Paris, hounded by headlines that told of the invasion of Prague. In the photos I fruitlessly searched for the faces of student friends but didn't find them, perhaps because a smiling face is so different from a frightened one, an expression of hope is so different from an expression of disappointment; perhaps because a face that reflects its belief in a more beautiful future – no matter how uncertain or unknown – is different from one that reflects the darkness of the future that awaits it; perhaps because an uncensored face is so different from a censored one.

The camera roll is the same; what's different is the film a person shows himself and sometimes, sometimes doesn't want to look at, for fear of recognizing himself in the future.

When I returned to Santiago I went straight to the central station and took the first train to Valdivia in order to meet up with La Bella again before that damn poet showed up.

It wasn't the Orient Express; it was an ordinary train, but the smell of coal, the black smoke that clung to the collars of starched shirts, was the same. The old train crossed chasms on bridges that trembled as it passed, just as the earth trembles in southern Chile. It crossed wild jungles where the occasional white *copihue* flower, a *madre de la culebra* beetle, or a moon beetle would appear, and before my hungry eyes a willow basket full of *tortas curicanas,* delicacies filled with *dulce de leche*, with *alcayota* squash and walnuts, pastries that, due to my situation as a poor student, used up all my money to buy a single one, not the biggest, but the smallest and most dried out, wishing it were bursting with juicy, delicious filling, waiting to surrender to me.

"Two rooms, and with single beds," the pastry next to it said snidely.

Surreptitiously I mashed it with my middle finger so no one else would buy it, so it would dry up out of spite, so that . . . and a sigh of hunger and memories escaped me as I continued on my journey to meet my destiny.

His car left the main route in Antilhue and he took a detour to Valdivia while the main section of the train faded in the distance, on its way to the lost time of Puerto Montt. He never suspected that the train's conductor could be the poet's father. That was why the 620 roared, throwing off columns of black and white smoke in its wake as the bridges creaked in fear, supporting the third class cars over the turbulent rivers that separated him from La Bella. That was why the conductor stopped the locomotive at the entrance to the Valdivia station without pulling into it as was his custom.

So that he wouldn't penetrate history, or La Bella, either. Words do not surrender so easily.

A gray cloud shrouded the landscape and the dark thunderclouds told him that he was on his way to meet his destiny, but he hadn't yet learned to distinguish grayness from seriousness in the sadness of faces, in the gray cloak that clouded his thoughts, in the grayness of the fear in people's eyes at the horror of being spied on, in the grayish-brown mantle that smothered men's dreams.

He did not yet know that the grayish-brown mantle was woven on both sides, in decay and in construction, and the Old Man and the New Man had crossed paths in a no-man's-land, and he couldn't quite understand at which curve in the road they had taken the wrong turn, how they'd come to walk hand in hand on their way to our destruction. And he never found out if it was necessary to disappear in order to be reborn in the arms of others who were also stripped from history.

40

What goes away, what remains, what is discarded, what is recoverable, what makes me tremble, what makes me survive, what validates me in my queries.

But how distant was the hour of lies and of having to skirt around the interrogations, on the one hand, and indiscreet ears, on the other.

I ran after my destiny, ignoring the warning signs; it's just that it was still a time for dreaming, I tried to rationalize.

La Bella had turned me down; she had escaped her conscience, I consoled myself as I stood in the university amphitheater, about to deliver my last speech as student leader, and my first as owner of my own thoughts. But I didn't know that, since I've never wanted to accept reality. Reality ties you down, keeps you from dreaming, keeps you from breaking down barriers, and turns you into an acolyte. Reality is the refuge of the mediocre, those who hide their ignorance and their inability to think and dream.

Reality surrounded me and still does.

It was the month of October of 1968. One year before, Che had confronted reality in the Bolivian jungle, at the little school in La Higuera.

"You always learn something new," I thought, grabbing my knapsack, leaving Valdivia and its memories behind forever and fleeing from reality just to bump into reality head-on.

Rise up brother, be born with me

Give me silence, water, hope
Give me struggle, iron, volcanoes.
Fasten your bodies to mine like magnets.
Come into my veins and into my mouth.
Speak through my words and my blood.

Pablo Neruda,
Heights of Machu Picchu[1]

[1] From *Twentieth Century Latin American Poetry: A Bilingual Anthology,* ed. Stephen Tapscott, trans. David Young, University of Texas Press, 1996, p. 213.

V. Of how he kept silent so that the word could blow through his mouth

The first stop was Santiago. I went all around the city, searching for my destiny. I took a ramshackle bus that followed the Matadero-Palma route, passed by the central market that offered the fruits of the sea and of my land to the curious, crossed the waters fed by the Mapocho that carried along the castoffs of history, and, at the slaughterhouse, stepped in puddles of blood that opened a window to my future.

To my left was the insane asylum. There they offered cold-water baths and electroshock to clear the mind. The last stop was the entrance to the cemetery: there they offered wreaths as a sendoff on the voyage through eternity to those naïfs who believed in death.

I pulled the cord to ring the bell and got off between the two stops.

The next morning I set off for La Vega Central market. I hailed trucks laden with produce, begging for a seat till finally a sympathetic driver said, "Hop in, young man."

I climbed over the wooden railings, making a space for myself among sacks of onions, heading north, north to my destiny.

On the truck I was thinking: faithless traitor, she chose the poet instead of coming along with me on my travels around the world to find my people and their struggles, instead of coming along with me, a liberator, to liberate, to get covered with dust and blood, to rise up, brother, and be born with you, and to fall and disappear in the sea.

La Bella stayed behind on the sidewalk, cracking up laughing.

"Apparently sacks of onions ruined the solemnity of the moment, and the odyssey turned into a comedy."

I peeled off the first layer of my story: it was 1968 and the world was ours.

Leaving Santiago, El Negro Álvarez, a student at the State Technical University, Valdivia campus, joined the caravan. Hidden behind the partially destroyed turret that had defended the old naval shipyards from Sir Francis Drake's attacks, he heard about the journey, of the rewards awaiting the intrepid, about the difference between boring, everyday life and facing the unexpected at each of death's turns.

He grew a scraggly mustache, since he couldn't manage a beard, and, looking like a plucked Jorge Negrete, sneaked aboard the old, ramshackle truck.

The trip took 72 hours along Route 5, the highway that crosses Chile from north to south. As they neared the sea, they passed close by Neruda's house in Isla Negra, Nicanor Parra's in Las Cruces, and Vicente Huidobro's in Cartagena. Cartagena: the beach where he had gone as a child, his private parts covered by a burgundy wool bathing suit, as if his life had already been marked, hand woven – a pair of trunks that sagged and gaped open when he got to the beach, leaking water between his legs and leaving his family jewels exposed to the caress of the sea breeze or of some friendly fingers, wrinkled by water or by age.

He never found out who the fingers belonged to, since he always closed his eyes as soon as he felt that pleasurable sensation.

However, I always kept them open, not out of pleasure, but because a person can fall into the abyss when going from a third-class car to one in first.

As they entered the desert, the voice of the poets was silenced by that of the stars, and the three of them, together with Gabriela Mistral, kept respectfully silent before such beauty, hidden in the bottom of my knapsack. "The Poetry Mail" had been born, and my knapsack filled up with verses and light to help me find my way.

To one side lay the cordillera and the miners and history; to the other, the sea, with its waves washing the wounds inflicted by history, and in the air a mild wind of forgetfulness swept the desert's surface of all traces of muffled groans.

And my knapsack filled up with groans, with silent cries for help, with "Rise up, brother, be born with me," not knowing that we were already walking outside of history.

As we grateful travelers decamped in Arica, we helped unload the sacks of onions, joyfully throwing them down so as to hear the noise of the onions as they hit the ground. We lowered the knapsack with reverence, not because of its material value, but rather for its spiritual worth, because its muddy depths, soaked in onion juice, could raise its verses over the old wooden bars that enclosed the truck.

Rise up, brother. Come fly with me.

At the back of the grocery store, sitting atop history, was Valente Rossi, a senator from the Republic of Chile. He was the one I had seen out of the corner of my eye when they had me sitting on the crate with shards of broken glass after renouncing my candidacy for the presidency of a student association and for having seen what I shouldn't have seen behind the peeling scenery in Sofia, as well as the tanks of liberation that were advancing, answering the call of the people to quash the Prague Spring. And in spite of everything, he gave me his hand, a marraqueta roll lavishly slathered with butter, and a cup of coffee, and he said to me, nostalgically, "I have a brother across the border. He will help you."

I never figured out which border he was referring to.

The next day, after a purifying bath in the sea, I walked across the border, the first one, the earthly one. The brother really existed, and just like the one in Chile, he too had a bar and a grocery store. Unlike the brother in Chile, he had no rolls and offered me a plate of lomito saltado.

We were in Peru.

That was the beginning of the mirror refracting his image, reflecting both reality and the individual, torn between the anguish of other people's suffering and the unbearable pain it inflicted on oneself, a refracted image in a language incapable of effectively reflecting the urgency of the cry that was suffocated by convention or by slowly turning one's back on one's conscience and looking the other way.

My thoughts were assaulted from all sides: by the poets at the bottom of my knapsack who clamored to come back to life, by the reality surrounding me, by the news reports I wanted to use to feed my scripts, the first of "The Poetry Mail," so as to give meaning to the word. But what sense did it make when the land was being sold in all its length and breadth, with all the animals and souls that inhabited it, clay-colored souls with cracked feet, curved backs, toothless souls who dragged themselves through the mud of their ancestors' land to rip open its belly and give away its bounty. It wasn't clear if it belonged to them or to the land, if these were new souls come to replace the aging ones, or the fruits of a land that was no longer theirs.

And for me there was no difference between fruits, just as there was no difference between souls, between the one who carved the stone with his story in it and the one who opened the belly of the earth with wooden plows to feed those who would pass his story on; between the verses of one poet or another, as long as those verses didn't conceal the bloody feet, the weather-beaten hands, the dried-up breasts that had nursed those almond-eyed children, descendants of the Inca.

This time he didn't bathe in the waters of the sea to purify himself; he rubbed the dust of the road into his skin, mixed with rainwater to make himself worthy; he ripped the collar off his shirt to avoid being tempted to wear a tie ever again; he let his hair grow, as there was no Bella anywhere around to cut it for him; he exchanged his worn-out shoes for a pair of Ho Chi Minh sandals; he punched another hole in his belt so his raggedy jeans wouldn't fall down; and, with his knapsack over his shoulder and his script in his hand, he walked into the first amphitheater.

"Excuse me, did you say jeans?"

The mise-en-scène was extremely simple and direct, to ensure the effectiveness of the poetic discourse.

With the help of a group of boisterous local poets, the chicken coop was torn up, and we headed for the doors of the amphitheater. With theatrical flair, the poets opened the doors to the new arrival: flanked by them and followed by the students, we went over to the stage, in the middle of which they deposited the knapsack and withdrew, turning the set over to us.

I climbed up to get a command of the stage; before the audience's eyes I constructed an improvised set: a cross where a portrait was hanging, and beside it a flag, ready to be unfurled.

Nothing was concealed; everything belonged to everyone. Bathed in humility, iconic poets plunged in with neophytes and the newcomers with those yet to come. The individual voice took on the strength of the collective, the silences maintained the rhythm, musicality, meaning, and progress of the reading and the story.

And in that new communion I became one with my destiny.

I took a few steps forward toward the center of the stage, pulled a poem from my knapsack, the one that would begin the recital. But first . . . a pause, a silence in which words hung suspended, the balcony holding its breath expectantly.

"A deliberate silence: it rocked one's thoughts, broke the mold, challenged traditions. Definitely belongs to the '68 vibe," the critics would say.

Yes, of course, it was 1968, and the initial, silent pause, wasn't deliberate. It was the result of his natural shyness. Later he got over it, maybe through practice – who knows if he overcame it or if they kicked it out of him.

As the first verses hit the audience, El Negro entered from the back of the room and noisily made his way down the aisle, creating a barrier between the listeners and the word. He mounted the stage and dropped a pack of newspapers at my feet, then turned toward the audience and pronounced, "Here is the new poetry, without filters, without rhyme, and when you read it, it'll make you jump out of your comfortable seats. . ."

And everyone squirmed uneasily, as if an attack of pinworms had invaded the amphitheater.

"The poetry that's written by those behind the news, the forgotten ones, the invisible heroes of history," he concluded.

El Negro drew applause, a cunning and easy attack that immediately divided the audience while at the same time capturing its attention.

It was '68, and even the word poetry was frowned on.

A forest of black banners rose up in the auditorium.

That declaration in the purest May 1968 style left not only me, but even the author of:
I can write the saddest verses tonight,
Write, for example
The night is starry

And the stars twinkle blue in the distance . . .

facing an uphill climb, to stanch the explosion of shouts of reproval and condemnation with:

Rise, up, brother, and be born with me, from the depths of the earth . . ."

And so I got the words out after a pause disguised as hesitation, while a forest of red banners rose up in the auditorium.

And we went on with the script in a friendly duel, in a joint speech by two actors, a discursive dialogue in which half of one fed into half of the other, in which the response was a question, not a statement, in which doubt gave rise to certainty, a certainty that had to yield again to doubt.

To conclude, I walked over to a far corner and read a poem by Uncle Ho, while my mind replayed the image of a naked girl, running with a grimace of pain on her lips and not a single tear in her eyes, her small body scorched by napalm.

El Negro turned the portrait over, and a threatening Nixon appeared, challenging us from his position of absolute power; he uncorked a bottle, sprinkling the portrait and the flag.

I extended my hand toward the flag in a military salute, and from the side of the arena, looking intently at the cross, exclaimed:

"Ave, Caesar Nixon, morituri te salutant."

And I threw a lighted cigarette on the altar.

Then came the explosion, an explosion of applause, an explosion of flames, an explosion of consciences, and, at the risk of burning up in the bonfire, we slowly walked back up the aisle, receiving new poems to feed the insatiable knapsack.

In the auditorium, anonymous hands extinguished the flames and swept the ashes, attempting to erase this part of history.

But history cannot be erased: it can be distorted, ignored, appropriated, used, read without really wanting to read it, rewritten, but not erased. An uncomfortable witness – it always shows up the poor guy who erected the statue, not the one who unveiled it – but we didn't know that yet, not the guy who was sweeping up and not me.

The party that followed was just like those that follow any premiere: merriment, verses here, verses there, genuine embraces, embraces that feel like knifings, the inevitable, "I would have . . .". the stranger taking notes in a corner, the darkest one, and who keeps on taking notes even in the darkest corners of the salons of exile, from Stockholm to Paris, from Québec to Berlin, passing through Sofia, through Sofia and Prague.

And La Bella? La Bella was fading from memory between the thighs of other beauties who, première after première, generously opened their legs to me, offering me access to their insatiable sexes, as insatiable as the mouth of my knapsack.

But a beauty, when she is truly beautiful, acquires the dimensions of history: she cannot be erased, she does not slip between your fingers, she doesn't disappear; she reappears in every lovely, insatiable sex offered to you before disappearing – yes, disappearing – in your memory of her, until one day La Bella entre las Bellas comes into view, the one I had glimpsed in my destiny from the very beginning, the only one, the one who will never disappear.

At the dawn of a new chapter, one of the poets said, "Let's go and see Caesar," and we set out in a couple of run-down VW Beetles for Trujillo, a land of poets, not where poets are born, though – where poets are born there are no amphitheaters. We lost our way at a curve in the road, and instead of Trujillo, we found ourselves in Tumbes. We were halfway to the center of the world, a place where there were amphitheaters.

More than an amphitheater it was something like an events hall where the town festival was being celebrated. On the program they wrote in by hand, "and with the participation of the internationally acclaimed group "The Poetry Mail," recently arrived in the lands of Tumbes to pay homage with their verses to the beauty of our local women, whose loveliness enhances our illustrious city."

The mayor's daughter sat down at a grand piano and masterfully interpreted the Tumbes anthem, followed by a wobbly toccata and fugue. The hearty applause told me it was time to make my entrance onstage.

I opened the door and walked down the center aisle of the enthusiastic auditorium, crossing paths with the mayor's daughter. Once I had reached center stage, I turned around slowly, playing with time, rhythm, and silence, and started to sweat copiously: half the hall was occupied by military; even the mayor was a commandant who had been appointed to guard the border.

After the first poems, El Negro entered, creating a ruckus as was his habit, and at midpoint he looked out at the respectable audience in preparation for his first lines and fell silent in astonishment. He looked at me with his eyes wide open like two fried eggs, not knowing whether to go on or turn around and leave me with the poetry, but without the reality.

The rhythm of the recital changed naturally, adapting to the hall; the silences grew shorter, the ending changed – it was kind of dangerous to pour gasoline on the fire that invaded half the auditorium, and to make matters worse, we were Chileans in the land of the Peruvian military, so the "morituri te salutant" took on another dimension. As we were leaving, out of the corner of my eye I observed that the only one of the beauties to spread her thighs was the mayor's daughter, and to our further debasement, her father had taken notice.

The alcohol vapors surrounding the local poets dissipated, they got wind of the danger, and sympathetic hands helped us traverse the final yards of the aisle. They lifted us – first the knapsack (profession above all else), then the performers – into a ramshackle Volkswagen and deposited us across the border, not without first giving us a strong embrace.

We were in Ecuador.

VI. Of how he made the leap from solitude to the masses, only to continue on his solitary journey throughout the continent

I fell into the hands of the Tzántsicos, or headshrinkers, an endangered tribe that took refuge in the jungle and in the pages of the books of a group of poets.

The end of the sixties was approaching and the barricades were beginning to tumble: those I had left behind in Chile, fighting for university reform and a budget for the Technical State University; those of the Latin Quarter in Paris, made of solid cobblestones that were now beginning to be sold as souvenirs; the invisible ones that slipped in among a forest of banners in Sofia; the ones in Prague that were unable to resist the onslaught of tanks; those that were yet to come, the ones that, instead of protecting us, would aid in our destruction; those made of cardboard that couldn't halt the advance of barbarity; those made of iron that chained me to my destiny.

The situation was changing: the president of the National University opened its doors. In the audience, several men flaunted their long hair. They had yanked off their shirt collars and gotten rid of the ties that stifled their cries of protest. Anyone who couldn't get his hands on a pair of Ho Chi Minh sandals simply went around barefoot. The beauties showed off their thighs, offering them up to the wind.

And after the initial pause, looking at the audience, in the very center, a gentleman in a suit and tie, with a slicked-back coif from which not a single hair escaped, behaving just as his mother in far-off Valdivia had instructed him, El Chico Ojeda, a classmate at Universidad Austral, in those days the southernmost university on the planet.

Summer had vanished from the meadows of Isla Negra only to reappear today in the center of the world; he had left Valdivia to stand on tiptoe – El Chico was really short – to spy on both halves of the world and complete his studies in Quito.

From that afternoon on, he began following the group around, since two is a group, and for a director it's a crowd.

At each reading, El Chico sat, with composure but never with pinworms, unflappably observing, his gaze fading every once in a while: without knowing it, he was writing his first short story. A tremendous guy, El Chico.

He invited us to see a bullfight at the bullring in downtown Quito. Allegorical, that's what El Chico was, I thought, recalling Tumbes.

At the final reading he was once again among the audience, in a suit, hair slicked back with a kilo of Brilliantine, so that not even one hair would be out of place and . . . I stammered. For the first time, I lost the thread, the rhythm, and missed a line: El Chico wasn't wearing a tie.

I knew what was coming: to rewrite everything for three voices. Trying to concentrate, I asked myself how I would have El Chico come onstage. The texts weren't a major problem: El Chico looked professorial and would lend a certain academic air to the show, but, how could I recapture the rhythm, I wondered, how could I incorporate the new voice, find a new perspective in the diagonal movements so as to maintain the balance of the stage and utilize the set. Three axes represented the cross; the script had to work with three roads.

But I was wrong.

That night, at Casa de la Cultura Benjamín Carrión, the atmosphere was thick enough to cut with a knife – not since my flub, but since the beginning; walking down the aisle among the public, I felt off-balance, pulled toward one side or the other.

On one side were those who had invited us; on the other, those who had put up a barricade after being thrown out of the scene. Directed by an Italian, Fabio Pacchioni, they had had the temerity to include Indians in the scene, making themselves up like those who lived in Santo Domingo de los Colorados, replacing creams with chicken shit and *achiote*, which added a new look to the actresses' cheeks, and, all of them kneeling, dressed in black, they raised their imploring hands to the audience and to the souls in César Dávila Andrade's epic poem, *Boletín y elegía de las mi-*

tas:

"*Break the baby's hand,*" they beseeched, "*so he will not become Viracocha's slave.*"

"*I have broken it,*" responded the coryphaeus.

But I didn't know that – the part about Viracocha, yes, but not that I had unwittingly agreed to trample on the ashes left on the stage by others.

That night we went out to celebrate with the recently expelled members of "La Barricada Theater,"[2] jolly drunks who held no grudge against us despite the fact that we had taken over their space.

In time I realized that one has to take over spaces, that those who came before me wouldn't blame me, that spaces were public in the sense that they exist for the public's sake, and that my role was to occupy them just to disappear later, allowing someone else to tread on my ashes and throw me out in turn.

Before El Chico opened his mouth, I said yes, but on one condition: onstage, and only onstage, put on a tie.

We left the party singing in four-part harmony; the base of the cross pointed to the center of the earth; a Colombian actress-singer started packing her bags.

The "Tzántsicos" filled our backpack with their blowpipes – or *pucunas*, in the headshrinkers' language – from which they ir-

---

[2] Independent theater group formed in Ecuador by the Italian director Fabio Paccioni.

reverently launched their poisonous poems.

With their verses and their blowpipes well hidden, the poetry continued on its way, surreptitiously crossing borders, those that existed between countries, those that suffocated Ecuador, those of mediocrity. We were at the end of the decade, and those who had been offended by the verses managed to silence *Pucuna,* the journal of those poets who escaped from the depths of the jungle of mediocrity.

> *Break the hand of the poet*
> *so he will not become the patron's slave*
> *so he will not write in praise*
> *of the patron.*

I have broken it.

The first half of the world lay behind us. We were in Colombia.

The group had grown to four members; from my neck hung an engraved metal disk that Guayasamín had given me at his studio on top of a hill, from which it commanded a view of beautiful, colonial Quito and where the hands of what would become his *Hands of Rage* twisted on the canvases.

In the knapsack, together with the poems, several sketches of the hands of rage – so you won't forget the hands of my people – Oswaldo had told me.

VII. Of how he traveled halfway across the world in search of a righteous man

History didn't stop in Pasto, and yet the residents held no grudge against me; on the contrary, thirteen years later they would lend me a kind hand to help me move forward so that our history wouldn't disappear forever.

Three men and a singer changed the rhythm of history.

The rhythm changes only if you dare to change the rhythm, the songs, and life – not reality – life and thought, thought and the heavy blanket with which they try to smother it.

Depending on the news and the state of his soul, or if the memory of La Bella crossed his mind, he would include:

> *Though love is human, it harbors the divine*
> *God Himself loved, so loving is no crime*
> *And if the love is pure and the desire real,*
> *Why would they want faith from my heart to steal?*
> *My blood, though plebeian, runs red and dyes*
> *The soul in which my matchless passion lies*
> *She, of noble birth, and I a humble commoner . . .*[3]

"Which part do I sing?" El Chico interrupted.

---

[3] Felipe Pinglo Alva, *El plebeyo*

If the news wasn't good, from the bottom of the knapsack and from the Colombian Department of Chocó, to the accompaniment of drums, came:

Even if my master kills me, I won't go to the mine . . .

I hadn't yet become acquainted with Maestro Escalona and his house in the air; Gabo got there ahead of me.

And while yellow butterflies fluttered around the former, the latter brushed away the lowly horseflies of southern Chile, perhaps because, although they were both born on the sixth of March, latitude kept them apart.

"Besides, you would've locked the lady in that house in the air, for sure, and taken away the ladder, because, remember, the gentleman was Chilean. And besides, you didn't yet have the sense of humor you needed to include "La Piragua.""

On warm Cali nights we took a break from our journey, caressed by the breeze and lulled by the barking of a dog – we even had a dog in Cali! – thanks to the generosity of the widow of a liberal leader, one of those who were stained with red, assassinated by a bird at a time when the Goths – the conservatives – had set loose flocks of "birds" to raze the Colombian countryside, the Colombian cities. Violence devoured the peasants' innards; violence left the peasants' tongue lolling over their chests, decorating their shiny Sunday suits with the dreaded "Colombian necktie." The "birds" made a gash on each side of the neck, followed by a cross-stroke with a machete blade, and with a similar blow they ripped out their tongues, leaving them dangling over their chests.

The violence was creative and left their signature on their deeds, just as Josef had left his in other latitudes.

"Chico," I said, "you'll never wear a tie again, not even on-stage, out of respect for the audience and so as not to give those *bandoleros* any ideas."

And on one of those warm nights, the Colombian actress sang into my ear:

If you don't love me, I'll slash your face
With one of those razor blades
I'll rip your eyes out
And I'll kill your mama

No doubt about it, we were in Colombia, and since good things always come in pair, the actress sang *à duo* with her younger sister.

Years later, the actress died in Spain, drowned in alcohol and memories; her children had locked the sister up in an insane asylum in Stockholm.

"In an asylum or in one of those halls . . .?"

"I never learned how to tell the difference," I replied, before my memories could start interrogating me.

The tropics can definitely drive you crazy, I told myself as an excuse for interrupting the story line, because what does all this have to do with the story?

And yet, on entering Colombia, when you enter the hot lands – and along its borders there are no cold lands – the damp heat clings to your body; the mosquitoes cling to your body so they can slake their thirst for fresh blood; its history clings to your body and to your history, and try as you may to ignore it, it rises through each one of your pores.

The Colombian actress and her sister were children of the violence that had lashed Colombia. Their father murdered, they had joined the hundreds of thousands displaced rural families in a long march. To escape her fate, one of them mounted stages; the other took refuge in *bel canto*. One escaped toward the south; the other began walking toward madness in order to escape from madness.

One possibility was to take charge of history and integrate it into my script. The other was to ignore it, remain ensconced in the scenery, in the drumbeats, and not those of Leonor González Mina, la Negra Grande de Colombia. To stay mired in the vapors of one *aguardiente* after another, or to lose myself on the warm, white sand beaches of Santa Marta or Cartagena and submerge myself, shielding myself behind the stone walls, shielding myself in stories from afar, projected in the clouds and portrayed by other actors.

"But that's not what entering Colombia is like. Stop screwing around."

The first stage of the violence had ended. Gaitán's assassination was tiptoeing toward oblivion while Galán began treading makeshift stages on the way to his death and to a new violence, its flames fanned this time by drug trafficking.

And so it was: the first time he arrived between two famous dead men, together with and holding the hands of those who don't count, those who, like him, disappear from history.

Cali opened her hungry womb to us, insatiable for adventure and adventurers, for open dialogue, for realities and poems, for young beauties and old prostitutes vying for my body and soul, and I bounced from one to another, seeking an answer and my destiny.

It was the first recital for four voices, and yet thousands of voices slipped in among the lines, and three became one, and one became a bridge between the stage and the disembodied voices that struggled, not to come back to life, but to disappear peacefully and to be sought not in the past, but in the future, so as to rest in peace at last.

At the back of the hall someone was watching: Nicolás Buenaventura, brother of Enrique, the director of the Experimental Theater of Cali. Nicolás was a man of two worlds, the world of letters and that of politics. He was a bridge between the stages and the audience, between the voices and life, between history and the danger-strewn path that traverses it. A hornet crossed the stage from left to right: it was a lucky omen, said the folks hidden out in the mountain.

It was a time of little massacres that gave way to big massacres, of great ideas that preceded small ones, of generosity that gave way to greed. It was a time when, though surrounded by death in the mountains, one was capable of becoming a cloud of smoke and materializing again on the peak of another mountain, and history became verse before it morphed into a peeling, empty stage set.

Without a doubt, it was a time when dying was worthwhile.

And for the first time he desired her, because a beauty, if she is truly beautiful, carries a scythe.

We started down the flight of stairs only to climb back up to Bogotá, which awaited us with open arms. Bogotá has no womb. We stopped for a second, dazzled by the magical green of Manizales. When we left, we contributed two pages of poetry to the Sunday cultural supplement of the local paper – and a short story, added El Chico Ojeda, who had definitely become hooked on the smell of fresh ink. One of the pages of the Sunday paper flew over La Línea, the infamous peak, and fell into the hands of a reporter from Bogotá, and so it was that Gloria Valencia de Castaño opened her heart and the microphones of her program to us. Peeved, Bernardo Romero Lozano came to see me in the Policarpa Salavarrieta neighborhood – "el Pola" – a shantytown where I had set up my temporary nest, a neighborhood that had spread its muddy legs to take in the uprooted of the earth.

"One hour," the friendly producer said to me. "One hour. I'll give you air time and pictures on national TV."

His only condition was that no bad words that might offend the audience could be uttered.

I accepted. I didn't want to offend anyone's ears and was never a fan of *ad hominem* attacks. What I was after was infinitely more dangerous. And they knew it.

Thinking is dangerous, my friend.

When we finished the recital where Neruda and César, Javier, and Benjo went up and down the stairs holding hands, with the headshrinkers alongside the poet Gallinazus, the phones began to ring. Some calls didn't respect the rules and pelted us with curses; others were happy, and joy reverberated in their voices. A black hornet crossed from right to left. A voice, dry and cold as a Bogotá winter wind, asked for an address where the four of us could be found. They didn't need photos; they had recorded the program.

There are reviews that hurt and demolish you. The group shrank back to two; two others returned to Chile.

"La Candelaria" opened its womb to those of us who remained – theater is fertile – and Santiago invited us to one of the final rehearsals of *The Good Person of Szechuan,* a Brecht work they were putting on.

We entered the hall as one enters history, crossing ruins and gardens, cobblestoned floors and walls that kept their balance precariously in the air, but as we were in the theater, we entered the hall after dousing ourselves with hope and happiness.

On stage, an actress played the main character of *The Good Person of Szechwan* in the double role of Shen-Te, a kindly prostitute who in order to protect herself is forced to create an alter ego, Shui-Ta, her merciless cousin.

At a desk, three gods, waving goodbye, are about to return to their place on heaven rather than face the reality of earthly life. The play begins in reality. Wang, the water carrier, had been tramping through fields and cities selling water, but of course whenever it rained, no one needed his services, while during times of drought, wretched poverty spread throughout Szechwan and no one could afford a pitcher of water from the good Wang. Wang, taking the audience into his confidence, informs us, "No one will take pity on us and change our situation unless the gods come," and in so saying Brecht immerses us in the plot. There are no longer any secrets or solutions, only to wait for the gods and their gift, that is, if they haven't already pulled out of the game.

At the end of the story, when the gods discover that Shen-Te and Shui-Ta are the same person – apparently they were the only ones who didn't know, since all the rest of us saw her transformation right on stage in front of the audience – she rebukes them:

SHEN-TE: Yes, it's me. Shen-Te and Shui-Ta. Both of them.

Who can persist in being good
when the hungry are dying?
Where could I find everything I needed?
Only within myself.
But how could I do that without losing my life?
The weight of my good intentions
was crushing me, but all I needed was to commit a single
injustice
to become powerful and eat my fill.
Something is wrong with this world of yours.
Why is evil rewarded,
and why is such suffering inflicted
on those who are good?

To which the gods replied . . .

And while I was thinking that this was a brilliant Colombian adaptation, Carrasco, the third of the gods, came crawling between my legs, stripping off his clothes till he was completely naked, and tirelessly repeating, "I am god."

Definitely brilliant, I said to myself. It outdoes Brecht.

The reality outdid Brecht, and the adaptation wasn't an adaptation. The Third God had split; three days later they found him, crazier than a goat on a hill, near the church of Monserrate, naked and chatting casually with the gods as if he were one of them.

A messenger ran the 42,195 meters separating La Candelaria from Policarpa Salavarrieta. On the third day, the Third God was resurrected from the dead.

"Santiago needs to talk to you."

And so it was that traditional Chinese theater became Greek tragedy with glints of comedy, only to become Chinese theater once again.

Life's twists and turns – that must be the road to my destiny: circular.

In Bucaramanga I rose to heaven, transformed into the Third God of *The Good Person*. In Santa Marta I discovered Nedjma's love and the madness surrounding Kateb Yacine, who fought, went into exile, endured prison, triumphed, returned, became disillusioned, mounted the stage, faced death in Nedjma's arms, while in one corner of the stage *The Tricycle* slipped in, or else an impromptu *Picnic* was set up on the battlefield before the astonished eyes of *Père Ubu.*

The world was invading the Colombian scene, perhaps the only way to embrace what is one's own.

As a transition to collective creation, we all locked our-selves in the Charenton asylum, the one that opened its cold water baths to the burning passions of the Marquis de Sade: Sade chat-ting with Marat, thanks to Peter Weiss.

Persecution and Murder: that was how the play was adver-tised, and that was how the arrival of a new tempest was an-nounced; a flirtatious, Mephistophelian Ariel fluttered over the Soacha district, over the Palace of Justice in Bogotá's main plaza, but not without first taking a turn through the mountains of Colom-bia, sweeping us closer to the candle flame so as to burn our wings and the New Testament.

Humidity clung to my skin again. Tipsy with *aguardiente* and beauty, sitting beside a beauty, I descended into hot lands once more. When I got off the *buseta* – I had spent a long time in Colombia – she directed me to a small grocery store. In the back, sitting on some sacks of coffee, was the recipient of the message that the beauty had carried: a humble Colombian peasant.

The only thing that differentiated him from any other *cam-*

73

pesino was his work boots, and they weren't props. We talked for a long time. He knew about Chile and about Allende; he knew about coffee and how to make it; he knew about humor and love affairs. I treated him with a certain respect, though I didn't even know who he was. He told me of his life out on the mountain, of his fear of airplanes, of his deprivations, of the importance of salt and brown sugar.

"The next time you salt your food, think of those who don't have access to salt. And it's not because of the food, it's because we walk endlessly, and salt lets us retain the water in our bodies. It's not a matter of pleasure – that's why we guard it so carefully, with our lives if necessary."

I didn't understand.

"Go get your boots ready," he said to me, as he was about to leave, before turning into smoke to be reincarnated on a mountaintop.

I was sorry I didn't have a *marraqueta* roll to offer him.

The Colombian beauty whispered in my ear, "The man's name is Manuel."

I trembled: that man was Tirofijo – Manuel Marulanda, the notorious leader of FARC.[4]

---

[4] FARC, the Revolutionary Armed Forces of Colombia, are the most important guerrilla movement in the country. Founded in 1964, in 2016 signed a peace deal with the government.

It was a time of tremors, of believing that one could change the world, that coffee was coffee and no garbage had been added to it, and that one fought for principles, not for easy cash to hide in *guacas*.[5] Besides, the Beauty was really beautiful, queen of the National University and the Policarpa at the same time; her voice was velvety and her lips tasted like coffee.

Among the tremors was one that had slipped in without my recognizing it, similar to the one that slipped into the café of "La Candelaria" in February 1969, when Jaime Arenas walked in. *Compañero* Jaime, the heroic commandant of the National Liberation Army, the one who organized the first student march demanding free access to culture, to books, to dreams for all, to the same opportunities, so that books might help build a new society, the society we had all been dreaming of. *Compañero* Jaime, the cowardly deserter, the one who left the mountains because he had challenged Fabio by asking for dialogue, when Fabio insisted on shooting the other traitors, ideological traitors, the worst, lowest kind, those who had been caught stealing salt or brown sugar, traitors because they undermined discipline, and without discipline revolutions are lost, *compañero*.

The traitor, until yesterday a heroic *compañero*, one who came down from the mountains running from death, arrived to assist as a spectator of the production of Kateb Yacine's *The Encircled Corpse*. He came to stain the love of Nedjma for Lakhdar with his presence.

---

[5] Caches to hide treasures.

At a quick meeting of the actors' collective, we decided that the show would go on, the show always goes on, and we are people of principle, we members of the collective told one another. *Sotto voce* we instructed our audience – everyone except the deserter and his bodyguard – not to display their feelings, to remain silent, and not to applaud at the end (and for a group of actors to forego applause requires great moral strength), but just to leave the auditorium while we swept up the ashes.

Firmly grasping the broom handle, I asked myself: At what point does one go from leaving ashes on the stage to sweeping ashes off the stage?

And I wasn't sure which ashes I was talking about or what part of history I was sweeping.

What sadness was reflected in the traitor's eyes! What sadness there was in the eyes of Lakhdar!

Among the traitors, one of the interrogated commandants was spared. His name was Juan de Dios. Stripped of his rank, during his self-criticism, and as a gesture of good will and sign of loyalty to the movement, he pointed the finger at his second-in-command, *compañero* Commandant Víctor Medina, to whose name he added, for good measure, those of two other commandants, Julio César Cortés and Heliodoro Ochoa, three traitors who were shot in the Colombian mountains for trying to strike down the direction of the movement, as stated in the revolutionary communiqué, *compañeros.*

We had unwittingly begun to close ourselves in, and unwittingly, too, we became Lakhdar, the hero of *The Encircled Corpse*, the eternal lover, and we marched forward toward our own murders. Jaime Arenas was murdered in the cold streets of downtown Bogotá in 1971, as he was coming out of an art cinema, near Carrera Sexta and Calle 24.

How far in the past lay the march led by the student leader from Santander, that march of more than a half million people demanding educational reform in the smiling streets of Bogotá in 1965.

And I didn't believe it, it's hard to believe it; but just in case, I stopped drinking water with brown sugar, and I ate my rice mixed with rage, with a side of tasteless, unsalted eggs, repeating to myself, those are others, not mine, as I covered up a crack in the faded scenery with the cowardly salt shaker.

VIII. Of how he was trained in the techniques of warfare

The era was giving birth to a new epoch. In Chile, Allende had won the election, which led me to follow the spiral of return. It was the fourth time he had run, the first time in history that a socialist was elected president through the democratic process.

"Democratic? What democracy are you talking about?"

I took off my work boots when I arrived in La Paz.

"La Paz? Peace? What peace are you talking about? Or did you make a wrong turn?"

It seems there are people who don't allow even their feet to be enclosed; their dainty little feet had grown accustomed to walking freely, bluish, floating in their Ho Chi Minh sandals. Besides, a straight line is the shortest distance between two points, but it's the most boring: destiny doesn't follow the rails.

"And the sad halls . . .?"

"Those are coming – allow him a moment of joy, let him believe he's climbing the staircase when in fact he's sinking down into the guts of the Siglo XX."[6]

In a corner of the tunnel, the miners had carved out of the rock a cave to take shelter in – come down and be born with me, brother –. In a play of light and shadow, the shadows of the earth, the lights of their helmets, El Tío, the Uncle, appeared, guardian spirit, spirit of the mine that protected them at the moment when the dynamite exploded, ripping open the belly of the mountain, while Uncle and nephew chewed coca leaves and had a shot of *aguardiente*. Once the smoke had dissipated, both Uncle and nephew trembled and held their breath, waiting to see if the opening to the surface was still clear.

Siglo XX radio repeated through its loudspeakers, "Grand celebration tonight at the Union Hall: following their performance in La Paz, world-famous international group . . . will join us . . . Women and children free."

Stone faces with slits for eyes, a ball of peace rolling around in their mouths, dignified clothing, threadbare and patched a thousand times over. Merciless judges if poverty hadn't managed to be transformed into beauty, prepared to lash into shreds any sign of pity, hardened hearts that nonetheless trembled at the offer of a friendly staircase; even an occasional tear, repressed for centuries, opened a furrow in those hard, stone-sculpted cheeks:
Rise up, brother, be born with me

---

[6] Siglo XX, Spanish for "Twentieth Century," is a tin mine in the Department of Potosí in Bolivia.

The *altiplano* public doesn't warn; it judges.

At the back of the auditorium was Juan Lechín, another legendary, one-time mining leader. At the exit, crossing the plaza of the Siglo XX country house, a field where, interrupted by the barking of skeletal dogs, attracted by my Ho Chi Minh sandals, he told me of his struggles, his exiles, his returns, and the attempts on his life. As we parted, he said to me, "I'm leaving now; tonight I travel on to Colquirí. Tomorrow I have a meeting with my *compañeros*."

Colquirí? The coldest mine of all, the one where even on St. John's Eve, the night of bonfires, the flames froze; the one where our performance was already scheduled, and the one where we would arrive late. I asked Lechín to let them know we would get there a day later.

His secretary, whose secretarial dignity was offended – and offending a secretary is serious business – took me aside and chewed me out, "You've just treated Juan Lechín, the next president of Bolivia, the one who's taking over after Torres, like an errand boy."

The secretary aspired to become the secretary of a President.

However, a black condor with sharp talons was already gliding over the continent.

But at that point in the story, neither the secretary (who, incidentally, was a notary and thus disappeared from the story); nor Juan Lechín (who went into exile once more by crossing the border hidden in a coffin); nor Juan José Torres (who would be assassinated in 1975 in Buenos Aires during Videla's administration); nor I, (who crossed the Chilean border thanks to a false document identifying me as a journalist from a European press agency); nor anyone else yet knew that an overthrow of power was being planned, this time directed by Hugo Banzer.

"We warned him – the thing is he didn't speak Aymara or know how to read the silences or the stones or the coca leaves, and while that stuff doesn't do a thing to us, it fries white folks' brains."

In the shadow of the stone wall of La Paz's cathedral, on a lovely little street there was a cultural sanctuary, la Peña Naira. In it painters' voices blended with singers' brushes, poetic discourse with politicians' verses, and the only thing they had in common was that no one had boots or uniforms. Even Juan José Torres wore civilian clothes to celebrate his birthday at the *peña* by dancing a *cueca* and singing in chorus:

> *Long live my homeland, Bolivia,*
> *a great nation,*
> *I'd give my life for her . . .*
> And a silence ran through the *peña*.

But before that, in the shadow of the old stone wall, sitting on the curb, we ate *chola* sandwiches, (the best in La Paz), impregnated with the odor of printer's ink from the University of San Andrés, where a new edition of an anthology of songs of struggle and hope that we had written together with the Colombian actress fruitlessly awaited the light of day. Our new friend assumed an instructor's role and taught me, through songs I had never heard before, about Bolivia's recent history.

Songs that gathered up the pieces of the Che Guevara epic so as to scatter them throughout the world in the mouths of other young people, songs that traveled from Cochabamba, the land of Coco and Inti Peredo, to the little school in La Higuera, from the mountains of Colombia to the Peruvian *altiplano,* from the Chilean desert to the jungles of Vietnam.

To feed my pride he spoke of songs in my accent, those from the column of Chileans under the command of Elmo Catalán and the younger daughter of Salvador Allende, those from the Argentines under the command of Antonio. When Inti was killed he was replaced by El Chato and a new song; the new songs traveled up and down the continent.

The last representatives of the epic in Bolivia climbed down the staircase on the pretext of teaching the inhabitants of Los Yungas jungle to read and write. They asked the army to transport them since it was a matter of social improvement, and they descended 2027 meters to Teoponte[7] and their destiny.

1251 soldiers went after the 67 students who emerged

---

[7] A town in the Department of La Paz, Bolivia.

82

from La Paz singing songs to begin the new offensive. Among them was Elmo. His role in this epic achievement earned him the distinction of having hundreds of *brigadistas* sign their names to hundreds of murals that adorned the Chile of the Unidad Popular Coalition. Among the students was Beatriz, la Tati, Salvador Allende's younger daughter, who years later, after the Chilean coup d'état, would take her own life during her exile in Cuba. Her death was kept a secret for a while because of who she was and because there was no place for loneliness and despair, not even on the isle of hope; just as her father's suicide was concealed for many years, and when I mentioned this for the first time in one of the halls of exile in Paris, the room froze before quickly returning to the preferred mode, that of lies.

Off they went, singing, into the arms of a fatal trap, despite the fact that on June 1, a colonel had dropped by the *peña* to warn them from the depths of a *charango*: Be careful, the army knows that you're not going to teach reading and writing. He lent them two trucks because they knew what they were getting themselves into and he wanted to keep close tabs on them. They mustn't even think of hiding at some curve in the road.

"Tell the kids not to go."

The warning was issued; they didn't believe it. It wasn't a time for believing.

Three-and-a-half months later, on November 1, 1970, history declared the odyssey, which had begun on July 18, 1970, over. Nine survived and managed to escape to Chile, among them El Chato, thanks to a safe-conduct issued by the government of J.

J. Torres.

After the massacre, a messenger came to the *peña* asking for the name of the military officer who had issued the warning, so as to bring him to justice.

"But," stammered the defender of the arts, "he warned us in order to avoid the massacre."

"It doesn't matter – somebody's got to pay for those deaths, and if you don't give the names, it'll be you who pays."

He pulled him out of the shelter, and luckily for history, the *quenas, charangos,* guitars, and verses came together at the threshold and protected him.

Nine months later, on August 21, 1971, the telephone rang early at La Casa del Poeta. The army had organized an uprising: it was the Bolivian Workers' Union calling to defend the president of Bolivia, General Juan José Torres.

I joined in his defense: I, the defenseless defender, I, the combatant whose only weapon is his heart. When I arrived at the San Andrés amphitheater, where I had instructed my actors to be if this moment should arrive, I found that the stage had opened its belly to the real world, and from there my actors and actresses drew out machine guns, dynamite, and rifles. For months they had been rehearsing on top of a powder keg, and like all creative acts, speeches are bidirectional, first from the script to the actor and then from the actor to the audience. Also, all scenes hold more than one interpretation in their bellies.

That was where we parted ways: I don't use weapons. I defend, yes, but without weapons or else with weapons made of cardboard. In front of the COB, the Bolivian Workers' Union, I listened to Simón Reyes, to Lechín. A poet handed me his unloaded rifle with no lever: a lovely, poetic gesture for a poet to hand me his harmless weapon for my self-defense before he disappeared, empty-handed, into the crowd.

With unprecedented bravery, armed with a useless firearm, accompanied by a group of young miners from Colquirí and Siglo XX, I felt obliged to go on with the script. In homage to the audience that surrounded me, I exclaimed, perhaps as a balm for their fissured lungs, "We're going to take over the COMIBOL!" the Bolivian Mining Corporation. At the end of Avenida La Paz, with a warrior's gesture and an emboldened stance, we passed through the unguarded doors of the semi-abandoned building. We asked a secretary who was trembling in an office to point us to the office of the president of COMIBOL. Two floors up, I kicked the door open; the president couldn't manage to pick up the machine gun he had placed on his desk while he ate.

"In the name of the revolution, from this moment on COMIBOL will be returned to the hands of the people."

We ordered him to leave his position, and, while he was at it, his food, as well: none of us had eaten a bite since breakfast.

Jubilant and emboldened after having taken over the management of the bowels of the earth, I proposed taking over the space.

We headed for the radio station in front of La Casa del Poeta, near the army's general headquarters.

The radio station was an easier target still: its pleasant

owner opened her doors and microphone to us; the young miners launched their revolutionary proclamations; I slipped in a few verses and lines from the play we were putting on – as propaganda, I admit it: if we won, we'd fill the theater.

At dusk, tired and out of proclamations, we left the radio station. Out in the street we ran into the poet and the secretary general of Bolivian Communist Youth.

"And now what?" we asked them.

The poet stared at me silently. After staring back, we both looked at the secretary, who, in the face of those silent stares, said, "Now we take over the general headquarters of the insurrection."

Good idea, we told ourselves. We were 4000 meters above sea level and thousands of kilometers from reality.

The poet had gotten his hands on a pistol, without bullets. He was a good poet. The secretary passed me a handle, but no bullets. Cunningly I threw it away at the first curve, lest I find a bullet and feel tempted.

We advanced, clinging to the walls. There were between 200 and 300 of us, and clinging to the wall like the shadows of thousands we covered one, two, three – thousands, as far as I was concerned – meters, till we got within fifteen meters of the main door of the barracks. At that point . . .

At that point the door began to open.

"They're surrendering, godammit!" we shouted in chorus, and we ran toward the barracks in order to be the first to arrive and unfurl banners in the heart of the insurrection.

A small tank emerged from the barracks. We stopped in

our tracks. "Run!" we shouted bravely, withdrawing in a swift exodus. The little tin soldier in the tank's turret fired into the air. He must be a miner's son, whispered Ramiro Necochea, the poet, speeding past me like a bolt of lightning. Yeah, sure, I replied as I left him behind, breaking all my speed records.

At midnight we learned that we had lost, and together with Ramiro and a couple of friends we started our retreat toward La Casa del Poeta. The young miners took the long road back toward the tunnels of Colquirí and Siglo XX, where they would continue to leave pieces of their lungs.

At a corner we ran into an Argentinean friend, enjoying a smoke and resting his back against a wall, his rifle dangling. He offered me a drag, and we stood there silently contemplating the beautiful stars that cover the sky over La Paz with their mantle.

"And now, brother?"

"I don't know. I'm going to Central America. They say there's action there."

"Me? I'm going down to Chile. People are waiting for me," I replied to his unspoken question.

How much time had elapsed since I received that fateful phone call in Colombia, announcing, "We won! Come back" and took the plane from El Alto shielded by a false journalist's I.D. from an international agency. *Merci, mes amis.*

How much time had it taken me to go down the staircase to meet my destiny in Chile.

The Unfathomable Depths

You shall leave everything you love most dearly:
this is the arrow that the bow of exile
shoots first. You are to know the bitter taste
of others' bread, how salty it is, and know
how hard a path it is for one who goes
descending and ascending others' stairs.

Dante Alighieri[8]

---

[8] Barolini, Teodolina. "Paradiso 17: Back to the Future." Comento Baroliniano, Digital Dante. Center for Digital Research and Scholarship. New York, NY: Columbia University Libraries, 2015. www.digitaldante.columbia.edu/dante/divine-comedy/paradiso/paradiso-17/

IX. Of how he managed to put ballet slippers on the miners who hauled copper from the depths of the mines

The banners flapped, held up by smiling hands; the walls sang to life, and life had meaning.

I breathed: after such a long time, I breathed and thought about La Bella.

I washed my feet in the sea; the smell of onions returned to my thoughts.

At the Communist youth headquarters, I informed them that a column of young miners was crossing the *altiplano* and was on its way. They asked me for the names and a description of the leaders so as to receive them properly.

They put me in a car and two days later I got out in Santiago just in time to run – it was urgent – onto the stage of the amphitheater of the State Technical University, where, planted right in the center, the Czech translator was concluding a meeting of the World Federation of Democratic Youth by describing how the Warsaw Pact forces had entered Prague to save the revolution, the Czech people, and their socialist democracy from the imperialist offensive.

He explained how capitalism had infiltrated the Czech government; a prelude to the invasion by capitalist forces bent on destroying our beloved and admired Union of Soviet Socialist Republics, the Great Fatherland.

With the monotonous tone of a student who had a bad professor, he repeated that the Warsaw Pact forces had responded to the people's anguished cry for help, begging to be liberated once more.

With a vague, distant gesture, he pointed toward the window of the beautiful castle, a window through which the enemies of the people had again been hurled.

Slowly at first, then picking up the pace, and rhythmically and uniformly, as was their custom, they filled the hall while the World Youth Anthem could be heard over the loudspeakers:

> Gathered before us
> From every nation
> This youthful chorus
> In acclamation
> Raises its voices fervently,
> Ever persisting, ever insisting:
> We shall be free, we shall be free.
> And these, our voices,
> Will not be silenced,
> Whate'er the choice is,
> Through peace or violence,
> We join together, as one we rise.
> Never disbanding, ever demanding:
> No more betrayal, the death of lies.

"What freedom, what democracy are you talking about?" The distant words with which a young Chilean student leader once rebuked Dubcek echoed in my ears.

Without a doubt, anthems give a different tone to the scenery; they are used to make hearts beat faster, to keep marching feet in step and marching at the same pace, and how effective and catchy they are, how they make you blend into the crowd! That's why you've got to alternate them with *El plebeyo,* to break the rhythm and be able to think.

I had arrived late. I turned around and headed for the mine, where a new stage awaited me.

In the copper mine of El Teniente, Marcial Balladares explained the clauses of my contract and what was expected of us – the Colombian actress and me: the mine, according to the quota system, is under socialist leadership; the second in command is a communist, and so on in all supervisory positions, except when, due to an opening, it is to our advantage to offer positions to MAPU – the Popular Unitary Action Movement, to the Christian Left, the Radicals, etc.

And so, suddenly and with a single blow, they had yanked a couple of planks from my stage.

"You're expected to put on plays with the miners that reflect their story and their interests."

"No problem," I replied. But one of the planks, the one representing interests, creaked dangerously.

"You'll have to bring Casa 50, the Casa de la Cultura in Coya, closer to the workers. We want you to stay in Rancagua; in Coya you'll work with Pancho Gazitúa, the sculptor. Silvia Urbina's handling music, Ana María, a militant with the JJCC and member of the Ramona Parra Brigade, is in charge of the murals. A local artist, Germán Ruz, not involved in militancy, will take care of arts and crafts; another painter, Víctor Hugo Núñez, is the director. By the way, we expect a detailed account of your trips – the old-timers, the ones from Teatinos, insist on it."

At that point everyone knew Teatinos meant the Communist Party.

"And also," he added, lowering his eyes, "the position requires that you pay a fee."

And who's playing the clown in this circus, I said to myself. Luckily, no one heard me.

Since paying a membership fee somehow implied committing myself to following the rail, I never paid, and I spent my money on books instead.

"He learned to keep his trap shut. You always learn something in this life."

Marcial led me to my office: a desk and a leather chair, all for me.

"Like for an executive," he said, proudly, "with two chairs for the future actors."

They had placed an announcement in the miners' weekly paper with my office hours, "Actors needed. No previous experience necessary."

There's nothing more beautiful than an empty stage, a stage awaiting the entrance of characters about to be reborn.

94

– Rise up, brother, be born with me – to give life to space and to shine again with its own light, waiting for a set to reveal the guts of a play.

There's nothing more terrible for an actor than an empty hall, lovely with its seats, tremulously waiting to be possessed by bodies, as the poor actor tremulously waits for someone to give a response to, offer a speech to, beg a smile from him.

There's nothing more terrible than a forced silence, the silence that haunts empty stages, books, pictures, songs, guitar chords used for tying up hands, bodies trapped under a carved stone, a complicit silence, the reflection of a new and ancient cowardice, hidden so as to avoid the stigma of being called cowardly.

A shiver ran down his spine, just as it would years later in the rooms filled with refugees from Stockholm to Paris, from Québec to Berlin, this time including some from Moscow to Sofia, the golden capital of Bulgaria, and some from Teatinos.

There's nothing more terrible for a director than a leather armchair, like the ones executives use, facing two other empty chairs, and some secretary slinking down the hallway, looking out the corner of her eye at the beast nailed to one step of the staircase.

On the third day I closed another door on myself: I climbed the *cordillera* to dive into the belly of the mountain. While some folks extracted copper, I extracted actors, all of us looking for a vein, though with different tools – while some drilled through rock, I unearthed souls.

It sounds lovely, but just try extracting a miner's soul, try putting ballet tights on him and making him stand on his head doing yoga, try to pull a voice out of him that will range from the throaty cry, "Watch out, cave-in!" to the delicate, ethereal tone that echoes in your brain and aims toward the moon. Try making his hands melt into a caress, and, removing the steel-toed work boots they use to protect their feet in the mine, try putting him in ballet slippers. And, hardest of all, just try to find a pair that will fit him.

These and other tasks awaited me, awaited us. Perla, the Colombian actress, convinced the miners to bring their wives to rehearsals. I tried to win them over by talking about Hamlet, and they went around like little goats with dead mouse heads, running through the mine shafts in search of the mad Ophelia.

They accepted. They accepted with the promise that they wouldn't have to appear on stage in tights because there would be one hell of a row when the first of their *compañeros* gave them a pinch in the butt. It convinced them to learn that leaders like Recabarren, Elías Laferte, and others had mounted the stage of the heroic saltpeter workers' association and that they were considered the fathers of the workers' movement, and pity the guy who laughed at Recabarren in makeup!

And with these examples taken from world theater history, they became part of the group. We called it TEC, Teatro Experimental del Cobre, and we joined efforts to find the vein.

Groceries in Chile were in short supply: toothpaste, toilet paper, rice, oil; butcher shops opened their doors to customers with a display of lungs and tripe. The meat had been put out on the spur of the moment and was sold over the phone; the employees slipped away, their bodies clinging to the walls, only to exit through the side door and be assaulted by platefuls of loin, both smooth and fat-streaked, and ribs. Sugar was sold at night, from large bags, and by the quarter or eighth of a kilo during the day, that is, when there was any, and "Doña So-and-So sent me" was the magic formula that opened the cellars. Others opened different doors, saying, "My *compañero* or my *compañera* sent me" and received not an eighth, but up to a quarter kilo, and with any luck a carton of cigarettes. It's not the quantity, massive or drop by drop, that matters; it's where that road leads.

A drop, no matter how small, added to another makes a downpour, was an adage that slipped in among the forest of banners.

There was a shortage of everything except ballet tights; we were even able to find ballet slippers for exercises.

It's a fact: there's always an excess of useless things.

As I waited for the characters to arrive, we borrowed other characters. We brought to the Sewell y Mina union Fernando de Rojas *La Celestina*, the tragedy of Calixto and Melibea, the first book to be smuggled into the continent in the steamer trunks of the *conquistadores*. The tragicomedy arrived hidden behind a brightly colored poster of a beautiful woman, her skirt hiked up, an offering to the Chilean miners from the Spanish bawd Celestina. The hall was filled; 800 spectators arrived, roaring. Ana González, who played our procuress, rushed out onto the stage throbbing with emotion and giving her all in a one-woman show; the rest of the characters lay sleeping in the miners' imaginations, though they didn't yet know it. The stage, draped in back, overwhelmed the audience and their thoughts.

At Teatinos they criticized the poster as being opportunistic and even having *petit-bourgeois* elements, which is a terrible accusation. Francisco Gazitúa, a former seminarian and the bold designer of the poster, came out with a brilliant *riposte*, "As Lenin said, 'the end justifies the means,' *compañeros*."

The Teatinos people had to suck it up. "At least they could've put in a raised fist instead of a raised skirt," insisted the head of the Control Committee, glancing nostalgically at the box with broken shards of glass that lay in wait, empty.

Someday I'll put the box with broken glass onstage, and it'll be the lead actor.

While they were waiting for the miners and their wives to walk confidently toward the stage, they invited Gorki's *The Mother*, in Brecht's adaptation, produced by the theater of the Universidad de Chile, ITUCH, and directed by Pedro Orthous.

Onstage, an actor (an actor who disappears to give way to a character, which is more Stanislavski than Brecht): the son, who, looking out at the audience (and distanced appropriately so as to stimulate reflection), following his mother's complaint about his working while his comrades were on strike, asks the audience, "If my comrades refuse to go to work in defense of their rights and I go back to work, what am I?"

These lines, which at the Antonio Varas Hall in Santiago were followed by a loud and uncomfortable silence, and which had to be repeated and repeated and repeated by the actor losing force in the repetition before provoking a timid, polite response from the audience, "A scab?," at the Sewell y Mina Union Hall received an immediate reaction from the audience: on their feet, as though a single person, the 800 miners stood and pelted the actor with curses.

Distancing effect, my ass! I had to go out and calm them down so they wouldn't stampede onto the stage and beat the hell out of the actor.

The miners began to earn a reputation for being a fierce audience. The actors began to envy the man who played the role of the son; no actor had ever gotten such a response from his audience. Groups from Santiago began to request invitations to the mine; apparently theater entails a certain amount of sadomasochism. Directors began to wonder what the hell was going on in the *cordillera*.

They had started down a long road to stand up as actors,

only to disappear as individuals; of pride, only to show humility; of risk and moderation; of love, only to make themselves hated. The miners wanted to stand up without steel-toed boots to protect themselves from the characters and speeches. They wanted to stand up with the humility of every actor in order to take over the stage and allow themselves to be taken over by their public; they wanted to stand up like actors, like those who are capable of taking the future into their hands. What the hell was going on in the *cordillera*? For just as copper had changed hands, the theater was demanding a changeover in any of its roles, whether spectator or actor.

What monsters the theater creates!

There's nothing more terrible for a theater director than for a group to get all full of itself and even have the nerve to stick Shakespeare in its pocket.

To calm things down we brought *Cloudy Skies in Chiloé* by María Asunción Requena to the union, a melodrama that tells the story of a young sailor who's in love with a beautiful girl from Chiloé who, in turn, is in love with the captain of the *Caleuche*, the ghost ship that appears in the canals of Chiloé on stormy nights, docking suddenly and without warning, and whose captain seduces and inevitably impregnates innocent young ladies.

The young sailor, the flesh-and-blood one, spent the whole play declaring his love to the beauty without even daring to hold her hand. The phantasmagorical captain of the ghost ship did not declare his love to her, but instead passionately took her sailing through the canals of pleasure that fill nights in Chiloé whenever a storm is unleashed.

It took no more than fifteen minutes for the enterprising miners, and especially the crafty miners' wives, to take sides, and for the rest of the play they drowned out the young, inexperienced sailor with jokes and advice. The actor, not the character, began to blush, not with love, but with shame. He had never felt like such an idiot, so he refused to come out on stage, not even to take a bow.

Here's the thing: love, when it happens in the theater, is real and not pretend. La Bella entre las Bellas taught me that.

Getting back to reality, we climbed one step of the staircase and invited the theater of the Central Workers' Union to put on *Onion Skin*, the story of the many forms of exploitation that the women in the recently nationalized textile company, Yarur, were subjected to. Next came the group from Lota, the coal miners, the ones who, with their black clothing, their black faces, their dust-filled lungs, swept the stage clean of bad memories.

And our people kept advancing, learning, assimilating, eliminating. They started to tell their story through short improvisations, first just for a few spectators, then for more and more miners: those from the Caletones foundry, those from the Sewell mine entrance, those from Rancagua, even some executives who got up from their leather armchairs, put on their steel-toed mining boots, and came to see what the hell was going on in the belly of the mine.

The TEC actors could now stand on their heads, assume the lotus position, do cat stretches – a collection of Jerzy Grotowski exercises that, in his Poor Theater, demonstrate that an actor's best tool is his own body. They put in their eight hours of work in the mine, traveled two or three hours in order to arrive, out of breath, at rehearsals, took off their boots, their heavy miner's clothing, the red girdle that protects the kidneys from excess weight or treacherous stab wounds, and put on tights and ballet slippers to begin their warm-ups. When it came time for improvisations, they put forth their lives, without saying so, out of modesty. In seconds, their bodies came together to form a mine shaft, to extract the mineral from the vein and deposit it in the conveyor belt, their hands manipulating imaginary drills to perforate the rock. Seconds later everything was in chaos and smoke: a forge had caught fire at one of the entrances to the mine. It wasn't the flames, but the smoke and carbon monoxide that caused the deaths. In one second they represented onstage the grandeur of those who are about to die and dare to give one more second of life to a comrade. Down below, news of the tragedy spread. The company, at the time the Braden Copper Company, didn't release any information. For three days the women gathered in front of the mine entrances, blocking them, until they were given the names of the dead, until they were told the truth they already knew.

It took three days to rescue the bodies: 355 miners succumbed to carbon monoxide poisoning. A distant 19th of June of

1945 came back to life before my silenced eyes.

Nearly at the end of the improvisation, as a chorus of women accompanied the funeral cortège toward an exit of the stage, an actor entered from the opposite side with a table and chair on which he placed a sign, "Now hiring workers."

Some of the actors left the cortège and went to line up in front of the table.

A woman walked over to the hiring agent, "The men in my family are in those coffins, every one of them. I need to work."

A miracle of stagecraft: Zola had gone beyond the boundaries of life and death. *Germinal* had come back to life.

Life went on and still does.

Neruda explained the deaths in his *Canto General,* "It's not gas, it's greed that kills in Sewell."

They had shown me how to teach them to tread the pathways of the theater. Of all the plays we read, Perla suggested *Los que van quedando en el camino* (*Those Left by the Wayside*) by Isidora Aguirre, the story of the first rural workers' union in Chile, but everyone knows that! That play was chosen because the miners came from rural families; they became miners at the entrance to the mine shafts. They were born on the earth's surface; the color of their skin came from the dust raised by the wind before it snatched them from the furrows and threw them into the depths, far from the light of the sun.

Casting wasn't a problem; the problem arose when it was time to give life to Naranjo, the traitor. Everyone looked the other way, clutching their ponchos – we already had costumes – staring at their Ho Chi Minh sandals, their hands gripping the pickaxes, hats over their eyes. They preferred being called Peasant One and Peasant Two to Naranjo: that traitor had a name that wasn't written in fine print in the cast list, and crisscrossed the play from beginning to end.

When we started rehearsing the following day, I said, "Just between us, what a great character that Naranjo is! Sure, he's a traitor, but from a theatrical point of view, he's one of those characters who make the scene sparkle, who attract attention and grow and mature before the audience's eyes. He's the kind of character who wins prizes – traitor or no traitor."

It was a tough job recruiting Peasants One and Two. I was definitely working with actors.

Gualterio, a carpenter from the Caletones foundry, played Naranjo. Gualterio was nobody's fool; he knew that he was being led to the slaughter, that for sure he would be more popular than the actor who played the son in Brecht's *The Mother*, but he made the sacrifice with that wonderful gesture that demonstrates the great soul of actors when, with courtly elegance, they give away lines that are guaranteed to earn applause for another actor.

One night we climbed another step and, gazing at the horizon, surprised, said to ourselves: We're ready; it's time for the birth. We have to come out of the womb of rehearsals to take the first steps onstage.

We set the date for our opening night.

Every opening night has its preview where you measure, study, adjust the rhythm, check the balance of the stage, gauge the blocking so that nothing appears to be out of place and the triangles allow everyone to see and be seen. You follow the direction in which the audience is looking to see if it will be a highway leading them to their destination, or, conversely, if it will lead them down the wrong path. You listen to the sound of silences shattered by the precise gesture of a hand, a breast, a hip that protrudes. This is useful in making sure the mass movement is clear, and within it, that the detail that lends meaning and relevance to each individual movement is justifiable, allowing the individual to exist without fading into the crowd, the detail that gives the mass movement its *raison d'être*. It's useful in determining if the fourth wall has been leapt successfully and the transition from the stage to the audience has been achieved, allowing the public to judge.

Every theater group has its preview before the opening, and ours was already an established group that had earned, step by step, its right to the stage and to be judged.

Rise up, brother, and tell your story with me.

The executives, without a word of protest, freed the miners of their obligations in the mine; the dignity of the mineral was at stake. They gave us a bus for our preview.

The nervous actors wondered where it would be. We left Rancagua for Santiago, the capital, taking the curve that wasn't a curve, and made a detour in Graneros. The paved road vanished and we followed a dirt path deep into the countryside.

The welcoming committee consisted of the leaders of a rural settlement – they copied our costumes, Naranjo said, identifying himself with his character. The set was a row of empty chicken coops. Before appropriating them, the farm owners had let the birds die, thousands of birds. In front of them some tree trunks, outlining an amphitheater; in the middle, wood for lighting a bonfire; all around it, our stage. The trunks served as bleachers for the audience to sit on.

"What about the dressing rooms?" the actresses asked.

"The third chicken coop – that one has a light bulb."

That night, for the first time, they tugged on our ponchos to warn us, "Watch out for Naranjo; we had one like that."

That night there was no applause: at the end the peasants were on their feet, looking at us with reddened eyes. We melted into an embrace, audience and actors alike, before sitting down in a circle to devour a chicken stew, the kind you can find only in the country, and we talked until the entire sky was sprinkled with stars, stars that, to me, resembled my actors' eyes.

Our opening was three days later. The union was abuzz with activity. The group from Caletones was there, along with those from Sewell, from Coya, from Rancagua patio, *compañeros* from the boys' school, from the girls' school; we had the sons and daughters of miners, and before them, the empty stage.

Among the audience were the critics – but not the usual, professional kind. The night before, they had called me from CODELCO, the national copper corporation, saying, "We're sending you two cars with a pool of journalists from Santiago. We can still stop them, if you'd like."

Images of the first day paraded before our eyes, when the miners had exchanged their heavy pants for delicate tights, their work boots for ballet slippers, when they had asked one another with anxious looks, 'what the hell are we doing here?' till the night when, rising to their feet, the peasants had exploded into silent, thunderous applause.

"Let them come. We know what we're doing."

And in a gigantic, mass movement, six on each side, the peasants of Ranquil walked in through the wide door, advancing down the two aisles that divided the union hall and calling on the public to join their ranks.

Together they bobbed back up to the surface and into history, bringing to light the most important detail, the one that revealed the meaning of the story, the one that challenged us, the one to which we neither had nor proposed an answer.

The critics got into it, too; the only thing lacking was for them to tug on our ponchos to warn us about Naranjo. But no: they were from the capital, and we were in Rancagua.

"It's a trick," they shouted. "Some of those actors are professionals disguised as miners." To prove it, they published the photo of Naranjo, "We've seen that guy before."

No, they hadn't seen him before, and maybe that was the problem. We had grown accustomed to looking without seeing, to skimming over details, in case they carried dangerous messages. To mold society it was necessary to mold our minds. Only when everyone was of a single mind could we achieve well-being and happiness: that was the ideal formula for non-thinking.

"Help!" I cried.

The country was on fire. A country where at one time Sunday family dinners had been a tradition, turned into a nightmare. Families were divided, dialogue was cut off, insults, not ideas, were interchanged, nothing positive could be recognized in one's neighbor; one's neighbor became a beast to be cut down. There was no room for discussion.

Discussion is dangerous, my friend.

We were living in times of the unreason of reason. Divisions arose within the Unidad Popular party. Criticism (not the box-with-shards-of-glass kind) was received with mistrust and the messenger was placed on the black – or was it red? – list.

"What freedom are you talking about, my friend?"

The other side constructed its own lists. In the union hall, during the opening, several people took notes. One of them furtively folded up a program and hid it in his pocket. I would see him again during my interrogations, before they blindfolded me. Coward that I was, I didn't have the nerve to tell him that the program contained errors; we'd missed a couple of accent marks. I had the feeling it wasn't the right time for such refinements.

There were scarcities and the problem wasn't production. The truckers, led by Cumsille, blocked the roads with their trucks. On the copper road, the one the miners took to the mine, you could hear explosions that didn't come from the mines. At La Moneda, the presidential palace, Allende called for dialogue; in Isla Negra, Neruda called for dialogue; at the National Stadium, in a ritual that prefigured the end of a tragedy, Allende offered up his body to the people of Chile.

In the bleachers the audience applauded, goading him on to sacrifice. In the bleachers, I was the audience and I was an actor, adding my voice to the chorus. The black shadow of a condor began to spread over the southern part of the continent, advancing toward Chile. In the distance the Sixth Fleet revved its engines.

The night lost its calm; within it, conspirators moved about. Incredible as it seems, both sides considered military action to be the way out. Sometimes people from both sides came together. On the left, some were demanding the creation of a new army made up of armed civilians, and they met with military officers who supposedly were loyal to the Constitution in order to execute a coup and thus defend the revolution. On the right there were civil sectors that silently shouted their demands for the army's intervention; together with these, military officers who, from the shadows, planned the coup that would end the rule of law.

Both groups thought they would take over without opposition. For the good of the people.

What had already been taken over was taken over again. Meetings changed direction: they no longer had to do with work; they had to do with putting things in order, with carrying a Party ID, without dissidence, with supporting the straight and narrow. In their midst, just like during our opening, some people were taking notes.

"It's essential to control information. History shows that if it's not controlled, you run the risk that anti-progressive forces will destabilize the process of change. It's necessary to support our principles on a solid base, and the best way to do this is to eliminate the possibility of choice or comparison. The enemy takes advantage of our weaknesses," a Teatinos member declared.

They had summoned us to a meeting in which the *compañero* from Codelco who was in charge of public relations would introduce Valentina, the new editor of the weekly paper at the mine, and they wanted us to be there. Not everyone: the list was drawn up by Teatinos. Valentina smiled from behind her huge, thick glasses. Her smile concealed her thoughts; it was a decorative smile, just as we were decorations at the meeting. Every so often a spark flew from her eyes as the *compañero* went on with his song and dance about the virtues of control.

It was late. The streams of the *cordillera* flowed down, infused with colors, creating a new landscape. The chords of Silvia Urbina's guitar echoed among the trees, singing to the human and the divine; looms wove new designs; copper plates came to life; my actors walked to their own rhythms: the established norms had been broken.

My actors weren't invited. Not all the norms had been dismantled. Nor would they be.

And the dismantling will return. As always, it will return.

It's terrible to live without norms, my friend. You'll have to think for yourself.

We had isolated ourselves without realizing it, and we had let ourselves become isolated. We were unable to differentiate the detail from the whole, the superfluous from the essential, the necessary from the useless. We had lost the humility of those who know how to give up, just to let ourselves be won over by the pride of the bad actor who tries to stay in power. And it's not always the main actors; it's those who believed they were major players, which was why they attacked the first class cars and assumed the power of driving the worn-out locomotive to the edge of the cliff. However, Allende, the conductor, had found a way out of the situation: he informed the politicians of all stripes, the military of all stripes, that he planned to call for a plebiscite to determine which course to take, with the possibility of a unified national government and even of resigning if necessary in order to open up a pathway to dialogue and the preservation of democracy.

On September 12 he would broadcast his proposal on the national radio and TV stations.

The TEC added a new play to its repertory: *Freedom, Freedom*, a Brazilian work by Flavio Rangel and Millord Fernández, a work I adapted to our reality and experience. No one said a word when it came time to turn the floor over to Shakespeare, not with *Hamlet*, but with Marc Anthony's speech accusing Brutus and the Roman people after the assassination of Caesar, whose lifeless body lay on the steps leading to the forum.

Seven knives passed through Caesar's body; seven knives pointed to the backs of the Chilean people, the last of them held by a military officer with the name of an emperor, Augusto. He had reserved his backstabbing wound for Salvador, who had the name of a martyr.

Even the rules of theater were broken: there was no preview; the group went directly from rehearsals to the stage. There was a sense of urgency. We had to install loudspeakers facing Avenida Brasil, as the audience didn't fit in the union hall. Radio El Libertador, the Teatinos' radio station, set up microphones to transmit the play live. We had gained their confidence.

Like the chorus of a Greek tragedy, we entered through both aisles, twelve and twelve. We advanced slowly, questioning ourselves even as we walked. The coryphaeus laid Caesar's bloody toga on the empty stage and the people occupied the set.

Afterwards, we loaded our costumes and props on a bus that was waiting to take us on a tour heading for Chuquicamata, so as to climb one more step of the *cordillera* and bring me closer to the encounter with my destiny.

The bus stopped at La Serena for a performance in the land of Gabriel González Videla, the twenty-fifth president of Chile, elected in 1946 by a coalition of left-wing parties, the same guy who in 1948 issued the law of the defense of democracy, the damned law that declared the Communist Party illegal. The same guy who created the Pisagua concentration camp, the very same one who persecuted Neruda, a senator of the republic at the time, forcing him into exile.

A performance in La Serena was a moral obligation.

First stop: Chuqui! Everybody off!

We entered a lunar landscape: the stones along the road told us their stories, stories of secret loves, stories of tough men's sighs, weeping for their lost loves; the stones along the road sang cantina songs that blended laughter with miners' crude, innuendo-filled pickup lines.

As we reached the peak, the *cordillera* immodestly spread its legs to surrender its fruit. Above those legs lay the infinite. In Chuqui, even more important than steel-toed boots were the helmets that protected our heads from the shooting stars that plowed the firmament.

From the bowels of the largest open pit mine in the world there arose a spiral of life; from the edge of the mine to the bottom there plunged a spiral of death. The enormous trucks returned us to human condition in that region of giants.

How could I find a speech that would reply to the stones, to the loves that had ripped their skins and dried out their veins in the desert, to the gaping mouth of a sad, lonely skull that cried out for its lost words so it could tell its story.

We mounted the stage to perform for the last time on September 10, 1973; the performance ended on the eleventh. A black mantle shrouded the stars and our dreams. At the back of the auditorium, as usual, someone was taking notes.

We hung around chatting about the past and the future with El Cachencho, the director of the Casa de la Cultura in Chuqui, and El Palta, a Uruguayan actor. We gave the present a miss. Deep down we were talking about a future that didn't exist, in order to exorcise the present. I said goodnight. The next day we continued on our way to the nitrate fields: we had another show scheduled at 11:00 PM.

The spiral path was descending.

My jaws ached, my fists ached from clenching; I had dreamed of cockroaches. I was sitting in a room, talking with my

114

wife and children, when, from the back of the chair a cockroach climbed onto my shoulder. I grabbed it with a paper towel and stood up to throw it in the toilet. As I took my first step, another cockroach appeared on the carpet, with a transparent, orange, gelatinous egg sticking out of its mouth. From the egg another cockroach emerged, took flight, and landed on a curtain. Still another one was crawling up my daughter's leg; cockroaches were coming out of everywhere, it was impossible to control them; I would kill the mother, and there I'd see the baby, running to escape and hide under the chair. With two cans of insecticide, I ran from one side of the room to the other, exterminating them. Whenever I moved I sensed the unpleasant sound of cockroaches exploding under my feet, and they kept on spouting more cockroaches from their mouths, in retaliation. I snapped my mouth shut and looked in a mirror. A cockroach crept out from between my lips. The cockroach was smiling. I threw up.

X. Of how he confronted his cowardice

The bus had disappeared. The descent to the infernos began. We entered limbo.

In the wee hours, silently, the driver had taken off in the bus, following the spiral of death, the descending path. The worst nightmare. The costumes and scenery were on the bus! The idea of a poor theater is all fine and good, even a challenge, but – a naked theater? The thought began spinning around in my head; I would make it take shape in Paris.

The bus emerged, regurgitated from the bottom of the mine. It parked in front of the guesthouse and stopped purring; it had come home. The miners, the very same ones who had been our audience, walked right by, ignoring us, heads down, their shoulders hunched with the weight of invisible tools. Their heads were adorned with white helmets, and when they reached the lip of the mine, they threw themselves belly-up on the ground, offering themselves in sacrifice.

I did the same.

Like the others, we fell into the first loop of the spiral, the one nearest the stars, the one where life began, or where death ended.

David Silberman, the manager of the mine, was the last to fling himself into the mine. The giant amphitheater held its breath, waiting for his halting words: coup . . . uprising . . . fighting . . . Allende is at La Moneda Palace . . . he's defending himself . . . the military cars are coming up from Calama . . . we don't have enough munitions . . .

Disperse, hide among the rocks, turn into dust and blow away in the wind, and when night falls, follow the stars; go down and disappear amid the lights, the shadows of the city; there a friendly hand will always open a door for you. If the military stops you on the road, don't resist, surrender; no one knows which way things are going.

No, we didn't know; we suspected. But after repeating it so often, we ended up believing our own story – you know, history shows that the Chilean military . . . and once again we forgot part of our history. Julio Durán, a right-wing politician, prior to Allende's triumph had threatened that blood clots would flow through the streets of Chile. We responded immediately: it's the Reign of Terror, and yet the reign of terror was no joke.

Years later irresponsible politicians, to cover up their uselessness, began using that slogan again, alleging: A reign of terror is being carried out against our candidates.

You can fool around with everything, but that "everything" has a limit. Decency marks that limit. Uncomfortable moments in history can be erased with an elbow, but you don't fool around with terror. In this life there is nothing more awful than facing a terror that has no limits, and our terror can't be sold for a handful of votes.

The most senior of the old-time political leaders approached Perla and me, saying, "*Compañeros*, we're organizing David's exodus to the desert. There are two seats left in the jeep."

We looked at our group; their voices echoed in our ears. Surely they had understood everything, but in a gesture of supreme cowardice, we didn't step forward. We stepped backward, instead, toward the guest house, this time *en masse*, in which the beauty of the group was provided by the beauty of our actors.

We waited with the same anxiety with which we wait to go on stage to face the audience, but an audience that marches, an audience in uniform, is no kind of audience at all.

And David? David never crossed the desert; he was captured on September 13, 1973. A military tribunal sentenced him to ten years in prison. He was taken to the penitentiary in Santiago, from where an unidentified group removed him 21 days later, on October 4, 1973. The last time he was seen alive was at the Cuatro Álamos infirmary. He was in bad shape; he had fallen into the hands of Manuel Contreras.

"From that time on, there was no more news . . . He was 35 years old . . . They even searched for him in Paraguay . . ." said a faltering voice in the belly of the mine, "up there in Chuqui . . ."

Or was it the wind?

For three days we stayed in the guest house, never going

outside. Through the slits in the curtains we could see the military's movements, sometimes alone, in uniform, sometimes accompanied by men and women without helmets. From the prisoners' hunched shoulders, from their bent heads, there rose a dignity that flew over the rifles. Our audience had become lead actors.

At nightfall Cachencho and Palta brought us food: a box with baby food – they'd stolen it from the hospital – and a book, "to kill time."

To kill time!

It was one of those times when you feel like stopping time, one of those times when you wish that the road to your destiny would come to a dead end or branch off at the wrong turn, or leap into the void. A time like the moment just before the stage lights up and you disappear as you take your first step, smiling; that moment when the whole play rushes through your mind and you forget about everything and are reborn with a new face as you step into the spotlight, in the shadows of the interrogation room. A new time that's no longer yours is created.

On the third day I was escorted to the military command. Two officers were chatting together, the area commander-in-chief and a colonel. To be honest, I never recognized the significance of the epaulets, stars, decorations, medals, or braided gold threads that hung on their puffed-up chests.

Between them, me, and the door lay a machine gun. I mentally measured the distance: it was closer to me than to the others, who were still chatting away among themselves, ignoring me. Everything was laid out in a straight line, almost like mapping out a maneuver. I've never allowed my actors to follow those rigid sorts of movements onstage, which don't lead anywhere and kill the balance of the stage. I could move in a semi-circle, I said to myself; it's longer, but it would give me a wider view, and instead of just sensing the presence of the closed door behind me, I could sense what was behind the door; I could, with a single, circular movement, grab the machine gun and cover the stage, aiming it at those two officers who are yakking away, oblivious to my presence.

Oblivious to my presence! For an actor, there's nothing more painful than to be ignored; for a director, there's nothing more dangerous than to have the actors shoot off on their own and for the scene to lose its meaning.

For me there was nothing more dangerous at that moment than for the machine gun to be loaded, and I'm against the death penalty, for others, not myself.

I ignored it, I ignored it utterly; it wasn't one of my props, and what I don't use is more than I need. I tore my gaze from the machine gun and fixed it on the two officers.

I read their minds: coward.

"We didn't know what to do with you guys," said the one who appeared to be in charge.

So they didn't know either, or at least not all of them did; but knowing how to do their jobs, yes indeed. The limits of terror: nobody knows those.

"We're sending you back. The others are already on the

bus. Just one is missing."

"Get him out of here."

The engine of the bus purred like a cat. We were on our way back: the bus was going home, and I was about to descend another step to meet my destiny.

Even the stones kept silent; the skull lost in the desert clamped its jaws shut; the remnants of clothing shredded from wear and the wind seemed to be trying to recreate a forest of banners, this time without songs, a forest of silent, faded banners, a sad forest in the vastness of the desert and of my people, a forest of banners waiting for someone to restore speech to the dry skull and return its music to the wind.

To die, to sleep.
To sleep, perchance to dream: ay, there's the rub;
For in that sleep of death what dreams may come
When we have shuffled off this mortal coil . . .

Respecting the pause in the story, we traveled in silence.

We passed through Santiago at night. A black mantle covered the city. From time to time the darkness was ripped open by beams of light that fell on us from the Puma helicopters. The noise of the helicopters produced shivers, noise, silence, noise – occasionally the sound of gunfire. We're resisting, I told myself by way of consolation. The light from the bus, a single headlight, a Cyclops advancing in the night, illuminated a red banner that lay

121

abandoned on the avenue.

It ran over it.

It ran over it and continued on its way, as we kept descending the stairs.

I fell asleep. When I opened my eyes, my actors had disappeared. Perla had disappeared. I was the last one on the list. It was a local list, not a national one, but it *was* a list. I was in the newspapers again, and for an actor, for a director, appearing in the newspapers brings great pleasure; it means recognition, even if it comes from that list.

"Wanted," read the headline: simple, direct, threatening because of the hidden meaning that lurked behind it.

I got off at the next stop. Membrillar Regiment, said the façade of the set. The orchestra conductor was a former high school teacher of mine from my days in Temuco. At that time he was area commander-in-chief, Commander Cristian Hackernek San Martín. My destiny was tailing me; unwittingly I was heading toward it, about to meet it face on.

How easy it would have been to look behind me or to have taken the jeep along with David!

Inside the entryway, sitting across from me in another waiting room, was a soldier in an unfamiliar uniform, apparently from the Air Force. Silence, suspicious glances colliding with one another, until, at the right moment, the little sensei arose from his bench, walked over to me, and broke the silence.

That was his role.

Now I understand why they called it the Membrillar Regiment.[9]

Without saying a word, they loaded me onto another bus, seating me in the middle. I was chained. I looked all around: I was alone. In front of the bus, a military jeep; behind it, another jeep filled with officers. They paraded me along dangerous streets through the center of Rancagua. They drove by dangerous places. One of them made note of any reactions.

In the plaza, a local beauty flashed me a smile. I smiled back. As I traveled along Calle Zañartu, the blinds of a local theater snapped shut.

Sometimes it's better not to see, my friend.

On Avenida Brasil they passed by the Sewell y Mina union office. The doors were chained closed. In front of us, the public jail. It was at that moment when I realized they hadn't asked me any questions, thereby leaving me without the possibility of responding. There's nothing more terrible for an actor, who has been preparing his replies for 1665 kilometers, than not to be given a chance to utter such carefully rehearsed lines.

They were learning: denying me the use of words was part

---

9 In Chile students throw quinces (membrillos) against a wall to soften them for eating. In this regiment the soldiers are the "students" and the prisoners the "quinces."

of the punishment.

The Rancagua jail, an old brick building that occupied the entire block, spread out before my eyes. On the façade, two palm trees, one on each side of the front door. In the corners, an impression of towers from which the prisoners were observed. Inside, two patios, one for minors and one for regular prisoners, separated by a concrete block. The block was two stories high; a metal staircase at the end of the passageway led to the second floor. To the left, a pipe that released a stream of icy water; to the right, a cement block with three holes: the toilets.

At the top of the stairs, a corridor that split in two, distributing people in tiny cells. On the left-hand side, just past the middle, was number 55.

My cell.

Number 55, second level, had previously been occupied by two regular prisoners. They relocated them to make room for political prisoners. When they threw me inside, there were twelve people living there.

Six slept on each side, and the extra one, the most recent arrival, slept in the alcove by the door.

During the day, the improvised sleeping quarters were turned into a living room: six on one side, their legs folded beneath them, six opposite them, legs folded. In the space between, amid folded legs, ran a corridor. No one was unaccounted for in our 3x4 meter cell. All of us were "the 13"; we took turns walking in perpetual motion.

Four meters forward, turn, four meters back. The secret was in the length of your strides, in how you stretched your leg to propel your entire body forward and returned the foot that had dared to leave the ground back to the corridor a single sigh forward.

The Poor Theater, exercises, stretching cat, scenery in motion, two walls of folded bodies, and between them an unstoppable surge along the staircases in pursuit of our destiny.

The first door closed behind me. In front of me, in the prison reception hall, a line of prisoners; before them, a gendarme. I reviewed the script: gendarme, it said, the last cog in the wheel among uniformed soldiers. They weren't officers, they weren't cops, they weren't aviators, they weren't from the navy – they were gendarmes, a sort of untrained guard dog that watched over prisoners.

I trembled. They nicknamed me "the cat."

Short, semi-toothless, with a prominent belly, the pants of his gendarme uniform half falling down beneath his paunch, shoes whose holey soles you could easily imagine, the senior gendarme strutted up and down the line, shouting insults.

He must have gotten water in his shoes during the cold, windy days of winter in Rancagua, I thought.

With a critical eye, I studied the development of the scene:

he shouldn't shout like that – he loses all authority. Besides, he doesn't enunciate well, and in the reception hall there's an echo; his movement is linear, always in a straight, parallel line and at the same pace, which eliminates any element of surprise. He comes up too close to our faces; he should keep a greater distance, and – I wasn't thinking of Brecht – he has bad breath.

A smile betrayed me; without realizing it, I smiled.

Mistake, huge mistake: you have to keep quiet, and your silence ends up quieting your body.

This fact was brought home to me by a blow with the butt of a rifle.

Though it was a time for dreaming, I learned to conceal my dreams: though it was a time for thinking, I learned to conceal my thoughts; though it was a time of disobedience, I learned to obey. I learned to keep quiet – I, who had learned to listen in order to put the word onstage, I, who adore the word – and may La Bella forgive me.

I learned to speak without words; I learned to recognize details in a forest of uniforms; I learned to let my thoughts run along one side and my body along another; I learned that neither of them would betray the other; I learned to speak in "I," forgetting "we." It could endanger the others.

I the Director was replaced by I the Prisoner, and in both cases, that "I" subsumed the "I/We" so as to allow my actors to survive onstage.

What I couldn't manage to learn was to prefer marching to singing, the masses to the individual, submission to dignity, greed to generosity, corruption to honesty. I noted the lack of principles disguised as principle, generals – always generals – so generic that they seemed to be made of cardboard and could serve as props for any play.

I learned all that because it was a time for learning, even though it might have been out of that need to feel human when "I the Human" was moaning like a wounded beast.

Some people didn't learn and never will.

"It's because they don't want to see the difference."

XI. Of how he learned to make silence scream

A stint in jail is of no use if you don't learn something, and that something varies, depending on whether it's from the perspective of the jailers or the jailed. The size of the jail doesn't matter. It can occupy a single block or a whole country, a country or a group of countries; it can occupy – and this really *is* terrible – an individual, his mind imprisoning his body or his body imprisoning his mind, and from that kind of jail it's hard to escape.

From the door lintel I watched all twelve of them. Very early in the morning, they spread the word: in that cell there are a couple of people that no one knows – be careful. Daylight was filtering in between the three bars of the narrow window; as time went on, the bright rectangle created by the sun's rays moved from one face to another, stopping time long enough to examine it. The tension was unbearable. I didn't recognize any of the twelve, and those twelve had been part of my audience. Not a single detail betrayed them, but I was afraid my nerves would betray me, and that one or both of the unidentified prisoners would recognize me, which would be like signing my death sentence.

The air became unbreathable; the slow pace of the jailhouse two-step grew faster; backs became hunched; the silences screamed.

That one? No. That one over there? Or maybe that one?

That night even the bedbugs refused to come out of their caves. Nothing was moving in cell number 55.

The next day at dawn more information arrived: they knew them. One was from Codegua, the other from Lo Miranda, militants from centrist parties. Their terrified families hadn't come to see them or ask about them.

Life recovered its normal rhythm: morning head count outside the cells – military officers had taken over the jail. The pudgy gendarme kept up his rhythm as he assigned us numbers so that no one would call out the same number twice. As a prank, we picked up the pace; Fatty picked up his. As a prank, one guy went back into his cell before roll call was over so that the count would come out wrong. As a prank we put the noose around our own necks: no one knew exactly how many of us there were, how many came in, how many went out, how many disappeared.

Some pranks are dangerous.

Fifteen minutes to use the bathroom: a gutter that crossed the floor downstairs allowed for a massive flood of piss. In front of the three holes that served as toilets: lines. It was a place of ritual, an altar where you climbed up with your pants down for greater efficiency, turned around to face the faithful, and then the officiant evacuated. When there weren't too many people in line you could even enjoy a bit of social life.

After fifteen minutes, a shout, and we all ran back to our cells. Along the way, some contact was made: we could see who had gone back in. With trepidation we glanced toward our friends' cells to make sure everyone was there.

At night, the clanking of deadbolts.

There's nothing more terrible than the clanking of a bolt in the middle of the night, a noise that interrupts your nightmare, turning it into reality, a noise that showed that you were leaving the moonlight behind and entering the darkness that covered the southern part of the continent, and when you disappeared among the shadows you didn't know if you would return to safe harbor: number 55, my longed-for cell, the anchor that connected me to life.

There's nothing more terrible than one of those cells where the locks don't open, those that will never allow thoughts to recover their words, or for smiles not to need a hiding place anymore, those that don't allow dissidence, those where decisions are made by the group, and we all know how small the group is.

I should have staged *Marat/Sade*. It's better to play a madman in the midst of generalized madness.

And yet I was and will continue to be: the thing is, my "I was," unlike their "we are," contains the pronoun "I," my own and that of every one of them.

I am, dear Carlos; I am, Pepe; I am, Gracia; I am, Guillermo, I am, Pancho; I am, *compañeros*, even though they deny me the right to "I am."

"*I am* exists, but it's reserved for those who travel in the first-class cars. Everyone else is *us* and belongs to *us*," replied the group.

You could hear the noise of locks and deadbolts sliding, clanging shut on my life.

I climbed up/down another step of the staircases, the two steps that led me to my seat on the bus carrying the prisoners.

That morning they had called my name over the loudspeakers. I was one of the twelve heading for the DA's office that day.

"I'm the thirteenth," I said, trying to get out of it.

The local government seat of Rancagua awaited us in the Plaza de Armas, to the left of the cathedral, with a beautiful enclosed patio, a real explosion of greens, with its offices and assembly room, its long, central nave crowned with a chimney, with wide windows facing the plaza, a reception hall.

Standing in the middle, Lieutenant Medina, our hangman.

There was a nave flanked by two aisles, one steered by the Air Force, the other by a combination of civilians and military officers; the largest – the one in the middle – which served as the reception room for the *intendente*, the President's representative, the mother ship, the most fearsome, was reserved for Medina.

Even though he received us one by one, Medina needed space.

Corporal Lara, the one in charge of transporting the merchandise from the jail, deposited us in the enclosed patio of the *intendente*'s office. Silence fell: no one spoke; even our breathing was contained. Time stopped; our eyes were fixed on the door leading from the lovely patio to the three naves.

The first to appear and select from the merchandise was Medina, his silhouette menacing in the half-light. He took a step forward, stopped, smiled. His eyes scanned us slowly; he didn't blink, not a single blink. The only thing we asked for was one blink, a humble sign of humanity.

He didn't raise his hand to point to anybody. He turned around without a word; we breathed; he crossed the threshold; his body disappeared. After a few seconds a hand reappeared from the shadows. He extended a finger.

It was pointing at me.

Even the plants breathed a sigh of relief: it wasn't their turn yet.

I moved forward slowly, with a movement learned in the jailhouse two-step, gaining seconds that were centuries of well-being. I went over the dialogue in my head, making sure it sounded natural and not automatic, that it flowed spontaneously. In my mind I buried what I had to bury: the fear that had accompanied me since my childhood.

I moved forward with my head high, trying not to let my body reflect my fear; I even rehearsed two or three innocent ploys.

In the hall, in the middle of the stage, Medina. I swept the hall with my gaze, recorded it in my mind for the future – just in case, I told myself.

"Some people never learn."

He was on to me. They blindfolded me. Without intending to, they helped me: I could concentrate.

I waited there while terror began to creep throughout my body. My fears were confirmed: horror has no limits.

But questions do, and since they have limits, they have no answers. They are classifiable questions, the kind that can be shot out with a formula or a meaningless phrase that carries with it a gesture of dismissal. I had wasted time miserably rehearsing for more than two thousand kilometers, from Chuqui to Rancagua. I felt frustrated.

During the three days that followed I focused on exploring myself. My mind had exploded; I learned to recognize the sunbeams that crossed my brain and burst, wounding my blindfolded eyes. My senses perceived even the tiniest sound; I could guess where the next blow would come from, the significance of a door opening and another closing, how a straight line can veer off and explore other routes. I became familiar with my body and its reactions: predictable, my body. I became disheartened, responded to electrical impulses that weren't my own, but rather came from outside; I reacted to blows, not those of life, but those of death – those hurt less. I taught my body to respond by hiding the answer; I taught my voice not to betray emotion, but to show fear – it was necessary to give them that satisfaction – and not what I was really thinking.

"The cardboard scenery, remember?"

I taught myself to recognize voices, among them that of a former schoolmate at the Marist High School in Rancagua. At the local government seat, civilians and military were mixed; in the hunt, civilians and military were mixed; in my aching body military and civilians were mixed; in my mind I recorded the details.

I used them years later when I staged a red, Latin American *Oedipus* in France.

The stage was outlined by cloth columns, some white, others burgundy. To one side, the right, downstage, was a small platform; slightly behind that, diagonally, a pedestal.

The rest of the stage was empty.

An actor crossed the shadowy stage, climbed up on the platform altar; a faint white light illuminated him.

Slowly he began to undress.

Not even a fly buzzed in the theater. One could feel the sacrifice of the actor, offering himself in public for the first time. A huge, raised scar crossed his belly, a memento of some bar brawl in the north of Chile. As he removed the last garment, the pedestal behind him began to brighten slowly. On it, a pair of military boots:

Medina.

The actor started to hang himself from a non-existent cross. His body disappeared, giving way to someone else's body, which raised its eyeless head and uttered its first line:

"I recognize your voice."

I wanted him to know it.

No questions, questions lost in time. Onstage my responses blossomed, those I had so carefully prepared from Chuqui to Rancagua. I hadn't wasted time while I was covering those two thousand kilometers.

At the end of the third day I returned to cell 55, with all the privileges of someone who was returning from an interrogation: the right to a makeshift bed assembled with my *compañeros'* clothing – with room to stretch my legs!

Nobody asked me anything. It wasn't a time for questions; it was a time for compassion.

I didn't speak – not out of bravery, no way! – but, well, just ask my body. Even today I jump if someone sneaks up quietly behind me; even today I wake up at night screaming and bathed in sweat.

I didn't speak because horror has no limits; I didn't speak out of simple curiosity. I wanted to see what there was behind the limit, peek at the last step, or maybe just because Medina, without realizing it, had stopped one step ahead of me. We all have our limits.

Make no mistake about it: there's nothing more terrible for an actor or a theater director than to occupy the stage, the main aisle, and say: I didn't speak; and yet I was happy. I laid my head down and fell asleep.

I was shivering, at last, shivering with dignity.

Months later, I had just finished taking a shower; beside me, Moraga, a member of the Communist Party Central Committee, had just finished telling me his story: In case I don't get out of here, he said.

Over the loudspeakers I heard my name; I was being summoned to the prison reception hall. I trembled, wondering if I would survive another step. After a pause, the voice added, "with all your belongings."

I crossed the patio, scanned the faces of my *compañeros*, those that remained behind. There was no envy in them. They had forbidden us to applaud releases. As on other occasions, a double line was formed and everyone – all of us – gave the freed man an affectionate pat on the back.

"Don't forget my story," Moraga added.

I walked out the main door in the opposite direction; on both sides, obscuring the palm trees, women. Women who kept vigil when we went out to be interrogated, not to give us courage, but rather to tell us, "We saw you." Women who awaited our return to tell us, "We saw you come back," and who themselves went back to their homes, devoid of men but so full of warmth. Women who, when we were forbidden to applaud those released, applauded for us. The brave women of Rancagua.

Next to me, two envoys from the U.N. On the avenue, a car with two flags bearing images of the world; they had gotten me out. I understood why Moraga had told me his story. I felt awful, as if traveling in a car that wasn't third class. I did what I was told not to do: I raised my fist.

"You always learn something new, but some people will never learn," said Víctor, the driver, smiling. He was an actor from the CUT Theater, one of those involved in *Onion Skin*.

"What the hell are you doing here?"

"Collecting little *huevones*," he exploded into joyous laughter.

He forged ahead toward Santiago; the *cordillera* blurring before my eyes, the road blurring before my eyes: I was crying.

In Santiago, on the way to the U.N. office for refugees, we passed by Teatinos. From within you could hear an emphatic: Men don't cry. At the U.N. office, a member of the International Red Cross filled out a form on letterhead and wrote my name. It would serve as my passport and I.D. to get to France.

I existed.

Without his past – distant or immediate – a man doesn't exist, though sometimes it's worse to exist knowing his future.

The telephone rang. It was Medina: He'd received an urgent call from Santiago; in his absence, his replacement had authorized my release without his knowing, which was a mistake, since he still wasn't done with me and I needed to be returned.

A change of plans. The driver would take me to Father Hurtado's refuge, where the U.N. had gathered those foreigners it had managed to rescue from jails.

I would leave the country as a foreigner. To tell the truth, I *was* a foreigner: I recognized myself without recognizing myself. The country was no longer the same.

The driver hadn't changed, "We're going to see La Moneda Palace."

We went: the Chilean flag was still standing atop the burned façade.

I was overcome by something like a wave of patriotism: Allende hadn't lowered the flag.

We went to see UNCTAD, today the Gabriela Mistral Center, where the military junta governed.

I was overcome by rage.

We stopped at the Café Haití for coffee.

I was saddened by something like nostalgia for the greenery of Caldas, the coffee-growing area of Colombia.

At Father Hurtado's refuge, among the foreigners, was a Colombian actress and singer: Perla.

Among the faux foreigners, a lot of Chileans with fake accents. I joined them.

Three days later, once more on the bus, my countrified Colombian accent started to sound Cuban, so I changed to an Argentine accent: It was safer. On the road ahead, a checkpoint.

Everyone gets off. This time they were looking for Chileans.

That didn't prevent the fear from spreading to the foreigners: terror knows no borders.

A three hour delay, and yet when we arrived at the airport, the Air France plane was waiting for us. The pilot had refused to take off without his cargo.

They rushed us through passport control. In the commotion, my mother had sneaked me a cardboard box: they made me open it.

Books: Brecht. Complete works, theater, theoretical tracts, and poems, Grotowski, Stanislavski, *La Celestina*. The bawd was going back to the Old World.

The little tin soldier looked at us, closed the box, and smilingly let me through. I almost felt him tugging on my poncho.

I told you so, I heard in my memory.

I boarded the plane. Given my condition, they offered me a seat in first class.
For my people,
for those left behind,
for myself,
I sat down in third.

The Reason of Unreason

or

The Critique of Impure Reason

For 500 years you will be doomed
to wander the earth.
After that time
you will disappear,
consumed by flames,
to be reborn from your ashes
And to walk blindly
toward your destiny.

XII. Of how he once again followed the road back to his original solitude

"UP" read the sign on the façade of the stone building in
the center of Paris, at 14 Rue de Trévise, to be more precise. The
UP had opened its arms to refugees from Chile, their first refugee
shelter in the center of the City of Light.

"Hmmm," said the Teatinos, "that's where it all began, in
Paris."

Turning right at the lobby exit and in the left-hand corner, a
total of fifty meters away, was the entrance to the Folies Bergère.

Turning left at the lobby exit and in the right-hand corner,
the grand boulevards, the grand avenues; where the road splits,
the Paris Opéra, and in front of it, the Café de la Paix. If you turned
left – which would be natural – you'd reach the office of the French
Communist Party daily, *L'Humanité.*

Mere details, since if you entered the lobby, after passing
underneath the UP sign – which didn't refer to Unidad Popular, as
we had believed, but rather Union de Paris – there was a hall; in
front of it, a little to the right, a cafeteria, and, turning left, six paces
beyond that to the right, two wooden doors: solid, nice, marked by
the passage of time and the hundreds of hands that had caressed
them. It was the entrance to a 300-seat capacity theater, an aban-

doned theater hidden in the center of Paris.

It was a meeting of two solitary souls, two beings robbed of their *raison d'être*, a director with nobody to direct, a stage with nobody to mount and take possession of it.

I entered the hall, walked down the aisle, stroked the seats, sat down in one of them to feel the caress of its arms, breathed the dust; my ears cleared so as to capture the last lines suspended in time. It was Monsieur Bip, who, from the set, smiled and said: You may speak; people who come back from the dead have the right to speak.

Without waiting I climbed the stage, and my body silently exploded in a scream that released the pain contained in my soul.

The thing is, I still use words. My body said all it had to say during the interrogations, and they didn't pay it any heed.

The warmest response came from the balcony, the nosebleed section or chicken coop, as they call it in Chile, just as it had issued from the abandoned chicken coops in the countryside near Rancagua in the seventies.

I got down from the stage, walked through the hall, was re-born with the lines, passed through the door. Once outside the theater, I took a step, the kind that has nothing to do with the jailhouse two-step.

I was in Paris.

In the cafeteria, a French woman, the same one who had been at the airport the night before, taking notes. Before her, a large cup of coffee and an empty chair. She beckoned me over; I obeyed. I'm a coward: I can't resist French women or coffee.

She took out a list, part of her notes. I was taught to read upside down: they were familiar names. My mind traveled back to Rancagua's local government seat; my hands moved upwards to the same rhythm, bringing the coffee cup to my lips. I tried to avoid moving too fast so she wouldn't realize I was buying time while searching for the right answer.

I lowered the cup, picked up a paper napkin, one of those semi-transparent kinds that don't absorb anything, and dried my lips. With my fingertips, so as not to stain myself, I took a croissant and brought it to my mouth. One mustn't talk with one's mouth full – it's bad manners.

Monsieur Bip smiled from a corner; I gave him a wink.

"You always learn something new."

"Rancagua?"

"Mmm."

"In jail?"

"Mmm."

"Was Pepe D. one of the prisoners?"

"Mmm."

I grabbed a brioche – they're bigger.

Jacqueline started telling me her story; I remembered Moraga. I wondered, why do we theater directors and actors seem like priests?

Everybody thinks they've got the right to tell us their life stories.

And afterward we have to go around munching brioches

like crazy so we won't betray their confidence.

Cavaletto, the one in charge of the refugee shelter, brought us another tray filled with brioches and croissants.

Good old Cavaletto.

"You never learn. Cavaletto wanted to see the list, too."

She had traveled to Chile, summoned by adventure; she had participated in the demonstrations of May of '68, but she didn't want to be considered a *soixantehuitarde*, or, in other words, a former combatant trapped in nostalgia and in the past.

In Chile she fell in love with a young guy, a photographer from the paper *El Siglo*. The photographer fell in love with the *cachet*: a French girl swept up in the revolution was a special case. Right around the same time, Catherine, another French girl, was swept up in the revolution in Arica, fell in love with a watchmaker, who would later become one of my actors; in Concepción another French girl . . .

Enough already with special cases, I said to myself.

"Sour grapes – French girls didn't go to Rancagua."

You know, you can tell, you can smell when someone is telling the truth, when someone is one of yours. You know for sure whether someone's been part of the action or is part of the fake scenery.

She was one of us; I trusted her.

Pepe wasn't in jail. The former elementary school teacher and then head of personnel in the mine, with 15,000 workers under his supervision, had gone and disappeared. He was a member of the clandestine regional Party leadership we kept in reserve in case of a coup. Pepe was in charge of organizing; I, of agit-prop. Every weekend we went out walking in the *cordillera* to clear our heads, to exercise, he said. He was trying to find and recognize unused paths, unexplored caverns. Pepe had read the story of Neruda's escape route at the time of the Ley Maldita.

Some people *do* learn. I, with my head in the clouds, was busy reading my destiny. I know, some people never learn.

And yet . . . added my mind.

"And yet what?" asked the Teatinos.

"And yet what?" asked Medina.

"The old guys want to see you," Jacqueline said, as she said goodbye with a certain sadness in her eyes. She and the photographer were breaking up; apparently being a French woman in Santiago wasn't the same as being a French woman in Paris.

Those were times when, in Paris, it was better to be a Chilean woman.

In a bread basket on the table, a croissant languished, a brioche grew stale, an abandoned *pain au chocolat* was left behind, never having surrendered the fruit of its womb. A few crumbs lingered at the bottom of the coffee cup. The echo of laughter floated down the staircases; moans of couples making love escaped from the showers. I climbed the first step and heard singing coming from the rooms.

"Latin America sings to Chile."

"L'Amérique Latine chante au Chilli."

I looked at the old theater and said to it: We have voices, we have a name. We open in two weeks. I knocked at the first door.

I phoned the number Jacqueline had given me; I was connected to the Chileans' office.

Mistrustfully, they asked me who had given me the number; mistrustfully, I replied, "Jacqueline."

They asked me if I knew where their office was.

Without elaborating, I said yes.

They asked me what shelter it was in.

"Nearby," I said.

"Ah," they replied.

"Tomorrow at 10 AM," they said.

"Okay," I accepted the appointment.

"Salut!"

"Salut!" I hung up.

I was learning how to use the language of exile.

When I arrived at the newspaper office, I went to the reception desk to ask where the Chileans' office was. Out of the corner of my eye I saw two Chileans, one on each side of the door. Instinctively I measured the distance between them and my back.

I had a bad feeling, and yet they were my people, mine

though not mine. They considered me to be one of them; I even became a political leader, but I was from the "I" band: even as one of them, I was still myself, and I didn't like them to tell me what I had to say, and if I wasn't pleased with the line, I would improvise and break the rhythm and veer off the rail. I even prefer "we" to that "belonging to," that "of," "one *of* them." That's what I think: I, who sometimes have my doubts even about the "I."

In the chapel it's a sin to veer off the rail, even when you're heading for the abyss.

At the office, two people: he, Claudio, the one in charge, who happened to be away from Chile during the time of the coup, and so I introduce the first category of exiles: those who were in the country on September 11, 1973, and those who were elsewhere. Beside him, her, Mónica, a young journalist from *El Siglo*, and so I introduce the second category: the institutional or bureaucratic ones – she was the *compañera* in charge of press relations and propaganda – and the mere mortals, a bunch of folks in charge of nothing whatsoever.

"Nothing gets published without my approval," Mónica fired at me point-blank.

It was a time of censorship.

"It wasn't censorship, it was the era. This would change when the era did. The day will come when control won't be needed anymore; whatever's controllable will have disappeared, or else it will be controlled."

"Whew, what a relief!

People said she was the one with the power, and they called him "the Black Hand," though no one could tell me why.

During the conversation, those who held power in the various areas went in and out: Quenita: UNESCO and international relations; fat Gustavo: organization; as for Pepe, the guy from the mine, they were waiting for him to take over the box with broken glass. As for culture, culture – a lot of people. Apparently it was a difficult area to control. Besides, this was Paris: where else could we go?

In charge of the commission, Carlitos, former president of a university; the head of music, Sergio (in fine print, "substitute member of the Central Committee"); of literary criticism, Lucho (in fine print, "supposedly a friend of Neruda's, but for some reason Matilde detests him; find out about this"); of literature, Carlitos, formerly of *Quimantú*, the government publishing company (in fine print, "loyal, extremely loyal"). The painters rounded off the commission: Pepe (in fine print, "tried and true; he was on the *Winnipeg*, the ship onto which Neruda loaded refugees from the Spanish Civil War to give them asylum in Chile in the days when Chile provided asylum and not asylum-seekers").

From afar, from Moscow, the one responsible for the group was Volodia (in fine print, "everyone respects him" – and it was true).

Nobody asked why, but when he visited us, we all had to recommend something to him, whether it was a book, a play, a film, an exposition . . . "Remember, you're in Paris," Volodia would say. Then he joined the others and left us alone to create in peace.

"A good guy, that Volodia."

The musician, an elected substitute member of the Party's Central Committee, using his double-talk, said: If I were an official member and not a substitute, how different things would be: everything would go smoothly and methodically. The old folks applauded, obviously moved: What strength our *compañero* has! For the first time one of the guitarists from Quilapayún was out of tune at a concert. A chill ran through his fingers. In the future, the musician-substitute would accuse them of using witchcraft as a revolutionary tool in the song "Malembe, Malembe." "And if I say this in front of the commission it's because my *compañeros* from the Cultural Commission of the GDR called me to warn me about it."

Since when is witchcraft revolutionary? *compañero* Honecker had inquired. And *compañero* Honecker knew about rails and what needed to be done to avoid derailing.

The musician-substitute knew his way around and was familiar with the statutes: It's dangerous to think out loud, my friend, and you should never badmouth a higher-up till he's fallen into disrepute. Volodia never fell. Others did, Volodia didn't.

Luckily.

The editor of *Araucaria*, the Communist Party cultural magazine, whose director was Volodia, got confused and thought that editing meant following the rails.

Apparently culture was the most fucked-up department, but

since this was Paris, the old-timers had to go around wearing kid gloves. Potentially it was the department with the greatest sounding board. . .

"Besides, it's better to keep them together than spread out. At least this way we know what they're doing," Mónica said.

The editor hadn't gotten confused; on the contrary, he'd understood quite well, and he played his role as a petty politico who dreamed of escaping the fine print and someday emblazoning his name on the cover of the magazine. In time he got derailed; it was during the era of the Great Derailment.

"It wasn't a matter of principle. What happens is that there's not enough mother's milk to go around."

I left the office, trying not to turn my back on anyone, just in case. I walked downstairs. The elevator was a very enclosed space; once I was out on the grand boulevards, I directed my steps toward the theater. Perla was working with the singers, and I needed to finish structuring the show.

News, poems, songs. The Gamma Photography Agency gave me a series of slides that were taken during the coup. Cavaletto lent me a projector. "Latin America Sings to Chile" was a gesture of brotherhood, a way of offering my apologies for the military's brutality against strangers who happened to find themselves in Chile when the coup took place – not all of them; some participated in the coup – a way of extending a hand through the songs of the Latin American people.

It didn't calm things down, but it helped.

It had testimonial content. The hardest part: it had to breathe solemnity; it had to be true without allowing a single tear; it required heart, heart and mind, but without turning into a melodrama that would draw cheap applause; it had to win compassion and solidarity.

"You need to be careful," Willy Odó said to me, smiling.

The hour of lies had already begun to tempt some people.

Invitations had been sent out; press releases as well. Everything was ready.

"Everything?"

Damn, I had forgotten to notify Teatinos and Mónica. They'd have me sitting on the box with broken glass again, for sure.

To my misfortune, journalists arrived. One of them asked me to write a story. An article appeared on a page of *Libération*. Jacqueline secretly fretted about the correctness of the French, which wasn't Molièresque, but Parisian.

Claudio and Mónica called me again. "They're going to congratulate me," I said to myself.

Some people never learn.

They might have ignored the business of the invitations, but a whole page in the press with my signature, not that of the woman in charge?

With an iciness that I reproduced years later when I staged Enrique Buenaventura's *The Autopsy* (you always learn something new), they informed me that I couldn't accept any other interviews, and that before contacting other journalists I had to inform Mónica so that she would cover the press.

"Are there any other interviews scheduled?"

"With Antoine Acquaviva, the one in charge of Latin America at *L'Humanité.*"

Mónica nearly fell off her chair.

For months she had been asking for a meeting with him, with no success, despite the fact that he was just two floors above the Chileans' office.

As I left the office, I saw Mónica erasing my name from the magazine article with saliva and an H2 pencil and writing in her own in block letters. For the records.

They had begun to erase me from history.

Through the show Perla and I made some French friends, and how hard it is to be friends with the French. Workers, intellectuals, people from UNESCO, from the Chilean Central Workers' Union, simply friends; good ones, real friends, not the kind that insist on naming their supposed friends so as to live in the shadow of their names and triumphs, to give color to their greasy, wrinkled gray suits, those who need to slip into other people's skins because they can't stand their own.

"Don't be nasty – they need to find the meaning of their own existence."

"I'm not nasty. I'm warning them: every time they put on someone else's skin, it starts to shrink. Balzac, *The Magic Skin,* remember?"

154

"It's part of *The Human Tragedy*."

"No, it's part of *The Human Comedy*."

Sergio showed up at the refugee shelter, hugged me, hugged Perla, and said, "I've got good news for you: in three days you're leaving for the German Democratic Republic. There you'll meet some of the actors from the Chilean Central Workers' Union, those from *Onion Skin*. They're waiting for you; they're going to form a group that will travel to stages around the world."

What words are more beautiful for an orphan director than, "You're going to reconnect with family and travel to stages around the world!"

"And what's more," he added, "since you've had health problems ever since you left Chile, we need to get you some treatment."

My coffee was cold; maybe that was why I didn't understand what kind of treatment he was referring to. It was a time of censorship; we had to preserve the integrity of our convictions, was what I heard him say.

I descended another step of my staircases.

A taxi was waiting at the lobby door; in the Hall, Cavaletto. I said farewell to the old theater. It might have been a brief romance, but that didn't mean it hadn't been a great one. The seats embraced me; Cavaletto embraced me and said, "A piece of advice and a gift."

The advice: Never hand over your documents. It's like

handing over your soul, and without a soul you can't travel.

I had exchanged the paper from the Red Cross – the document with which I was expelled from Chile – for one from OFPRA, Office Français de Protection des Réfugiés et Apatrides, CH No. 0060835. I had exchanged my safe-conduct from the Red Cross for a Titre de Voyage, a travel document that served as a passport. I was protected by the Geneva Convention of July 28, 1951, and the Préfecture de Paris had given me an official residency card and a work permit, valid for six months.

I existed.

Useless advice, I said to myself. Who's going to ask me to hand over my documents? My *compañeros* respect the soul.

The gift? A map of the Paris métro and two first-class tickets – for when you come back – he said to me. He had marked the route from the airport to the refugee shelter.

I laughed. What a joker, that Cavaletto.

I ended up using both of them.

When I arrived in the GDR, the first thing they asked us was:

"Which of you have papers? Hand them over; we'll hold on to them. It's for your safety."

I hid them.

"They took them from me when I left France," I lied, even though it wasn't the hour of lies.

Those were times of mistrust.

"Hmm . . . this guy didn't read the statutes," the Teatinos folks said to one another.

To tell the truth, the first Bella entre las Bellas had forgotten to give them to me at the first meeting. It wasn't a night for statutes or rules.

XIII. Of how he learned to use shadows to recover light

From the sky the city looked like it was cut in half, one part lit up, the other in fading light.

They're playing with contrast, I said to myself, recalling that this was the land of Brecht. They've gotten rid of the superficial, leaving only the essential. Distracting elements have been eliminated from the spectator's view, so as to leave the actor, the story's protagonist, naked – the new man atop the ruins of the old. The essential message gets through; the scenery is provided by each one according to his possibilities.

The ruins of the buildings destroyed during the Second World War passed by like scenery before my eyes. Mother Courage trudged along with her cart, skirting the survivors and the dead. Maître Puntila entered the glittering bars of West Berlin, and in a drunken haze crossed over to the Eastern sector to sleep off his binge in the shadows.

He had a dual personality and a dual language, Herr Puntila did, but unlike that other character, Dr. Jekyll, he didn't have two names, and he staked it all, not on good and evil, but on the dividing line between classes being erased by the magic . . .

" . . .of the revolution!" exclaimed my comrades, enthusiastically.

"No, of booze."

Shades of black and white played in the landscape, lending

it a gray tone that reflected sadness, weighed on one's shoulders and one's mind, and wiped away smiles.

What part of the script hadn't they read? I wondered. They understood and could explain certain things: the horror was still very fresh in their memories. The wound was still open, and there are some wounds that shouldn't close, those that aren't made of cardboard, those that injure the conscience of humanity, unlike those that, because they *are* made of cardboard, require a deputy or senator's signature to exist at the hour of lies, dirtying, stealing, staining, hiding suffering, trampling dignity yet again.

Horror has no limits. But pain does, and it's unbearable when our own people are the ones who make us feel ashamed of saying that horror has no limits because they are part of our horror, and that complicity can make it return, or at least justify it.

Berlin was not waiting for me. Berlin, political Berlin, was for those riding in the first-class cars. Paris, on the other hand, was for the third-class riders; those in first got lost, on the métro there were too many destinations.

The bus headed for a castle on the outskirts of Potsdam; 38 kilometers separated me from Berlin and the "Berliner Ensemble," the theater of Brecht and of the "Volksbühne", directed by one of his friends and disciples, Benno Besson. He offered his theater to the third-class folks, I said to myself, recalling that Brecht never signed; Helene Weigel[10] had forgotten to show him the statutes.

Luckily, *las bellas* exist.

Brecht admired Chaplin because his words ridiculed those who held power, because with an explosion of laughter he stripped the powerful and clad the workers. I admired Brecht because I carried his works and the epic path hidden in my suitcase.

At the entrance to the castle, *Genossen*[11] Willy; beside him, Konsomol members bearing flowers; behind them, the Chileans. I didn't see the actors. Next to me, the painter Guillermo Deissler, who didn't see the painters. They had told him a different story.

The actors had disappeared, as had the painters. For ten days we devoted ourselves to investigating this. Nothing. In the GDR you didn't investigate: you were investigated. *Genossen* Willy's lips were sealed, even though he had grown to like us.

When I asked him for some paper so I could keep writing, he said: You're just like Patricio Bunster[12] – the only thing he wanted was paper. That's how I found out that Patricio had been there. The old-timers came, and they were a bunch of kids who asked questions, as old-timers used to do, serious questions, other, infantile ones; some were touching, others sent chills down your spine.

---

[10] Helene Weigel (1900-71) was a well-known German actress and director and the second wife of Bertolt Brecht.
[11] Comrade
[12] Patricio Bunster (1924-2006). Distinguished Chilean actor, dancer, and activist. Member of the Chilean Communist Party's Central Committee. Bunster lived in exile in the GDR.

Whether politicians or musicians – a guitar peeked out from underneath the poncho of one of them – their questions and their tone never varied.

The person in charge of the Chilean Communist Youth – la Jota – at the castle, a young scholarship student studying in the GDR, was a bigmouth. He appeared to be alone and lonely much of the time, like a man without a *bella* or a *bella* without a man (other combinations weren't permitted; we were in the GDR). A few beers, some good talk, and his tongue grew loose.

"There are other castles: you cross the forest and there's one with Chileans in it."

"Are they painters? Actors?"

"Chileans."

Better than nothing. At least we had a clue.

We complained about the lack of exercise; we told *Genossen* Willy about the two-step, about how narrow the cells were. We needed to regain confidence in our legs, be able to look forward, keep our balance, and there's nothing better for keeping one's mental and ideological balance than riding a bicycle. Good old *Genossen* Willy got us bicycles.

In effect, at the other end of the forest there was a castle full of Chileans, who also suspected that not far from them were even more castles with Chileans.

There were no painters: they were in Dresden. The actors from the theater of the Chilean Workers' Union were there. We embraced.

We talked our heads off. "Sergio told me about the assignment," I said in a language the listeners could understand.

"Sergio? What assignment?"

I would rather have been in Dresden with the painters. There's nothing more terrible for a director than to be rejected by his own people.

On the other hand, a dancer from the National Ballet of Chile said, "I'm in. They cut my wings."

I gave her a hug.

On our trek back through the forest, trailing behind us, a green car lit our way so we wouldn't take the wrong turn.

Straight lines get on my nerves; besides, I was furious with Sergio. I changed my pedaling speed; the chain broke. The one on the bicycle, I mean; things are not that easy, with GDR bicycles, as with the Party, you couldn't change speed.

"Some people never learn."

Genossen Willy was waiting for us at the door, looking serious. He led us inside, opened the kitchen door: he had saved us some sausages, black bread, and beer.

"In case they didn't feed you well. And then, get some rest. Tomorrow I'll take you to Potsdam to buy clothes, a gift from the GDR unions," he said proudly.

"What about paper?"

"A gift from the unions," he repeated. "Paper isn't on the list, but I'm authorized to make some exceptions."

True, instead of normal shirts, he brought me two artist-type shirts, a purple one with ruffles, the other white with more ruffles. Both made from a nice, transparent synthetic fabric. They don't hide anything in the German theater, I thought; it's must be Brecht's influence.

"Shirts for an artist of the people," he said in a proud tone.

I accepted them. You should never turn your back on a union. Beside the shirts there was paper and carbon paper.

Guillermo had better luck: he discovered that in the city of Halle they were putting on Neruda's opera, *Splendor and Death of Joaquín Murieta.* Joaquín Murieta, the legendary outlaw who ravaged California during the Gold Rush era, a Chilean bandit, vindicated Neruda, and to prove it, sang of his love for Teresa. Only a Chilean can love like that; the evidence was irrefutable. Incidentally, Murieta stood for the Latin American struggle against North American expansionism and announced the arrival of the *fearsome greyhound*, coming to kill dark-skinned children . . .

It was '67; Che lived on in Murieta.

Guillermo managed to communicate with those who were putting on the opera. "Managed," I say, referring to certain problems with language and control. He had studied set design. They came to see him, spoke with him, explained to him. He drew a couple of sketches. They loved them. They decided to take him along as part of the team. It made him happy.

It made me sad – no, not out of envy, but because I had been planning to ask him to design the scenery for an empty set for my next play.

He started packing his suitcase – we traveled around the world with a suitcase, one suitcase, and our dreams and fears hidden in our hearts.

We threw him a farewell party. They were coming to pick him up the next day at noon. At nine one of the leaders from Berlin arrived at the castle, announcing that a group would be leaving for Bulgaria; he had brought a list. I remembered the window with its three bars separating the armed guards' patio from the greasy plank on which, next to the guards, stood a microphone whose switch screeched before they began to read off our names from a different list.

I took a breath: my name couldn't be on the list; the musician-substitute had assured me . . .

It was.

When the leader from Berlin switched off the microphone – excuse me, when he stopped talking – I walked over to him, "there must be some mistake, *compañero*, my assignment is . . ."

His reply was like one of those you get from a politbureau, brooking no appeal.

"Unlike other people," he said, looking at me with disdain, "we don't make mistakes."

A shiver ran down my spine; my legs trembled. Thirty-eight kilometers was too much to cover by bike. I took the train toward Berlin, without permission; the *compañeros* would understand; it was urgent: in three days we were leaving for Bulgaria.

Lovely Berlin, lovely the house where the Chileans lived! A cold light entered through the window, freezing the atmosphere and blocking all shadows and gray areas.

"Party affiliation?" asked a *compañero* from his desk by the entrance.

I wasn't mistaken: they have no gray areas.

I thought of La Bella, the first one, and even though I had never signed or paid, I replied, "Communist." It was urgent and I needed to talk to someone.

He disappeared down the hall, returning fifteen minutes later.

"Third door to your left."

They let me in.

Before them a dossier, "What kind of work did you do in Chile?"

"Theater. I directed the Teatro Experimental del Cobre, in the El Teniente mine."

And I started telling them about the empty chicken coops, the performances around bonfires, about how they tugged on our ponchos, and even though I clearly understood that this wasn't Brecht's distancing effect, I added – just in case – something about the last tour, the Paris performance, about what the musician had told me . . .

"Do you like planting potatoes?"

That one I wasn't expecting. Here it wasn't a matter of controlling the contractions of my body; my mind had lost its agility. I simply wasn't expecting it.

They had caught me off-guard, and I had to ad-lib.

"If the Revolution requires it."

I shrugged: it had sounded phony, almost like a cardboard prop. Asshole, you incredible asshole, I self-criticized. I knew there were some speeches I couldn't produce.

"Now go pack your bag; you're leaving for Bulgaria, to plant potatoes."

Although I knew that the line is the line and that you don't question the rails, which lead to the box with shards of glass, I thought: I'd rather sit on the box than plant potatoes, and I said:

"There's an error. I demand that you call Paris, and they'll explain that I've come to do theater."

"Bulgaria," they repeated.

"Why?"

Punishment is more bearable when you understand the reason for it.

"So that you'll learn. It's because of chickenshits like you that we lost, you intellectual petty bourgeois."

As I walked out the door to catch the train, I ran into Guillermo. I didn't dare say anything to him; since his opera was by Neruda, maybe he'd have better luck.

XIV. Of how he learned that disrespect is a virtue

The punishment brigade, a bunch of guys from La Jota, got off the plane. They were happy: an actor from the Catholic University of Valparaíso and his wife (two, I added); a photographer, the son of a member of the cultural commission in Paris, the guy from Quimantú (three, I added); Conchita, the daughter of Pepe, who was in charge of graphic design; and his buddy, El Chacal – not Vladimir, the guy from Venezuela – this one was from a *población* in Chile (0, I added), Conchi had a belly like a watermelon; Perla; Guillermo; and I.

The only one with a return ticket was Guillermo, paid for by the folks at the Halle opera (one, I subtracted).

And what about this one? they wondered in Bulgaria.

"Our Chilean *compañeros'* orders are orders and we've got to respect them. However, the order doesn't say we can't bring him back," the Germans said. Those GDR *compañeros* sure were organized: the return flight was leaving in one hour.

Guillermo got on it, went back, and stayed and worked in the GDR. He died in reunified Germany, in the same city where he took part in the staging of *Murieta*.

It was a time of irrationality.

"It *was*? What do you mean by *was*?

They gathered us together in a room and once again asked if anyone had I.D. documents from any non-socialist country. They herded us into another room, a VIP room, where a choir of young Chilean communists who were studying in Bulgaria awaited us. As a tribute, they serenaded us:

We shall, we shall not be moved . . .

Just like a tree that's standing by the w-a-a-t-e-r,

We shall not be moved . . . they waited for us to reply.

I stood there, mouth agape. Yes, we were in Bulgaria.

"That's nothing – you should've seen Romania," the poet Lara whispered to me.

I was glad: that's what he gets for sticking his nose where it doesn't belong.

"Vengeful! And to a *compañero!*"

"So what?"

"Hmm, it seems like he's getting better," said the musician-substitute. "We'll have to *treat* him again."

Sofia beneath a forest of banners wasn't the same as Sofia beneath a wilted cluster of photos of the Leader, Todor Yikov. Sofia shimmering beneath the golden cupolas of its churches wasn't the same as Sofia languishing beneath their peeling, gold-colored paint. Taking trolley number 8 to go out and have a good time wasn't the same as paying 5 *stotinkis* to be forced to take it from Dervenitza to the center of the city.

Visiting Sofia wasn't the same as living in Sofia.

And it's not a question of being ungrateful.

The leader in Bulgaria, the former ambassador, was the

brother of Fernando Alegría, the one from *Lautaro, Young Liberator of America.* Maybe that was what saved me from planting potatoes.

With Guillermo in mind, I finished writing and began working on the production of *We Call You Pablo-Pueblo*, in homage to Neruda.

"As you guys see, you always learn something new."

Koleva said the same thing when she gave her first Bulgarian class. The most enthusiastic learners of the new language were the young people who were planning to continue their studies; they didn't know that many would end up in military instruction camps, some of which were in Bulgaria, and that they would help fill the ranks of the Manuel Rodríguez Front.

"You forgot 'Patriotic' – it's the Manuel Rodríguez Patriotic Front.' That's a bad sign, the Teatinos members said.

Repeating phrases in Bulgarian: *Kak se kazvash Vie? Kakvó ima?* or something like that, I wondered in what language I would put on the show, as my mind returned to Monsieur Bip, the cat stretch, disassociation of thoughts from their bodily response, the rhythm of silence, the musicality of the word, the magical sound of lines rolling down the staircases.

I began to look for bodies as well as voices; I began to play with spirals by crossing diagonals, the balance and imbalance of the stage, the lights and shadows of the Black Theater, masks and choruses. I decided to interrogate the audience using the solitary coryphaeus, transcending the language barrier.

"Actors needed," read the little sign. "No experience necessary. Enter without knocking." Instead of an executive style leather armchair, I had a hard, wooden chair and a rustic table in my room.

They lined up.

I left Koleva and her laboratory – *dovízhdane tovarich* – and determined to stroll around Sofia. I needed to decipher the secret hidden beneath the peeling roofs of faux gold; I needed to find the place where Cyril and Methodius hid the Cyrillic alphabet during the 500 years of Turkish occupation; I needed to question the women who had been raped during the occupation; I needed to understand what the silence of the dusty, expressionless portraits of the leaders concealed; I needed Dimitrov's Komsomolsk to loosen their tongues and explain to me what they were fighting for; I needed to see the theater: not the uninteresting, official one, but the underground theater, the one that was hiding in the University's basements, so much richer, more authentic, joyful, like the *Joró*, the name of the Bulgarian dance. I needed to see the national student theater festival on the Romanian border.

"A border represents a threat and therefore a challenge."

I needed to learn the language of my new public in order to find a way for us to communicate. I studied hand movements, different kinds of smiles and their duration. I studied cries of love and their different types, real and faked. I even paid attention to the way people walked, those who held power and those who feared it; I needed to learn how to position my actors onstage.

I shielded myself from the sun in order to disappear beneath the shadows of the national heroes, including Lenin and Stalin. I studied the changes in temperature beneath each one, looking for a way to bring warmth to the hall.

I didn't need to see *Santiago, Hotel Carrera*, a play staged by local actors and directed by its author, the *compañera* of the *compañero* in charge of culture and a distinguished member of the political commission of the Bulgarian Party, but I learned all that too late, after they asked for my opinion. I talked my head off.

I know, some people never learn.

What I didn't know, and neither did the leaders, was that the *compañero* senator who joined the leadership had come because he was crazy and they had sent him from Bulgaria to be locked up in an asylum to recover. Not so crazy, though: the senator hid the letter.

The senator was the one who laid into me the hardest when I expressed my opinion: that there was no structure, that not even Snow White would believe the story, and she believed everything . . .

The play was about a member of the political commission of the Communist Party who had escaped from La Moneda Palace, taking refuge in the Hotel Carrera, in a room belonging to a United Nations bureaucrat.

She: elegantly dressed, the script said; he, in revolutionary garb, the script said. They dressed her in a tailored suit, like the ones they put on *compañera* Valentina Terechkova for press conferences; she looked like a black pudding with feet. They dressed him in a red vest with yellow stripes, threadbare at the elbows; he looked like a traffic light flashing a warning signal.

She was a cultured Bulgarian intellectual; he, a cross between Superman and a hero of the Russian Revolution. He emerged from the wardrobe where he had been hiding and walked through the room as if he were descending the staircase of the Winter Palace. All that was missing for it to look like a scene from *Battleship Potemkin* was the baby carriage; to tell the truth that was the best part of the play. Unfortunately, the unbearable tension broke when he opened his mouth, looked the intellectual international bureaucrat in the eye, and, raising his fist, spat out his first line, "We shall overcome!"

The Bulgarian intellectual replied, "With Chopin," and kept banging away at the toy grand piano that adorned the stage, recreating the elegance of Hotel Carrera.

From that moment on, every bit of dialogue that came out of the leader's mouth ended with a "We shall overcome!" and a raised fist, which, by the tenth time, made Conchi look at me and say, from her seat, "We shall overcome, Pedro!", raising her fist.

It was the starting signal. All the Chileans in the audience began raising their fists and repeating the dialogue without rhyme nor reason.

The Bulgarian audience was touched, and the spectators, in turn, began raising their fists. From their boxes, the old folks were moved by this homage and they, too, raised their fists in the air. Apparently both groups needed a distancing effect.

But I left all that out of my critique.

I took along a diatribe by the *compañero* senator, which resembled a monologue straight out of the Charenton Asylum. He was no Marat, of that I was sure – maybe the Abbé de Coulmier, the mad abbot, the former legislator who ran the asylum. I promised myself I would read *Marat/Sade* again, and next time I would pay attention to the senators' speeches.

They can serve as an inspiration, not the way they think, but in their rhythm, their cadences, the way they pick up speed when they think they're being heard by humanity, the emphasis placed on those words that seem like monuments. An extraordinary use of words! The pauses are more problematical, and let's not even talk about the content.

International solidarity . . . comrade in charge of . . . the people . . . the struggle . . . leader . . . gratitude . . . realism . . . socialism . . . the senator-abbot prattled on and on.

From the shade of my chair I was tempted to raise my fist and reply, "We shall overcome," but I restrained myself. I had the impression that the senator had lost not only his mind, but also his sense of humor.

When we got to Dervenitza something had changed. Youthful fists weren't happily being brandished in the air along the corridors; The guy in charge of the Jota Jota had fallen into disgrace, and there was a new guy: the actor from the Universidad Católica de Valparaíso, the only one who hadn't wanted to be part of the theater group.

I listened to him repeat to a young girl: international solidarity . . . a comrade in charge of . . .the people . . . the struggle . . . leader . . . gratitude . . . realism . . .socialism . . .

"We shall overcome," the girl replied with a touch of humor.

I promised myself that I'd put the actor from Valparaíso onstage in some production. Years later I included that type of character as a prop in Buenaventura's *The Orgy*. He was the carpet that stretched out at the feet of an old whore.

They ruined my rehearsals: every time I turned my back to them, my new actors raised their fists and laughed. Since I have eyes in the back of my head, I used their laughter, their shining eyes, their bodies twitching with laughter, their cunningly clasped hands, and if any of them didn't hold hands, I forced them to, to keep them from making fists onstage.

I deleted some words from the script; they had lost their meaning. I left a space between one pencil mark and the other, in case in the future – maybe, you never know – they might regain their meaning someday.

Opening was in two weeks, once more without a preview. I went to see Alegría, the man in charge. I waited patiently on the corner for the senator to leave; I didn't want him to be there when I requested the hall, nor did I want him to ask what for. That guy was capable of requesting a supervised preview, and for sure I'd ended with no opening night. In any case, my actors were prepared; if the senator were to show up, they had to raise their fists in unison; that would dazzle him, and he wouldn't see the rest.

Raised fists are a forest of banners.

I longed for Paris, where I could elude censorship by simply not signing my name to my articles. Though later the musician-substitute came up with the idea of pre-exhibitions, to cast the texts in a good light, naturally using democracy as a pretext. Remember, he was a musician, but a musician with the soul of a senator-abbot. There was a lot of activity at the office, comings and goings, and even Volgas, shiny black cars for the crème of the first class – unlike the dull, gray Ladas – parked in front of the place where the embassy used to be.

Luckily for me, the senator left and didn't come back. I hurried to the place and managed to hand in my petition. The former ambassador would take care of requesting a theater space from the Fatherland Front.

Time had passed; my documents, both from the U.N. and from the French government, were dangerously approaching their expiration dates.

That night we were invited to a closed meeting. Leery, I wondered why I was on the list of those invited. In the hall of the Fatherland Front we were advised that if we recognized anyone, we were not to say his name. I took a deep breath: it wasn't to ask for a preview. A heavy wooden door opened wide. The first to enter was Caputo, an economist that La Bella had introduced me to in Santiago. We got along well, though I suspected he was in love with her.

He had paid for his schooling by loading and unloading trucks in the central market. Behind him, Coke, a member of the secretariat of La Jota, then of the Party, and future leader of the Party in Paris.

I was glad: real heavyweights who had managed to get out of Chile alive were walking in. They gave a boring report, nothing new, stuff we all knew about; they added a drop of hopefulness and kept mum about the most interesting part: them, their escape, acts – not names – acts of greatness and of infamy.

They were lifeless.

Even Neruda had described the human aspect of his persecution and escape, though concealing the name of the love of his life, Matilde, because officially he was still with Delia del Carril, the Argentine painter, the little ant, who introduced him to Paris and the avant-garde. He didn't name the love of his life, but *The Captain's Verses* put his life on the line to protect Matilde. At the end of his days in his *Isla Negra Album*, he apparently put life on the line once again: this time her name was Alicia and she was Matilde's niece, a dark-skinned, ample-bodied beauty, except that Matilde, a ballsy woman, wouldn't put up with it and threw the new love of his life out on the street. The thing is, Matilde was a real *chilena*.

"If you ask me, Neruda joined the Party 'cause he was a lover."

Just like the entrances and exits of the heart, you have to take care of the entrances and exits on a set. They determine the direction of the scene and guide the spectator's eye, even more so when you're dealing with a different language that can make comprehension difficult.

Opening day arrived, that yearned-for, feared day, the moment when the doors are flung upon to reveal your soul, your guts, your dreams and fears, your most secret desires exposed onstage.

Like all directors I arrived early, the first one, alone, to ask the hall to treat us well, to apologize to those who had given life to that theater before for trampling their footsteps, to beg the seats to receive their new guests – my executioners, for better or for worse – with love.

I asked permission to go into the technical booth: I wanted to turn on the spotlights one by one, rouse them from their torpor, ask them to dissolve in the characters as they illuminated them.

"The orders from the Fatherland Front mention a theatrical hall, but there's nothing about the use of spotlights. We can't let you turn them on," I heard, paralyzed.

Darkness has no limits. All those geniuses combined couldn't turn on a 15-watt bulb.

Outdoors, the moonlight was enough for me: moonlight adds a different tone, a different dimension; the communion becomes sacred. Around a bonfire, light and shadow play on the actors, emphasizing them or making them fade from the scene, allowing the dialogues to shift in waves on clouds of smoke. The scene plays with hard reality and the softness of velvet, and the play floats in space.

In a closed hall, without windows or lights, the lovely scenery becomes an interrogation room with a blindfolded public. Before their eyes: nothing.

Although, perhaps, why not play, not with past interrogations but with the challenge of the imagination, with an absolute void, so as to feel the intention, the direction of the word, the reconstruction of the image starting from nothing, the nothingness and the everything of every spectator? To give birth to a new kind of theater, the ur-theater, the one from Plato's caves.

But, careful: I was in the present, and that night the old-timers, among them the senator-abbot, were coming.

Calmly (a few months had gone by and I had assimilated the local rhythm), calmly I said, "It doesn't matter, *compañeros*. Please, someone get me a phone so I can call a senator, a member of the Chilean Communist Party's political commission, and ask him to phone the *compañeros* from the Fatherland Front."

The reply was what I expected; I had learned from the GDR and from Bulgaria, "It's not necessary. There must have been an oversight. Take the keys to the booth; we'll even leave the cabinet with filters open for you."

And from beneath a table they took out a shoebox, adding, "We'll even lend you these colored filters. They were left behind by a French group that took part in an international festival. You can mix them with the red ones. Oh, and tell the *compañero* that we solved our Chilean *compañeros'* problem."

The doors opened at the appointed hour; the audience filled the hall. Behind the curtains, the actors waited anxiously.

The house lights went out; the stage lights went on, and . . .

A warm round of applause greeted the first actor, a congressional type of applause: slow at first, rhythmic, and then growing faster and faster and ending in an ovation accompanied by the requisite "bravos."

The second actor was about to come out, and they covered

the stage with flowers, in the purest *compañero*-welcoming fashion.

A fly flew across the stage from left to right; hearty applause. I was struck by doubt: Is left-to-right an unlucky sign, and is right-to-left a lucky one?

"Not when it's a fly, only a bumblebee and it has to be blond. And not in the theater, it's in guerrilla warfare, and that kind of stuff happens in Colombia, not in Bulgaria."

I peeked through the hole in the curtain; every respectable theater has a hole in the curtain through which the actors can see the audience and do a head count: half-empty hall, half-filled hall, full house. It was a full house: old folks, young folks, young Colombians, young Cubans, young Ecuadorians, young Chileans. Not a single Bulgarian among the spectators, nor a Russian – even on loan – though maybe, just maybe, the shadow of Dimitrov hung suspended in the air.

I had suspected as much, but even in the worst nightmares there is a moment of relief. Everyone applauded, even the guy who swept up the carnations so that my actors wouldn't slip and break their necks.

I, the sweeper of dreams, swept up the flowers, called back the actors, exited to the left – it made no difference that it was a fly and not a bumblebee, and the newly emptied stage, threatening in its silence, imposed order.

We had begun again.

Months of studying gestures, movements, tempos, months searching for a way to break the language barrier, months finding a common ground to communicate in while preserving the beauty of the word and the poetry.

Not a single Bulgarian!

They had robbed me of my right to the word, and there's nothing more terrible for a theatrical director, for an actor, than to be silenced; there's nothing more terrible for a theatrical director than for his blood, his people to think he's speaking Bulgarian.

I'll have to adjust the language; I'll have to check the filters in order to create different atmospheres with the lighting; I'll have to change the pace, I said to myself, and I was prepared to do all that. What I couldn't manage to figure out was how to change the forest of banners in their heads so they could see beyond the masses, see the detail that allows them to distinguish the cardboard scenery from the idea and its essence, to see without getting lost along the way and continuing blindly.

How could I teach them to see that Homer, a blind man, saw more than the sighted did, I asked myself, plunging into the masses, guided by Jocasta. Unwittingly I had sullied my mother's womb: I asked her forgiveness and closed the doors of that theater in Sofia, ripping the images from my eyes.

Stumbling, I returned to Dervenitza.

Years later, in my staging of a Latin American *Oedipus*, I took the blind Oedipus, his body covered with a heavy, frayed sheepskin blanket, clutching the eternal branch of a Fontainebleau tree as his cane, and had him walk back and forth onstage, guiding the hundreds of thousands of peasants who had been displaced by the violence in Colombia along the way.

"Assembly!"

They transported us on buses; it must've been a serious business. The most optimistic among us exclaimed, "The dictator has fallen!" We all wanted to believe it: it was a time when believing was necessary: *Credo, ergo existo!*

The *compañero* senator chaired the assembly. No, the dictator hadn't fallen. The senator-abbot read the decree,

"With the consent of the Fatherland Front, we will allow you to study." I looked at the Jota members: they were all school-age kids, and from the beginning they were convinced they were going to study, like all their peers who were in Bulgaria.

He continued with his speech, trying to erase the happy expressions from the youngsters' faces.

"I want you to think about how right now your *compañeros* in Chile aren't able to study, how they're persecuted, tortured, how they haven't got enough to eat, how they don't get money like you do to take the bus, how many of them have lost their parents . . ." and he went on enumerating.

All of that was true, but it was equally true that he had no right to make them feel guilty because they were going to be studying. It was immoral to erase the smiles from their faces. I recalled the play *Santiago, Hotel Carrera,* especially its refrain.

No, I didn't feel like raising my fist.

The former ambassador asked if there were any questions before his *compañero* read out the list and destination of the Jota members.

El Chacal was the first. Mistake, I said to myself, but I didn't have a chance to warn him.

"*Compañero*, we all admire the heroic Soviet people for their love of the arts. The whole world admires their dancers."

No dummy, El Chacal, I thought. That guy wants to go to the USSR.

"La Conchi and I . . ." – (he was talking about the daughter of the guy in charge of graphic arts in Paris; another point in his favor, El Chacal was definitely no fool) – " . . . studied ballet at the Universidad Católica de Chile."

That explains his clothing, then, no doubt designed by Pato Bunster: a parrot-green velvet suit, bell bottoms, and yellow, high-heeled shoes, like an escapee from *The Magic Flute*. That drove La Conchi crazy, making her give up the security of her parents' house in the upscale neighborhood of Santiago for a squalid little room in a shantytown. I could imagine El Chacal dancing in toe shoes, but imagining La Conchi, with that belly of hers and in a tutu, I couldn't contain my laughter.

"We all know that the Bulgarians are the Russians' best students . . ."

El Chacal blew it: you could be a *compañero,* a disciple, but not a student. Besides, he'd forgotten that Nureyev, the Bolshoi superstar, on his return from Paris to Moscow following a tour, when it was time to board the plane, after passing through security and with tensions relieved, had turned around, and, in a leap that would make the ballet's swans die of envy, flew over the airport's barrier wall and sought political asylum in France.

Even though a person might forget, the Party has a memory like an elephant.

"Faggot professions aren't accepted into our programs," roared the senator.

"The Party had its principles."

Chastened, El Chacal sat back down. There were hints that they weren't accepted among the populace. But we were in Bulgaria. La Conchi fainted, as she usually did throughout her pregnancy. That saved him.

Immediately afterward, the actor from La Católica stood up.

"*Compañero*, I studied theater at the Universidad Católica in Valparaíso," quickly adding, "but I understand that it's necessary to study for careers that will serve the revolution . . ."

(Not only was I about to use him as a prop, but the carpet would be grimy, too).

"That's why I'm asking permission to study philosophy, so as to explain to our people the writings of Marx, Engels, Lenin, and the reports of our glorious Party" concluded the actor.

"Approved," said the abbot.

I spent the rest of the meeting studying the peeling, golden ceilings of Sofia's palaces.

The next morning I went back to the office and asked to return to Paris. My documents were valid for another two weeks.

Crestfallen, the former ambassador said, "In Chile, Pinochet referred to the refugees as kings and queens traveling around the world. To disprove that, the Party decided that as of last week nobody moves from wherever they are."

It was a time of irrationality.
"What do you mean, *was*?"

A husband remained in one Berlin, his wife on the other side of the wall, both of them unable to cross; a son in Sofia, his parents in Paris; some in Argentina, others in Venezuela. It was as if a gigantic iron curtain surrounded the world.

Traveling was a crime unless you happened to be on one of those first-class missions; the lucky ones who owned passports and moved about were punished with ostracism, while those of us on the other side of the curtain were simply denied permission to leave, and without permission no one got on a bus or a train, let alone an airplane. Without permission one was a pariah, and I was a theater person, not a dancer. Besides, the barriers separating Sofia from Paris were higher, and I, the distinguished actor-dancer, was barely able get into first and second position; in third or fourth, I broke my head.

I need to leave, I insisted; I insisted a thousand times. Time went by and the documents approached their expiration date.

I was going crazy.

At the French Consulate I asked what was happening with

my case. By showing up before the fatal date, I would keep my refugee status and my documents could be renewed; otherwise, I would lose my refugee status, and in order to get in back I'd have to start all over again, but the Geneva Convention was clear: one requested asylum in the first country one entered. To request it I would have to register Bulgaria as my country of departure. I would become a refugee from the East, and I wasn't prepared to do that – not for their sake, but for mine.

Without papers no one would accept me in any part of the world. I would be stuck in legal limbo.

I went back to see Alegría. I spoke to the intellectual, not the *compañero*. He agreed to consult with Moscow.

Time flew by, and just as swiftly the former ambassador arrived with the news: Moscow had granted permission.

The Fatherland Front gave the green light; the Jota members accompanied us to the airport. We were happy; we were sad: we had established links beyond the ephemeral lifespan of a play.

Ciao, Pablo; Ciao, people.

Sofia lay behind us, without her forest of banners, her paint peeling in huge strips; the Jota members standing proudly, fists held high.

In my airplane seat, I wondered: Moscow? But who? The same question I had asked myself as I left the Rancagua jail: Who authorized my release?

They brought me a tray with salad, and passed me a salt shaker. When I saw the grains of salt, I smiled. Volodia, son of saltpeter[13].

The clouds parted. In the distance, the lights of Paris began to twinkle.

I climbed up another step toward my destiny.

---

[13] Saltpeter mines in the north of Chile had a profound impact on the country's social history. *Son of Saltpeter (*1952) s the title of one of Teitelboim's novels.

186

XV. Of how he climbed onto the great stages in search of the cornerstone

I spent the first night wide awake.

"Ah, you know, Paris is Paris!"

No, not the first night, the other one, not the first, the second, the one at the refugee shelter near the Folies Bergère.

"Ah, Paris is Paris!"

I missed the silences of the corridors, the heavy darkness, waiting for bolts to be unlocked.

"The treatment definitely left you with a screw loose."

From the lobby lounge, a light sent out intermittent signals from an arc lamp that illuminated my robotic steps. Hypnotized, I crossed the threshold. A rickety leather armchair occupied the middle of the lounge. No sounds came from it, it was unoccupied, waiting; there were no other chairs in the room. In front of it, a table; on the table, a TV set, and on the screen *King Kong*.

I sat down to practice the language. It was the original *King Kong*, in black and white, a masterpiece of silent film.

We clicked right away.

Today, my first night in Paris, not that one, the first of the third, I spent wide awake. I walked into the lounge; the armchair was unoccupied, as though waiting for me. I sat down. The TV was in front of me, on the table. It was turned off.

I flashed back to my second time, trying to figure out why

they had pulled me out of the heart of Paris and sent me to the other side of the Iron Curtain.

After the opening of "L'Amérique Latine Chante au Chili," not only did an article appear in *Libération* the next morning, just as I was about to dip my croissant in a steaming cup of coffee, but Georges Dememay also appeared, dressed in his best finery. He greeted me with a noble gesture, the haughty, southern gesture of a vine swinging on Ñielol Hill in Temuco. I pointed out the chair before him and offered him some coffee. Cavaletto was paying.

Georges was the public relations representative of the Théâtre de la Ville. Jean Mercure, its director, had read the article and ordered him to acquaint us with Paris, or rather "le tout Paris" of the theater world.

That night he came by to pick us up and take us to see the play that Mercure was staging. As the lights were turned out and the enormous stage of the Théâtre de la Ville lit up, a peasant in Ho Chi Minh sandals and threadbare silks appeared, carrying two buckets. As he reached the edge of the stage he looked at us and pronounced his first lines, the ones with which the play began:

"I am Wang, the water carrier."

The Good Person of Szechuan! At the end of the play, when the gods were waving goodbye – remember? – and leaving Shen-Te and her unanswered questions all alone, at the moment they were about to ascend to the heavens, the stage began to generate before the audience's eyes, before my eyes, a staircase that emerged from nothingness and disappeared into the infinite space of the Paris skies.

In the dressing rooms, when the play was over, I told Jean, the First God, that I had played the Third God in a Colombian production and that my heaven was reached via an old, broken-down chair. We exchanged a divine embrace.

And so, in a spiral of life we explored the theaters and neighborhoods of Paris.

The next day I embraced Phaedra in a dressing room, in the person of Silvia Monfort, a beautiful and legendary actress. In the 18th *arrondissement*, Montmartre, we climbed the staircases, only to disappear behind Sacré-Coeur through the Porte Saint-Denis and enter Paris' lively "red belt." There the Gérard Philipe, one of the eight national theater centers of France, awaited us; at its entrance José Valverde, its director. The son of Spanish refugees and a man of the theater, he opened his arms and his theater to us. We were home.

Like a flash of lightning, the image of Monica erasing my name from the newspaper and from history crossed my mind. Behind her, a shadow was smiling. I tried to identify it but couldn't. I recalled someone entering the lobby, announcing me . . . I've got good news for you.

From that day forward I made my way through lobbies with a lantern in my hand.

"It's tough to overshadow someone, my friend," Icarus

whispered on the way back, while I directed my returning footsteps to the office of *L'Humanité*. Gustavo, le Gros, the one in charge of the organization, was sitting behind the desk.

With that unfocused stare so typical of certain political leaders, except when they've got you sitting on the box with broken glass or when they're about to deliver some "good news," he said:

"You have to talk to Pepe, the miner."

I smiled. He was the guy from Rancagua.

"Now he's in charge of the Party's Cadres Control Committee.

My smile vanished.

This time I spoke, "If it's about my leaving Bulgaria, you know that nobody leaves from the other side without permission, and in my case, they consulted with Moscow." I thought of El Chacal, vowing I'd buy myself a green velvet suit.

"They let you leave, but they told us that you were being sent away as a punishment. They let you go. You have no right to participate in a cell as a militant; it's to make an example of you. Since you left, there's a bunch of people who have asked to come back."

Once more I was left without a cell, without a cell but not without assignments. In any case I'd have to sell Quila's[14] records, but I didn't have the right to decide where.

"However, the punishment doesn't say anything about committees, so you'll join the cultural committee. They're meeting tonight in a room upstairs."

---

[14] Quilapayún, one of the most famous Chilean musical groups in exile in Paris.

The room upstairs – I felt like I was in heaven.

"Try to be discreet," Pepe the miner advised. "I'm inviting you to dinner this Saturday. Elisa's here." The living room of his apartment was filled with life, music, and tuna noodle casserole, the French culinary specialty of Elisa, his wife.

At precisely seven PM Carlitos, the one in charge, entered the conference room along with Lucho, the critic (of art, not of the rail); Pepe, the painter who spent the entire meeting drawing us (sketches that Lucho kept openly in his ring binder); an editor, the same friend who had banned my prologue from a song collection in Quimantú; the musician-substitute, the only one who didn't smile when I occupied my post. It wasn't personal; it's just that it was hard for him to smile. He thought it might detract from the seriousness of what he was saying.

That day he was the first to speak.

"A singer has just arrived, a perfect voice, a promising *bel canto* that will take popular music to a higher level. It's our duty to find her a prestigious hall and introduce Ana María to Paris and to the world.

Silence: everyone was concentrating on the painter's eyes, and with a barely noticeable movement, he gave me the floor.

"Let's have El Quila introduce her at one of their concerts."

"They refused. Besides, Ana María isn't the kind of person to be introduced by anyone; she's destined to shine in the sky with her own light."

I wouldn't have recognized Ana María at a dogfight. What could have happened in my absence? I questioned the others with my eyes. Some of them gazed down at their nails; others closed their eyes, not to see better, but to avoid seeing. The air grew strange.

"Maybe she'll have to do like everyone else," I ventured – "start from the bottom, or maybe the French guys from Chant du Monde can take her on, record her, and then cut a disk."

"Let's change the subject," Sergio, the musician-substitute, urged. The atmosphere cleared.

At the exit, as I walked toward the grand boulevards with Lucho and Pepe, they asked me, nearly in chorus:

"You really don't know who Ana María is?"

I confessed my ignorance.

"She's Sergio's wife."

No doubt about it: I'll never learn. From that day on, every time an uncomfortable silence invades a meeting, just like everyone else, I cleverly turn my eyes toward the ceiling, but of course, since I'm an actor I overact, accompanying the gesture with a drumming of my fingers, my hand discreetly pointing at the one presiding.

"It's not overacting; it's calling attention to yourself. It's a well-known fact among theater people that the slightest movement of a shoulder, a thigh, a hint of a glance, are enough to call attention to yourself and then divert that attention to its real target."

Once again *I was*; without being, I was. Life followed its normal course, and I could once more worry about serious things. I needed actors, and if I didn't find them I needed to create them. Since they had cut my wings and my contacts, I had to start from scratch. During the day I worked. My brother, who lived in Paris, not as a doctor, but as a writer, helped me find a job; without intending to, he helped me. I was invited to speak at the cell in his neighborhood, near La République. A worker from the book union was there; we spoke; he made an appointment to meet me three days later while he made certain arrangements. He wrote the address on a piece of paper: it was the newspaper!

The job wasn't on the third floor or on the second, either, or in or near the Chileans' office. I breathed a sigh of relief. It wasn't a bureaucratic position, little gray men occupying the offices of the revolution, puffing out their chests to keep a whisper of criticism from filtering in, guardians of purity who allowed La Bella to dry up; a beauty filled with hopes; not their bottomless pockets – those would never, ever dry up.

I thought about the GDR; I thought about Bulgaria; I thought of the translator and of some of my *compañeros*.

It was a third floor, but underground, the third basement, a worker's space.

My tools: a broom and some cleaning products. Little by little, as I kept learning, I even managed to clean the rotary presses that gave birth to *L'Humanité.*

I had arrived.

With my worker's salary I was able to pay for métro and bus trips for the actors. Not everything, though. Perla cleaned floors in the offices of a prestigious newspaper. With her earnings we could offer a light *casse-croûte*, *sánguche* in Chilean, halfway through the four hours of daily rehearsal.

To work their bodies, their voices, their imaginations once again. To make them forget everything from the past that had smelled of theater and acting style, to stop raising their fists after every set of lines. I taught them to laugh at me so that at some point they might be able to laugh at themselves.

I looked for them in every act of solidarity, at every airport arrival, in bars and universities, seated at a student's desk or at a professor's. I snatched the *bellas* from other men's arms just to turn them over to those of armchairs, and, once virginized, put them onstage. I taught them to love without the need to touch one another. In Rancagua it was my job to teach sweetness to the miners' coarse hands; in Paris it was my job to close wounds.

I even went to the office on the second floor, took a shower, changed out of my old blue sweater, whose color I had chosen in homage to Rubén Darío, took off the overalls that reeked of ink, sweat, and gasoline – I had begun cleaning the rotary presses – slipped into a clean pair of pants, the artist's shirt they had given me in the GDR, and climbed up another step.

Appearance matters. As I walked into the office I realized that I had forgotten to change out of my canvas espadrilles: I was stepping on slippery ground.

"I'm here to ask you to help me find actors."

"What a coincidence," the musician-substitute replied. "A great French director was here asking us the same thing and we told him that unfortunately there were no Chilean actors in Paris, just one in Avignon" (and it was true that there was one in Avignon, but not true that she was an actress: she was a *grande dame* of the Chilean theater, Marés. I had met her in Chile when she received us in her house like a queen). "Pierre (he was referring to Pierre Debauche) is putting on *the* play (emphasis on *the*) about Chile. I'm doing the music. It'll have actors from different countries from around the world, will be produced in five languages, and a horse will wander among the audience."

Six languages, I thought to myself: he has to count the horse, and besides, it's not all that original. Peter Brook and his group at the théâtre du Bouffes du Nord in the 18th *arrondissement* had Vietnamese, Indian, French, Iranian actors, etc. . . ., but they performed in French no matter where the play was from. They had just presented *The Conference of the Birds*, based on an Iranian tale, in a bare room except for a Persian rug draped over the bricks at the back of the stage. Beautiful! The rug was worth a pack of horses or 100 camels, and birds from all parts of the world paraded before our eyes, and we all felt like birds, reflected on the bare stage.

Nazim Hikmet, a Turkish director, had students from around the world in his group at the university, among them two from "La Candelaria" in Colombia, Emiliano Suárez and his partner, Elvira.

"I was hired as a historian," said El Flaco Thayer, a history professor who taught in Vincennes at the time. "And I was hired to organize the files," petulantly added his wife, who was known by everybody as "Mrs. . . ," a sad title acquired by some women.

"The ministry of culture, the city of Nanterre, and the Council of la Seine et Marne are financing the play and paying our salaries."

"And you? What resources do you have, and what language do you plan to act in?" the musician-substitute asked.

"Me?"

I looked at my people; from a distance I looked at my people, the ones nobody wants, those nobody chooses, those whose people fondly tug on their ponchos when they're acting, who spend hours working their bodies, their voices, the lines that were denied them.

"Me? My resources are these canvas espadrilles, my blue sweater, and we're going to act in the only language we all know: theater."

I made them stand as actors at sixteen international theater festivals, maybe out of pique, but I made them stand. Proudly, they stood.

"And without a horse."

But before making them stand on stage, I had to make them stand in the rehearsal room. I lost count of the newspapers I saw go by and of the bags of dirty rags I had used to clean the rotary presses. I lost count of the news I read while waiting for news.

Jean Vilar is the name of the hall where the première of *The Land of Bloody Tears* was to be presented. To tell the truth, during rehearsals, we ourselves had shed bloody tears. The little hall was full; once more *le tout Paris* in exile, our *tout Paris*, not just the Chilean one, was ours: Uruguayan, Paraguayan, Ecuadorian, Colombian, Argentine, Bolivian, French: curious, throbbing, expectant, wondering about the result, about the content, about the actors, who were mingling, as equals, with one spectator after another.

There were no reserved seats.

"Do they have a horse?" the musician-substitute asked.

I sensed a sort of bad faith.

When it ended, silence. Then one, then two, then three, one by one, out of turn, beautifully out of turn, the applause multiplied: one, then three, rose to their feet.

One brought flowers for everybody, except for one. I began with the actresses.

In the distance, the regular, congressional applause faded. At the cocktail party, a Chilean journalist came over to me to introduce me to a Frenchman who was in the audience taking notes. He had been sent by Jack Lang, director of the Nancy International Theater Festival.

A Frenchman and a Cartesian, he had to see it to believe it. He saw and he believed. They handed me an invitation.

When the lights went out and the last actor or audience member left (by now they were one and the same), I respectfully bade the stage goodnight and left the theater. In front of the hall, smiling, an arrow pointed east: Nancy, 281.71 kilometers. Another arrow, pointing toward Paris, read: Joinville, Charenton Asylum, 3 kilometers.

The spiral, that of life, had opened up; another one of my staircases remained behind.

I looked at the invitation, I looked at the clock: I had to hurry. In three hours, at six AM, my shift would start: the rotary presses awaited me. My hands ached.

I fell asleep after cleaning the first machine; in my dreams I thought I saw the figure of Thierry le Gros, one of my guests, removing the bucket of gasoil from my side, along with the paper bag containing scraps of cloth and the bagful of trash.

Newspapers and announcements filed through my mind, blending with scenes and moments. The music of Los Calchakís rocked my dreams. Their director, Nicolás, had composed the musical score for the play in a studio in the fourth *arrondissement*. It was more like a basement, the walls lined with egg cartons to muffle the sound. A group of friends led by Bibí, Jean-Marie Binoche, an actor and theater director, reproduced the music on reels like: tapes for rehearsal, for tours, backup. They were prepared to lend their voices, if necessary. We wanted to reproduce part of Allende's last speech, but in French. The first actor came in; we listened to him; he silently returned to his seat and filled his glass of wine. We were among family. A look was enough to decide, and no one left with hurt feelings. They all tried out, last of all Jean-Marie. We listened; he sat down. Jean-Marie passed me the microphone; I refused.

"No, not to record it – to see how you feel it. You're the director."

I traveled back in time, passing in front of La Moneda. I

looked at the flag that was still raised on the façade: it came to life. Afterward Bibí handed me another glass of wine.

"All set," he said. "Now to make the copies." They had been recording.

Nailed to a gray wall in the living room of a rent-controlled apartment in Montreuil, someone had left a couple of braids. It was the editor's apartment; the braids belonged to La Chica, his daughter, one of my actresses when she managed to get out of Bulgaria together with her brother. She thought she was ugly; they had made her feel ugly. She, who was beautiful even in her final moments, had cut off the braids that her father loved to pull and jumped out of a seventh story window. Her fragile body was scattered on the concrete of a badly-lit parking lot in the working-class neighborhood of Montreuil, on the outskirts of Paris.

That night I didn't rehearse; my actors and I were paralyzed with grief.

She was about to turn eighteen.

Eighteen, after having lived a century.

Perhaps that was why, at a meeting to which I hadn't been invited, one of those where the past, present, and future were proclaimed, when control was a necessary tool (to prevent any possible derailment), a meeting where La Jota demanded control of cultural groups from the Party, the editor raised his voice and said: The theater group belongs to its founders; El Quila and El Inti[15]

---

[15] Inti-Illimani, another Chilean musical group in exile (in Milan, Italy).

belong to their founders. Without them those groups would not exist. I demand respect for their creators.

The musician's whinnying could be heard as far away as Nanterre.

"Did he have a horse?" I asked.

"Not that, either. Don't take advantage of the situation."

An internal squabble had broken out to determine who was who, who gave orders to whom, who would keep the locomotive and who would travel in third class.

They tried to control everything. A shadow fell over our exile.

The time to create los Manolitos[16] and to take power was drawing near. Los Manolitos was created; as for taking power – patience. Moreover, taking power doesn't mean sharing power, much less pluralism.

"What democracy are you talking about?"

Governing is for the common good, but not everyone governs or counts. And the élites want to stay in power, and internal squabbles were called purges in the past, are called purges in the present and will be called purges in the future. Depending on the degree of power attained, you're either purged or erased from his-

---

[16] Nickname given to members of the Manuel Rodríguez Patriotic Front, the clandestine arm of the Communist Party.

tory, or else you're assigned your role in their history – and watch out: you'll never budge from there!

I recalled Quevedo: between a carnation and a rose . .

"And if for once we didn't choose?"

The whole stage would be something like a huge doubt, and each movement would lead to a circle of life, which upon dying would generate another circle of life, because the circle would be open, not self-contained, and each speech would respect the right to a response, and the stage would be balanced and would include each and every one, and . . .

"Something like collective creation?"

"Yes, but in view of everyone."

I awoke in the car; we were on the A4. To the east, passing through Verdun, we traded scars; the trenches crisscrossing its surface offered us protection. From the depths of one of them, a small tank, almost like a toy, as little as that one in Prague, silent witness of the First World War, puffed out its chest and pointed, tenderly, almost like my childhood toy, toward the sun that lit up the plain, marking the first and last line of defense, the Maginot Line. In Colombey-les-Deux-Églises, the four arms of a cross welcomed us. Nancy and its festival opened their arms – and a performance space – to us. The next day all performances were canceled in order to give us a stage in a circus tent at precisely eleven AM. The stage grew smaller and smaller; the tent fuller and fuller; the actors made their way to the stage and sat along its edge, then at the edge of the circle of lights, and finally in the circle of lights itself.

In view of this new reality, I gathered the actors: Move around as best you can, but there are two golden rules. One, never in a straight line, and two, don't trample the audience. They might not applaud at the end.

I closed my eyes. The tent came to life.

As I entered the newspaper office, not from the side of the grand boulevards, but rather through the side door, the workers' entrance, the one that faced Rue du Faubourg Poissonière, the *compañero* in charge of raising the barrier handed me a letter.

Whenever a letter is delivered in this impersonal way, it's almost always bad news.

It had a French stamp; a Marianne smiled at me from the upper right-hand corner; it bore my name and that of the group, and it said: Director. The sender: Paul Puaux. The city: Avignon.

When a letter has a sender, it almost always erases that initial, unpleasant sensation. I went downstairs to change, prepared my work tools: the bucket of petrol, a bagful of clean rags, and another bag for dirty rags. I soaked a rag, ran it through the inky roller, and left it beside the rotary press. That's the first thing any good book union worker does at the beginning of his shift; you never know when one of the bosses will come by.

And like everyone else, I went to eat my *casse-croûte*, a breakfast consisting of ham, cheese, rustic bread, garlic sausage, and a glass of red wine. You needed strength to work. Not only did I learn to clean the rotator presses; now I was a *prolo* and I even spoke the lingo, *mon pote.*

"And yet you never sat at the center of the table, always to one side and in the corner; you were an *intello*."

"It must be because after the first glass of wine I switch to coffee."

I opened the envelope; silence at the table. I shouted for joy – everyone waited.

"Avignon, the most important theater festival in Europe; I'm going to be in it with my group."

"*Ça s'arrose.* That calls for a drink!"

Following custom, I stood up and brought over two flagons of red, Côte du Rhone. Turning to my charming tablemate, I said, "Claudette, today I'm not drinking coffee."

The squad leader asked, "How many days?"

"Fifteen."

By way of apology, I added, "They're giving me the CGT local.[17]"

During the festival, even the most insignificant local opens its doors, and during the resistance, Jacques Duclos, the revolutionary tailor, the man of the resistance, had been at that one.

"*Ça s'arrose.*"

Two more flagons, this time paid for by my *compañeros.*

It was one of those moments in France when we're all *prolos* or we're all *intellos* or else we simply all *are*.

"*Ça s'arrose*," said the Compleat Freedom Fighter's Manu-

---

[17] CGT Confédération Générale du Travail, General Confederation of Labour is the most important national union in France. It was founded in 1895.

al.

In general, before the festival, the theater critics conduct interviews. They don't cover the whole festival, and it's just another way to make a pre-selection according to the degree of interest the groups generate. We were no exception.

Chatting with José Valverde about the possibility of finding a place to hold the press conference, we rejected the options for various reasons: the Théâtre Gérard Philipe might give the impression that we were being sponsored or compensated; the Jean Vilar was a little too far away for the Parisian press, and in general they don't visit the same place twice. After rejecting one after another, we were left with my workplace, but not the rooms on the third floor, which might give the impression of dependency; nor the Chileans' office, for the same reason. If at the beginning my actors in Chile had come out of the entrails of the mine, why not come out of basements in Paris?

The journalists arrived through the front door; the receptionists at the main entrance called up to the second floor, "Are you having a press conference?"

Mónica suffered a series of attacks.

They asked, "Where's another Chilean?"

A worker passing by said, "In the third basement."

Intrigued, the journalists trooped downstairs, listened to the story, asked questions, asked one another. It didn't sound like outmoded '68 rhetoric; it sounded like a part of France's theater history, that of Vilar and the People's National Theater (not to mention the Avignon Festival), that of Planchon in Villeurbanne on the outskirts of Lyon, that of Vitez in the Palais de Chaillot where, a poet after all, he staged an eight-hour *Hamlet*. Even the Eiffel Tower felt cramped on the esplanade.

No, that's where they were wrong: how far we were from them. We had just barely gotten on our feet, from work, getting on our feet, emerging from the caves. Let's not exaggerate – not from the caves, from the belly of the Cordillera, from the depths of the cells, from the concentration camps, from death and from life.

"*Ça s'arrose,*" and we all went upstairs to the first floor for an *apéro*.

I had climbed another step of the staircase and was standing full-on in the light of day.

Paris is also beautiful by day, I discovered.

XVI. Of how he learned that only love lets you leap from one spiral to another

We left Paris through the remains of one of the gates of the walled city. As I passed through, I thought: I'm crossing a border again and I never know if I'll return, if once more I won't belong, if they'll close the gate on me forever, if I'm being thrown out or punished. I've never been able to figure out if the walls are made of stone or cardboard, or if my date with destiny is nothing but my encounter with the word: the word, that beauty I never possessed.

The sunlit road echoed in our ears; lights went on and off as we passed by; rivers extended imaginary bridges so that we could dance across them; scents invaded our minds. Six hundred eighty-nine kilometers separated us from the city of popes, from the city of stone.

Dizzy with the fragrance of lavender, from the lights that exploded into rainbows before our eyes, we climbed up to the infinite before descending into the warm, pleasant belly of Provence.

The Rhône opened its arms and its legs to us; beyond, the sea called us, wiggling its hips, the ships' sails separating to show us their fruits and waiting to satisfy the wayfarers' desires.

We sailed, just as we would sail in Marseille.

The bells of the plaza clock brought me back to reality: find Rue Ledru-Rollin. Luckily the hall was located at number one and was easy to find so as to begin the ritual: meet and greet, unload, set up, and *ça s'arrose.* Then, walk up and down the side streets, sit down in the plaza to drink a *Moresque*, a combination of Pastis and almond syrup, in memory of history, fling open my arms and embrace players from around the world. From a walled city, from a vacation spot for popes, from a palace for one man and his retinue, Avignon had been transformed into a world stage, a theatrical palace for the multitudes. On the patio of the palace, in the streets, on corners, in the open air or in basements, a silent theater, a spoken theater, a rich theater, a poor theater, theater, nothing but theater, just as Vilar dreamed it when he left the city of light to go and knock down the walls that held the city of stone prisoner and give birth to the festival.

Our reviews were good. One of them affected me for a long time: it spoke of my smile when I spoke and the sadness in my eyes, and no matter how much we rehearsed, that sadness was hard to hide. There were things in which Stanislavski took the lead over Brecht's distancing or estrangement effect.

Distance we had, but we weren't strangers. We had never been more a "part of" something than in that set, we and they, the characters.

If the Rhône had opened its legs to us, the hexagon offered us its body, from Finisterra to Brest, to Nantes, to Strasbourg, from Calais to Marseille, from Paris to . . . and to . . . and to . . . With that first play we covered the forests, castles, battlefields, meadows, heat, cold, snow, and ice more than a hundred times. France, the beautiful, had her whims, and Marianne changed from one region to another. She surrendered, but her surrender wasn't the same; a beauty never surrenders the same way twice, just as one show will never be the same as the last, and the next one will always be different, as well.

If it isn't, and if it's a repetition, they're cheating you, or you're cheating your audience.

Beneath our dreams passed roads, landscapes, good – and bad – news from Chile, a friend released from prison, another who fell prisoner, and eyes that had started to smile evoked sadness once more.

Evoked, not revealed.

The third basement lay behind me, the punishment had been dispelled, and I began to get involved in militancy without being a militant. The Cultural Commission laughed openly, till the one in charge, at the start of a meeting where no one was paying attention and we were having fun gossiping about love affairs and trips – travel was possible again! – he, a university president, he who had never been heard to utter a bad word, pronounced with Shakespearean elocution, "Just shut up, assholes," breaking the rules.

The actors from the Chilean university theaters whom I had invited to perform for the copper miners would have loved to have such control of the audience! There was an immediate silence; we all riveted our eyes on him. No actor had ever commanded so much attention.

Silence, tension, fixed gazes, attention, a body made of five bodies hanging on the next speech.

In the next play I'm going to pull something like that, I said to myself.

It wasn't the word "assholes" – it was the element of surprise, the rupture, the abrupt change of direction that throws you off, that makes the future cease to be future and become a question, and the theater acquires its true stature when, in the hands of the audience, it turns into a question.

Roads opened up, one stage followed another, surprising us. Traversing the soul of France, we got to know her. The actors started coming and going: some went off to study; others were called away by life, the other life. They loved the lights – what actor doesn't love being in the spotlight! But the road to the spotlight wasn't easy. It required something more than experience; it required nourishment by their peers. As they lost sight of the forest of banners, their movement had to lose its coarseness and learn sweetness. We brought Bernard in to teach us classical dance so we could dance a *cueca criolla,* one of those with plenty of foot-tapping. In order to lend the element of surprise to our movement, Françoise arrived to initiate us in modern dance. Integrating the various languages demanded complicated new choreography; precise movements to bring us back to natural, free-flowing moves. We needed to *know*, to know and to command in order to possess, to be possessed, and to surprise.

Borders began to fall.

Borders don't "fall," not in that impersonal way, as if it were the force of destiny at work, that irresponsible, facile, cowardly way of describing things that won't let us sleep in peace, lest they catch us unprepared during the night. They don't fall, they're torn down; and again, watch out for that dangerous impersonality. Once again you've put things into the hands of those who wait, those resistant to change, God forbid they might have to make a decision.

No use waiting, my friend; it's dangerous to wait, *compañero*. They might be locking you up within other borders.

We pushed them back, pulverized them; we flung open the floodgates. We summoned the world to occupy the group. Actors arrived from Ecuador, from Mexico, from Colombia, from Peru, from Poland, from France. We returned to origins: we gave movement to the word, transforming the body into a trunk, lower extremities into roots, and arms into branches rustled by the wind. We took possession and set roots.

As actors who had been buffeted by the storm for so long, we were able to resist it, face it head on, but to do that we needed to learn. A university professor from southern Chile arrived, bringing the tireless tinkling of rain on metal roofs, the mist around the campfire, and by bringing with him the repetition of the gesture, he taught us to break the monotony. A watchmaker came from the north: an alcoholic smuggler, full of life, he brought us the habit so as to break the habit and showed us the roads so we could avoid checkpoints and get through without being stopped.

Even Teatinos came to believe he was an infiltrator and was about to eliminate him for security reasons.

"Whose security?" I asked the head of Security, a worker from the Fiat factory in Rancagua, fortunately my *compadre*. If not for that, we would have lost an actor.

The Polish actress brought Grotowski; the Colombian invited Jacques Lecoq; another Chilean brought mimes from Noisvander and Monsieur Bip; the Ecuadorian, the rituals of Santo Domingo de los Colorados, those that pervaded César Dávila Andrade's *Boletín y elegía de las mitas*.

Each and every one brought us a piece of the past so we could plow our present.

And yet, it seemed to me, something was missing; I looked at the picture and something was missing.

We recaptured the feeling of plunging our fingers into the mud, plunging our hands and arms slowly into the damp earth, separating the furrows to penetrate them and steep ourselves in their scent. We learned to work with clay so it would preserve our image, to cover it with mutilated bits of news, scraps of other stories that lent shape to ours, and that *papier mâché* eventually created our masks. We had stripped our souls bare onstage; we needed to cover our faces with the masks of the theater. We couldn't allow ourselves the luxury of masks loaned to museums or from private collectors, those who buy beauty just to conceal it, thinking that doing so turns them into cultured men, the lovely masks of *The Conference of the Birds*. And so we had to resort to those that had disappeared from history to lend us their faces, eroded by the desert wind, trampled by extension of an airport landing strip, buried in an abandoned mine up north, devoured by fish in the Pacific, mutilated faces that were reborn as mutilated faces, carried off by the wind.

We stripped our souls bare so as to bare our bodies on-stage. Not all of us, one: the watchmaker, in front of the pair of boots. Medina, remember?

In order to do it we had to learn how to wander aimlessly in the Marché Saint-Pierre, there beside Sacré Coeur in Montmartre, in the greatest fabric market in Paris, where the scents of *bellas* from around the world intermingle with the fabrics that will caress their bodies, arousing our envy.

I learned to tail someone without being spotted, to feel the contact of other hands on the fabrics extended before our eyes: Indian women stroking gold-embroidered cloth, Algerian women, their hands decorated with lovely filigree caressing fabrics that would shamelessly pop into the men's minds. I learned to imagine the way they fall, their movement as they float in the wind, the effects of a sunbeam reflected on the material, slipping and pausing, exploding in a thousand directions, or grabbing hold of it so as to make it disappear among its fibers.

The filters for the lights in Sofia had been hidden among the fabrics, changing their colors, bringing a blush to the actresses' cheeks and a pallor to those of the spectators.

"So, you were more a school than a group."

"No, we weren't a school. We were students. But we definitely weren't disciples."

La Escuela arrived later, recently liberated from the Chacabuco concentration camp in the north, in the driest desert in the world, where the daytime heat is unbearable and the nighttime cold makes the stones explode. Chacabuco, where even more than the fencelines, the walls are flat, hundreds of kilometers of sand and caliche; overhead, the only escape was the sky, to leap from one star to another till you reached the star where she, the beloved one, was.

Iturra, not the Black Hand, but Ricardo, his brother, had just arrived, and he told the story of the school they had created in the concentration camp, including – since they had the best teachers in Chile at their disposal – the fact that they had requested official recognition and authorization to issue diplomas and had even dared to hint at a stipend for materials. The teachers worked for free in exchange for food and lodging.

"Some people never learn."

On the contrary, they *did* learn, day after day. Astronomy, Geology, History within history: the handle of an abandoned shovel, a rusty rail uselessly waiting for a mineral-loaded train to go by, a worker's glove. They learned to recognize the sighs of love among the stones and to distinguish them from the sighs of political prisoners. They taught and learned writing, the ABC's for some, its meaning for others. The play ended with the first letter

213

written by a formerly illiterate worker to his wife – he, reading it aloud as he was writing it in the concentration camp, she, illiterate, in the shantytown, trembling with love, stroking the paper and imagining its contents.

For only one day did the spiral stop, the staircases reject their steps, and the stages call out to us uselessly; the *bellas* writhed in their beds wondering, what have we done?

It was September 11, the anniversary of the Chilean coup d'état. Grief froze all activity; parliament became a whiplash; the locomotive slowed down, and all of us were able to climb aboard the wagons of history.

From all over France, from everywhere, we arrived at *la Fête de l'Humanité.* Humanity, indeed, the kind found in the third basement.

After the liberation of Paris, newspapers once again circulated freely through the streets. The rotary presses blushed, adding red to the headlines; *Maréchal* Pétain's gray uniform disappeared; the prefecture emptied its jail cells, just as in the past others had opened the gates of the Bastille. When the French Communist Party's newspaper once more emerged into the light of day, the workers organized a huge party to raise funds and to guarantee, for at least a year, one page, the first, known as *la Une de l'Humanité.* And that, according to the workers of the book union, is how the most important cultural festival in Paris became a tradition.

The hymn emerging from the earth, from the plains, from hiding places, from fear and from courage accompanied us on our way to *la Fête de l'Huma.*

> *Ami, entends-tu le vol noir des corbeaux sur nos plaines?*
> *Ami, entends-tu les cris sourds du pays qu'on enchaîne?*
> *Ohé! Partisans, ouvriers et paysans, c'est l'alarme!*
> *Ce soir l'ennemi connaîtra le prix du sang et des larmes.*
> *Montez de la mine, descendez des collines, camarades . .*

Come down from the stage, *compañeros,* and join us; let us join you.

For once, riding the métro toward La Courneuve, toward the park in the shadow of La Cité des 4000, I said to the conductor, "Don't go off the rails, *compañero.*"

At *La Fête,* a million people in two days, *le tout Paris,* in a nutshell, that is, *la crème de la crème,* mixed in with *le tout Paris* of exiles, of everyone, arriving from the happysad-sadhappy refugee shelters that collected the footsteps of the old, smelly, worn-out shoes of exiles from all over the world, that is, the *ratatouille* of the castoffs of the world; from working-class neighborhoods on the outskirts of Paris and from the rest of France: workers, fishermen, professionals, young and old, and especially lovers of good music, good food, sausages and beer, snails and frogs' legs, wine and exotic drinks that were offered to their lips for only two days in September.

On the other side, lights and stages. The big one, the central stage hosting a Bartók concert; Anna Fratellini's circus troupe,

Los Colombaioni (Fellini's clowns); Ray Charles; a classical or experimental ballet. On the other stages, musical performances, sets that yielded to the word in endless discussions in which everyone could take the floor and contradict the next person, and if necessary they'd invent something, and whatever wasn't true at that moment might become true in the future, and certainties became uncertain.

It was the largest popular festival in Europe.

And in it, La Cité Internationale, a privileged space for traveling through the beauty and squalor of the earth. Kiosks from around the world representing every country, every liberation movement, every overthrown regime, every disappeared child, every displaced peasant, every man, every woman standing to be heard, at the very least, to be heard.

And those more fortunate ones pledged, as they passed by, to lend a hand, to offer a smile and a hug and to have a drink with their *compañeros.*

In the middle of the International City, the Chileans' food stand, decorated like a thatch-roofed *ramada*, with a string of little plastic flags dangling from it, with a reproduction of *El Siglo* to be given away, signaling with our eyes the tip jar conveniently displayed beside it (Mireya Baltra's kind suggestion), baked empanadas stuffed with ground meat, hard-boiled egg, and raisins, kneaded by the *compañeras'* chubby hands while the men cut branches to add cachet to the kiosk, to turn it into one of those *ramadas* filled with life and hope. And the indispensable *completos* and *lomito* sandwiches on home-made bread, and the hand, waving proudly and continuously from right to left, pointing out the lined-up components of a *completo*: sauerkraut, pickles, diced onion – just like at the Fuente Alemana restaurant, the Santiago women explained.

Up front, a space for receiving guests and striking up discussions. It was easier with outsiders; we tried to respond without ruining the party for them. It was more interesting among ourselves, though, because deep down we knew we had no answers, or that the ones we had could make shivers run down our spines.

As for me, they had to whisper names in my ear: a soon as I saw a new-old friend approaching, I would hear: Jean, La Vendée, and after the French-style hug and kissy-face, I managed to squeeze in, "*Jean, mon pote, ça va La Vendée?*" His reply would help me place him and he could go back to his set. It's just that there were too many of them, and after I offered to buy them a glass of red wine, or they invited me – *ça s'arrose* – by the tenth performance, all the lights, characters, and names were jumbled up in my mind.

Coffee break time, they whispered in my ear.

One eleventh of September, everything changed. Springtime: the weather was with us, and in a rare moment of relaxation a group of us – the leaders of the Central Workers' Union, political leaders, Lucho the critic, and I – were chatting in a circle of life.

I was talking, in my Molièresque artist's shirt, the wide sleeves floating in the wind, gesticulating to emphasize or deemphasize a word when I was struck by a beam of light. I kept talking, and not even my actor's pride made me try to hear the reaction. I

217

looked without looking at the other part of the circle so as to be able to set my sight free. And there she was, walking from center stage toward our *ramada*, La Bella entre las Bellas, La Bella who would mark my destiny.

She was with a Chilean; a bolt of lightning hit him. Guillermo dissolved into smoke, our friendship gone forever. She came closer; each one of the members of the circle froze out the others, while they kept moving their lips like fish out of water.

I had heard about her beauty, I had heard about her intelligence, I had heard about her smile and those beautiful dark eyes, I had heard that she existed, and I had heard of how hapless suitors had crashed into her long eyelashes, but I had heard it during the hour of lies and I didn't believe such beauty could be true.

Guillermo came up to me first and said, "I was looking for you. I want you to meet Pris, a Caribbean actress."

My toes curled up in my Ho Chi Minh sandals; I hoped she hadn't noticed.

As it was *La Fête de l'Huma*, I made a chivalric gesture: I took her delicate hand, and, like Gérard Philipe playing D'Artagnan, I leaned forward to kiss her hand. "Enchanté," I muttered.

Lucho the critic copied my gesture, but he had to stand on tiptoe to reach La Bella's hand. Carlitos, the editor, had to climb up on Lucho's shoulders; the two union leaders gave her a firm handshake with sturdy hands, the sort of hands that develop calluses from using a hammer, even though one of them was a bureaucrat whose only acquaintance with a hammer came from looking at the posters covering the walls of the cadre school. The politicians put on their "first class car" faces to impress her, and Quena, the woman in charge of relations with UNESCO, left the group, in order to avoid witnessing the ridiculous spectacle, even though she was famous for loving comedies.

In the *ramada,* the old women suffered various attacks; Quena's sister, a psychiatrist, had to see to them. For half an hour the empanadas came out flatter than pancakes.

"Look at her hips," they said.

I looked at them gratefully. Sometimes, unwittingly, the effect of an utterance differs from expectations, or maybe it just contains hints to direct our thoughts, like a kind of liberation.

The International City was a gathering and dispersing point; there the world came together to establish its differences; ideas, to be born or to die; some eyes closed to make way for others that would light up the stage and people's thoughts. It wasn't a matter of destroying; it was a way to provide an opportunity for the future.

La Bella entre las Bellas – her presence eclipsed even her legend – told me about her life in the theater, her experience forged in El Yunque rain forest, her first lines rippling down from the mountains toward the sea that bathes Puerto Rico, her dreams, her disappointments.

Slyly I removed my robe so that she wouldn't think it was a cassock; I've never managed to understand why people tell their life stories to us theater directors

"They don't tell you their life stories – they're trying to return to their lives onstage. Some people will never learn."

With the fragility of an orchid, but bending voluptuously like a palm tree in the midst of a hurricane, fanning the air with her eyelashes, smiling through those lips that were opening the door to my destiny, she said at last, "I want to act. Do you need an actress, *monsieur*?"

I needed one. That *monsieur* put me on alert, though: I asked myself which the hell king I would have to dethrone. I looked at her eyes and regained my composure.

From that moment on, I stopped looking at her to observe her instead. I measured the reach of her gaze, the broad movement of her thighs, the height from which her speeches would fall, the arc of her legs and how the light slipped between them, as if in play, her fingers tossing orchid petals whenever she gets nervous or explodes with desire.

"Do you have commitments?"

She smiled.

"No."

And we both talked about the theater-within-the-theater. Anything else would have been too simple, and when you're La Bella entre las Bellas, you don't let anybody read your thoughts. "No" means "yes," "yes" means "no," a smile is a "maybe," and a fluttering of eyelashes is the start of a war – and may all hell break loose!

Thirty-three years later I still don't know for sure when a "no" means "yes," a "yes, "no", or a smile "maybe."

I was putting on Enrique Buenaventura's *Documents from Hell*. I had ascended another step on the staircase.

La Bella was familiar with the play; alone in the hall, she on stage, I in shadows, she trembling, I separating my feelings from my critical eye.

"Right. Nobody believes that one."

He was about to commit an error: in the theater, emotions are part of the critical eye. It's not a scalpel slicing through the scene; it's a feeling ripping you apart to give life to the scene.

I had set aside one of the roles, from *The Autopsy*. Until that moment I hadn't found the right actress to bring the female character to life. I needed a couple onstage that could, with scalpel in hand, in their eyes, their smile, one gaze avoiding the other – perform an autopsy of thirty years of marriage, without a single shout, without raising their voices, without either one raising a hand or an eyelash at the other, where a "yes" could be a "no," where a "no" could turn into a "yes," where everything might be a "maybe" for the audience.

Yes and yes: I had the actress. No and no: I didn't have La Bella.

I needed a dwarf – deformed, ugly, someone who could use the attraction of her ugliness to manipulate men, who could put the actors behind a veil in order to make them stand out, and La Bella underwent a transformation. Modestly she lifted her mini-skirt and removed a stocking, making a knot in it and placing it on her head; before my shadow, she shrunk down till her skirt touched the floor, turned around slowly and smiled at me. Irresistible!

I knew something had been missing in my life!

Pleasure flooded me; I had found the actress to perform the bishop character in *The Orgy*.

For *The Autopsy* I stripped the stage bare, and once I had it set up to my expectations I dressed it in white. I covered the floor with a big white screen, the back wall with an enormous white cyclorama; I created a circle of white light that defined the space and assaulted the spectator's eyes, slowly adding throughout the duration of the play a touch of blue light that gradually introduced coldness to the scene and to the hall, until a tremor went through the audience as they crossed the borders of the theater into the redoubt of an operating room.

In the middle of the operating room, two black plastic chairs. Seated on one of them, La Bella entre las Bellas; standing behind the other, the actor-professor from the University of Concepción, both of them dressed in gray, which gave her an elegance that bore her pain and gave him the appearance of a bureaucrat, a petty bureaucrat escaped from one of Magritte's paintings.

The leitmotif was apparently simple: he, a doctor who performed autopsies during the time of the dictatorship; she, his wife, a housewife. That day, as usual, he went to work to perform another autopsy, only this time it was on his son. I had to construct her character; she carried the weight of the play. For him, at least, there was a guideline: doctor. For her, the darkness that shrouds a housewife. What a challenge!

Nothing is harder for a director and his technical staff than to achieve a perfect whiteness on the stage; there's nothing more exciting for a director and his actors than to build characters from nothing; the doors to the universe open up to them; bereft of guidelines, they must navigate the stage, trying to find a point of support and set the scene in motion.

We had thirty days till opening, thirty days to adjust the Latino characters and rhythms to French, to universalize the characters, to go beyond the literal translation to the language of theater, with the danger of distortion that a double translation implies.

On opening day, the unforeseen. All openings have unforeseen events, but predictable ones. With La Bella entre las Bellas it was the first time performing in my group, and the first time can never be predicted. As usual, I was listening behind the curtains: the silences gave me the rhythm of the play; the outlined silhouettes like Chinese shadow puppets against the cyclorama backdrop, the tension between both characters, and just then – a jingling. There was no music in the play; the music consisted of silences, the cadences of the word, the coldness of glances, and yet an uncontrollable jingling, coming from the earth, was taking over the stage.

From the shadows I checked those other shadows. An undetectable movement was coming from beneath La Bella's skirt: her knees were knocking.

Fortunately her desperate attempt to control them added

tension to the dialogue.

Heaven and hell can meet; climbing and descending stair-cases can cause the spiral of life and the spiral of death to cross at a given moment. La Bella's transformation into the dwarf woman can make a dead speech, blessed by her sacred canticles in the midst of an orgy, be reborn between the legs of an old whore.

From the immaculate whiteness of an operating room, we invited the audience to eat their fill at a banquet, to sell their seats and their souls for a handful of rice, to rip off their masks and cloth-ing and enter the grotesque world of the wretched beggar protag-onists of The Orgy. The ragged guests at the orgy were invited to cast off their tattered garments and don the kind audience's ele-gant attire, which hung on their scrawny, deformed bodies. A bish-op, a colonel, a politician, a thug, the deaf-mute son concealing his defects and the shame of rejection, his love for his mother, that love that was bursting with the desire to replace his absent father.

A handful of rice and a few miserable coins to recreate the fantasies of the old whore, her sex dragging along the ground, groped by the beggars, her fantasies ascending, sublimely, to the heavens, escaping squalid reality.

The stage was transformed into a dim mirror that reflected a sinister, but lively, reality. One was no longer oneself, and under those circumstances everything is permitted, including being one-self.

Life addressed the stage, and the stage addressed the public. The old whore, acting as theater director, assigned roles, dressed and undressed them, lewdly observed their pitiful attributes, and with a director's malice invited them to assume their roles before the panting audience.

"You speak now, Señor Governor . . ."

And she invited one of the beggars to climb to a wooden box and play the part of the candidate to Governor.

He smoothed the sleeves of his threadbare tuxedo; the jacket, like a showcase of the world, left his ribs exposed. The beggar-businessman draped him with a dirty scarf, like a presidential sash, which the spectator, if he was a careful observer, could imagine had once been white. The candidate raised both arms toward the rabble – the audience – made a "V" for victory in anticipation of his triumph, and launched the first line of his carefully prepared speech into the air:

"We're hungry – we want to eat something!"

The rabble exploded into applause.

The halls filled; politicians from all around the world made reservations. Others clenched their fists, made their teeth chatter, and looked out of half-closed eyes so as to avoid seeing the whole picture. No, not the whole picture – the details that lead to the whole picture; the whole uniform is part of their being; it's the tool that allows them to avoid reality.

However, they smiled, and the *compañeros* from the Chilean Central Workers' Union in exile agreed to include the play in a performance at La Mutualité: 8000 seats, a cathedral-hall, the central nave of workers' events in Paris.

"Who can refuse to participate in an orgy?"

225

The first loop of the spiral spun endlessly; the hexagon had opened its vertices and thrown us into the European current. We crossed the highest peak of the Alps and dizzily descended on the Swiss side; step by step we leaped along the stone roads where the Romans had trodden. We came across a lost elephant, slaked our thirst in an aqueduct, and, impelled forward by the winds, fell into the throng that hid Bern and its festival.

We began to spin incessantly; the tenth time we crossed the bridge, La Bella exclaimed, "The maelstrom, the whirlpool so feared by sailors."

There's nothing more fearsome for a director, for an actor, than to spin and spin around the stage without being able to latch onto his life preserver. Scenes paraded before our eyes; characters wandered aimlessly, unable to find their speeches; costumes bounced from body to body; lights went on and off, creating ghostly paths.

Emerging from the depths of the whirlpool, like a theater god, the festival director led us along secret pathways to the city buried in the middle of the mountains and took us to our hall.

At precisely six in the afternoon, one hour after Federico García Lorca was assassinated, streetcars carried the castaways, those who cleaned streets, houses, statues, away from the city so as to clean up streets and consciences. At 6:30 they deposited them on the outskirts, in commuter cities, wasteland cities, lawless, godless cities, cities of despair, so that they might reproduce and recover strength.

At night the city came to life. People strolled along its

streets, and even the tiny beings that lived, motionless, atop the columns stepped down from their pedestals and headed for the theater.

At precisely 9 PM the hall didn't reflect a single flaw in the audience. At 8:59 I peeked through the little hole in the curtain: they had kicked the poor wretches out of the hall, the Gavroches of the entire world, the guides who led the disabled, the plunder from the castaways tossed by the maelstrom.

By precisely 9 PM they had taken away our *raison d'être.*

I, who was born in the sinkholes of the *cordillera*, I who had devoured the wild jungle, I of the empty chicken coops and halls that reeked of sweat, was about to perform for the nobility. I, who like Jean-Baptiste Poquelin had been born to perform my dreams for common folk in public squares, found myself enclosed in a freezing, sterilized chunk of history.

We swam against the current, clutching the walls of the spiral, clinging to the steps. We had to return to the spiral of life; the spiral of death, the most fearsome whirlpool, was absorbing us, the one that attempts to take over the director's dreams, the actors' dreams, and swallow up their last words, making them disappear from history forever.

"The maelstrom!" exclaimed La Bella, horrified.

We escaped. Ljubljana awaited us. Avignon once again opened its gates, the gates of a city that had knocked down walls. Nantes offered us its hidden shipyards in which to polish and protect our lines. In the deepest underground channel we deposited the word. The crucified victims of La Vendée gave us a cross and nails, the bourgeoisie of Calais, the noose around their necks, handed us the keys to the city.

We escaped! That night, while applying our makeup to return to reality, we saw our images in the mirror crowned with white hair: we had lost our innocence.

And that allowed me to climb another step toward my destiny.

"Come down – look which way the spiral is going."

XVII. Of how he learned to read history in the vacant eyes of its castaways

From the summit you can see the plains, and behind them the sea shamelessly caressed the land; wave after wave, lick after lick, it eroded the defenses of the holy city.

Since we were descending, we crossed the Alps via a lower peak.

Huge mistake: you mustn't descend from the heights. In order to pass through checkpoints, you should always try to cross via the highest peaks, the ones the officials can't reach.

Without realizing it, we were starting to go around in circles, not in a spiral, and the whirlpool threatened to swallow us. The clouds offered us their breasts, and the unleashed winds penetrated our ears. Once more my senses had opened up to the signs of the world and wounded my brain.

I started to climb to the final level of the pyramid, the third, the one that touches the sky with its hands, the one that looks out over the universe, the final level, the one at the edge of the precipice.

Let the sleeping forces of the universe awaken,
let the wandering spirits of the earth draw near.
I,
the great Burumbún,

implored:

Let the storm be unleashed!

We left on tiptoe, we left carrying our hopes, we passed the Arc de Triomphe, we were suffused with lavender, we crossed the Alps again, we stopped underneath the statue of Columbus to beg for his protection, we dipped our toes in sea water, we crossed ourselves, and we embarked on a journey to a festival that opened its arms and its secrets to us on the other side of the Mediterranean, the holy city of Hammamet.

Nedjma of my first loves, Nedjma of the swaying hips and jasmine-scented sex. Nedjma and the cry of the Arab women who were watching the sea to announce our arrival.

I, orphaned by the world, man without a country in which to lay my punished body down, I who was robbed of dreams and the secret paths of the *cordillera*, plunged into other worlds, into another civilization, in search of the balm that might soothe me by feeding my soul and my actors.

I was burning my ships, not knowing if I would ever return to Genoa or wander deep into the desert to disappear from my world.

La Bella entre las Bellas, jealous of Nedjma, stretched out among the lemon trees, spread her legs to be possessed by a lemon, perfumed her orange blossom lips and surrendered to me with a cry that was a blend of palm trees and orange blossoms.

That night, amid shouts of elation, Columbus came onstage from the sea. Taken aback, he wondered if he hadn't made another mistake. Flirtatiously he touched the shore with his left foot first, swept his gaze over the audience from right to left, looked over his shoulder at the lights of the holy city of Hammamet, and while the music of *Carmen* filled the open-air amphitheater, two thousand spectators formed a barrier of love to stop him before he got lost in the desert.

One of the *Santa María*'s sails waved in the wind, in it a hole so that I, the mast, could observe the world that was being born.

That night, at sunset, after the show, we sat down with my brother Tahar and my brother Mediuoni in a circle on the ground, around a huge tray of couscous.

Beforehand we had cleansed ourselves; it was the start of Ramadan.

Because we were theater people, the women were given permission to sit in the first circle.

Amid the shadows, La Bella entre las Bellas observed a descendant of Nedjma who, herself, was sadly observing. She broke the circle to go over and talk to her; the sadness in her eyes broke through the ring of shadows and the circle of light.

I remained seated. It was the start of Ramadan.

Anaruz – that was her name – told her that she wanted to be a theatrical director in her own country. She asked if actresses in La Bella's country could get to direct. Laughing mischievously, she asked what it felt like to dance in front of men, wearing flimsy clothing and adorned with feathers, if her husband allowed that and didn't punish her. She offered to teach La Bella to dance with the sensitivity of an Arab woman, standing on tiptoe on just one foot to emphasize the movement offered up by the hips; she would teach her and the other actresses, but in a closed room, just among women and in the presence of the female elders. She could teach her how to decorate her sex to attract her husband; she could teach her so many things if La Bella entre las Bellas would reveal a single secret: what a beauty has to do in order to sit in the first circle, that of light, and how to outshine the sun without being burned at the stake, and how . . . She fell silent, lowered her eyes, and withdrew to the circle of shadows. The men were watching.

As we left the hidden city of Hammamet behind, little stalks of jasmine fell from the men's ears, opening a path of flowers to Columbus. Our Atahualpa, reborn in Columbus, fanned the faces of his admirers with a fluttering of his eyelashes. La Bella entre las Bellas exchanged her miniskirt for men's clothing to make her way through the horde that loudly pleaded with the director to trade her for carpets, camels, and corals. The French actress bade her Tunisian lover farewell, and altering the famous speech, sweetly said to him, "We'll always have Hammamet, my darling Mustafa." Steph, our French technician, an *enfant de France*, an abandoned child who had been brought up in an orphanage in Villejuif, like the actor Depardieu, and just as fat, squeezed his concubine (as he liked to introduce her) into a suitcase and in a single movement tossed it into the truck.

We left the sea behind to enter the desert, and after crossing it, to reach the sea once more. We were searching for the Phoenicians and the galleys that plowed the dreams of my childhood.

The festival of Tabarka and its castle awaited us. Since this time the set was the castle and the stage its central patio, Columbus didn't arrive from the sea, but rather descended from the heavens, and the sail waved, entangled in a tower.

The rest of the actors followed the route taken by the Turks, the Romans, all the seafaring men who had invaded them until Columbus and the great Burumbún arrived.

Our eyes filled with a forest of coral, sun, and friendship, we left the sea to enter the desert. Nomads of the world, we started out for Djendouba, a no man's land, a land of nomads, to join the remains of dreams trapped in the sand and the ruins of a Roman theater built in the third century.

The staircases are definitely a spiral where the first and last of my ruins come together, the burned chicken coop in the Chilean countryside, the ruins of a Roman theater; and each ruin, my lovely ruins, brings me my *raison d'être.*

Swept in by the desert wind, emerging from the depths of solitude, the audience traveled through the night, including a handful of Palestinians from a refugee camp, stragglers from the Black September Civil War, a standoff between Jordanians and Palestinians, men forgotten in time, space, and history.

"When brothers face off against one another, history, embarrassed, forgets them."

"History? Or the brother who wins?"

"Not everyone – there were 3000 dead. Those in the audience are Fedayeen who survived. Hussein asked us to hide them."

Their huge eyes, two shiny black olives, interrogated the stage. The sound of their souls interrogated the actors. Time stopped, allowing us to connect with them for a second, only to continue on our way again along unknown paths: we to our destiny, they to oblivion.

"Next time you see them, tell them I said hi."

You always return to Genoa, just as you always return to Valparaíso. The acoustic shell of its mountains creates a symphony that irresistibly beckons travelers. You return for its semi-clandestine hotels that welcome illicit love affairs, because a sex *al pesto* is *un bocatto di cardinale*, just as a sex decorated by a sea urchin that adds tickles to lovemaking is a seafood stew where the poets of my land go fishing.

You return to Genoa holding the hand of La Bella entre las Bellas in order to climb the stairs before requesting a room with a view of the bay, leaving the lights of the port behind at night so as to be guided by the lights of Paris.

In Paris love tastes like a delicately decapitated *religieuse*[18]; it tastes like tears of a fading love and tears of a burgeoning one; it tastes like the words of lovers beneath the Pont

---

[18] Religieuse, meaning "nun," is a French pastry made of two choux pastry cases, one larger than the other. The small one, representing the nun's head is eaten first. Popular imagery associated to the French Revolution.

Neuf, of breasts exposed to the lights of the *bateaux-mouche* that cross the Seine.

In Paris love tastes like songs and silence.

That night the theater became love; orgasmic moans were all in unison. That night sex was lost in a spiral of life, and both of them, holding hands, climbed the staircases, their accomplices, that let them slip into their perspired bodies.

That night they decided to leave for Greece.

"On a tour?"

"No, running away."

I had a date with Sophocles. I wanted him to give me back the word, to make our love and suffering human, to allow me to be part of the people, to be the chorus, to be an unmasked mask, to be human in the sight of humans; I wanted him to give me back the time beyond sunset or to turn off the projectors; I wanted him to give me the sacrificial knife and lead me to the altar of my destiny to offer my life and disappear from history in order to confront my errors and to rest at last.

XVIII. Of how he learned that destiny is written as it's being read

We arrived on the 6th, having crossed plains, mountains, and waters. We knew that our days were numbered, that our destiny was beginning to be traced in the clouds, and that the womb of La Bella entre las Bellas was preparing to receive the seed.

We arrived on the 6th, just in time to enter Delphos at dawn on the 7th, that momentous day, and to learn our fate.

At the entrance to the grotto we separated. La Bella entre las Bellas went to consult Aphrodite; I continued along the path I had started on the route of Aguas Santas on Ñielol Hill. I had to face the answer alone.

I returned from the bowels of the earth.

She returned from the depths of the waters.

And, joining our bodies, we began to shape the clay that would give birth to the next *bella.*

The answer was not in the grotto; it could not be found in magical gases that issued forth, clouding our minds, nor was it in the crystalline water that bubbled up on the peak of the *cordillera* to slake the lost traveler's thirsty lips.

"Aphrodite came closer to the answer," said La Bella, revealing the Seine flowing between her legs and her breasts exploding with desire.

The answer is on the surface, in the space where the powers rising from the grotto and the gale winds descending from the heights come together, in the space where lava mixes with the great waters, which calm their yearnings. The answer is in the speeches that leap into the abyss and take shape in the body of the audience.

"And what did you ask, in the end?"

"The question is a secret. If it's revealed, the last step of the staircase disappears."

The answer began to materialize in the enormous stone theater, where one among ten thousand, I the director, I the actor, was transformed into me, the spectator. I got rid of my sandals so I could step on the stone and take root, I, one among ten thousand, saw Oedipus, mother earth, and my people appear before my eyes.

In Epidaurus I was able to join the chorus, becoming part of the ten thousand with the same rights; together with them I answered the Coryphaeus' questions, and when it passed alongside me, a flash of lightning crossed my mind. I tugged on its tunic and whispered, "Be careful. Naranjo is a traitor."

As I abandoned the old theater (and neither theaters nor *bellas* are ever abandoned), I offered a sacrificial lamb to the gods, but like all directors or actors, as a man of the theater who is hungry for affection and food, once it was roasted I began devouring its flesh as I sat propped against the stone seats, with La Bella lying across my lap.

The gods understood.

But that didn't prevent me from being assailed by doubt, no matter that I had all the elements in hand. I became intoxicated, trying to find a certainty, and it was useless: at the base of the Parthenon I slipped into a play and interrogated the audience, and it was useless. In the Agora I asked the wise men, and it was useless.

"The only one you didn't ask was yourself."

"And would I have gotten the answer?"

"I don't know. Go consult the Oracle, but remember, in order to be sure of receiving a reply, you have to reach the last step, the one that's at the last turn of the labyrinth. But keep in mind that asking implies a risk: there may be an answer."

And, for the record, making you disappear from history, condemning you to ostracism, was only one way to prevent you from becoming a threat to the riders of first-class cars. The punishment is only for third-class travelers, and some of those cars have windows, though most of them have none. That's how you keep the *demos* in blissful ignorance. "The people" doesn't necessarily mean wisdom, and a vendor of favors who travels first class can be replaced by a blood-sausage vendor in third, and *demos* can turn into demagoguery: it all depends on the curves in the road. And if your car has no windows, you're traveling blind.

From drama I moved on to comedy, and in both I was au-

238

dience and actor; in both I was mask and flesh, tunic and body, voice and silence; I was one, and I was ten thousand.

And where I come from, in the third-class cars they didn't sell blood-sausage; they sold *tortas curicanas,* pastries filled with *manjar*, with *alcayota* squash and the most expensive walnuts. The cheapest kind, the kind I ate, had no filling.

Every play leads to a different destination: in one, to the sacrifice of a lamb to the gods, in another to lost youth and taking up the journey again.

> Aphrodite plucked me from the nightmare,
> lent her eyes to the traveler who had gouged out his own,
> as punishment for not seeing which way his destiny was leading;
> she was a balm for my flayed body,
> she was an elixir for my shriveling heart
> so great was the love she demanded!
> Aphrodite led me to the depths of the sea
> and delicately,
> with the force of a cyclone,
> drowned me in her juices.

The road before me split in two; uncertainty once more. On one side: mountains to be scaled, the forests of my childhood to revisit and explore, but this time in Yugoslavia, slipping along the road of Aguas Santas and falling, arms flung wide, into the Mediterranean. On the other, plunging into the eyes of the woman I loved and walking on the waters to descend, with my body re-newed, into the port of Brindisi, from where I would embark on the road of life, drunk with perfume.

I took both roads: the rooftops of Paris awaited us.

"You always learn something new."

XIX. Of how he learned that the past is the worst border because it can become the future

Beneath the rooftops of Paris, Madeleine Renaud buried over her waist in a mound of earth in Beckett's *Happy Days.* At the end of the play, Jean-Louis Barrault, the actor who played Baptiste, the mime in *Children of Paradise*, reached out his arms to her, trying to save the word, trying to save his love, trying to save the actress who was sinking both into old age and into the character.

Cries of "Garance!" were heard once more at Le Théâtre des Funambules, reincarnated at the Rond Point of the Champs d'Elysées. Once more a heartbroken Baptiste proclaimed his love for *la bella.* For *la bella*, for his wife, for the theater, and for the character, even if in his efforts he had to sacrifice his character and give the mime speech.

La Bella entre las Bellas, eyes brimming with tears, took my hand and dried my lashes with her own. I was crying.

As we made our way silently through the Tuileries, crossing the Pont Neuf, Paris trembled at our sobs, and the two of us bowed down before the greatness of that love.

There's nothing harder for a *bella* than to bow down before the fading beauty of another *bella*. There's nothing more terrible for a director than to have a sob elude him before he can put it onstage.

Several nights later we walked into one of the salons where *le tout Paris* in exile used to meet. Luckily for us, Willy Odó had seen both the play starring Renault and the Carné film, *Children of Paradise*, which allowed us to break the routine of parties – the hour of lies, the hour of jokes – to wind up, at the end of the party, with Teatinos' announcement of the next meeting.

Leaving the salon, I realized that something was missing from the set. Beneath the rooftops of Paris, the Black Hand had disappeared, and when one of the leaders disappears it's better to become a mime.

On our way back to the apartment, walking along the banks of the Seine, the Left Bank, La Bella asked me, "Why do people disappear? Under a dictatorship I get it: it's part of their nature, their bestiality, their need to annihilate us . . . but to disappear among ourselves?"

I turned around. Medina had left me a conditioned reflex: you should always look to see who's following you. We walked in the opposite direction. I wondered how to explain it to her; I wondered how to explain it to myself.

"The theater – to restore meaning to the word."

I told her I had returned to the GDR at the end of '77, beginning of '78, after ten years of Mays in Paris, this time not deceived by the musician-substitute, but through the theater. Benno Besson, who directed the Volksbühne, the People's Theater, invited me to an opening in Berlin. José Valverde, my good friend, took care of the details: tickets, money to buy *tortas curicanas* – sorry, I mean sausages – along the way. Benno took care of sending out the invitation on letterhead, including a carbon copy: he'd gotten his hands on some carbon paper!

"I came back of my own free will," I told La Bella. I spent the night, alone, in West Berlin. The lights wouldn't let me sleep, the lights that crept through the windows of my room, the lights that smashed helplessly against the Wall. The next day I took the subway, the U-Bahn. I buried myself deliberately in the bowels of the earth. After a little while, the tunnel turned a single color due to the absence of tones; from behind the columns of deserted stations there emerged the vigilant shadows of soldiers keeping watch. Giant "miguelitos," twisted pieces of metal, blocked the way along abandoned rails – there was a single rail, and it was controlled. As I descended, a brilliant, cold, impersonal white light – *The Autopsy,* I had used that sort of light in *The Autopsy* – illuminated the line that advanced slowly between enormous wooden boxes. In them, or behind them, were a window and a small circle that allowed for communication. I was pulled aside. I handed over my travel documents, identifying me as a Chilean political refugee, a pariah with no other papers, protected by the Geneva Convention, and even so, they pulled me aside, my *compañeros* did.

I thought of the noise when the microphone was switched on in the Rancagua jail, the feeling I had whenever I heard my name called, as I passed by the armed guards. Once more I was filled with terror. And yet I was in friendly territory, among friends. In a well-lit room, a *Genossen* asked me pleasantly, in perfect Spanish:

"Reason for your visit?"

I showed him the invitation from the Volksbühne, the original and the copy.

"Do you have an invitation from your Chilean *compañeros*?"

I didn't have one; I didn't think it was necessary. I started to talk to him about theater, of the importance of a people's theater, of Brecht. I was going to tell him about the chicken coops in Chile, the Teatro Experimental del Cobre, when, like a flash of lightning I saw myself in the not-too-distant past saying the same thing to my *compañeros* in Berlin. I shut my mouth, shrugged, and smiled.

"I'll need to save that idiotic expression for another play," I said to myself.

They let me through.

That night, after the opening, we went to the party at Benno's house (or his wife's, or Benno's *compañera*'s), a small apartment with a view of the Wall.

I had never felt more *protected.*

We spoke of everything and nearly everything, of the difficulties of creating and at the same time the ease of creating, of how it was possible to use the word and the stage without crushing or defiling them.

We spoke of Yverdon, his hometown, beautiful, friendly. Its waters soothed the traveler's feet; the courtyards of its castles opened on the theater: the city generated theater. I told him that I first became acquainted with Yverdon when I was invited to participate in its festival. He didn't know Chile, though he tried to go there in the days of Allende, and while he didn't talk about Chile, when he spoke of theater, he was talking about my world.

For Benno the problem lay in the freedom to create, the attempt to lock him up in a cell, to curb dreams, to impose lights and colors, to flood the stage with cardboard scenery in order to cover up the reality of another world, their world. For Benno the problem lay in the lack of a critical viewpoint, of someone in the audience who would have the courage to stand up and say something that went against the current. For Benno the problem lay in his conflict with Brecht's disciples who had taken over the word, petty bureaucrats, little gray men in dark suits who tried to control the uncontrollable, who crushed the seeds of creativity because they were afraid of seeing its fruit; little gray men, mediocrities who latched on to the railings of the first-class cars and traveled hanging off the sides, begging to be let in.

As we were about to say goodbye, Benno announced, "In two weeks I'll be in Paris. Let's meet with José at 5 PM at the Café de la Paix, in front of the Opéra."

"It's a deal! And you?" I asked his *compañera*. "Are you coming?"

"Me?" she replied. "I can't leave; I'm the guarantee he'll come back."

In '78 I received a phone call. I met José at the café. Without preliminaries, he came right to the point:

"Benno wants to come here on a tour with his group."

I was glad.

"They want to seek political asylum; they need to breathe."

After a pause, he added, "We're collecting signatures to support him. Will you sign?"

I saw the twisted rails that kept the cars from passing freely from one Berlin to the other, the sadness in the eyes of the hostages in the apartments lining the Iron Curtain; I saw the Paris Opéra as I had seen it ten years earlier, in '68, with a red blanket waving on its roofs, its doors open, songs climbing the staircases, the stage ablaze with hope, "prohibiting is prohibited" scrawled on the walls.

I signed.

"Do you know what this means and what risks you're taking?" José warned me.

"I know. To be able to sleep."

They allowed him to leave. No one looked at the signatures. The Ministry of Culture welcomed him with open arms; the stages received him. He carried Brecht and beyond Brecht in the bottom of his suitcase, the bluebird of happiness.

"He was about to be erased," I explained to La Bella, "but he was saved."

Eleven years later, on the 9th of November of '89, a ray of light passed over Germany, the Wall was demolished by friendly hands on both sides, and just as in the past, the shadows fled, seeking refuge among other shadows. One of them, *Genossen* Honecker, arrived in Chile. Others, as in the past, learned to adjust.

"*Genossen*? My ass!"

Up till now the Teatinos folks have never found out what I

had signed, and now it's too late; today the signature is worthless. If they look closely, in the photos of the halls of exile, they'll see that another person is missing: me. At that moment they had begun to erase me from history.

We had reached the heights of the Renault workshops. We turned around and made love at the foot of the replica of the Statue of Liberty.

As we approached the apartment, we crossed in front of the studio where Picasso painted *Guernica:* in the painting, the tree of liberty was still standing.

We dreamed.

You always have to look back over your shoulder; the past and its mistakes might catch up with you. The lights reflected in the Seine tried to warn me with their movement. Images shimmered, giving life to the reflection of the buildings and monuments; rooftops twinkled just as they did beneath rainy skies in far-off Valdivia; bridges threw phantasmagorical shadows across our path; the Morris columns reflected the face of La Chica, my actress, who took her own life in order to live on in memory. The rails of the only road had permitted the controllers to leave, little gray men who multiplied in the sad halls of exile.

They tried to stay in control till the hour of lies, the hour that allowed us to smile.

I even missed the Black Hand and his *compañera:* how I

must have been hurting.

For everyone's sake, to enrich our ranks, to achieve democracy – the supreme good – the musician-substitute-who-was-
no-longer-a-substitute proposed forming larger committees that
would include representatives of our people, the ultimate target,
the *raison d'être* of our being, of our existence, in order to be nour-
ished by the sap, the roots, the wisdom of the working class, our
guiding light.

Lovely, it sounded lovely, like those speeches that guide
the spectator and keep him from derailing. No, I wasn't thinking of
Brecht or the Poor Theater. Something told me I would have to
delve deeper into the past, to the birth of the walls of history.

The first to enter the hall for the meeting was the painter, a
canvas, not brushes, in his hand; a canvas that was to be shown
to us before obtaining permission to exhibit it before other eyes.

The doors were flung open to admit the representatives of
our people, but there was no one in sight. Maybe it was the back-
lighting – or had they installed *svobodas?* – that ingenious creation
of Czech scenography, the one from the Black Theater, which allows you to create an invisible wall that lets the actors disappear
from the audience's sight by simply crossing it. Nothing – not a
scrap of cloth, not a piece of cardboard – only light, allowing new
movement, its non-existent walls transformed into a symbol of liberty.

They're learning, I said to myself. You always learn something new.

The sound of steps climbing the staircase was the first thing to fill the meeting room, following by somber gray clothes, the men and women who had come to judge us.

I was overcome by uncontrollable shaking.

They asked him for a little more red, a broken chain, like those one of them had seen on those gigantic monuments that are a paean to the glory of man and the system, during a visit to the Great Fatherland.

"And a raised fist," the other woman added.

There's always someone who adds an extra flourish and ruins the balance of the work, I thought, smiling to myself.

We cowards all lowered our eyes, avoiding the painter's gaze: Well, you know, considering our situation, and besides, it was the people who asked for it.

When the meeting ended, I bolted out of there, but I didn't manage to cross the wall of light and turn invisible to the eyes of the musician.

"The next step is the theater: bring the script of the play you're staging and we'll analyze it. Personally, I'd like to have a copy to study beforehand."

Just like on the inner patio of the local government seat in Rancagua, the other morons were smiling; they had been freed.

Walking with the painter and the critic toward the grand boulevards, I asked the former, "How did you feel?"

"It's like throwing water on a fish – they slip, but they'll get over it."

I don't know if they got over it. I didn't return. I tried to go back, but I didn't.

"I don't get it," La Bella said.

"To Chile, to go back to Chile. They gave me a passport."

For a few months now they had been issuing passports. La Quena went back; the painter's wife went there to see what was what and to dust the furniture; I felt like it was time for me to make my entrance.

"Our entrance," La Bella corrected me. "We're part of the play."

The clay was coming to life.

We began our farewell tour, though you never really say farewell to Paris. The tour took us all over France, though you really never say farewell to France; all over Europe, though you never really say farewell to Europe. The final farewell took place in the UNESCO Hall of Honor, though you never really say farewell to the world.

How terrified I was!

During the farewell tour, Pinochet made public a list of 5000 Chileans who would never be able to return to their homeland because they represented a threat to State internal security.

When they handed me the list, I said to myself: I don't see why they're showing it to me: I can't possibly be on it. They gave me a passport, and a passport means worldwide travel, including Chile. The document from OFPRA, the French Office for the Protection of Refugees and Stateless Persons, allowed me to travel all over the world, except to Chile. It would be illogical to issue a passport and forbid me to use it. I smiled: no, I couldn't possibly be on the list.

I was.
234.
I was.

I cast my eyes toward my staircases and once more started to explain: there must a mistake, and I started to tell them about the theater . . .

"Some people never learn."

While I waited for the mistake to be corrected – because I was sure it was just a mistake – I began working on staging my return.

My tears would bathe my farewell, and I would offer up my back in sacrifice to the universe. My tears would bathe my return, and I would offer up my chest to the universe. At the distant port I would launch the fourth Punic War, the most personal one, my own, in order to reach that far-off land of mine.

With your help, Athena.

Mounted on a white elephant, I would climb the carved staircases of my *cordillera*, stone by stone. The brakes, exhaling air, would free me from my shackles and hurl me forward in a frenzied race.

At another port with an evocative name, I would bring the

elephant aboard. Hidden inside it would be wisdom: nearly two thousand volumes containing the history of World Theater, studies of staging, scripts – since no one can know life's twisted paths and mine was a spiral – *Les Cahiers du Cinéma*, film scripts and movie directors' notes. To feed the present it was necessary to devour the past.

In the middle of the piles of books, in the place of honor, I would return a small cardboard box, crumpled with the passage of time; inside it, the complete works of Brecht, Grotowski's Poor Theater, and Stanislavski's manual. Along with them, hundreds of volumes, the books that launched my childhood travels, that provided my childhood rest, treasures of world literature, hundreds of books without borders.

Fabrics from all over the world would be smuggled in to adorn its bowels; moonbeams and sunbeams and eclipses would hide within it, only to emerge later and light up the stage, the actors, my characters. A battered old pot, an aged prostitute's only treasure, would settle inside, only to rise to the surface, begging charitable souls to fill its belly.

Adorning the white elephant's trunk would be two concentric rhomboids, where the word "Renault" could be read, and below that, "35 tons."

In the shadows, the teachings of Jean-Jacques Ezrati, lighting maestro, would help me try to break through the mantle of shadows that would cover my future sets.

"Lighting for its own sake doesn't work," he had told me.

"It's a matter of illuminating life and death, comedy and tragedy, of the famous actress taking the stammering, stumbling neophyte and thrusting her onto the stage. You have to climb up to the stars, if need be, to correct the angle of a beam and achieve the desired effect. You have to understand why sometimes a beam of light refuses to obey."

You have to create light so that it will disappear from the audience's view and be born in the word, so that it will shed light on it or hide it, depending on the audience.

I was traveling back home to reconnect with the word and with my public, and I was not the same.

I would make my entrance through infinite space, on Air France – since it was on Air France that I had been expelled from the country – in third class, since I refuse to travel in first. During the trip I would write the first speech. I needed to see the *cordillera*, fly over Chuquicamata,[19] descend into the desert, soak up peaks, precipices, coasts, the sea, trying, like a poor director, to penetrate the earth where I would plant lemon trees, orange trees, olive groves, so that the audience could reach out their hands as they walked into the theater and feed their bodies in order to feed their souls. An aisle of jasmine would perfume the *bellas* as they entered the hall; a wall of lights would hide it from the eyes of inquisitors of every stripe.

I needed the oak and the *araucaria* to support my charac-

---

[19] The largest open-pit copper mine in the world, located in northern Chile.

ters; I needed the *boldo* and the cinnamon tree so they wouldn't fire off a monologue; I needed Oedipus and his bloody eyes to restore sight to my miners and dig my own grave. I needed – ye gods, how I needed to offer myself in sacrifice!

With my feet swollen from walking all over the world, I would smooth the ground; with my bloody hands I would build, stone by stone, a theater without walls to hem in the speeches, a theater which, like the one at Epidaurus, would allow – oh, audience of the people! – those speeches to be heard without interference, a theater with no first-class cars.

A theater near a hotel where I could ask for a double-bedded room with walls covered in empty egg cartons, cardboard boxes so that screams couldn't escape down the corridors.

And at the entrance to the theater, a simple poster that would read: After being away from the country on a long international tour, now back on the national scene . . .

Once I was settled in, I would cross the *cordillera* in the other direction, the way out, to make sure the doors were working.

11,905.42 kilometers would be the distance the truck would travel, on the deck of a ship, to discover its new world: Buenos Aires! The direct flight from Antwerp to Valparaíso cost a fortune.

The Reencounter

. . . we have seen the sea in motion, they say,
. . . we have seen ships capsize and cities tumble,
*   razed by earthquakes,*
. . . we have seen towns in distant lands destroyed by war.
*   This is what we have seen in the house of living imag-*
*   es.*
*   And there is one of those houses in every village.*

Trade Winds, Harry Martinson

XX. Of how he learned that the best answer is the one that leads to a question

As I dozed in a third-class seat, my dreams flew over me. My heart thumped. Down below, in the immensity of the ocean, on a wave, a cargo ship; from the prow, the white truck smiled. I called over the pleasant flight attendant and asked:

"Any signs of a storm?"

"Not at all – not in the clouds or in the sea or on land or on anybody's mind."

I had forgotten that there are one-track minds that can't even deal with storms.

"I prefer storms."

A shiver ran down my spine, just like during my interrogations when a question came back and back and back and would keep coming back forever because it had no meaning.

On one side, the *cordillera*; on the other, the sea. The sky: clear; light flooding the landing strip. In Rancagua they cleared out a warehouse to receive the visitor and secretly add the books that had been rescued from burning to those that had arrived to replace them and multiply them. Love filled their pages.

Everything was ready, including those in charge of marking off the checklist. On either side of the staircase two of them waited for me. They let the other passengers through, all but one.

There's nothing more terrible for a theatrical director, for an actor, than sensing that his audience awaits his entrance, and, in a moment of panic, forgetting his lines and not coming out on stage to face his public.

Two dun-colored little men blocked my entry into Chile, they below, I above; between us a flight of stairs. My ticket said Santiago, Chile; the list said no. In Paris the *Genossen* had assured me that the list was a bluff, that people on it had gotten in, that people who already were in the country had been on the list and nothing had happened to them, that the Vicaría[20] was on alert, that you could enter as free as the wind, that there was nothing to worry about.

"I should have worried."

"Some people never learn."

One step separated me from the flight of stairs; one step would distance me from the safety of the plane. It would place me in the hands of DINA, Pinochet's secret police, and return me to the jailhouse two-step, four walls, lights exploding in my brain – but I had already lived through all that. I didn't go down those stairs. We took off.

Far away a brood hen shed a tear and went back to her chicken coop.

I disembarked in Buenos Aires. They had brought me there for free.

---

[20] The Vicariate of Solidarity was an agency of the Catholic Church in Chile during the Pinochet regime. Its charge was to halt the abuse and abduction of Chileans and to defend human rights.

In front of the Obelisk, I looked around – not a circular glance; I looked to one side. The *cordillera*, once so welcoming, rose like a sinister wall between me and my destiny.

I remembered Berlin.

I hopped on the subway, heading toward the port, got off, sat down. My bare feet sought relief in the water.

I exploded into tears.

"Chickens don't cry," said a voice.

"I do, and I'm no chicken."

On the third day I dried my tears and observed the fat cats who had capsized in Buenos Aires.

The first cat had white hair. Lucho had been sailing from Italy; he would go under in Valparaíso. He fell into misfortune by trading the cold waters of the Baltic for the sultry ones of the Mediterranean, for exchanging the cold waves of the South Pacific for the sensuous caresses of Mediterranean waves, and for taking photos that showed him in the circle of power when that power was fading.

In Italy Enrico had taken on the Piazza del Popolo and the Party ministry and had changed his ways. It was no longer necessary to march in processions (oh, you atheist!); it was no longer necessary to make pilgrimages to Moscow to form the cadres of the Italian Communist Party.

Enrico, who together with Santiago Carrillo of the Spanish Communist Party and Georges Marchais of the French Communist

Party, had begun to walk the walk that would lead to the so-called Eurocommunism, the movement which, by breaking with custom, would come closer to social democracy and end up with the dissolution of the Italian Communist Party. And together with them, smiling in the photo, is Lucho, digging his own grave.

In Cuba Fidel said, "Don't come to me with your stories about change: you might know where they begin, but you can never tell where they'll end up."

"He's no fool, that Fidel."

In France the Chilean Communist Party began to marginalize those who were growing closer to the French Communist Party. The age of great purges had begun, some of them for growing closer to . . . others for distancing themselves from . . . and others simply because they were hard to swallow. Just like those combatants who had fought in the International Brigades on the side of the Spanish Republicans and who, on returning to their countries of origin – Poland, Czechoslovakia, Russia – were interrogated, placed in solitary confinement, and expelled because they might have been contaminated by the germs of the Republican plague, the white-haired fat cat was thrown out into the cold, murky waters of the Mapocho. Apparently he had been contaminated and was demanding a change to what was immovable.

I was reminded of *The Confession*, the Costa Gavras film that tells of the interrogations administered to a Czech minister who had fallen from grace, accused of treason to the Party and the fatherland, and the treatment they subjected him to until they squeezed a self-criticism and a confession out of him.

"To me, to do this to me!" Guastavino would lament in the future as he wandered from Los Placeres hill to El Barón, begging for a rail.

Evidently in Charenton Asylum they're treating out-patients, I said to myself.

The second one was a former senator, the same woman who sat around a fire pit in Teatinos, knitting wool socks for the *compañeros* and elevating her varicose-veined legs to reduce their swelling. I could never figure what kind of fat cat she was: not Siamese, and certainly not Persian. Cheshire maybe, but no – that one smiled.

The third fat cat was a former *compañero* from the time of La Jota. He went around on pins and needles, waiting for his beloved to cross the *cordillera* with the good news and a passport. She crossed over, the beloved crossed over, returning his ring. Their marriage had crashed and burned along some curve of loneliness.

We had all arrived in Buenos Aires; we all embraced at the Argentine Communist Party's celebration. There weren't a million of us, barely a hundred, but we shared the same loneliness, and we, the spoils of battle, embraced in the patched-up web, on the other side of the *cordillera*, before starting to tell lies.

In one corner of the park, a theater group, Osvaldo Dragún's, was putting on his *Stories and Jail.* The first plays, his

Tales to Be Told, I already knew because I'd read them; the ones about jail I knew in my bones. I preferred the first ones for their liveliness; the second group gave me chills. I looked all around and saw the walls and bars that grow inside us. I need a hammer! my mind cried out.

"Didn't I tell you?" said the crazy abbot at the Charenton Asylum. You can't trust Robespierre and that fucking universal voting, equal rights and the fucking republic. Charlotte Corday was wrong; I sent her to murder Robespierre."

"Along the way she fell in love with Marat and killed him out of jealousy. Marat was the only one who could notify Danton. The two of them were sitting, one next to the other, on top of the mountain."

"You know how a curve in the road can change history?"

"Or were they the curves of a *bella*?

From the shadows, Gorbachev was smiling.

I moved my chair out of the circle to keep from being closed in.

Trains have always been a part of my life and my destiny, from the sleeping car that carried me from Santiago into the dense, wild forests of Temuco; the old locomotive that carried the father of the first *bella* on the Antilhue line to knock me off the rails for the first time, straight into his daughter's arms; the Orient Express that offered me the mysteries of the East; even the trains of Calle Lavalle – no longer in existence – that carried me to the

Teatro Cervantes, the Colón, and the red-light district, my first refuge during my stay in Buenos Aires.

At the end of the aforementioned party, a Chilean woman caught me off-guard and took me to her house in the San Telmo district. It was on Calle Chile, and the street had cobblestones. Her house was a three-story pyramid that reminded me of the set of the last play I staged in Europe: a moveable pyramid that revealed its inner workings, the other part of the scenery, as it spun. The play took place in the cardboard structure, and behind the cardboard – where passages allowed the actors to perform on the first, second, or third level and emerge from the scenery or be swallowed up in it – it created, through small movements, a prehistoric bird projected on a white background, or a brothel from which the *bellas* called out to their customers, offering their curves and reaching out their arms, begging for help.

Yes, just like trains and pyramids, brothels are also part of my life. They were in Chile, in Santiago and distant Valdivia; they were in Paris, on the Rue Saint-Antoine, when it was a street of brothels and not elegant hotels like today; they were in Barcelona, in the neighborhood of old whores; they were in Cali and Bogotá; they were at the port of Sête, where prostitutes and sailors gave me refuge when I capsized during a tour; they were in Buenos Aires.

They were and will continue to be, corridors of mysterious doors hiding secrets, treasures, sobbing caresses, distorting two-way mirrors, masks, and, at dawn, the horror of a wasted face, devoid of masks, love, and makeup; faces of weather-beaten earth, revealing a dearth of caresses; creaking beds and foul-smelling mattresses, torn stockings draped over a sink and a half-full bottle to help get through a bad moment before picking up my pyramids again and giving my audience the sunny view of life, the one they paid for so as not to see their real faces reflected in the other side of the mirror.

"Which one, the one on this side of the mirror or the other side?"

I directed my steps to the seashore, and we sat down to wait.

Those who were bereft of life wanted to see how the waters parted and gave way to the white elephant of the last battle.

The first to arrive was the word, the word transformed into the deep sound of a horn. The libretto said *Carmen*, but no one has ever followed a libretto – or a line, or stage directions – word for word, except for those bureaucrats who, lacking ideas of their own, copy the content blindly till they unintentionally hit the void, which suddenly blows up in their faces along with the manuals, and the street is left with no answers, not for the audience, not for the actors, but for them – the hawkers of dreams.

The sound of the horn knocked down the walls of fog hovering over the port.

And the other walls? Those are harder to knock down.

Before the truck left France, the customs agent who handled the embarkation and disembarkation paperwork warned me, "There's a rumor going around that a truck loaded with weapons is about to leave, its final destination, Chile. I want to see the cargo, and in any case I'll see which border post I'm going to let you through so you won't be detained. We have just enough time to get you through."

The most dangerous thing for those ignoramuses wouldn't be the books, but rather a powerful projector that resembles a missile launcher and projects a beam of light that can follow an actor's movements, isolate him, make him stand out, and, depending on the angle, light the way before or after him, confirming or anticipating his trajectory, pulling him out of the "we" and sacrificing him before the audience.

"Dangerous if you don't know how to use it."

For once the truck followed the script: it was arriving on the prow of the ship. I cried, we cried with emotion, we embraced, we followed its movement with our gaze; the crane lifted it up into the air, balanced it over our heads, and deposited it, not in my mind, but in a trailer that carried it alone, without an escort, without our being able to liberate it, to a gate-enclosed patio.

The last vision I had of it that day were the two half-open back doors: Rap, rap, rap, they went, like those three knocks that had echoed a little while earlier in my Paris apartment at midnight, the hour of nightmares. I got up without waking La Bella. At the door was the comrade in charge of security for the Chilean Communist Party in France. The dictator fell, was the first thing I thought. I looked at his face: no. They forgave me, what the hell for, I don't know, but they forgave me. I looked at his face: no. He's come to give me an explanation. My *compadre* wasn't capable of giving explanations; rather, he was the executor of lowly errands.

"Volodia sent me."

So Volodia is back in Paris: I remember feeling suddenly happy.

"Tell him I recommend *Happy Days*, "I said, thinking that Volodia wanted me to recommend a play to him.

"Some people never learn."

"He wants you to read this document," he went on, "and to send us your opinion in writing."

"I'll read it and leave it in the office for you tomorrow."

"No, you've got to read it now and give it back to me. I'm sorry, but those are my orders."

That said, he stepped away from the door.

Even now I still wonder what bug had bitten Volodia to make him give me that document to read: it was the declaration that would give birth to the Manuel Rodríguez Front. I had seen the "Manolitos" around; one of my actors had even allowed himself to be seduced by their siren songs, and it wasn't the voice of the people that called him.

And so I began my report to Volodia, asking him where he had gotten the idea that the people were asking us to rise up in arms and take power.

When someone declares that he's acting in the name of the people or responding to the people's call, or *is* the voice of the people, you mustn't trust him. He's lying, hiding his personal or Party ambitions, the desire to take power, and that's why he uses the time-worn cliché "in the name of the people," which forecasts dark days for those "people" whose words he has usurped. In the past the worst crimes were committed in the name of an emperor, a king, a general, a party, an ideology; that paved the way for conquering, enslaving, imposing, robbing with total impunity. It became frowned upon. Today it's more impersonal: everything is done "in the name of the people," and "for the people's welfare." You have to look out for your image, especially because "the people are calling you."

Damned if we haven't made progress!

Just then I understood the movements – martial, almost soldierly – that were taking place among the leadership. I saw the young guys leaving in sneakers and coming back with combat boots.

They left with a smile lighting their lips: the people were calling them, and when the people call, you answer. My actor disappeared; his *compañera* remained in Paris. I wondered what his last lines had been. I thought of Teoponte.

> *I'm off to Cochabamba,*
> *to Cochabamba, señores,*
> *the nightingales will sing,*
> *I'm off to Cochabamba.*

Ratatatatá, they're gone,
Ratatatatá, they're back,
Ratatatatá, it was a lie
that the guerrillas are done for.

Lovely! And yet something was off-key: in the mountains of Colombia they were being killed for a bit of sugarcane; in Peru the Shining Path was spreading darkness and brutality in the Cusco area. They even went as far as to cut off the peasants' hands to teach them not to vote, that voting was anti-revolutionary, that it was playing into the game of the system.

"It wasn't inhuman– it was a revolutionary lesson, *compañero*."

In Chile, apparently, the *compañeros* forgot to notify the people to wait for them, and those who awaited them were the military.

After the return to democracy, some Manolitos or Lautaritos, since there had been a split, still remained, taking over banks for their own benefit – in the name of the people, of course.

"You always learn something new."

You have to be careful when working the lights; you might cause a general blackout. That's how I ended my report to Volodia.

I closed the door.

"Rap, rap, rap." The doors of my truck took me back to Buenos Aires.

It took me three months to get the papers to break the chains that held my truck in bondage. I filled out hundreds of forms, and each form needed to be accompanied, not by a carbon copy – *ay,* I still kept the one I had been given in the GDR – but rather by a green bill.

Something had changed on my continent, not dreams – those were still there; if they weren't, no one would survive – but something had changed, and I am against immobility: a frozen scene is a frozen life, just like a frozen speech, a frozen gesture, the endlessly repeated music of a scratched record. Something had changed, but more than a change, it was a nightmare. Not the nightmare of dictatorship – that one we already knew. Corruption had crossed our path and become the obligatory toll without which your journey, your dream, your life would come to a halt.

At what point, I asked myself, did it leap out from behind the fake scenery and make its way across the stage as though it belonged, like a natural character naturally delivering its lines. At what point did we stop paying attention and assume that it was part of the staircases, just another step, the one that was missing.

The nightmare of dictatorship is something we're well aware of – no, what we're aware of is that horror has no limits; otherwise we would break. It has no limits, but:

Life deals us such hard blows . . . I don't know

They are few, yet there they are . . .
they open up dark ditches
in the proudest faces and in the sturdiest spines.

Life deals us such hard blows . . . I don't know!
Like the hatred of God,
Like the limit of limitless horror.[21]

That morning, from the other side of the *cordillera,* the black heralds of death crossed over to announce the horror of horrors. Three, three in the life force, three that embraced us long-distance, three that were one and at the same time thousands.

The little gray men of the dictatorship had slit the throat of Roberto and María's son, champions of the theater.

José Manuel Parada, for you, *compañero,* my stage goes dark today: they slit the throat of Manuel Guerrero, a professor. For you, comrade, I will dip my fingers in ink and silence my word:

They slit the throat of Santiago Natino, a publicist.

Santiago, for you, my brother, today my marquee will be blank in the hope that you may write justice with your blood, and in huge letters NUNCA MÁS[22] along the entire *cordillera,* my *cordillera,* our *cordillera,* but above all, your *cordillera.*

---

[21] César Vallejo, *Los heraldos negros* (The Black Heralds)
[22] NUNCA MÁS, never again!

The road of Aguas Santas was dressed in red.

That day I walked, I walked in circles. I walked the spiral of death, reached the seashore, and my heart burst with sadness.

Thank you, César, for lending me your heralds.

The customs office and its bureaucrats kept putting obstacles in my way, preventing me from continuing my journey; they had immobilized me. But the sea helped me remain calm.

My sea, whose subterranean currents held the dreams of the disappeared who had been hurled into her breast from the air; my sea, which, while El Plan Cóndor spread its brown mantle over the continent, extended its luminous blue waters in subterranean currents that came to life, advancing without asking permission, advancing without anyone's noticing, and coming to shore, began to uproot the foundations of dictatorships, the foundations of rotten institutions, the foundations of fake cardboard scenery.

Purifying waters that swept away those who occupied the stage, or which formed coral reefs, the only acceptable barrier because it filters away impurities, in order to stop those who have slipped in, trying to take over the stage again and shine their own light, ignoring the others, the earth's dispossessed, the owners of dreams.

Purifying waters, a compendium of currents – one would never be enough – a swirl of underwater currents that would sweep away those little gray men or women, along with their memory and their cardboard speeches, and the savage earth would spread her legs, swallowing them up to return them to the past, where they belong.

But how far I was from my land and its movements; how deeply submerged were my newly-formed ocean currents; how far my eyes were from reality. I took a little bottle, filled it with seawater, and set out to break the chains that held my truck prisoner and kept me from continuing along my meandering path.

For every horror there is a ray of light; every speech requires a reply; every actor who disappears requires a hand in order to scale the wall of oblivion, to leave his seat in the audience and return to the stage.

That morning Buenos Aires lit up.

A rumble of drums followed by a small group of women, their heads covered with white kerchiefs. Never before had the mix of colors heralded so much dignity. A small group of women followed by a multitude; a canvas was coming into focus inch by inch, palm by palm, invading – oh, tendrils of hope! – the beautiful avenues of Buenos Aires, advancing toward the Casa Rosada, the presidential palace.

"Lend a hand for the disappeared!"

They weren't asking for much:

just a hand,

nothing more,

nothing less,

a hand.

The sound of the drums linked the past to the present, making way for the chorus of women who silently called out for justice, their kerchiefs pointing toward the sky like faceless masks. Their tearless eyes focused on a drum filled with red paint in which we – one by one, as was our style – dipped our hands so as to imprint them on the canvas that unfurled, inch by palm, palm by inch, along the beautiful avenues of Buenos Aires, later to fly across the border and unfurl once more, invisible, along Puyehue, in Providencia, a 200-meter-long passageway where the Colegio Latinoamericano de Integración can be found, the same school in front of which Manuel and José Manuel had been kidnapped. They were wrong: Barrabás had managed to make his way to the large house on the corner. Today everyone plays in the street at the school door: the children together with José Manuel and Barrabás.

I dipped my hand in, not for my people, I swear; I dipped it in for everyone, and in that everyone *my* people, mine and yours, were all included.

I had been in Buenos Aires for three months; over the drumroll I let out a cry for help. They had bled me dry. Time was passing; my daughter – we knew she was a girl – was growing in La Bella's womb.

On the other side of the *cordillera* the error would not be corrected: the list of those denied entry would pursue me till the fall of the dictatorship. On this side of the *cordillera* I needed support in order to break the siege of corruption. They'd never let me through without paying a forfeit on each and every step.

"Some people never learn. You don't pay on each and eve-

273

ry step. It's not about climbing staircases; it's about corruption descending them. With corruption, it's better to pay on top; they'll take care of those down below. Corruption has its own rules; it respects hierarchies. Those down below think they're bosses, but they quake in their boots before those on top. That's the key to staying in power."

I checked my pockets; I shouted louder. From Bogotá, La Bella and Perla, the Colombian actress, replied.

"We need to find someone on top who the crooks are afraid of."

I looked around: the haystack was bigger than the *cordillera*. The dictatorship had fallen, the country had returned to democracy, and yet the road, like me, was a spiral plagued with obstacles.

With obstacles and detours, with bloody paths that bypassed roadblocks, with . . .

" . . .an actor, an Argentine actor in Paris."

When nobody believes in anything, it means that the moment has come to raise the curtain and let the theater in. Three knocks announce curtain time in Parisian theaters; three calls announced my departure: first to Bogotá, then from Bogotá to Paris, from Paris to Buenos Aires, to La Casa Rosada.

When Alfonsín[23] traipsed around the world announcing he would be president of Argentina someday, nobody had believed him, not even the actor in Paris who lent him a sofa so that he

---

[23] Raúl Alfonsín, President of Argentina from 1983-1989.

could regain his strength and continue his pilgrimage and his rants.

He made it. Maybe he made it because he deviated from the script, maybe because since nobody believed him, they let him through, poor, crazy, and innocent, or maybe because madness in a world of crazies is a good counselor.

Or maybe just because it had been written.

The call from La Casa Rosada to the customs office was never recorded. But its effect was.

"Get the hell out, Chilean."

In one week I worked out a new route, studied maps, bought myself a compass. From Bogotá they sent me fuel through Jacques, one of the French techs who had come to help us set up, to teach the Chilean techs, one of the two that had traveled, impelled by a thirst for adventure.

For a week Jacques flew over Buenos Aires; he came from Bogotá, high, as usual. I set him up in Lavalle, where he grew weary of barbecues and the wine he bought every afternoon with El Flaco and his wife, a platinum blonde, an Evita who had never left the *pampa* and was languishing in Buenos Aires, a blonde who, at the twilight of her body, put all her meat on the grill.

Poor Jacques – he ended up with a reheated chunk of rib eye.

The truck had traveled 11,905.42 kilometers before they stopped it cold. On Argentine soil it covered exactly zero kilometers in ninety days. Its reflectors languished with the desire to light up the stage; my books clamored for me to open them and stroke their pages. The pyramid, my pyramid, the one from the last play in Europe, jealously demanded my attention.

I had traversed hundreds of streets and avenues in Buenos Aires; I had gone up and down thousands of steps, knocked on hundreds of doors, asking for someone to open a window so that my dreams could escape from prison.

During my last week in the city I had assigned myself three tasks: the first, to study maps and trace a new route in my mind. Somewhere I had taken the wrong curve – lucky mortal.

The second, to falsify my French driver's license, turning it into an international license and putting little seals all over it, authorizing me to drive 35-ton trucks – or even more – if I felt so inclined. At the same time, and as part of the same task, I decided to read the manual on how to drive the beast.

The third, to buy a couple of books. It was the week of the Book Fair.

At the doors of the Book Fair, I wandered back and forth, unable to make up my mind to enter. The temptation was great, and I'm easily tempted.

"Life deals us such temptations . . . don't I know."

Temptations, the kind you can't resist, that parade before your eyes, stop for a second and possess you; there are eternal seconds like La Bella's gaze at the party at *L'Humanité.*

And I'm easily tempted, or at least I was tempted enough to buy two books. On the other side of the gate were thousands and thousands, just waiting for a friendly hand to pull them from the shelves. Once more unto the breach – which one? -- and, without an ounce of guilt, to choose.

"Life brings us terrible choices . . . don't I know."

That's where I found myself when suddenly a familiar shadow crossed my path: Volodia. He had come to give a talk, invited by Chileans in Argentina. He gave me a hug and asked:

"Do you know who has my invitation?"

Not a clue, and there were no familiar faces nearby.

"Me – they left it with me." I handed him the ticket I had just bought.

"Let's go inside," Volodia said.

"No, I'm waiting for someone. You go in first; they're waiting for you."

As he walked away, I murmured, "Thanks for letting me leave Bulgaria."

I never saw him again.

I got back in line to buy another ticket. I had just enough cash left to buy one book. Without a second's hesitation, I bought Puig's *Eternal Curse on the Reader of These Pages*.

I got into the truck.

XXI. Of how he went from the noble profession of actor to that of tightrope walker

I managed to bring Jacques back down to earth. Departure time had arrived. Argentine customs kindly put a guard in the cab to make sure I wouldn't get lost.

The Chileans watched from the sidewalk, a little sadly. They were staying behind.

"Where to?" asked the person in charge.

"Pa' delante – straight ahead," I replied, imitating Fidel and Arturo Prat. I peered into the rear-view mirror: behind the truck was a wall, which allowed me to complete the heroic phrase, "Not a single step backward, not even to pick up momentum." The truck thanked me.

Jacques flipped open the Renault manual, chapter one: How to drive the truck.

I started following orders.

"You always learn something new."

I moved various levers, disengaged the hand brake, up and to the left, on the dashboard. I grabbed the key, a little stick crowned with a lovely, ivory-colored knob, looked at Jacques, and both of us issued the war cry of theater folk: *Merde!*

I turned the key. The truck roared, snored, and died.

Embarrassed, I asked Jacques to read me the lines again; surely I had skipped some, "After a long period of immobility, the motor must be allowed to warm up so that the fluids can circulate, the air in the brakes can find their way, and the compressed air can lift the chassis, which will utter a sigh, and only at that point should you shift into first. For heavy loads, apply the auxiliary gear stick to duplicate the force."

A forest of banners sprang up on the sidewalk. At least, that's what I imagined, because the dust cloud didn't let me see anything.

We left the port, headed for Corrientes, turned onto Carlos Pellegrini and then onto Lavalle. Jacques wanted to say goodbye to his Argentine lover. At the corner we took Avenida 9 de Julio, the broadest avenue in the world. Through the rear-view mirror I could see the Obelisk.

I said farewell – *chau*, Buenos Aires – though you never say farewell to Buenos Aires.

Behind us the Obelisk disappeared. I was at zero meters above sea level; 1798 kilometers ahead of us was La Quiaca, at 3422 meters about sea level.

The truck turned its head, gave me a dirty look, and said, "You should have told me, *che*. In Paris you said it was 1590 kilometers and at sea level."

It had spent a lot of time in Argentina.

"What I think is, it used to escape at night and go dancing

in La Boca."

Twenty-four hours later, on Route 9, the truck didn't run – it flew.

On one stretch, a caravan of gauchos rode alongside us, waving their hats. We stuck our hands out the window and waved back.

"Wake up," Jacques said. "We're heading north, not to the *pampa*. There are no gauchos around here; the ones who were riding were following alongside a train, and the one they were waving to was Evita, not you."

"We're both part of the show," I replied. "You should never leave lines hanging in the air."

I shifted gears and climbed on a motorcycle, just like Che.

We stopped and they served me a coffee. Apparently it had been a huge effort.

"Twenty-four hours? A huge effort?"

"No, three months and twenty-four hours, not counting the years in exile."

We climbed the staircases, step by step, meter by meter, all 3442 of them. The trees disappeared in the night. At dawn a forest of *tamarugos* protected by a blanket of spiderwebs trapped the dewdrops; the first sunbeams extended along the road, gentling the hardness of the stones and bringing relief to our tired feet.

The stones, in turn, disappeared from the houses, giving way to mud, straw, adobe. Pachamama,[24] protecting her children from the cold and the lonely wind, though not from the gray men.

---

[24] Incan fertility goddess and earth-mother.

Rise up, brother, be born with me, repeated the wind.

I rose. I placed my foot on step number 3443, the one that leads to 3447, when the dispossessed of both sides, along with the dispossessed of no side, the dispossessed of the earth, come together.

Villazón, in Bolivia, offered us its wretchedness.

Argentina lay behind us. After collecting his cut, the guard showed us the only paved portion of road we would see for the next few weeks: the narrow bridge that crossed the Villazón River, marking the border between two groups of wretches that, in no man's land (because nobody cares about them), smuggled useless merchandise in a new order destined for those who were blessed by wealth, though not by luck.

Beneath the narrow bridge, along the water's edge, backs curved by the weight of their burdens and eyes fixed on the water in an attempt to read the coca leaves that drifted by at the bottom of the river, there crossed a new race of slaves, children of the earth, lashed together with a long cord: the rainy season had begun.

On both sides of the river, tithes were paid, crumbs that ended up in the pockets of those occupying the lowest rungs of the ladder of corruption, sad crooks who flashed their toothless smiles as they told themselves: We belong, we're part of the power structure, after which they would squat down, just like the others, just like me, in the marketplaces, to eat a chunk of greasy food served on a sheet of newspaper, bowing their heads even lower in shame so that their neighbor and their brother wouldn't recognize them.

Jacques and I devoured a roasted face, the only part of the sheep that reached those parts, the animal's head, complete with skin, which is tossed on the coals, rubbed with salt and *rocoto* peppers. The eyes are covered with coca leaves so they won't explode. The feast was accompanied by a nice glass of *chicha de maíz.*

We spread out our map, and horrors! Grease had spilled on the paper and the roads had been obliterated. In the distance you could read: Desaguadero, 963.65 kilometers.

"That's nothing, less than a thousand kilometers," said the truck.

"I want to learn how to drive," said Jacques.

"This doesn't even require a full rehearsal," said the director.

"Poor mortals," said the sheep's head. "The grease didn't erase the roads – there *were* no roads."

"Pay up," said the one who appeared to be in charge.

I paid.

They lifted the cord; I shifted gears; the truck roared. A couple of Bolivians shouted, "Hey, wait."

Argentina had given us a guard to make sure we would be dropped off at La Quiaca. Bolivia gave us two of them to make sure we'd be pushed out at Desaguadero.

The ritual of departure changed: the Bolivian guards handed us a little bag of coca leaves and some volcanic rock to grind up with our teeth, moisten with our saliva, and make a ball that we were supposed to lodge in a corner of our mouths. Now, along with the sound of gears and the sighs of the truck, we added *acullico*, the juice that would take away our fatigue, keep us awake, and help us endure the lack of food. The only thing it didn't take away was our fear.

Behind us was Argentina, struggling to return to the path of democracy.

"What democracy are you talking about?" echoed in my memory.

In the rear-view mirror you could see two single lanes: one of them on the right, leading to Argentina; another, on the left, leading to Bolivia; in both of them, the dispossessed of the border, stone men, heads bowed, awaiting the day when they will be able to raise them and shake the foundations of the walls and bridges that separate them from life.

I hit the gas.

Roads crossed by water, crossed by landslides, crossed by the absolute absence of roads, roads that were the negation of their *raison d'être*, staircases without steps, but which soared to the sky.

First stop: a cry followed by two explosions in the solitude of the *altiplano*.

I hit the brakes.

It flew: my heart flew toward my beloved; it flew toward my daughter, stirring impatiently in her mother's womb; the truck flew toward thousands of pyramids scattered along the path, stone pyramids that blocked the imprudent traveler's way, pyramids that demanded attention, females abandoned in the middle of the *altiplano* and awaiting their revenge against those who trod on them.

"Stones must be respected, picked up with tenderness, and you must pass alongside them step by step so they won't be offended and get in your way again. We told you to stop, but you didn't stop. Where's your equipment for fixing the wheels?"

We quickly consulted the manual, "In case of a flat tire, call . . ." There was a number, a calling center in Paris. They would send a truck with spare parts to change the tire. What luck – we were covered!

3542 meters high. We had ascended one hundred meters. Zero inhabitants for kilometers around; three llamas who watched us curiously. We weren't sure whether or not it was a road. Six hours earlier we had come across a shepherd's stone hut. I hadn't considered it necessary to check to see if there was a number on the scrap of cloth that served as a door.

We didn't dare ask where the nearest phone was or what the area code was to call Paris.

There was nothing left of one of the tires; with the other one, it was just a matter of patching a few holes.

Assisted by the two Bolivians we pulled the seals off the rear doors and took out the spare tires; now it was a matter of mounting them.

We sat on the ground, our backs resting against the truck, waiting for someone to come along and take us, along with the two tires, to the nearest town. The moon was beautiful, within a hand's reach; you could see the craters. The *altiplano* night was frigid; you could feel the cold cutting through the rocks. The wait was long; the llamas multiplied from three to six. The ball of coca became more and more perfect, and we spat the greenish saliva almost as far as the guards did.

Stories come together in space: Jacques spoke of French Guyana; even if he had been talking about Camembert, it would've been the same. We listened to him affectionately, the llamas, the guards, and I. The guards spoke of El Alto. We listened to them, fascinated; that meant there were places even higher than where we were, and if they call a place 3542 meters high El Alto . . . (at this point even the truck was chewing coca) . . . they spoke of their childhood without a school, of fathers swallowed up in mineshafts, of parents who ambled freely through their houses just as the llamas ambled freely through the *altiplano*. Me? I spoke of theater, of chicken coops, of international festivals, of Epidaurus, of possessed stages, of rapt audiences . . .

There's nothing more terrible for a director than for a captive audience to fall asleep on him. Even the llamas took off: it's almost like wanting to be the centerpiece at a table with no diners, with not even the Comendador de Calatrava at its head.

Thirty-three hours went by. Far away, in La Bella entre las Bellas' womb, the fruit continued to grow. At less than thirty-three kilometers from the border; we thought we had begun the descent into hell. La Bella intercepted my thoughts: an old pickup was ap-

285

proaching before our eyes. It stopped: if anything good can be said to come from the loneliness of the *altiplano*, it's that solitary llamas and solitary vehicles give one another a hand. They offered us llama *charqui*,[25] a cigarette. They sat down without a word, without asking questions, but they sat down beside us. It wasn't necessary to know who they were, where they came from, or what they were doing in that place, let alone what sort of cargo they were transporting.

We were brothers in misfortune, and surely with such a big truck with such odd license plates, we must be carrying precious cargo.

After we had finished chewing, we hoisted the two wheels into the pickup, along with a guard to help us reload it on the way back, and me. The other guard stayed behind, watching over the truck, Jacques, and the six llamas that had come back.

Apparently they were more interested in hearing about French Guyana than theater stories. Besides, in the immensity of the Bolivian *altiplano,* go try to explain the limits of a stage and spoken lines to a bunch of llamas. Having said that, I turned my head and regarded the loneliness of the landscape, my loneliness, my landscape, my stones, my audience.

I fell asleep.

"The wheels are ready," a voice woke me. I was in the middle of a hamlet; the truck had followed its route. They explained that someone had probably stolen the inner tubes of my tires, that under the tires there was only air, which was lucky,

---

[25] Jerky.

since, through some miracle, the air had stayed inside, but the holes caused by the stones had let it out. I needn't worry, they explained, because they had old inner tubes that had been left behind by other truckers who hadn't stopped in time.

"They never listen," the guard said. "If they see that a person is poor, they never listen. Sometimes we don't warn them, just to teach them a lesson. For the record, we did warn you in time, but you didn't listen, just like the others. And turning toward Vulcan, he added, "There's nothing you can do with these guys; their feet have no roots." He handed me a little bag of coca leaves and we started to chew, waiting for another pickup, jeep, or truck to come by in the other direction.

The next day we got lucky: I went back to the truck to continue on my way; the llamas had taken off. After all, Jacques was a technician, not an actor. Each to his own role, I thought.

I grabbed the bag of coca away from him and let him drive. Jacques was one of those who flew, and the truck needed to keep its wheels firmly on the ground.

We began to take over the Bolivian roads. In Bolivia distances aren't measured in kilometers, but rather in days; with luck, they're measured by the time it takes to haggle over tolls, over raising the ropes that cross the road every so often to exact the fee for crossing ancestral lands, occasionally passing a hamlet, sometimes in the middle of nothing.

We learned that you can't wait for a gas station to fill the truck's tank, that in hamlet after hamlet you have to ask if they have a barrel of gas and buy it in little quarter-liter cans; that days don't pass the same way in a globalized society as in a society suspended in time and in the past.

I asked if they had eighth-liter cans.

Time had lost its way around some curve; the tires had been patched and patched again, and you could barely detect the original part of the patch on the inner tubes. The wheels were no longer round and had lost the sense of the pavement; even though it was the rainy season, the windshield wipers refused to do their duty. We replaced them with tobacco dissolved in urine, spreading it over the glass. Never before had nothingness been so clearly visible, the moon so lovely, the rain like diamond drops exploding before our eyes.

"More coca leaves, please," the director asked, promising that when the right time came, he would supplement the orange and lemon trees with coca bushes that would lead to the door of his theater, and that instead of a box office, there would be a rope and a little can for the audience to deposit whatever they wanted. He would replace the *soupe à l'oignon*, with which he had planned to lend an international touch to the hall, with a nice roasted sheep's head, allowing its fragrance to escape in homage to the theater gods.

"Take that bag away from him or we're going to get killed," Jacques said.

The beginning of the ascent of the *altiplano* changed my perspective on things, and, just so you know, I've got circular vision. The theater had taught me to see to the left, to the right, entrances, exits, the top of the pyramid and the first step; prison had taught me to see through cracks, to make the bars that insisted on limiting my movements disappear, to travel out of my body so as to observe and measure its reactions. The absence of light in my eyes had taught me to turn sounds into images. My travels throughout the world, had taught me to puzzle out and avoid the traps of rigid signs. My rebelliousness had taught me to go off the rails. My fingers had taught me to recognize the colors of fabrics with my eyes closed so that I could see them in a light that transcended my own. The Renault manual had taught me to shift gears and control the truck's whims. The Party had showed me the walls that hem in ideas. History had taught me how some search for the ideal race and others for the ideal militant. My lack of discipline had taught me to sit carefully on the box with shards of broken glass. Love had softened my bad temper, which exploded every time things didn't turn out the way I wanted or imagined, teaching me that the outcome went beyond anything I had imagined, and that my task was to disappear along the route in order to show the way and illuminate the next step.

I learned to take myself seriously so as to be able to laugh at myself – all this and much more had I learned, and none of it did me a bit of good. I found myself in front of a mass of mountains that went up and down in an endless game of narrow, one-lane roads (a half-lane under the best of circumstances), partially collapsed bridges, landslides that announced their presence after plunking themselves down defiantly and blocking my way, jealous of the fruit of our love; dry stones, sterile mud that fell unexpectedly upon the traveler.

I found myself contemplating an infinite mass of *cordillera*, an endless wall that created new walls, closing off their secret paths to block our way.

Now I was really beginning the ascent, to 3452 meters above sea level.

XXII. Of how he discovered the meaning of the Delphic Oracle

First thing you've got to do before starting to climb a hill: honk the horn and listen. Watch out for the treacherous echo, the one that brings back your words or scatters them among the ravines.

"You already knew that: the flatterers, those who try to be accepted, make up part of that gray echo that endlessly reproduces words pronounced by others."

If you hear a sound that isn't yours, wait: another vehicle is coming down, and the road isn't wide enough for two. If there's no reply, change gears, pop a handful of leaves in your mouth, and may his god and ours have mercy on us.

Don't stop – never stop. If another truck appears right in front of you, the one going downhill is supposed to look for a turnoff and stop; the one going up doesn't stop; if he does, he'll end up in a gorge.

"You always learn something new."

The brakes will loosen up little by little. First the air will escape in a puff, then another and another, weaker and weaker, and so it continues; the brake pedal will start sinking into the floor; the truck will shiver feverishly; no matter how hard you shift, it won't go forward; you'll hear the scrape of metal and feel the truck slip backward, first one centimeter, then another, picking up speed till it's hurled into the void at the first curve. Remember, since the truck has power steering, it won't respond to you. After the third breath of air escapes, it won't respond at all.

I hit the brakes.

In front of us it appeared, in all its yellowness, one of those Volvo trucks that crossed the *cordillera* loaded with drugs. We had spotted them on other peaks; we had seen them disappear in the ravines. Ropes yielded at their approach, allowing them to pass: trucks without makes or models, Mafioso trucks, trucks that had been paid for in high places, haughty trucks with neither homeland nor law. Their imperious snouts looked down from on high; their headlights illuminated the single lane; a side beam searched out a hand-dug space in the *cordillera* for the truck to stop in, yielding way.

It found it, it found it, but its tail still blocked part of the road, at the edge of the abyss. I had a panic attack. I hit the brakes. I won't get through; I'll fall off the cliff, I thought.

The first thing we heard was a sigh from the truck; the air started to escape from the brakes through the safety valves; the gas pedal was coming loose. Then two cries in Quechua – unlike Oedipus' speeches in Greek, in Epidaurus, I couldn't understand them, but from the tone I imagined they weren't very friendly. The two guards jumped out of the truck on the side toward the edge of the cliff. Then another sigh from the truck, a second air leak, and a scream, this time in French: *Sauve qui peut!* with a noticeable Arthur Prattian accent. It was Jacques, following the guards. A third air leak, and then came my grand entrance. I thought about La Bella, about my daughter, whom I saw reflected in the moon, but whom I would never hold in my arms; I looked for an appropriate speech, vacillating between Racine, Molière, a Greek tragedy or something from one of Valle-Inclán's *esperpentos.*[26]

"Why not one of your own?" my ego suggested.

I'd have to project very loudly, since with the noise of the truck echoing over the cliff, my words would risk being lost. With any luck, the reflectors would give off sparks as they crashed against the rocks, lighting the way down. In the end, when the echo no longer repeated my lines, my body would be torn limb from limb, adding a classic touch to my movement, one arm pointing forward, the other backward, and my legs splayed open in a leap worthy of *Swan Lake* or a flailing pathetically like a lamb being sacrificed to the gods. They say that in the seconds right before you die, your whole life runs through your mind; for a poor theatrical director, it's his last *mise-en-scène*, the one from the second following his death in his march toward his destiny.

"So the last step is the first one?"

The truck came to a halt. The two guards had placed two rocks up against the rear wheels to stop it.

---

[26] A grotesque, ironic style cultivated by early 20th century Spanish author Ramón María del Valle-Inclán.

"They screwed up my *mise-en-scène*."

Air built up and the brakes responded again; the gears shifted successfully. I removed the two leaves of coca with which I had covered my eyes to avoid facing death. In the rear view mirror I saw the yellow truck slowly pulling away.

We agreed on the order in which the crew would re-enter the stage. First I'd honk the horn; if no one honked back, and once the truck started moving, Jacques would get in. Then the two guards, who remained behind to pick up the rocks and to prevent an accident. Jacques requested the passenger seat: either he drove or he got in last.

I honked: nothing. The only sound that echoed back was the truck's horn. The truck started moving forward, but after just a few meters and before picking up speed, the door opened and the first guard, followed by the other one, got in. Then Jacques stuck his head out before disappearing from my view. Gavroche had miscalculated; he lost his balance and slammed against the wheel.

I braked, this time with the approval of the guards, who had become fond of the Frenchie.

There are priorities in life: the first is life, the last, death. The first order of business was to place the rocks so as to prevent the truck from rolling downhill, dreaming of its past on European roads it would never see again, alone on the slope, sad and defeated, tumbling down the precipice of life.

Fortunately, the experience we had gained led them to put the rocks in place before the brakes sighed for a second time. I opened the door; on the left side, the door of memories. I saw Jacques' face as he fell: it reflected surprise. He didn't utter a scream, but remained just as silent as those actors who react to the written text and not to the text that emerges from the writing, unable to summon up words, astonished as they are by the power of imagination and their lack thereof.

Jacques had fallen toward the right-hand section of the truck, the one on the side of the void and at the same time that of the future. The truck clung to its six central wheels to stay alive in the present. Above us, the infinite; below us, the spiral of death clinging to our longing for survival.

We turned the truck around. Jacques, sitting at the edge of the abyss, the fabric of one of his pants legs gone, and with it part of his skin. Thirty-three centimeters without skin, revealing his muscles in operation, his flesh pulsing with fear as if he were being zapped with electricity, his open mouth incapable of replying to a question that vanished in an echo.

He was posed just like the Comendador, not a blink, his face a perfect mask, devoid of all expression, so that the audience could shape it in one direction or the other: death or life.

On the ridge two kites fluttered, just as kites do on the other side of the *cordillera* in the month of September. They came together in an embrace, then withdrew in circles like the country girls of my town, escaping, surrendering, awakening the desire and spiraling movements of the males. On one side, the fabric from a pair of pants; on the other, the character's skin, Stanislawski and Brecht, the scenery covering the wound, and on the other, harsh reality before the eyes of the director and the guards.

They cut off the rest of his pants, rinsed the wound with corn *chicha*, chewed coca and spat it on the wound thirty-three times, once for each centimeter. Then they applied coca leaves on top of it, perhaps so he wouldn't see the rest of the road and could rest from his fears. They tied the whole thing up with a filthy rag that we used for cleaning the windshield.

I honked the horn and we continued on our way.

In the cabin, sitting in the middle, Monsieur Bip, the lighting technician who had learned to practice the art of silence.

From that moment on, and for the next 100 kilometers, the task was to find a hospital or a First Aid station where a professional could assess the injury and apply a scientific treatment. We found a First Aid station; they laid Jacques on a cot. The room was painted white; the light was intense: it looked like the operating room in *The Autopsy*. Just in case, I didn't say anything. The nurses washed their hands and began to unwind the rag.

I was expecting a nest of worms – thirty-six hours had gone by since the accident. As they unrolled, the coca leaves started to appear, the second protective layer. The medical personnel, two nurses, nodded their heads in approval. They peeled off a leaf, and underneath there appeared a piece of pink flesh in perfect condition, thirty-three centimeters of impeccable flesh: not a worm or a drop of blood. I thought of Shylock.

They removed a little bag of coca from a white cabinet and began chewing. They replaced the guards' spitballs with those of the medical personnel, covered the wound with coca leaves, and wrapped it back up in the same filthy rag.

"Sorry, but we're short of sterile material," they said.

They handed me a bag of coca leaves, "For when you change the dressing." My head was spinning as I left the room. Portia and Nerissa were smiling.

"I want to drive," said Jacques, recovering his powers of speech.

He drove.

At dawn we were surprised by a lake filled with pink flamingos. Balancing on one leg, they dreamed of the time when the only creatures to disturb their sleep were the llamas. When they heard us approach, they took flight and disappeared in the horizon. That day, to punish our insolence, the mountain spirits extended their claws and dug them into one of the truck's sides. Jacques had taken the curve very tight. In principle, you're supposed to go to the edge of the abyss, and at the exact moment when you can't see the road and you feel the air scaling the rocky walls of the cliff, you turn the wheel − not before, not after − and above all, you don't stop, no matter how hard they've grabbed you or how deafening the sound of the cordillera's fingers are as they rip off the truck's tin sides.

Half the letters of the "Nuevo Teatro Los Comediantes" sign, six consonants and four vowels, remained: an eternal sign, its other letters remained stuck to one of the Bolivian mountains.

The books took advantage of the opportunity to peek out and delight in the scenery. One of them warned us: Careful, if you screw up on another curve, you might end up becoming a satellite of the moon.

"*Merci*, Jules."

Six weeks had gone by since we crossed the border at Villazón. We had traveled 841.65 kilometers, and we were 86 kilometers from Desaguadero, on the Peruvian border, 4065 meters above sea level. In El Alto, 400 meters below, at the bottom of a spiral road, was La Paz, the capital of Bolivia.

We rested. We had learned that distances in Bolivia aren't measured in kilometers, but in days, and more precisely, by adding, "God willing."

I covered one of my eyes with a coca leaf, leaving the other exposed. With one of them I looked at the past; with the other, what still awaited me.

In the distance I spied a hand balanced atop the Obelisk, waving goodbye. I kept it in my heart next to the hands of rage that Guayasamín had given me "so that you'll never forget the hands of my people." No, I would not forget them, neither those of his people, nor those of mine, nor those of my continent.

Balancing atop the peak of the *cordillera*, unable to distinguish sanity from madness, reality from nightmares, I saw the band of pink flamingos disappear. I wet my lips in the Uyuni salt flat, the highest and driest in the world. The tires exploded in my ears to the rhythm of Ravel's "Bolero" while an Argentine condor danced barefoot on a table in the esplanade of Les Invalides in front of the Eiffel Tower, the tires spinning more and more dizzily around the table and the condor. At one of the border crossings, a wedding band rolled down the sides of the *cordillera.* From the bottom of the spiral, the sirens called out to me, dressed in seven skirts offering me a *chola* sandwich.

"I almost went down to the depths of hell."

"Don't brake, never brake," echoed a lifesaving voice in my ears.

With my other eye I looked at the future that was calling me – rise up into birth with me, brother – and offering me its abandoned womb, a small column emerging from between its legs, spinning beside the sunbeams. Time didn't come to a halt, reminding me of the shadow, that whatever is to be learned is found in the future, not in the past, that the past is just its means of support, that in order to go forward I had two options: either pull the coca leaf off my eye or cover the other eye with a second leaf.

I headed straight for Desaguadero. I was about to go forward when a rope appeared in front of the truck. At each side, holding it up, one of my guards, columns of stone and flesh indicating the end of the familiar and the beginning of the unknown.

I had seen them before, when I consulted the Delphic Oracle prior to starting out on this journey, but until that moment I didn't understand their meaning: In order to cross over from the past to the future, you have to pay for your sins.

XXIII. Of how he ran across the demons of power on a bend in the road in Tahuantinsuyo

Behind us lay the past. We crossed the threshold of the sun to enter the darkness. Viracocha tried uselessly to hold out his protective hand, but a gray mantle covered the sacred valley. The waters of the lake had started to change color on the Peruvian side. President Ramiro had announced his emergence from the shadows by burning voting urns so that their smoke would block out the sun.

The black light of the theater allows you to see from a different perspective; it highlights what is hidden from the spectator's eyes, illuminates secret paths, and, next to a *svoboda*, it hides, reappears, romps around the stage, destroying preconceived notions, opening people's eyes to new ways of seeing.

President Ramiro's luminosity was brown/red/black: brown like the brown plague of the Second World War, red like Beria's red plague[27], black like the black plague of the Middle Ages, fatal like the plague virus that we harbor in walled-in minds and which, if we're not careful, can take root like a vine growing inside us, creep toward our neighbor and travel from port to port in the name of the majority, a body that will give its own blood to nourish it and allow it to survive.

"Luckily you were vaccinated, remember?"

---

[27] Lavrentiy Beria (1899-1953). Soviet politician named Chief of Security and the Secret Police under Stalin. Later condemned for treason by the Politburo and executed.

At 3827 meters above sea level was the bridge that marked a new border, newly paved, a new congregation of the wretched of the earth sitting there, offering flowers, food, or just killing time as they waited for their own to run out. Their faces lacked expression; their lips were sealed; their eyes looked neither straight ahead nor to the side, but their backs could see: with subtle movements they announced when someone was approaching; they ached with affection, warning of danger. Their cracked feet smiled whenever grease from their food spilled on them, cleaning off the dust that covered them. The children let their childhood escape through the holes of their threadbare llama-wool sweaters, decorated with Incan designs, woven by the hands of their grandmothers, by their mothers, by women without love or caresses.

Sad are the sweaters of the peasant child.

Their food, wrapped in election propaganda, announced the arrival of a new president, of change, of hope, of an end to violence, and yet the black ink ran together with the grease, lending the food a bitter taste.

On the opposite wall, a torn poster calling for a voting boycott; on the same wall, next to figures of indigenous people, Ayacucho's poorest of the poor, rose the image of President Ramiro.

I wondered at what point both inks mixed together, hidden from the audience's eyes, at what point both posters were jumbled together, one with the other, at what point, by manhandling the word, they made it lose its meaning, at what point the ones who spoke in the name of, and as the savior of, found themselves standing on top of the same pedestal, and they used the append-ages – call them the people or the citizens – to pave the road to hell. No more was there *a rise up and be born with me, brother,* it was a come and govern with me, brother, repeated by one, re-peated by the other, while behind faux cardboard scenery they hid their true intentions: follow me blindly, poor deluded creature; I need your vote and your blood.

I ate, but first I threw away the wrapper.

I ate, but I didn't pay. The area commander in chief, a dashing Peruvian Army colonel, gave me a safe-conduct, and al-lowed me through without guards. Amazed, I said to myself: He's not a bastard; he's a well-born, good-hearted, educated man who has climbed to the peak of the *cordillera* to help culture develop, to lend a hand to the word and the image, to let a poor director in, and to allow the stage to make its way again from chicken coops to theater halls, from theater halls to the abyss, from the earth to the sea, from which the word will emerge once more.

"Only a man with those traits and a pure heart like Your Grace is capable of letting the theater through without paying and without an armed guard," I said to him with a pronounced Cervan-tine accent.

"Please go ahead, Señor Director – you, your assistant, and your truck. Have a good trip, and wait for me in Puno; the safe-conduct is valid up to Puno," he replied with a distinct Andean accent.

370.5 kilometers of freedom, all downhill, and with no guards; the waters of the lake caressing our thighs, the whole cabin to ourselves; 2774 kilometers between us and the next border, and the world was ours.

Before our eyes, Puno, and at its entryway a guard, Cerberus in charge of the fortress. We stopped.

"The colonel asked me to accompany you to a *pensión*. He'll be here tomorrow to talk to you."

We were crossing another border.

At the side of the road two clowns were playing – "Theater, you know, in the street, in the hall, in the chicken coops – seventeen international festivals," they repeated in broken French.

The new festival sat on the ground, it was the street; it squatted on its heels; it was the hall; it tumbled in the mud, a new Roman circus of the heights: it was a circus festival. The rotten smell sprouting from the earth replaced the fragrance of sprigs of jasmine.

"With lights," said the technician, "depending on their angle, you can achieve a different effect: they enlarge, they reduce, they add a happy tone, a sad tone, they can wrap things in love, create a cold, hateful look, depending on the angle . . ."

The two clowns opened their almond-shaped eyes wide. The truck was sinking into the mud; half the street was filled with water, the other half with sludge. "Keep straight," the guard had said. "Don't drift off the road; never drift off the road."

I'd drifted off. The clowns screeched, "Don't drift off, never drift off!" and, like a Greek chorus, they added, "Some people never learn."

Not all genres can be combined in a production. In the search for supreme pleasure, pleasure gets lost. After which, lifting their left leg, they started tipping over to one side. Forty-five degrees, the perfect division of a right angle. No wonder they were able to build the lost city of Machu Picchu. At 45 degrees, the truck lost momentum; on the driver's side, my side, wheels suspended in mid-air over the wet side of the road, the left side mired in mud up to the window. Jacques took off the rag he had been using as a bandage, spat on the window with coca leaves, and closed his eyes to enter the center of the empire.

We got out from the left side of the truck. The wheels formed a platform so that we could climb down the stairs slowly, first one leg, then the other, stopping whenever the truck shuddered, holding back everything, even our breath, to prevent a sudden overturn, avoiding the temptation of accelerating the rhythm of our speech.

Unlike a play in which the director comes out at the end to greet the audience, this time I emerged first. Circling the truck, the audience watched us, talking among themselves. Some speculated that the truck would vanish into the mud, others that it had already touched bottom, that it had reached the Inca Trail, "Stone upon stone, I give you my past and my future," they murmured. Others, more realistic, offered up their backs as an improvised stretcher. One more degree of incline and it would have leaned backward before flipping over in the mud, its tires pointing upward toward celestial highways.

The spectators in the nosebleed section were the first to act: they rolled up their shirtsleeves and started hauling stones. I'll never know where they got them from – invisible walls, undiscovered ruins, quarries left behind following explosions of the maternal womb? They shook off their chains and formed a human chain. Some of the first-row spectators lent their arms, others their backs. With their arms they pushed huge wooden levers to straighten up the truck; with their backs they maintained the centimeters recovered. Those in the nosebleed section squatted, dug, collected buckets of mud and filled the holes beneath the wheels with stones.

There was something unreal about the scene: the truck spewed fire from its exhaust, enveloping it in a ball of flames. The inhabitants of Tahuantinsuyo raised the fortress that would house the new Inca, the one who, as the legend says, will come back to mark the birth of a new empire . . .

"Don't mess with me – those were the Aztecs, the one who came back was Quetzalcóatl, not the 'new Inca,' and the story took place in Mexico. You got your legends mixed up."

"And you weren't the one who found yourself sinking into the mud at 4000 meters, so don't *you* mess with me about the fucking details."

A monument arose before my eyes; can by can the earth surrendered; stone by stone a new road was built; centimeter by centimeter the truck straightened up; by steps and degrees I advanced along the staircase – 45, 46, 47, sang the chorus with each layer of stones.

"Ninety!" The circle broke out in applause, and then they squatted on their heels to watch the last scene.

"Rise up into birth with me, brother," said the truck, sighing.

I gunned it – though not enough to get the truck moving. I gunned the motor, and, looking in the rear-view mirror I saw that on the left side of the road there was water; on the right, mud. The road had disappeared, and the spectators had dispersed.

The next morning at 6:00, when we were hurrying on our way, a messenger handed us a *quipu*, a little knot, two little knots, three little knots. My fingers cramped counting those little knots.

El retablo de las maravillas, Cervantes' *Marvelous Puppet Show*, disappeared; the pure heart disappeared. A uniform appeared, its hand extended.

The area commander in chief's bribe was enormous.

I asked La Bella and Perla for help. Once more I had been stuck between a truck and a hard place. I, who for months now should have been listening to my daughter grow, talking to her, not just via the moon and the stars, but whispering secrets into her ear and telling her stories through her mother's womb; I, who should have been lending strength to La Bella entre las Bellas, who should have been broadening her beautiful smile and covering her expressive eyes with coca leaves so that she could see our future, so that she could escape from the past, so that she could discover new paths, so that our love could run freely in search of detours and delusions, leaving the main road, breaking down barriers; I, the theatrical director, I, who loved the radiance of the stage and dreaded darkness and rigid speech; I, who hate the love of cardboard and lines worn thin by false repetition; I, who long to reinvent the body's every second to stave off boredom, I, the eternal lover, the one who made promises without realizing that promises destroy reality; I, the adventurer, asked for help so as to offer the shadow of my protective shoulder.

From that moment on we haggled; in every grocery store, we haggled; over every basket of food we haggled. First we haggled with knives and forks and ended up haggling with mud-covered fingers. We haggled over wholes and halves; shamefully, like wretched political candidates, we promised without having the slightest idea of whether or not we could fulfill our promises. Unlike the candidates, though, we were ashamed, tired of offering French classes to the carefully-made-up *bellas* so that they could hike up their rates. From offering, we went on to barter: -- Oh, forgive me, my theater of lemon and orange trees! – a tube of light to light up the basket in exchange for two weeks, one week, three days, two, a meal, "please, we're hungry." We ended up haggling, for differential, but guaranteed payment, since our help arrived on horse-back along the *cordillera*, a plate for each of us, then a plate for two, and as the days went by, a bowl of soup with no meat, then with no potatoes, just whatever broth there was, and half a bowl at that, it doesn't matter, half, a quarter, a teaspoonful , "just a taste, *casera*," and there were days when we had to be satisfied with just the aroma.

For a hungry gut, there's nothing more delicious than a pleasant smell that evokes meals from other times.

"In my next play I'll include smells."

Even the memory of the international festivals reared its head.

"You must've been very hungry if you accepted cardboard," they rationalized.

"In my next play I'll create smells for the mind so that each person in the audience can be scented with his favorite dish," I added, staring at the last spoonful of that beautiful soup.

One day help arrived, proffered by a French actress who had joined in the adventure. It was a time when everything crossed the borders, when drug-toting trucks circulated with no need for the drivers to cover their smiling faces along the way, leaving little paper bags full of bills, different sorts of bags: fat ones, greasy ones, fat-bellied ones for the bosses, the guys who traveled in the first-class cars; smaller bags for the little guys, with inner folds and double bottoms to make them appear bigger; for the mid-level bosses, like my colonel, the area commander in chief; bags of holey, old socks to hide under the mattress for the lowest rungs of corruption. The French actress, no hips, no breasts, but with a pair of lips that stretched deliciously to pronounce her words, carried a little bag in her image and likeness.

"They're gonna crucify us," Jacques said, with the experience of one who has traversed three thousand kilometers and has seen hundreds of ropes going up and down along the road.

"*Mais non, mais non,*" Muriel repeated, trying to console us.

Miracles don't exist, except in the heights: a driver of yellow trucks gave the wrong bag to the colonel and disappeared along the road while looking for a port.

They kicked in the door of our squalid room. In the doorway stood the figure of the colonel in his fatigues, "Get up, you loafers!"

To be honest, he didn't exactly say "loafers." Fire spewed from his mouth and from his eyes. The coldness of that burning glare reminded me of the coldness of another military officer from my past; the memory made my knees tremble. His gaze changed only when he diverted it to the French actress' legs, a matter of seconds that was worth the eternity of a gesture, the kind for which an actor would be remembered *per secula seculorum.*

I'm referring to Sarah Bernhard's final cough as Marguerite Gautier in *The Lady of the Camellias,* Melina Mercouri's last fuck in *Never on Sunday,* Jean-Louis Barrault's heart-wrenching "Garence!" in the tightrope walkers' scene in *Children of Paradise,* the last cackle of a hen before it's killed in the Rancagua chicken coops, only to be reborn in *Those Left by the Wayside*.

Muriel shivered as she felt the colonel's stare between her legs; I, the cowardly protector, blocked her sex with my thoughts.

The colonel reassumed his role. In an authoritarian, military voice, he roared, "Get in the truck; we're going after a thief."

Even the mirror hanging on the wall in the squalid little room was taken aback.

The pursuit was fierce. The wheels of the truck whirred.

"Where to?" I asked.

"Just follow my orders; I'll show you," the colonel said.

The military is like the Party: when you're in their claws, you've got to pretend to be following orders – you always learn something new – a pretense that allows you to live till you find a detour, the right place to run off the track and be derailed.

Right, left, up, down – it reminded me of the ridiculous lieutenant who was my gym teacher in Temuco. At each checkpoint, the colonel stopped to get information; at each checkpoint he issued orders that would misdirect the yellow truck, raising walls that would force it to take the path he wanted it to follow. As for us, we took shortcuts: for once during this journey the ropes were lifted, and the infuriated columns made way for us, their empty hands awaiting an old, darned sock with a few miserable bills in it.

I stopped. Along the road you always reach a point where you have to stop and calculate the next move.

"This is as far as I go," said the colonel.

We hesitated, like the audience at a concert hall that isn't sure if the movement is over or if it's just a pause, and if they can applaud without looking ignorant.

We took a sip of *ayahuasca* water – the coca leaves weren't enough – which brought us back to past experiences. All our senses were heightened. It had the same effect as torture, albeit without the beatings or electric shocks: our minds exploded with images and allowed us to access fleeting experiences, opening roads that had been closing, detonating lights that illuminated every fiber of our being. Yellow trucks paraded before our eyes; we trembled with fear and laughter, turning that old childhood game of cops and robbers into robbers and robbers. However, the *ayahuasca* water didn't help us figure out whether or not to applaud.

With a dismissive expression, the colonel pointed out our route. A jeep emerged from the jungle and took him down a blind alley: he had been trapped.

"Bon voyage," he said before he disappeared.

Yes, culture changes man, and theater is transformative: it breaks rigid formulas, including that of the military.

We stood at attention; we three assholes stood at attention.

"At your command, Colonel!"

Shamefacedly, we continued on our way.

That's how it starts – they lead you down the garden path

with the sense of pursuing an objective, and you go after a victory, not a goal, a victory that implies the other guy's defeat. And without realizing it, you end up applauding as if you were at a rally, or you stand at attention. In both cases, the "at your commands" or the "vivas" – "long live the glorious so-and-so. . ." lead to disaster: some don't let you in, and some don't let you out.

I've got to stop drinking *ayahuasca* water, a sacred plant that teaches you to learn, opens your mind, heals your wounds, allows you to understand your thoughts and fills your mind and your eyes with the terrible moment when one person blends into another, when one military police officer is confused with another, when both sides move in to surround and destroy your thoughts.

"Let's stop for coffee," Muriel and Jacques shouted in unison.

I parked the truck in front of a bank in the town's main plaza. To our left, a row of shabby wooden tables with benches; on the tables, steaming cups of coffee and pans of fried eggs in *manteca colorada.*[28] We dashed across the plaza, our stomachs quivering with happiness.

As I was about to soak up the third egg, I noticed some shadows advancing toward the truck. A brownish haze began to darken the heretofore smiling plaza. The red egg yolk grew pale; a drop of yolk sought refuge in the hair of my beard.

I slowly arose from the table – the cat, Grotowski. First I raised one leg over the bench, then stopped the movement in mid-

---

[28] Originally an Andalusian dish, *manteca colorada* (or *colorá*) consists of lard cooked with pieces of diced pork and seasoned with paprika, which gives it its reddish *(colorada)* hue, combined with other spices.

air. I pointed the toe of my canvas espadrille toward the sky, then toward the future, and finally toward earth. A Chilean Nureyev, I extricated my other leg, this time moving it backward, raising it proudly and gracefully. With both feet on *terra firma* I continued in a flowing movement, tibia and fibula, thigh, buttocks, flattened by the journey, hips, waist, chest of a defiant actor, or an opera singer who inflates his lungs with the winds of the universe before expelling a profound "do." I walked over to the truck, me, the coward, praying that I had managed to frighten the shadow away. I know, I know, some people . . .

"I see that the gentleman is interested in theater," I said, trying to start up a conversation.

One second later I was plastered to the wall like an Incan mosquito, my hands in the air, my legs spread apart, my stomach devoured by bedbugs.

"We've captured President Gonzalo,"[29] circulated throughout the plaza.

Curious, I turned my head to witness that historical moment. The only thing I saw was that they were dragging Jacques by his arms, his short legs (one shorter than the other following his fall) kicking desperately. Muriel, that intelligent French actress, tore her skirt, daubed her face in a split second, opened a lace parasol, and, swinging her hips, joined in as part of the scenery, arm in arm with La Colombiana.[30]

The one who appeared to be in charge of the gray haze in

---

[29] Nom de guerre of Abimael Guzmán, leader of the Shining Path, Maoist guerrilla movement in Peru.
[30] La Colombiana, a prostitute in Mario Vargas Llosa's *Captain Pantoja and the Special Service*.

that plaza, a lieutenant or a captain, kicked off the interrogation. At that level, "interrogation" is just a figure of speech. The guy didn't ask a thing; all he needed was to adapt the stage to his script: on one side of the conflict, the military; on the other, the Shining Path; and in that particular scene, as invited actors, us.

We felt like the filling in *chola* sandwiches, like the melted ham and cheese in panini sandwiches, dried-out McDonald's burgers – we felt like *the people*.

Even an actor, an ordinary cast member, has a *raison d'être,* and his ephemeral, but utterly necessary, steps, help give meaning to a work. On the other hand, in a bread-and-circuses situation our presence is not required, and the gourmet doesn't even notice, even though we might have adorned ourselves with the scent of herbs, balsamic vinegar, and little lines to make us look like we were sporting grill marks. And the more we adorned ourselves, the less essential we became, something like post-election votes, useless bits of paper waiting to be recycled and used in the next elections.

I had no election. I had to be cautious so that I could escape from the script. Jacques wanted us to call the French Embassy, UNESCO, the Gérard Philipe Theater, and, if necessary, his mother, whom he thought of since I mentioned her name when I asked him to shut his trap.

"To the barracks!"

"Whatever you say, my Commandant," I replied, blushing again. I, the rebel, a fawning follower of orders; I, the proud one, bending over; I, the man of the people, enclosed in a squalid little town plaza; I, the noncompliant, complying while waiting for the

314

curve that would allow me to recover my lost dignity; I, the innocent, declared guilty; I, the guilty disguised as innocent; I, straying
from my path once more as my time ran out.

They took Jacques away in a jeep. I had to drive the truck.

We took a turn around the plaza, with the natives watching.
La Colombiana and the Frenchwoman kept up their work.

We headed down a side street; the barracks were practically outside of town. The procession was starting to march inside
me; I had throngs spinning in my stomach; my hands dripped
sweat; my foot slipped on the gas pedal; the truck jerked forward
as though overcome by an attack of hiccups. Sitting beside me, an
olive-green clad Indian, machine gun in hand, greeted his acquaintances – just about the whole town – smiled at La Colombiana, and asked the Frenchwoman for a discount.

I slammed on the brakes. The little tin soldier nearly landed
on his snout. He pointed his weapon at me.

I pointed out the electrical cables hanging down and
stretched across the width of the street, weaving a web right above
the hood of the truck. To my gesture I added these words:

"We can't get through."

"If my commandant said so, we'll get through."

Military logic is unassailable.

"Your wish is my command, Sergeant," I said, topping my
reply with a dollop of irony seasoned with secret revenge.

"Sure, he's sarcastic with weaklings. The moron doesn't
realize that they're more dangerous than the rest, since they

themselves have been humiliated, and history shows that anyone who's been humiliated turns into a humiliating hangman if he comes across someone even weaker than he is."

And he wasn't just talking about the military, I said to myself; he was predicting my future.

I hit the gas.

I knocked over three or four posts before he yelled at me to stop.

I stopped.

On both sides of the street (that it wasn't paved goes without saying), women emerged like beetles from their shacks, brandishing brooms nearly twice their size and emitting guttural cries.

We froze: the truck, since it was French, might have recalled the shouts of the women in the Kasbah during the Battle of Algiers; I was reminded of the women of Hammamet when they saw La Bella in shorts during Ramadan, or the little tin soldier, as he thought of his wife.

There's nothing more terrible for a theatrical director than to see masses of spectators approaching and rolling up the windows to avoid being pummeled by brooms.

When they began sweeping us out of history, the little tin soldier reacted, stopped pointing his weapon and at me, and aimed at the masses.

A blessed remedy: the crowd froze in place – not their shouts, just their movement. In order to clear the way, the soldier negotiated, "Come to the barracks tomorrow to see my commandant; he can order the posts to be repaired and the electrical cables to be picked up."

Smart little soldier – he knew that the area commander in chief wouldn't lift a finger; you just had to see the women's holey clothing.

He climbed back into the truck and ordered me to keep moving. Tough little soldier.

With a circular gesture, I pointed out the tangle of cables that we still had to cross and the number of brooms we needed to avoid.

He got it! He hopped out of the truck, borrowed a broom, and walked in front of the truck, picking up the cables, one cable, a third of a wheel . . . On top of the truck's metal roof you could feel the cables slipping. My mind hesitated between imagining the play of sparks confronting the angry sparks of the women and deciding what to do with the machine gun that the soldier had left in the cab in order to walk, like a priest in a religious procession, in front of the truck.

The old women crossed themselves.

At the barracks door, blocking the entrance, waited the lieutenant or captain, legs spread wide, arms akimbo, in combat uniform.

The little tin soldier came to attention and presented arms with his broom.

"To the dungeon," barked the area commander in chief.

Obediently, I got out of the truck.

"You, not that one," he said, pointing toward the soldier. "It's all his fault; he was the one who warned us about a truck with foreign plates and strange people who were getting ready to hold up the bank, about how one of them looked like Presidente Gonzalo. The Shining Path denied they had caught him and the Peruvian Army was put to shame."

"Excuse me, you can be on your way, but for verification purposes you have to report to army headquarters in Lima."

When I got back into the truck, I looked in the rear view mirror. The little tin soldier was smiling mysteriously as he walked toward the dungeon.

No doubt about it, I was back home.

In Latin America nothing is what it seems to be, and you never know whom you're talking to, if he's friend or foe, corrupt or more corrupt.

We crossed the plaza to pick up the Frenchwoman; she tried to charge us.

Ayacucho: the land ravaged by the Shining Path. We entered head-on and turned off the lights. It was better to advance in the darkness like a shadow so as not to be seen. Just in case, the Frenchwoman traveled that part of the journey with one breast in the air: Marianne! Jacques clutched a little red flag as he sang:

Montez de la mine,
descendez des collines,
camarades

A little disoriented, our Jacques: the only thing I didn't want was for *les camarades* to come down from the hills and block our way.

Seeing Muriel and Jacques' disapproving faces, I took off the little Lenin medallion I once was given for protection and hung it from the threadbare scarf with which I protected the word. Didn't want to catch a cold, after all.

We took a sip of *ayahuasca* water and started singing that Boris Vian song, *Le déserteur:*

Monsieur le Président
je viens de recevoir
mes papiers militaires
pour partir à la guerre

Je ne veux pas la faire
Je ne suis pas sur terre
pour tuer des pauvres gens

Each one of us was thinking of a different president. I thought about the times when I had taken up arms, always unloaded. I wasn't the kind to kill; I was the kind to be counted among those present.

"He didn't realize that they were already erasing him from history, and that those who tell about it only tell what's in their best interest to tell."

The truck, the only thing that had its feet on the ground,

continued on its way to the rhythm of a *huaynito*:[31]

> *You swore you'd love me,*
>
> *love me forever.*
>
> *It's been two, three days,*
>
> *and you've gone and left me.*

"It must've been thinking about a French van, and everyone knows that the vans in France aren't famous for their faithfulness."

We had to add a glass of *ayahuasca* water to the gas tank so it wouldn't get depressed.

The white city waved goodbye to us, regaling us with the aroma of its *chicharrones* and a glass of *chicha morada* to give us the strength to go on. In the distance, in Cali, Colombia, my daughter got the hiccups in her mother's belly. La Bella frowned.

We awoke by the sea. Muriel tucked her breast in, Jacques rolled up the little red flag, I stuck Lenin in the trunk of memories, and the truck fell in love with a little Peruvian minivan that coquettishly dipped its wheels in the ocean at the edge of the shore.

We decided to look to the future and forget the past. We had forgotten to show up and register in Lima. In fact, we had passed Lima right by without seeing her. I had sniffed the fragrance of jasmines that called out to me, but La Bella's perfume was more powerful. From that first day, when a million people had crossed my path and surrounded me, the perfume inside the cab

---

[31] Traditional Andean dance.

confirmed the magic of her power.

In anticipation of the next bridge, we asked Colombia for help. Perla, the Colombian actress, prepared the last little bag of dollars and started her descent to join up with us on the Ecuadorian border so that we could continue on our way.

My love remained behind, alone, in Cali, accompanied by our daughter, who asked from inside her womb:

"When will Papi be here? He promised to catch me in his hands."

La Bella told her stories; she told of the lemon trees that sheltered our love, of how we had chosen her name at the theater in Epidaurus, of how the blanket she was knitting to keep her warm on the high plateaus was coming along. She didn't mention that every night she unraveled what she'd knitted, awaiting some kind of sign from the heavens, the sea, in dreams, a sign that would reveal my presence disguised as absence, or that the moment of my arrival, as promised, was soon to come.

There were barely 1720.42 kilometers left to go before my promise could be fulfilled. It was impossible to calculate in terms of time; the roads unfurled in one dimension, our roads in another. The calendars weren't the same: on some roads they were Gregorian, on others Julian; but ours was a solar moon on the *altiplano*, Gregorian by the seashore, non-existent on my staircases.

La Bella disentangled another skein of golden wool to give legitimacy and viability to my promise.

When we arrived at Tumbes, on the northern border, poets

threw verses at our feet as a reminder of other days, knapsack days, hungry days– like the present – the days of "The Poetry Mail," the first step of my staircases.

At what point did the verse turn into a speech, they wondered; at what point did the word become flesh and the whisper become a word in motion.

And yet, from the beginning of the journey the word had been in motion; it leaped from the book to the stage, from a solitary pleasure to a collective pleasure, becoming a pagan festival where even the gods danced and rules flew out the window, terrified of being affronted.

From the beginning it was us, word and image fusing in an act of love. It was us, the affronters.

XXIV. Of his struggle against a mosquito that reigned at the midline of the world

As in the past, a ladybug led the way for us; as in the past, a wall of words rose in our wake to avoid persecutions; as in the past, on the other side of the wall, Perla, the Colombian actress, awaited us, having struggled for three days and three nights in a wretched room against a little mouse that insisted on devouring a bar of French soap, the only reward remaining from her seventeen international festivals. In the end, with her actress' heart, she gave it away: The theater has to surrender even when it comes to soap, she explained.

We had deodorized, perfumed, awakened, and washed the road since bidding farewell to the Obelisk.

Those corrupt folks who travel in first-class cars swoon over jewelry, cheap trinkets which they think afford them worth, not realizing that they simply call attention to their own tawdriness. Lower-class corrupt folks adore perfumes, soaps, and French deodorants, believing they cover up the sewer smell of the shantytowns that witnessed their birth and which cling to them even in the sad halls of local society.

We had given up our perfumes; the Frenchwoman had given up her underwear so that a guard could give it to his lover, a social climber who dumped him for his boss, a boss whom she then shed along with her seven indigenous skirts, thus becoming the most desirable "female escort" after La Colombiana.

Jacques and I had nothing left to offer but ourselves, and even the Frenchwoman cut us off, not even for free or with promises to pay on an installment plan.

On the other side of the border Perla was waiting with increasingly squalid little bag, a gnawed bar of soap, a trained mouse, and the fearsome headshrinkers.

In beautiful colonial Quito, Guayasamín, from the heights of his studio, said to me, "You should have been more careful with the amulet I gave you. It was for controlling anger and avoiding dangerous thoughts."

I didn't understand; even today, I still don't. It's just that there's so much pain, so much injustice, so much suffering around me, so many who gargle with destitution, with inequality, that it all conspires within me, causing uncontrollable rage to rise up into birth on my stage, even if I'm left without an audience or applause.

There's nothing more terrible for a poor theatrical director than to bow to cheap applause and close his eyes so as not to see those who are left lying on the ground.

"Against rage we have our hands," Guayasamín said, once more lifting the hands of his people in protest to the heavens.

"And against destitution, we have *esperpentos*," said Valle-Inclán.

Make them laugh, laugh till they cry, laugh till they realize that they're laughing at themselves, laugh till the laughter of the toothless ones explodes in their faces and runs freely along the streets, laugh till the laughter freezes in the mouths of those who gargle with the laughter of the destitute, with our own laughter, the dispossessed of the world who wander the earth.

Carried along in sedan chairs by hands of rage, protected by the barricades of "La Barricada," our presence reduced by los Tzánsicos, we crossed gold, stone, and wood, the order of the rows of native people running along the byways and the disorder of the native people in the markets; between Rumichaca and Ipiales, we crossed the midline of the world.

We stopped; we observed a moment of silence; we changed hemispheres, held hands. Behind us, sadly, lay my future; before us, sadly, my past; at the midline of the world, my present.

A mosquito buzzed back and forth between both worlds, disoriented, a lost soul that crossed over to the northern hemisphere after eating, but fed itself by biting in the southern one. I didn't walk with the speed required by the circumstances in the north: my left leg refused to leave the south, and at that moment of hesitation, in that fraction of a second that would herald victory or catastrophe, it bit me.

I felt that my blood was deserting me.

"Obviously, since you looked like a skeleton dressed in beggar's clothing."

I crossed my leg; I crossed the imaginary border; I crossed the path that led to the lost city, a city of silver in the south, of gold in the north, the road of Aguas Santas, the road to the fountain of youth. In my delirium, I asked for a bottle of *ayahuasca*. I didn't care about reconnecting with my past; I needed strength to face my present, to be there for the birth of my daughter, who summoned me from her mother's womb, "You promised!"

My ankle disappeared. I missed the Bolivian guards. I had to stop and buy an espadrille that could contain my swelling right foot. My toes looked like baked empanadas, those hot, overstuffed, juicy ones, like those that covered the Sunday table at my parents' house. My pants were squeezing my leg tight, just as my memories squeezed my head: both of them, my right foot and my brain, were about to explode. The spiral was spinning faster and faster – The maelstrom! I exclaimed, terrified – and my fingers gripped an imaginary steering wheel, issuing circular instructions to put the scene in order. The chaos was so overwhelming that no one could figure out their lines, no one could find a way out, no one could find a mirror to feed a romantic line to.

Some *ayahuasca* water and my actresses' tears allayed my fever. The mosquito begged my forgiveness: I didn't realize your resistance was so low and that in your condition even the tiniest bite would be a disaster.

"It must be a theater thing, you know?"

La Línea

And so, as you approach this place, as I ordain . . . dig a
hole with an angle at each side;
around it drink a libation to all the dead,
first with mead, then with sweet wine, and the third time
with water, and over it sprinkle white flour.

Soon the soothsayer will appear . . . to tell you which road
you must follow, how long it will take, and how you may return to your homeland, by crossing the fish-laden sea.

The Odyssey, Canto X

XXV. Where he explains how madness allowed him to avoid the violence that scourged Colombia

Over centuries, water – that diamond-tipped drill – built the bridge that connected us to the steadfastness of the miner who dug holes in the highlands to harvest the fruit of the earth, and it pierced the rock, forming a natural bridge, a symbol of my continent, a stone shell whose heart had been removed.

Huayna Capac crossed that bridge to conquer southern Colombia; we crossed it to conquer stages. From Cusco, his shadow accompanied us; from Cusco the water of his aqueducts slaked our thirst; from Cusco it repeated in our ears: if you hadn't divided us, Tahuantinsuyo would have grown to be even more powerful, for the common good; but the ambition of the first-class travelers, the little gray men, caused it to stop working for the Inca and the common good, instead sating the appetite for riches and power among those who had been there and lost their power, those who aspired to power, those who wore corruption stuck to their skin, like ivy on a wall.

¡Ay, sí, sí, sí!

At the other side of the Rumichaca Bridge, it was impossible to detect the beautiful, multicolored greens of Colombia: drugs had invaded the land.

A new empire, the empire of the *narcos*, reigned in that

part of Tahuantisuyo, unsheathing its claws on the rest of the country, from Rumichaca to the Sierra Nevada. Not even the wall of jungle, stone, four-nostrilled-serpents, and Darién mosquitoes could contain it.

What nobody had managed to achieve – neither Huayna Capac from the south nor Bolívar from the north – the *narcos* achieved: emperors who trampled souls, bodies, wallets, beliefs, and principles. One after another, those who unlawfully held power or some aspect of power or who longed for power, that of the ballot box, of weapons, of money, surrendered before the white plague, the century's new evil in that oasis of violence.

I started to feel the first contractions. I had to get moving, yet once again I found myself sitting on a hard wooden bench in the city of Pasto, waiting impatiently – it was a Friday, and on Saturdays and Sundays the customs office closed its hands. We had no bags left; besides, prices in Colombia had gone up for that form of the drug. The only thing of any value, I thought frankly, was an official invitation to participate in the Manizales International Theater Festival.

A military officer, the area commander in chief, walked by our bench, kept going, stopped, came back, and pointed a finger at me.

He reminded me of Medina, my hangman from Rancagua. I started to shake.

I stood up. Like a robot, I spread my legs – not too wide, just enough to keep my balance and at the same time to block the trajectory of his boots toward my testicles. I crossed my hands behind my back so they could cuff me; I closed my eyes so as to keep the layout of the room in my mind and calculate where the blows would come from, as I waited for the blindfold and the first question.

"What are you doing around here?" asked a voice with a trace of genuine interest and a pronounced *Paisa* accent[32].

"I'm a poor theater director," I said pitifully, and I started talking about international theater festivals. I managed to get as far as Avignon, describing that walled city, its stone bridges, the groups attending from all around the world, a place that had been transformed from a laid-back city into a dynamic one where a new theater project sprang up on every corner . . .

"Just a second, maestro," he cut me off.

Maestro, not *doctor*: a good sign for those of us who have lived in Colombia. He ordered a couple of *tinticos*, Colombian coffee, and sat down next to me to listen to the rest of the story.

" . . . and that's how I came to Pasto, for the Manizales Festival and to be there, as I promised, for the birth of my daughter, who, along with La Bella entre las Bellas, awaits me in the shade of a mango tree on the patio of the Teatro Experimental de Cali."

"At Maestro Buenventura's?"

"Yes, at Enrique's."

He stood and raised his voice. Even the stone bridge on

---

[32] A coffee-growing region in the northwest of Colombia.

the border trembled, and not a single emotion had crossed in in such a long time.

"In Colombia no one stops a theater group that's been invited to the Manizales Festival. Bring some more *tinticos* and the signed, stamped papers so you can be on your way."

He was familiar with the festival; he knew Enrique and his group. He had seen them pass by, their caravan going back and forth, into the wind, for the glory of Colombia. He had been part of the audience! And when you're part of the audience, you're a participant, you're the word, you're the dialogue, you're the actor, sitting there and spouting your lines; you're a member of the family with the soul of an actor.

I felt another contraction; I had to hurry. They brought the signed papers five minutes before the customs office closed its doors.

As I was about to climb into the cab, the area commander in chief whispered to me, "You were the Third God, weren't you? Tell the other gods that you found a good soul in Pasto."

Even Wang, the water carrier, was surprised.

385 kilometers separate a promise from empty words tossed on the wind. The bells of Popayán, comradely survivors of violence against the earth, the only kind of violence that leaves survivors in Colombia, pealed to lend us strength as we went by. In Cali, La Bella left the shade of the mango tree to perfume her body in an orchid bath and soften her skin with coconut oil. She put on a white tunic that we had bought in Greece and sat down to

sew the final stitches on the blanket that would protect our daughter.

In her womb our daughter turned over – "I'm ready now" – she said, relieved. Three days remained until her birth.

Proudly the truck stopped at the Teatro Experimental de Cali. Perla, Muriel, and Jacques got out from the right side, while from the left, I, the expert driver of heavy trucks, I, the promise-keeper, the pagan who wandered along roads with the theater on his back just to deposit it, along with my weary body, on the stage in the temple of my halls.

The jealous sky opened up as La Bella passed by, just like the jealous mob that opened up for her that first time in France, allowing my gaze to get lost in hers.

"I want to hear your voice to make sure they didn't change you along the way," said my daughter from the womb. "Remember, in Latin America not everything is what it appears to be."

I drew up close to La Bella's womb in order to talk to my daughter without go-betweens. Sorry, moon, it's just that I had never been so close to her. My daughter wrinkled her little nose and flipped over. Her mother wrinkled *her* little nose, but didn't flip over.

What a challenge for a theatrical director to stage a play within a play!

"She's a wild one – you should have felt her kick my belly when she didn't like *Caligula*. I had to leave the auditorium."

I would've left, too: I endure evil and destruction, but I don't stage it, lest someone be tempted to unchain the horror and try to impose blind obedience to his whims through random acts of murder.

A monster lay in ambush along the roads of Colombia; it darkened Colombian skies, infected Colombian rivers and seas. A new tyrant, building monuments to his madness in absurd defiance of sanity. Reviled, feared, beloved, a rustic Caligula enforced his law by means of new praetorian guards: hit men.

So great was the madness that at his death they erected monuments to glorify him, adding madness to madness.

"Sanity, adding sanity to madness. They were defying us to find out what was hiding behind the monuments."

A shiver ran down my unborn daughter's spine.

May the theater gods protect us!

"Have you guys thought about where that little bundle is going to be born?" asked Enrique after giving me a hug.

Only at that moment did I become aware of my madness and the madness in which I had gotten my loved ones involved. I thought of the lemon trees; the Greek theater appeared before my eyes; Hammamet offered me its white sands, its sea, and its swimming pool, surrounded by jasmine. Paris spread her legs over the Champs Elysées to make way for an ambulance en route to Pitié-Salpêtrière Hospital.

Clean her with coca leaves – no, give her *ayahuasca* water; that will make her labor easier. I cried tears of guilt, of guilt over having arrived too late and without even one measly bag of coca leaves.

The gods took pity on me: so great was my sadness, so great my guilt, so little my remorse, that three days later, when the contractions had become uncontrollable, a little leaf fell from the mango tree on the patio of the Teatro Experimental de Cali, a leaf with the name of the best clinic in the city. Its owner was Enrique's brother.

In Colombia madmen, poets, and theater people will always find a helping hand to allow them to carry on with their task: to fight over occupying center stage in order to represent life.

I entered the birthing room. "Wait for me," said La Bella – this time I go first."

"Prima donna," I muttered to myself.

It wasn't the right time to explain to her that every theatrical director is the first to enter the hall: he needs to be alone to talk to her, to hear her story, to win her love and ask forgiveness for possessing her, explain to her that he's not jealous of those who possessed her in the past, that every *mise-en-scène* is a new act of love that begins in the past but which possesses her for the first time.

La Bella spread her legs, resting her feet against the lintel of the door to the birthing room. The stretcher jammed; our daughter practically shot out: the blinding, white light was the cause of the jam.

The Autopsy, it reminds me of *The Autopsy*, La Bella said, and despite her starring role, she didn't want to go into the birthing room.

"It's the light in Greece when we frolicked in the lavender fields; it's the light of the lemon trees, of your eyes, powerful reflectors that lit my path; it's . . . " I said, to calm her.

"Time to close your legs: the doctor's at the movies watching *Amadeus* and it's still intermission," said the nurse, with the authority of a cardboard cut-out.

She crossed her legs and we waited, holding hands. It wasn't customary in those days, but they let me into the room. It wasn't customary, but they let me cut the umbilical cord. It wasn't customary, but it would become customary after the news of her birth leaped from the nosebleed section to the balcony, from the balcony to the orchestra, till the lights bowed their heads before her beauty and her honey-colored skin, and nestled her among its rays.

As promised, I caught her in my hands. Never before had I held anything so delicate between my hands; never before had such beauty emerged from the depths of flesh. Everything about her was imperfection, and just as with her mother, the sum of her imperfections resulted in such great perfection that it hurt to look at her.

I purified her body with olive oil, wrapped her feet in two bay leaves, like buskins, cut the umbilical cord with the sacrificial knife, and said to her, "You are free; go run along the stages of life."

Never since have I lived through such a beautiful May

night.

As I had left the baby clothes behind in the truck, the nurse wrapped her head in gauze and fashioned a tunic from a white sheet.

Forming a chalice with my hands, I lifted her body and faced it toward the south, then the north, then the east, and finally the west, so that she would learn that all roads were open to her, all but the road leading back to our past.

She raised her little head and opened her eyes. Two brilliant lights illuminated the month of May. She turned her head and leaned back, looking in a different direction; she had entered the world of the theater without a cry, without music to announce her arrival.

Her beauty arrived crowned by a smile.

She was born during a pause in the time of madness.

I, the one who takes care of all the details, had forgotten the coca leaves.

And that made her vulnerable.

It was four AM. The moon was beginning to fade; the sun poked its head out timidly so that its rays might caress her skin, and just as with her mother, it left seven marks, the road to happiness.

The taxi headed for Calle Séptima; expanses of sugar cane greeted the newborn. The taxi driver, a Valluno[33] through and

---

[33] Name given to someone from the Department of Valle del Cauca, Colombia.

through, asked:

"Is it a boy?"

"No, a girl."

"My sympathies. The next one'll be a boy. You don't always get what you want."

And yet we had gotten what we wanted.

In the heart of heaven's branch office, at the door of his hall, waited Enrique – "Let me see that little bundle," he demanded. He took her in his arms. Beneath the mango tree he made her listen to one of his poems. Then he entered the hall and walked her up and down the stage. "Welcome to the family," he told her, painting a spiral on her belly with iodine.

Meanwhile at the port, near Buenaventura, at that very moment the car that would transport the actors along the roads of Colombia, along the roads of Venezuela, along the lost roads that would bring me back to my country, was arriving.

In France I had bought a golden car, not for royalty, since I come from the minstrel caste; not out of arrogance, since I shed that when I put on theater clothes; not to give pleasure to the nobility, since I prefer the audience in the nosebleed section – I bought a gold one because even in the land of the fleur de lis it was considered cheesy and therefore was cast aside and given away at a price that even a penniless wretch could afford.

But that was in France. In Colombia it was the envy of the drug traffickers, of the ministers, of those who frequent the first-class cars, and it was a source of amazement for those lost souls cultivating forbidden fruit in the fields, who watched countless times as a bit of sun from the lost city of Guatavita flashed by.

The truck was jealous and refused to leave till we painted a golden fleur de lis on its rear end.

Reality is terrible; reality strikes blows; reality forces you to make decisions you're trying to avoid, to assume terrible responsibilities. I assembled the pyramid: home and theater set, fake cardboard that depicted reality on the outside, cardboard innards, a pale reflection of a new reality, on the inside. The lights emerged from their boxes to hang from the clouds of Cali; the costumes stretched and yawned after such a long journey. The moment I long feared had arrived – I, who had been thrown out of my time and my calendar: I had to replace La Bella entre las Bellas, the mother of my daughter.

Mother and daughter turned their backs to me. My daughter wouldn't allow me to change her diaper. I tried to explain to her that there was no other way, but lacking words and gestures, I headed for the door, walked out, and went away as a sad father, but a happy director, to the rehearsal room.

A new actress was waiting for me, a rough stone, an eternal frost, a dry thistle in a flower bed, a flower withered at the seed, with eyes . . . at least she has two of 'em, I said, enthusiastically. Better than nothing.

There's nothing more exciting for a theatrical director than to work with nothing. There's nothing more beautiful than to transform a rough stone into a diamond, or at least into charcoal. There's nothing lovelier than to make the word sprout in dry earth, to set a disabled imagination into motion so it can run along the stage. There's nothing more important in a director's life than to be able to start at zero and offer infinity.

In three weeks the Teatro Experimental de Cali would hand over its stage to me. There's nothing more beautiful in the theater than for a group to hand over its heart to someone else, and a friend's heart is not to be betrayed.

I started rehearsing day and night.

Alone at first, I had to teach her to love so that later she could love her audience; to hold back so that later she could surrender, body and soul; to hide one breast, so that, by later revealing the other one, the audience would explode with desire; to walk like cotton and not like stone; to leave the bad actor's rail for the infinite tangle of paths; to walk a diagonal line when she had only known how to follow a harsh, straight one; I taught her to sing so that when the sound was taken away, she would give her speech a musical lilt; I taught her to look at the other actor so as to kiss him long distance with her lashes – I taught her so many things. I, the sorcerer's apprentice.

In my lifetime I had turned an alcoholic beggar into a great gentleman and a great gentleman into a hell-raising beggar, La Bella into something revolting and a revolting thing into beauty;

hatred into love and love into a sea of jealousy; the only ones I was incapable of transforming were myself and my torturers.

Two weeks later the doors of the theater were flung wide and in walked La Bella carrying a straw basket. In it was my daughter. I recalled the women who sold those delicious *manjar* or *alcayota* squash pastries at the train station in Curicó. Both of them had parked themselves in front of the stage and declared, one with words and the other with a howl, "We're the assistant directors."

There's nothing more terrible for a theatrical director than to have two rearing, snorting divas at the same time – one can be controlled, but two? I wouldn't wish it on my worst enemy.

La Bella nursed my daughter and the stage with her breasts, transmitting love, patience, sweetness, and jealousy; she discovered the secrets of her footsteps so that others could follow in them; she surrendered just as she had done in Hammamet.

The littlest one imposed limits on the scene; certain things should stay within the family.

Columbus was reborn in Cali, but the city's heat, the perfume of hot lands, made him sway in his bullfighter's suit more than a palm tree, and more than conquering he wanted to be conquered. The prostitutes were a pale imitation compared to the local hookers; they had to make a superhuman effort to compete with their odors, their lewdness, their offerings. Using the basest cardboard trick in the book, I pulled the Frenchwoman out of my sleeve and stood her beside La Colombiana.

The play picked up momentum: even the sail went off to one side while Columbus drowned on the high seas. I had to rein in the technicians; three times they left the neighborhood without electricity. They wanted to connect even the fireflies. The ghosts came to life, and one day at midnight, when the witches come out to chat with the magicians, three knocks resounded over the stage. An actor approached from the shadows. We were in Latin America.

"No, you were treading the boards of the theater; it's not the same thing."

Two months had gone by since the birth, two months and a week since my arrival, hours since we finished the run: we were ready to move on.

"Be careful, all of you," said Enrique. "You're going to have to cross La Línea, and that ordeal frightens even the bravest of the brave, not just during the ascent or during the descent, but even at the checkpoints at night, when the bandits come out of their caves to hold up travelers and offer fresh blood to the mountain spirits. It's 3250 meters high, and the theater gods don't reach that far."

"3250 meters, *ça c'est la rigolade*, a piece of cake," said the truck, showing its wounds.

"Just be careful." La Línea offers itself like a female who's impossible to reject; it traps you in its curves and tosses you down a cliff once it's been satisfied."

The truck grew sad and lowered its headlights, thinking of the flirty little Peruvian minivan.

"Be careful. La Línea divides the real from the imaginary, the past from the future, goodness from evil. La Línea is where the double spiral begins – that of life and that of death – and you can't tell which is which."

"The maelstrom, but one that spreads out in mirages that make you take a curve without knowing if it's the right one or the wrong one."

I didn't understand; I've never understood which is the right one and which the wrong one, or who decides that it's one or the other, where each one leads to. I've never been able to imagine what might have happened if I'd taken the one that wasn't or was without knowing that it was, and trembling with uncertainty, I, the driver, chose the route: Santa Fe de Bogotá.

I couldn't get lost there: I was coming from France, from logic, from numbers, and in Bogotá, unlike the rest of the world, everything was logical:

To the south, the poor,
and I was pure south;
to the north, the powerful,
and I was powerless;
in the center I would add nightmares
or subtract dreams,
I would advance or disappear.
In Santa Fe everything was Cartesian:
the higher the number of the street

the greater the wealth,

the lower the number of the street,

the greater the poverty.

And I, I was zero;

I was the one without a number,

Because I, the possessor,

never lined up with the beggars.

We will enter from the south, the place for those who have no number, the dispossessed of the earth; we will press on to Quevedo's fountain to slake our thirst, I promised, but the fountain had dried up. In Santa Fe de Bogotá – and this I hadn't known – cradle and grave, light and darkness, coexisted, both under the same roof; I create and destroy in order to be able to create, as though creation implied destruction. Something had changed in my Colombia; a white mantle had covered her up to harden her soul.

There's nothing more beautiful for an actor than to die in order to be reborn, to reach the last step on his staircases in order to offer himself voluntarily in sacrifice.

There's nothing more terrible for an actor than to be assassinated on his way to the sacrificial altar, to be surrounded and carried off into blind obedience.

There's nothing more beautiful for an actor than to have his eyes ripped out in order to see, behind the cardboard scenery, the paths that will lead him from his imprisonment and break down the fence that surrounds him.

"Even the brave tremble when they have to cross La Línea," Enrique repeated. And I, I was a coward.

I left Cali, treasuring in my memory the dreams of the beggars, the prostitutes, the barefoot children who sold themselves on street corners, the crazy priest who baptized my daughter, the theater tree, the one that would survive the bombardment of evil that afflicted my Colombia. I left, bearing on my back the pain of my memory, which had been destroyed by the arrival of a new era, that of the merchants who crawled out of the shadows to take over the marketplaces.

I left, directing my steps toward my dreams, my destiny, and my poor staircases.

When we reached the city of Cartago, there was a familiar figure, standing on top of a rock: Germán, an actor who, when we had to unload equipment, would show up out of nowhere and unload, and when he had to load equipment, would emerge from the shadows and load it. When someone forgot his lines, he emerged from the script and remind him. The costumes were all ironed, apparently without anyone's having done the job; the holes in the beggars' clothing were mended: we tore them before every performance and they'd show up again, repaired. Whenever there was a blackout, a flashlight would beam on, offering the precise angle to the designated actor. Whenever we took a rehearsal break, at the very top of the pyramid a shadow would appear; a Colombian gargoyle hung there, listening. When we arrived in Cartago a familiar figure was standing at the prow of a little paper boat floating on top of a rock so that we couldn't help seeing him: Germán, dressed as a Colombian Columbus, was waiting for us.

I hit the brakes.

Not a pin would fit in the car; not a pin would fit in the truck; but an actor is an actor, not a pin, unless someone asks him to be one.

He hopped into the truck with his belongings: a change of clothing, a threadbare sweater, and a flute. "I'm learning, in case I have to play music," he said.

From Cartago, a safe port, we entered directly into the magic of Colombia. The colors assaulted our eyes, even when it was men who were assaulting us. Our hands, held high, were caressed by clouds; inspections became our daily autopsies; the little bags became perfumes, deodorants, washing machines. We even offered our memories, minidramas that told stories; we, the tellers of hope.

"I've come from Paris to keep a promise . . ."

Heaven touched the earth, and above the front door of a farm, on a concrete arch that marked the beginning of limitlessness, a small plane. It caressed the truck with one of its wings; they regarded one another; challenged one another. Both had "crowned"; that is, they had succeeded in delivering their shipments, one, through the clouds, the other, at the highest peak of the cordillera. There was one resemblance between them: both had hidden themselves, one from the guards, the other from the

346

guards. There were many differences between them: one destroyed dreams by dreaming; the other offered a world where there was room for dreams; one contained hippos and giraffes; the other freed mankind from the ghosts of history; one was a prisoner, its feet chained to concrete; the other moved about freely in search of a stage where it could rest and then surrender again.

Nearby, in El Cañón de las Hermosas, beauty lost its beauty and the commandants were dressed like drug traffickers. Nearby, beauty grew in La Bella's arms.

There was one resemblance between us: we both hid ourselves to survive. There was one difference between us: one was death, the other, life.

We had almost reached Calarcá; to one side lay Cajamarca. Between them, La Línea, "Be careful, not everything is what it appears to be, and not everything that appears to be, is. You have to learn not to look in order to see."

We needed to gather strength again. You can't cross La Línea on an empty stomach. We ordered a bowl of soup, thick, steaming, not a ripple on its surface, smooth as one of those highways we haven't seen for so long, but as rich in surprises as a dirt road. I plunged my dirty, bent spoon into the soup, and who cares if the spoon is made of gold or silver or tin when you're hungry and about to face La Línea! From the depths of the bowl came a cockscomb, which must have felt rejected, since it fell off the spoon, submerging itself in the soup once more. Slowly, as if asking forgiveness, I dipped the spoon in a second time and . . . this time it wasn't a cockscomb, but a chicken foot that appeared, twisted, its toes shrunken, tendons in the air. To distract myself and stop thinking about La Línea, I pulled out the tendons: I pulled on one and a little toe moved. Even with chicken toes you could reproduce a melody on the edge of a tin bowl.

This time I didn't give it a chance to dive back in. I started sucking on the little chicken toes. When you're hungry, who cares where the rest of the animal went! For an actor the cockscomb and feet are more succulent than *coq au vin.*

We returned to the caravan. As we lifted the basket holding our daughter into the car, I realized she was happily sucking on a chicken foot. This little bundle is going to be a fighter, I thought.

We began our ascent to the inferno. The lights of Calarcá faded in the distance; once again we were on our way to touch the firmament. Thousands of curves teased us with the wrong road; one of them led us to eternal darkness, from which a peasant, wrapped in his *ruana*, emerged, shotgun in hand, aiming at us.

We stopped.

"Don't go on; it's not safe."

Seeking protection, we huddled at the edge of the road. It was cold at La Línea, the kind of cold that penetrates deep into your body and freezes your mind, the kind of cold that makes you shiver, but not from fear. La Bella wrapped our daughter in the blanket she had knitted during my absence.

We got in the chicken line; even the bravest were there. For a few miserable coins armed peasants protected our lives.

I fell asleep; ever since France I hadn't felt safe sleeping.

When we awoke, the darkness had dissipated; the peasant guards had disappeared, my daughter's chicken foot had vanished; the only trace I could find of it was a tiny scratch on her upper lip. "It must have been a fighting cock, and he lost," I said proudly, lifting the winner in my arms.

We formed a circle; I opened the book and read Chapter Seven, Verse 33: When confronting one of these apparently superhuman slopes, you should climb slowly, never stopping. When descending one of these slopes crowned with superhuman force, you should go down at the same speed with which you went up (slower is acceptable); anything faster than that will send you flying and no one will be able to stop you.

"Not exactly no one; you'll run right into the last wall in your wanderings on the staircases."

Don't brake, and if you have to brake, rest your foot on the pedal gently, like a hand on a breast, delicately, and not for too long: if it overheats, it'll get out of control.

I flipped the Renault manual shut and we continued on our way, downhill. Cajamarca was at 1800 meters; a glass of *masato*[34] and a slice of roast pork teetered precariously on the edge -- of the *cordillera* and of violence.

I'd rather face death on the *cordillera* than from the brutality

___
[34] A popular, fermented Andean beverage. It can be prepared with rice, yucca, or other ingredients.

of human beings.

Not everything in Colombia is what it appears to be: the peasants were peasants, the weapons, weapons; the fear was real; the protection wasn't protection. I had fallen into a *pesca milagrosa,* a miraculous fishing net. They were kidnapping and demanding money.

"You saved your hide because the oldest peasant recognized you. You had forgotten him, though; he was the one sitting on the sacks of coffee, in the hot lands, when you made that little turn, years ago. Maybe you didn't recognize him on account of the cold. That's what saved you, that and the fact that he saw the baby. He gave the order to leave you guys alone and to guard you while you slept. You never found out, and for your information, miracles don't exist. In Colombia sometimes everything is what it appears to be."

The engines hummed and we pressed on. As we passed through the hot lands, before ascending to Santa Fe de Bogotá, perched on some sacks of coffee in a grocery store, a memory was smiling.

We entered like the dispossessed, smiling; we arrived like wretches, full of hope; we entered like the *comuneros*,[35] our ears closed to the sirens' song; we entered like the dregs of history, in-

---

[35] The *comunero* revolt of 1781 was a uprising against taxes imposed in the department of Santander, Colombia. It was initiated by a group known as El Común. Four thousand *comuneros* marched on Bogotá, eight years before the Paris Commune.

visible; we entered like the bull enters the arena, ready to put up a fight he knows he will lose; we entered like the actor onto the stage, knowing that we would disappear at the end of the show. We entered along Carrera Séptima, got as far as Calle Doce, continued on to Segunda, and stopped in front of La Candelaria. We were in the *barrio*, the fortress of culture, the fountain of thought. We were at the mercy of the Second Prostitute from *The Good Person of Szechuan.*

To take on a whore you need a bigger whore: I matched my prostitutes to hers. It was a great clash: on the sand, drama; in the bleachers, desire; for every violent breast I put up another breast, distilling love; against the patchouli, the perfume of love; against the price of love in gold, the price of a humble tray of food; against the Second Prostitute's monastic cloth, the festive colors of transparent fabrics from around the world to undress my prostitutes; against the shrill soprano, I offered silence: I, the fighter, respect the music they denied me.

Even my daughter, flirting, poked out her chubby little leg from between the blankets to take part in the battle.

When it was over, I threw my arm over Santiago's shoulder and together we gathered up the tired, scattered remains of the actors and actresses.

"How about a nice *tintico*?"

"Of course."

We entered the theater, though through different doors: we headed for the "Seki Sano" room, named in honor of the Japanese maestro who enriched his theatrical schema with techniques borrowed from Meyerhold, the disciple of Stanislavski, the actor from the Moscow Art Theater, the actor who had doubts, the actor who escaped from the uniformity and rigidity of interpretation to create his group and present a different model, the actor-director who tried to broaden the limitations of the *mise-en-scène*, drinking from the sap of the Commedia dell'Arte. Meyerhold, who in 1918, one year after the triumph of the Russian Revolution, joined the Bolshevik Party, believing in, dreaming of, a better world, attempting to break through the boundaries of intolerance, trying to forge new paths for the theater in that new society. Meyerhold, who later opposed the limit-setters, the creator who refused to accept the limitations of socialist realism and the little gray men, commissioners charged with enforcing their blind application.

Meyerhold, the man of the theater, opposed them. Stalin declared his theater "counter-revolutionary" and he was expelled from the Party and tortured. He signed a confession. They didn't sit him on top of the box with broken glass; they shot him instead. Those were different times.

"I prefer the box with broken glass. A person can get used to that, but not to being shot."

"What democracy and freedom to create are you talking about?" echoed in my memory.

Seki Sano, maestro and disciple, who had been invited to work in Colombia during the time of Rojas Pinilla, and who formed actors, gave, and gave of himself until he was thrown out of the country.

Silently I entered the hall, joining the convergence of stories suspended in the air, hidden by the walls, roots struggling to break through walls.

What makes the difference between the past and the present, between one story and another? I wondered as I searched for new paths, new bridges, new spaces, a new form of crossing halls and stages.

I need a curve to throw me off track, I, the derailed, and to bring me back to the dangers of creation.

Napoleon helped us. Half man, half fish, he moved between La Candelaria and the Colombian Theater Corporation. Like a dolphin, he had managed to survive by navigating the turbulent waters of the Colombian theater. He wasn't an actor; maybe that was why. He wasn't a director; maybe that was why. He wasn't anybody; maybe *that* was why. He didn't know a thing and yet he knew everyone's secrets. He wasn't good with words, and yet everyone asked him for advice. Without being a Don Juan, he soothed the conflicts among the *bellas*. Without losing his dignity, he collected the drunken bodies that lay scattered on the floor in the aftermath of parties.

Napito was an indispensable shadow. Life had taught him to take care of himself: boiling oil had sealed his legs together; only love could separate them, turning him into a murmur that glided along the walls. Maybe that was why he had managed to survive and live from the theater.

He never raised his voice, and he was the only one allowed his own speech when everything was collective, everything but the speech that I, the creator of the word, found slipping out in an improvisation.

For three words they killed one another. They gave themselves names: I, the illiterate playwright; I, the King Midas of scrap iron. Any word I touch turns into a speech and belongs to me, and if anyone has the gall to pronounce my words, mine, the Creator of Nothing, he'll have to answer for it.

No one could say anyone else's lines even if he disappeared into a world of never-before-pronounced phrases, of unfinished gestures, even if the Maker of Phrases' memory had faded with time – no one except Napito, who was forgiven everything because he was nobody.

Napito, the master puppeteer, hid the threads of his love for Vitito, a teenage kid, picked up from the street by a painter in Cali, who, hidden among the costumes, was transported by Napito, his white knight, a dolphin who raised him to the heights in order to deposit his love in the shadow of the Virgin of Montserrat.

They survived on Calle Primera, on the other side of the market square, protected from smells, tradeswomen, roots, platters heaped with cockscombs and chicken feet. Their love survived, nurtured by plants that heal wounds, burns from boiling oil, marks left by broken bottles tearing through skin, the wounds in Napito's heart, because Vitito was unfaithful.

Napito gave us shelter; as one of life's castaways, he felt a kinship with the castaways of the theater. When we arrived at his apartment, other nobodies started coming out of the rooms, other shadows like him, all of them messengers taking refuge at different institutes where the inquisition wouldn't come looking for them: the Colombian GDR, the Colombian Soviet, the Colombian People's Friendship Group . . . they had hidden their fragile bodies and their dreams in the maw of Colombian Stalinism, and smiling wickedly, they hid their secrets behind the door. It was their only defense.

The tour had been ruined; our late arrival was fatal; the little bags were left behind along the route; we had to book some new shows; the Manizales Festival was still some time away; the French contingent's time was coming to an end: they had to go home and take up their jobs again. We organized a block of performances at the "Seki Sano" to collect enough money to repatriate them; however something just wasn't working: the lights were delayed and delayed till they simply didn't arrive.

Something was darkening the sky over Santa Fe de Bogotá. Perla, together with Napito, managed to get a gig, but that same night it disappeared. The phones stopped working; they began to demand approval by a female commissar.

In Colombia there's a hierarchy; "This isn't Europe," they told us.

Certainly the regional Teatinos exerted their power and determined what was revolutionary and what wasn't, what followed the rules and what dangerously defied them. It was essential to maintain the established order and issue public chastisement, and yet we were talking about the theater.

The French contingent demanded Colombian rules; they didn't understand them, but they demanded them. Everything is collective; everything belongs to everyone. They asked for one third of the projectors and the sound equipment. They left us the costumes. The vultures started circling over the Seki Sano. At night they came in to negotiate and separate their share from the rest; in the daytime they offered to help mediate the conflict on our behalf. They ended up with everything and made a deal with the French contingent, including in it a French woman who was passing by the door. We asked for help; without their knowing it, we asked for help. Only Napito knew about it. We called La Bella's homeland and obtained a loan – not a big deal, but in Colombia any money at all was a big deal.

We entered the hall. The bureaucrat was presiding; she launched a flowery speech that had very little to do with theater. She spoke of solidarity, of the Chilean people's cause: lovely, it sounded lovely. She spoke of the dispossessed: it sounded very lovely. She spoke of an act of solidarity; they would take half of everything. They had already moved it from the truck into the hall and they agreed to return the French contingent.

Napito had told me, "You've got to get everything in writing" – the Shadow knew them well, and he knew how they acted in the light of day. He handed me a legal paper for them to sign, three copies, all stamped; then he handed me the little bag with bank-issued promissory notes. "Never in cash," he told me; "you've got to make them sign."

Eyes wide open, the commissar – the Second Prostitute – took the bank checks, verified the amount, handed them to the French contingent. Vacation time was over.

As I was about to leave, I turned around and asked them to reload the technical material and books that had been distributed back into the truck. Just so you understand, they're nothing if you don't know how to use them. It's not a matter of lighting something; it's a matter of knowing what's to be illuminated, what's supposed to disappear. It's a matter of using all languages in the service of a cause (their language was starting to stick to me), of giving life to the stage, drawing life from the walls that surround it, giving Oedipus back his eyesight, the beggar his smile, the character, his life, even if it requires the actor's death.

We were left without technicians. In any event they had come for three months; they couldn't get more time off from their jobs in France. Fantasies grew in their minds; they listened to serpent and scorpion songs; they allowed themselves to be covered by the mantle of white powder spreading throughout Colombia, powder and easy money to make more money with.

Nevertheless they fulfilled their mission. Without good old Jacques I don't think I would have crossed the *cordillera*. The other French technician, Laziz Hamani, registered my daughter's birth. He had asked to come and take photos, and he did.

I've never seen the photos; I hope he figured out that in Colombia not everything is what it appears to be. And yesterday's friend is today's enemy, without ceasing to be a friend, since my only enemy is a lack of imagination.

But even though we had been left without technicians, we hadn't been left without technique: Napito had learned; from the shadows he had followed connection after connection. Germán had learned to load and unload, which is a technique; Jean-Jacques had taught it to me at the Sorbonne. Time has to be on the side of the word, which the actor, not a projector, must illuminate. Music is born of movement and not from a loudspeaker. Cardboard reveals, not hides, reality.

We weren't alone; loneliness filtered out of their rooms and began to keep us company; other actors joined in. Hunger and thirst are collective; telephones rang in the void and were left off the hook there.

Muriel, the Frenchwoman, accompanied us to Manizales. She was a courtesan, a woman of the theater. Her husband came along, but that wasn't our business. He came to rescue her from other arms; she was the one who had to decide if she wanted to be rescued or if she would run into other arms, real ones or those of the characters, if she would remain at the altar of the theater or would wallow around in life so as to bring fragrance and sustenance to that altar, to steer the speeding locomotive toward a new life.

There's nothing more difficult for a theatrical director than to battle the human beast, to unleash passion and feed it without killing the character, to possess it, only to treacherously hand it over to the arms of the audience, forsaking what is most precious to a human being: the desire to possess, good, evil, love, hatred, power.

There's nothing more difficult for a director than to use his power and at the same time surrender it.

Because in the theater only death is collective; the rest is pleasure and sacrifice. You have to climb up one step without realizing that you're descending into the depths of hell. You have to turn pain into a balm, to make what is turn into what is not, and make what is not have the right to exist.

We were on our way to the Manizales International Festival, and once again we were crossing La Línea, but this time in order to reach another line, the main street of Manizales, a spinal column that balances dangerously, marking the highest point of the city and of the theater, and beside it, two chasms that blend into the greenery of Caldas.

Surrounded by coffee plantations, the city was boiling: at every corner a theater group, defying the abyss; in the hall, on the street, on the upslope of the mountain, on the downslope of the mountain, at the "Teatro Fundadores," and in the anarchist shoemaker's workshop in front of the theater. The Arbeláez brothers offered a rest stop for witnesses of the violence that lashed Colombia.

And if the violence appeared onstage, it was so that we might learn to recognize it; you don't face death until you want to.

If you're lucky.

We came from Chile, from Argentina, from Europe, from the other side of the world, from the most prestigious schools, from the gilded halls, from the market squares, from the street, from the shantytowns, with family names or as bastards; the theater came from its cradle and from its grave to be reborn amid the variegated greens of Caldas, where everyone shook hands, for their sake and for ours.

We were assigned the university theater; we decorated the hall for ourselves and for other groups that would be presenting there. The huge, naked amphitheater challenged us. We accepted the challenge: we possessed it; we pushed back the shadows to make way for the set; we emerged from darkness into light; the word put on its party clothes.

We leaped over barriers, establishing new bridges that would allow word and movement to pass through. We swept the stage so we could dirty it in our own way. *Mano a mano,* we restored the word to the ignorant, transformed the amphitheater into a theater, a temple of wisdom, and a brothel of passion.

We built scaffolding on the stage, *svobodas* in order to create walls that could be dismantled. We built scaffolding above the audience, in order to expose the source of a language.

Columbus crossed the stage, half bullfighter, half novice fighting bull. In one corner, Germán practiced his machismo by humming the tango "Rinconcito arrabalero." In the middle of the hall, Napito took note of movements, light, and sound. The pyramid occupied center stage. Off to the side, La Bella entre las Bellas, taking possession and allowing me to direct the symphony of colors from the auditorium.

There's nothing more beautiful for a theatrical director than for a body to sweep across the stage from left to right, from top to bottom, on the diagonal, in a circle – anything but that horrible straight line – to come to life and defiantly be possessed. For each movement I requested a certain angle of light, the tilt required to enlarge, to diminish, to suggest three dimensions, to strip it down, allowing the audience to rebuild it.

There's nothing more beautiful onstage than the complicity that allows you to explore limits; there's nothing more beautiful than watching La Bella act, with my daughter resting in a projector box, emptied of metal and filled with life, issuing joyful whimpers as she discovered the power of the stage.

I had set one condition: someone to look after my daughter while we worked; we needed to dedicate ourselves fully to the task.

I needed to hear everything, even the tiniest sigh, impregnate myself with the aromas, from the coffee plantations surrounding Manizales, from the actors, arriving with their spices from the four corners of the earth; I, the olfactory orphan, needed to recapture that sense so as to put it onstage. I needed to look around and not to miss a single detail, behind the wall of light, in the shadows, in the sky, and on the ground. I needed to absorb everything. For that reason, and for that reason only, I asked for someone to look after my daughter.

There's nothing worse for a theater director than to be told he can't have a certain angle, the one that will give life to the apex of the pyramid and will open the path to speech. You have to know everything to understand what you're asking for; you have to know the impossible to make it possible, Jean-Jacques had taught me in the hall, on the street, in the classroom, at the Louvre.

You have to learn not to see in order to see, Lieutenant Medina had taught me when he blindfolded me, depriving me of sight for three days. Never before had I seen so much, so much detail, so much beauty in the lost landscape, so much color in the absence of color.

I climbed up on the scaffolding; I couldn't quite get the angle I needed. I closed my eyes, imagining the light, imagining the actress; I looked down from the top of the ladder, I looked from the hall, I looked from the stage: a curtain served as a wall, a black curtain blocked my way.

I moved the projector.

I was on the top rung, keeping my balance in the gazes of my actors, who were watching; I had to move forward just so; I had to lean over just so; I had to . . .

A voice startled me out of my concentration, "The lady wants to know if she can take the baby and bring her back here at twelve, at lunchtime."

"At lunchtime," I replied automatically. As usual I hadn't been listening and repeated the final words so that no one would notice. I was studying the effect of the light on the stage.

"Some people never learn."

The lady had been hired by the Festival. She arrived in a nurse's uniform. She had been taking care of my little girl for three days.

Lunchtime arrived. Columbus had managed to walk across the stage to the rhythm of *Carmen*; El Enano had learned to tango; the Frenchwoman had made a decision: she would return to Paris with her husband, but she would leave him when they got off the plane. Perla straightened out the costumes and reviewed her lines. La Bella dictated the most recent lighting effects to Napito so he could record them, and at the same time she tried to put on the tiny carnival outfit – no, not tiny: a sigh that produced sighs. There was just one problem: every time the baby saw her, she got hungry.

I went down another rung, sat in the middle of the hall, and closing my eyes, looked all around.

My daughter was missing!

It was one o'clock!

I called the Festival office. Maybe there had been some

misunderstanding and she'd been taken there directly. Nobody knew the nurse. She had shown up at the Festival offices looking for work. They'd asked her if she had experience with babies. Of course, she'd replied, she was a nurse. No one knew her real name, though they did have her address.

I jumped into the car, arrived at the shantytown where she lived; the street existed, the number, existed. The nurse didn't. Nobody there knew her.

My daughter had been kidnapped!

The greenery of Caldas grew dark. Stories of paths where drugs were trafficked and babies were sold, whether to be adopted or dismembered and offered as spare parts, took on new meaning.

The actors and actresses stood in the collective dining room, leaving their plates half-empty, and went out into the streets to look for my daughter. They didn't need a photo. They had adopted her as the festival mascot. Never before had a three-month-old been in so many arms; actors and actresses, thirsty for love and family, fought to see who would hold her or tell her tales of other lands, steal a smile, suffuse her in the warmth that we actors so often lack.

The army and the police blocked all the roads and paths with access to Manizales, "If they haven't taken her beyond the city limits we'll find her," they told me, and I, the enemy of limits and walls, begged that this time, just this once, they would work.

Shadows invaded Manizales. I had never before witnessed such dark shadows, and yet, I hoped my daughter would emerge from the shadow and return to our arms.

The phone rang; never before had I felt such fear. I knew horror, but not fear. I trembled when they handed me the receiver.

It was the nurse, "Come to the university theater alone and cross the bridge. I'll hand over the baby on the other side. She's fine."

I went alone. She was on the other side. She left the baby on the ground, in her straw basket, turned, and walked away. What went through her mind I don't know, nor do I care. She hadn't asked for anything and I would have given everything; that is, nothing of value. A curtain covered my eyes, but it was a curtain of joy.

I went back to the Festival offices, deposited my daughter into her mother's hands. The news ran up and down the line dividing the city in half. The actors and actresses returned, and in an endless line they stopped by to give her a kiss.

In the dining room the food was growing cold.

XXVI. Of how he learned that turning off the lights doesn't mean the end, but rather a new beginning

You always learn something new, I said to myself, looking into the rear-view mirror.

Manizales was closing the festival, and I was hurtling headlong toward the ring roads of Colombia, looking for a way out of that labyrinth.

Decision time had come.

Uphill or downhill, left or right, forward or backward?

Forward, I said, opening my eyes wide so as not to see.

Some people wanted to send us via a labyrinth without forking roads, one-directional, life or death, simple as that, without room for doubt or suggestions; you accept it, you follow, you sign on, or you disappear from history.

The other labyrinth was full of hidden paths, detours, traps, defeats, and victories. There were no road signs; it was plagued with drugs, guerrillas, bandits, but also friends, community, and gentlemen. It was the road of doubt, of life or death, but on that road you could choose the moment of certainty and of your own accord take the curve that led to the edge of the cliff, concentric circles swirling on top of one another in different directions, a steel labyrinth spinning till it disappeared into itself, or an infinite labyrinth in which the path was made by walking. Here "forward" meant a surprise at every step, and every step revealed a new path.

Forward, I said, and when we bump into the law, we'll pass below the line, through the tunnel of time and of my destiny.

To the south, Popayán, the city that set its bells to ringing as we passed through. It welcomed us in the midst of ruins, and in the theater we found the ruins of a dream together with the ruins of a city, a reflection of the ruins of a civilization.

We melted into an embrace.

From each embrace a new path arose, from each knife wound a new nightmare, from each trap a hope, from each hope a new path leading to a new nightmare.

On each path a new labyrinth arose, all of them with a common center: La Línea and Medellín. Between both of them, a phone call from on high: the Second Prostitute ordering that we be denied salt and water.

We stopped along the road – an inspection. Since the roads were non-existent, we weren't sure if we'd been stopped by the army, the national police, the Colombian Revolutionary Armed Forces, the National Liberation Army, the Cali cartel, the Medellín cartel, highwaymen, paramilitaries, criminal gangs, or simply hungry peasants or some lost soul in search of rest.

All of the above. For the nine months our journey lasted, everyone stopped us; in the end some of them even called us by name and wanted to know how big the baby was. Others grew accustomed to seeing us go by and lit a candle to guide us on our way.

We had even started to resemble roadside shrines in body

and soul. The *guaduales*[36] cried when they saw us, since they too have a soul, though unlike us, they have roots.

"We, too, have a soul and roots; what we don't have is land. That's why we're souls condemned to be carried along by the wind for all eternity."

"Let's hope that it's forever and ever, since every time you pass by we collect a 'tip'," said the official in charge of the group after pocketing his share and letting us through to another turn of the labyrinth.

They didn't give a damn who we were or where we came from; they cared more about what we were carrying and what they could get out of it. On the roads of Colombia, the word didn't rule; arms did; light didn't rule; shadow did. On the roads of Colombia not everything was what it appeared to be, not even what appeared to be, was: a uniform, an insignia, a flag could just be a lowly piece of cardboard scenery, signifying absolutely nothing.

We learned to walk along its roads. We were, without being, and without wanting to be. We were not what we appeared to be. At first, for every one of those with firepower, we were members of the other band; for every one of those with any sort of power, we were suspect because we had no power at all. But for the wretched, we *were*, and among them we found refuge.

From that moment on, every curve presented a dilemma;

---

[36] A type of bamboo found in the Cauca region.

there was the circle of life and, spinning in the opposite direction, the circle of death. From that moment on we began to search for a way out; we'd get close to a border, and they'd close it; we'd get to the sea, and a wall of waves would separate us from our destination; we'd climb up one step of the staircases and reach the end, and right beside us, fading, we would see the real staircases vanishing in a different direction.

From that moment on we learned to build bridges in the clouds, to differentiate between siren songs and the songs of the earth.

From that moment on we learned to fight against the elements unchained by the Second Prostitute's fury; from that moment on we learned to ride out the storm by taking shelter in ports designated by mysterious lighthouses, friendly hands that lit them to guide us there and turned them off in our wake.

Colombia was transformed into a forest of fireflies, more than one of them leaving a little package in the labyrinth of life without being noticed by the labyrinth of death.

A way out requires preparation; a way out needs a point of departure. In my case, the way out no longer had a direction: it was forward or nothing.

The papers and the invitation to Manizales had expired; we renewed them. Friendly hands in the government renewed them for us without asking questions. We were living in times when asking wasn't a great idea: you might bump into the truth. We were living in times when knowing was dangerous: you'd risk talking too much and having someone end up dead on a deserted road or in the middle of Bogotá. We were living in times when even colors lost their meaning: before, the color red, the red banners would lift your spirits; before, the red of street lamps lit up the beauty of the *bellas,* who, for a handful of coins or a sob would grant you a caress and a grimace of love.

The red light district of my prostitutes had gotten lost in time. The red banners that once were joyfully paraded along the streets of Sofia had frozen. The militants' I.D. cards no longer had any content; they were used to beg favors or to get access to a portion of the booty. Corruption was no longer the exception, it was the rule. We were the exception: an army of foolish kids who still believed; we believed that roads still led somewhere, and we forced ourselves to believe it, even when we had passed the same curve again and again, not daring to take the one that veered off the cliff.

"I always thought you were a coward."

A way out is planned for so many years. I walked into the Chilean Consulate in Bogotá; they ushered me into a waiting room. I closed my eyes, trying to drive away my past. I tried to hide behind a smile, feeling like I was being watched. I had polished my worn-out shoes on my pants; I had even put on a vest, though not a tie: my cowardice didn't go *that* far. But I did feel miserable and humiliated, with the worst kind of humiliation, the kind you inflict on yourself. A jacket! But for the record, no tie; that's how I tried to preserve my honor.

When they called me in, I presented my daughter's birth certificate, dated in Cali, Colombia.

"I'm here to register my daughter and to get her a passport; I need to be on my way."

The bureaucrat looked at the paper, looked at me, and asked:

"Are you the father?"

Then, silence, no additional questions. He took a book with a blue cover out of the drawer and started checking the list.

His finger slid slowly down the page in a straight line; when he reached the bottom, he dampened it with saliva, knitted his brow slightly, and turned the page.

It didn't take long; his finger stopped, he looked at me, and I, coward that I am, in a gesture of bravery, had taken off my jacket and stared at him intently.

Tension flooded the office. Two backs stiffened: that of the representative of the dictatorship, that of the victim of the dictatorship. We both held our gaze; I, the combatant, knew that once again in my life I was fighting a losing battle.

All guards are the same, I thought: they observe you, they create a file on you, they shape you to the image they've formed of you, with the instructions they've been given; they spy, they listen, they scrutinize your movements, your comings and goings – there's where I screwed them up big time; they must have gotten dizzy – they make sure locks are working, and they leave your cell door open so they can study you, watch you closely in a larger cell among the infinitude of cells that make up the labyrinth in that game of concentric circles and cubes bouncing off the circles.

The office had a window through which someone was observing the guard.

There's nothing more beautiful for a theatrical director than to face a battle he's not sure of winning, a battle plagued with doubt. Avoiding arrogance, he tries to face it with a frank gaze, a circular gaze, since in both circles there's a way out: toward life, toward death.

A lost battle opens up the possibility of new battlefields. It's almost like leaving a stage behind: you leave it sadly, knowing it will forget you, that it will surrender to other arms, and that your memory will fade in the distance. And you feel betrayed, abandoned, punished, and you take a step and you betray it, forget it, prepare yourself to possess the next one, a new cell in the theater of life.

"Quick, bring him a little bag of cardboard dust so he can build himself a set."

They're crying, the *guaduales* are crying . . . my daughter started to bawl in the waiting room; the tension was broken. We both turned our heads to hear better. The bureaucrat, a little gray man on the gray spectrum, said:

"I'm sorry, but there's nothing I can do."

Apparently he really was sorry. Maybe he had a daughter

or a son somewhere far away; maybe, without his realizing it, that child had been left behind, locked up on the other side of the border he so zealously guarded.

"Your daughter was born in Colombia. The Colombians can issue her a passport."

The Colombians didn't give her a passport, not even for money. The situation was getting really ugly.

When all the doors had been closed in our faces, I looked toward the past, tossed the jacket into the wind, yanked the collar off my shirt, exchanged my worn-out shoes for Ho Chi Minh sandals, the old-fashioned kind, the ones that were made of old tires so they'd be indestructible, wrapped my daughter in poems and faded manuscripts, left the banners in the truck and in Sofia, and entered the American Embassy on foot, just as I had entered the amphitheater of the Universidad Nacional in Quito, Ecuador, through the main door, staring straight forward, head high, proud, a penniless millionaire, accompanied by La Bella entre las Bellas, and not, for once, by poets and madmen. We deposited our daughter on the counter, in the middle of the set, took three steps to the side, on the diagonal, directed our gaze to the middle of the counter, and without glancing at anyone, launched our speech from a distance:

"We're here to register the baby. She needs a passport."

They checked La Bella's passport. Puerto Rico, Puerto Pobre: regardless, it granted her nationality. They gave her a passport.

I, the granter of life, didn't grant a thing, not even a curve in the road. I, the barefoot wayfarer, didn't offer even a piece of earth to walk on; I, the dreamer, offered nightmares; I, the maker, offered only a life that gave birth to a new labyrinth.

My daughter smiled at me, "I forgive you, *Papi.*"

In Colombia my daughter had grown accustomed to sleeping in the truck or in the car. To tell the truth, she preferred the truck; she felt more secure. Her cradle consisted of empty projector boxes; her toys, the costumes and props; her family, the actors. Her lullabies were the songs of the *guaduales*; the snakes' hissing pierced her eardrums; she drank water from the sky when the water of the earth was undrinkable; she bathed in rivers and waterfalls, despised walls, adored the open spaces of the theater, a wild world that grew before her eyes and watched her grow.

There was nothing normal about her infancy; everything was abnormal, and she was happy.

Once more La Línea. Full stop, new paragraph.

"Someday I'll leave La Línea behind; I didn't know that my wish would be fulfilled or what I was getting myself into."

Searching for a way out, we left for Medellín. In theory we had shows to put on, and that would buy us time and food. We arrived there at night, having lost our way following a star; tired and with no inn to shelter us, we stopped in the darkness, closed our eyes. When darkness broke, the Belén cemetery appeared before our eyes; you could read that on the arch framing the entryway. Luckily, we had stopped in time; six meters more and we would have slept among the dead.

"Ah, what peace!"

We made a phone call and went down to meet the person in charge of the Colombian Theater Corporation in the city. He met us at a café. No performances: they had disappeared; no contacts: they had evaporated; everyone had turned their backs on us. Lend me your back in solidarity, brother, and we will build a wall of backs, and close it at the call of the Second Prostitute.

The wife of the man in charge fell in love with my daughter. They weren't able to have babies. We chatted for a long time, talking about theater, travel, festivals, about life. We avoided talking about death; we even laughed. We talked about persecutions, persecutors, and those who were persecuted, of light and shadow. Even the curves of La Línea entered into the conversation. Even the bravest fear it, such is its power, and La Línea took on a shape and a voice. La Línea, which was incapable of giving a speech, began to issue rules and decrees. La Línea ordered people through, forged the rail; there was no escaping it. La Línea, the queen, was promoted from Second Prostitute to madam of the brothel.

La Línea, like the ghetto, is self-sustaining, needs strict rules to guarantee its survival, needs to form its leaders in its image and likeness to guarantee its consistency over time. The boss designates his replacement; the boss determines when he needs to be replaced; the boss has the power to annihilate if the replacement tries to eclipse him while he's still in power; the boss is in charge of the box with broken glass, prison, or expulsion. He decorates or marks foreheads with a circle of ashes to make sure his aim is true. Nothing changes; nothing can change: the boss and only the boss has the right to be rejuvenated so as to hold on to his seductive powers.

"Everything changes so that nothing will change."

And yet, something had changed: the Second Prostitute had dyed her hair red. Even the banners from Sofia paled with envy.

A labor union, the Medellín city workers' union, offered us shelter – how symbolic, I thought. For better or for worse, we were accustomed to picking up trash and leftovers from the streets, and what were we but debris, the flotsam and jetsam of a shipwreck, floating in circles and trying to rebuild a *raison d'être*, debris looking for more debris to create a floating stage that would carry us off to disappear in the heart of the vortex, our public.

We descended from Belencito into the city, another step on our way out. We began working on a show at the Pablo Tobón Uribe, a beautiful theater that opened its doors to us. We were able to rehearse ahead of the symphony orchestra as long as we cleared the stage before they came in. We fulfilled that condition: there are no arguments between words and music; we're complementary, so complementary that the day of our presentation we discovered that the chairs from the brothel, our lovely French chairs, which lent the scene an erotic, Parisian tone, had disappeared. We had to replace them in a hurry with a couple of boxes that we had brought from the trash collectors' union, which gave the scene a neo-realist tone, à la Luchino Visconti or Vittorio de Sica.

"Vito!" exclaimed Napoleón, bursting into tears. Napito had been with us for three months.

"Personally I'd prefer Fellini."

"*La Dolce Vita* or *I Vitelloni?*"

"No, *La Strada.* We spent so much time on it that it became our home and our way of life."

"I'm partial to Buñuel's *The Young and the Damned*," said the Second Prostitute, sticking her nose into what was none of her business.

At his next concert, the symphony orchestra director and the first violinist appeared sitting in our beautiful chairs, which gave the concerts a French bordello tone and assured them a full house for the rest of their tour. They included in their repertory the melody of "A Man and a Woman" from the Lelouch film and started off by announcing themselves as "New Wave Concertos." They couldn't understand why the audiences left the theater dancing the samba until they went on tour in Brazil and the entire hall got up and danced. They asked why: they were told that the Brazilians adored Vinicius de Moraes.

It was a time when music came down from the *favelas*[37] –

---

[37] Slums in Brazil.

just as half a century earlier it had come up from the *arrabales*[38] –
to stow away on a boat heading for Europe, where it would conquer bodies and salons. It was a time when unfettered art could
still flourish.

They called us!

The call wasn't from Bogotá; the fateful phone call came
from the customs office in Medellín. The boss gave me a month to
leave the country; otherwise he would impound our work tools and
expel us.

Two questions immediately crossed my mind: where to?
and, would the baby's cradle be impounded, also? As I couldn't
decide which to ask first, I kept quiet.

"You always learn something new."

We headed toward Envigado. Along the road, to our left,
the Nevado del Ruiz, a gorgeous volcano that dominated the landscape with its smoking peak, awakening the uncontrollable desire
of the coffee plantations. A friendly fumarole that greeted travelers,
it had begun to spew smoke a year earlier but hadn't been a threat
to anyone for nine. The university had invited us; when we arrived,
its director proudly escorted us to the theater. We opened its
doors, I stepped inside as one steps inside a theater for the first
time, with love, with respect.

---

[38] Slums or poor working-class neighborhoods in Spanish-speaking Latin American countries.

378

"With caution," the director warned me.

He was right: the theater was half in ruins: the rows of empty seats teetered above the floor. At some point they had broken the rule and decided to make themselves comfortable in the hall in a dangerous rocking motion. The stage had been devoured by termites, and all that was left of it was something resembling a corridor.

"The plays can be adapted to a straight line," said the director.

During the day, the lighting came from the torrid sun, and at night, from the stars, whose beams tried to penetrate the holes in the roof.

"Let's hope it doesn't rain; last time we had to cancel the show. We forgot to tell the audience to bring umbrellas."

To tell the truth, the hall was pretty dilapidated. And yet, there's nothing more exciting for a theatrical director than to begin constructing his own space, to feel as though the hall is part of his being and he a part of the hall, to raise the altar where it will bring the word to life, where the characters will be born every night so that they can walk along the stage and among the audience.

Naranjo, Naranjo is a traitor, the spectator will warn the actor, tugging on his poncho – the spectator, not the director, since the spectator is the one who will finally give him life by accepting or rejecting him. There's nothing more beautiful than a theater with its guts exposed, concealing its cardboard-decorated skin.

To work! To sweep the dust, leaving it deposited to one side in order to put it back in place after we've passed through, yielding the floor to all the dusty characters who passed by before, them and the dust of our own characters.

We went to the nearest factory for assistance. They were accustomed to buying tickets, but no one attended performances. We took the truck: we needed the power to change that habit. We wanted them to attend; it was our right.

There's nothing more terrible for a director than to perform for a full house, but with nobody in the theater.

We stopped in front of the main entrance, beside a sentry box, and asked to speak with the manager. They called to some-one inside. They watched us from above, wanting to make sure we were what we said we were.

We were in hot lands, and in hot lands suspicion is king.

"In cold lands, too, incidentally."

Suspiciously, I looked at the wall and the symbol above the doors to be sure they weren't made of cardboard.

The doors opened; the manager appeared; we got out. He stood motionless, his eyes filled with tears.

It wasn't such a big deal, really; we were very thin, with bags under our eyes, poorly shod, but wearing the most elegant garments in the wardrobe – we, the actors, selling a show.

We opened our arms. The manager walked right past us and embraced the truck.

We were at the Colombian Renault factory, the first in Latin America.

"I'd heard about it. I was told people saw it coming out from among the ruins, disappearing into the night, reappearing on the sea in Santa Marta, and passing in front of the Government Palace in Bogotá before evaporating in the mist. I didn't believe it, I didn't, even though this was Colombia, after all."

He issued an order: the Renault factory in Envigado, Colombia, halted production so they could welcome us.

"May I drive it?" he asked. "I want to show them what a truck from the main factory is like."

He drove the truck inside: gravely wounded, blind, its brake lines tied up with diapers to keep the air from escaping, traces of urine and tobacco on the windshield, its turn signals out of order since they didn't know what to signal, mortally wounded along its flanks, it entered its house thousands of miles from the Seine, haughty, proud, defiant, smiling, and warning: Don't touch the brake, because if you do, I won't be able to start up again.

That night the manager hosted us at his home, a lovely house hidden behind the walls. In Colombia there was such a variety of walls, even the ones people created, not to lock themselves in, but to defend themselves, despite having paid protection money.

Quiche Lorraine: I hadn't tried one since the time when La Bella and I ate one in the Latin Quarter in Paris. I had forgotten how they melt in your mouth, the tenderness of the crust, surrendering layer by layer before yielding up their fruit, and the cream spilling over, enrobing a bit of bacon, golden, crispy, a symbol of love. Desire flowed straight down to my loins.

Snails, a dozen snails in their shells, swimming in a sea of butter, garlic, and parsley; a rosy roast beef, throbbing, blood coming to die in my hungry mouth, blood feeding my anemic body, animal pain to assuage the pain of wretchedness. All of it washed down with a variety of wines, offering up their flavors and the sunbeams of the *Midi*. When it was cognac time, a wave of something like nostalgia came over me, the same kind that had overtaken me in France when I thought of the tomatoes of my land.

The next day the Renault workers arrived to rebuild the theater hall. Not all of them: some stayed behind to work on the truck. "Don't screw with us, brother, we're not gonna let a beat-up Renault like that drive around here; it's a matter of pride," they said affectionately.

The day of the performance, we had a stage; the seats had been repaired and upholstered; the entry doors didn't make noise; the electrical cables had been changed to avoid having everything go up in flames; but most important of all, on the day of the performance, the hall was absolutely packed: all the Renault workers were there, not for us, for them. It was their show.

"As it should be."

The next day we took down the set. The truck was at the theater door, waiting to be loaded. It looked like a movie heartthrob; I wasn't sure if it looked a little like Jean Gabin, because of its experience, or if it resembled Alain Delon, because it was so dashing. They'd even washed it! And after how hard it had worked to plant roots on the continent!

"I think it looked a little like Lino Ventura, a truck with hair on its chest," said the golden car.

As we passed the Renault factory on our way to La Línea, all the workers came out to bid us farewell. A part of them remained on the truck.

I looked into the rear-view mirror and saw them disappear in the distance – in the distance, not in my heart.

We had to pass through Bogotá in order to get to Tunja, where another university and new friends awaited us. It was a new step, a new twist in the labyrinth. I didn't know it yet, but it would save our lives.

As was our custom, we entered from the south, prepared to cross the city from one side to the other; like cornered beasts, we wanted to mark our territory.

"Mark territory? What territory? The only thing you guys do is pass through," said the Second Prostitute.

To my right, the Government Palace, then the pigeon-filled plaza, then the Cathedral, and beyond that the Palace of Justice, and then . . . Pigeons, there wasn't a single pigeon in Plaza Bolívar. It was a November day in 1985. The M19[39] had taken over the Palace of Justice! The takeover happened on the 6th; counting employees, magistrates, and visitors, there were 350 people inside.

They stopped us; we couldn't move. In the plaza, soldiers

---

[39] The 19th of April movement, a Colombian guerrilla movement that later became a political party.

with their backs to the Government Palace, all of them aiming in the same direction, toward the heart of justice. At the main entrance, a tank prepared to launch the assault; inside, the chief justice gave the order not to attack; his voice was silenced by cannon fire.

Once again the word proved powerless in the face of blind force. By the 7th, order had been reestablished. I, the involuntary witness, saw how it was reestablished: they pulled out 98 corpses; all the files on drug trafficking and corruption went up in smoke.

The army and the police sang songs of victory; democracy was preserved; honor was preserved; order was reestablished. In Colombia not everything is what it appears to be, but this time, for once, what I saw was that the men and women who went up in flames were victims of the established order. Tears streamed from my eyes; I swear it wasn't the smoke. Those dead were just as much mine as my own dead, the ones in La Moneda Palace, were theirs.

A moment of silence ran up and down the continent.

That night the government issued its own version of the events on national television; shortly after the announcement started, it was interrupted by a march:

Guerrrillero, guerrillero

Adelante, adelante

It was the Helenos[40] paying homage to the M19. I took a detour. As I passed an apartment house, I honked the horn; it was

---

[40] The ELN or Ejército de Liberación Nacional, an insurgent guerrilla group in Colombia.

heard on the radio.

We smiled.

Ahead of us, the road north. Once we had entered the savannah, to the right was a convent, to the left, the Government country house – where presidents spent their weekends – and in between, a police roadblock. They collected a toll to drive into Bogotá; they collected a toll to get out. Looking left or right was free.

Bewitched, we continued on our way. Somewhere, about 50 kilometers along, hidden, was the solution to our problem, the honorable way out, the one that would ensure the birth of orange trees bordering the road to the theater, the one that would offer rest for the travelers. Somewhere was Lake Guatavita and deep beneath its surface, El Dorado, the city of gold, as I repeated to La Bella in an attempt to lift her spirits. It was the most real thing I could offer her in Colombian territory. "It's there, within reach of your hand. They haven't discovered it yet because they don't know how to look for it; you have to see with the eyes of your heart."

Luckily La Bella was in love; anyone else would have told me to go to hell.

In the distance we heard the tolling of bells. To keep from imagining they were death knells, I said, "They're the bells of the church buried in the lake; they only toll for a select few. Beneath this town is El Dorado; it's a matter of going up the stairs, not down."

Following this logical explanation, we pressed on, as was our custom.

"And El Dorado?"

"Don't be such a fool. You really believe in that nonsense?" I shifted gears.

We passed El Dorado without realizing it; all those curves in the road had made me lose my mind and see reality where there wasn't any.

The cold brought me back to my destination; I crossed over the bridge. Teatinos was prepared to launch a new battle: at the door of the Universidad de Tunja's theater, the director of cultural affairs and his wife were waiting for us.

We were on safe ground: a hall and some friends.

Boyacá was the same as the rest of Colombia; drugs circulated there, and where there were drugs, there were guerrillas, paramilitary units, the army, the police, and corruption. The only thing that didn't get through there was the sun; it was colder than hell, not like the nights in the Chilean desert or the cold of Colquirí in the Bolivian *altiplano*, but the sort of cold you feel on the banks of the Seine in winter: cold, but bearable.

Eduardo, who formerly was president of the university and who had invited us, had left his position. He was summoned by the Palace and became a government secretary. They charged him with the insane task of trying to establish a dialogue between the factions to put an end to the violence in Colombia. In a land that was on fire, the labyrinth toward peace needed to come from a cool head, and who better than someone from cold lands to calm tempers.

Once again, without seeking it out, another moment of

madness paraded before my eyes. That weekend we were invited to Eduardo's country house. We ate, strolled around, chatted; then other diners arrived, all of them heavyweights, those in charge, men of good will – or not so good – men of all stripes.

The *cordillera* kindly parted the branches of the trees that crowned its peak, allowing me to spot military officers, who, with rifles with telescopic sights and fingers on triggers, followed every movement.

The Rancagua prison ceilings returned to my memory, but this time they were there to protect us, or at least that's what our new friend claimed.

No one was convinced, neither the brand-new government secretary, nor the scruffy theatrical director. My daughter, on the other hand, was happy. She had never touched a cow before.

Back at the theater, we hurried along the mounting so we could get on our way, lest they develop a cramp in their finger.

Before us snow was falling, with increasingly copious flakes that made the road disappear from sight. I slowed down, fearful for those in the car. The mountains had vanished from view; the Nevado del Ruiz fumarole no longer existed. Despite the heavy snowfall, I didn't dare roll up the windows to keep the flakes out of the cabin; the heat was unbearable. We were in hot lands.

The Renault building couldn't be seen from the edge of the road; our one-day friends didn't come out to greet us. The dream builders had gone out on a new assignment: to snatch life from death.

The set had changed: where there had been trees, just a few treetops, the tallest of them, peeked out; where there had been walls, mountains of rocks, and yet there was no call for rejoicing. Under the walls and mud lay 22,000 people. Seven thousand wandered around with vacant stares, without a guide, in search of a present and a non-existent future. Armero[41] had been punished by nature, condemning it to moan for all eternity. Armero had climbed up one step too many of the staircases. Armero had tried to escape violence. Armero perished before our eyes on the 13th of November, six days after the Palace of Justice erupted in flames.

Colombia was burning on all four sides; it burned at each curve, on each path, on each abruptly blocked road. It burned in the hot lands; it burned in the cold lands. We, we in the midst of the violence, taking note, silent witnesses, so as to tell its tale tomorrow.

That is, if tomorrow came.

Along with the mantle of blood that cloaked the earth, along with the gray mantle that cloaked people's consciences, there arose a white mantle from the bowels of the earth. And joining those three layers, beams of white powder traversed Colombia, adding darkness after a brief moment of brilliance in the new paradise.

---

[41] The tragedy of Armero was a natural disaster resulting from the eruption of the Nevado del Ruiz volcano in 1985 after 69 years of dormancy.

"O gods, what sin is great enough to warrant such a punishment!"

"O gods, don't take away my last stage!"

I know, I survived, and those were times when even that was denied to me.

We were heading for Armenia [42]. The sound of the *guaduales* filtered in through the windows, piercing the cloak of fake snow. In the city life's wretched women awaited us with *tiples* [43] in hand, mini-dresses and garishly painted faces. In our travels along the staircases we were received with open arms by those women who opened their legs for a couple of pesos: the whores of Armenia. The merchants of false love received the merchants of illusion in their embrace. We reserved the front rows of the theater for them; they were our guests of honor. This was how we honored their profession.

Their brightly painted faces stood out in the audience. My daughter smiled in their arms; they had painted her face, too, as homage.

It wasn't easy to leave the security of their arms, but the road was calling us, the road and time, which was running out.

For the first time we took an unnecessary risk.

"For the first time? Some people never learn!"

We traveled at night. At dawn a deafening noise guided us,

---

[42] A medium-sized city, the capital of Quindio Department.
[43] A guitar-like instrument, popular in Colombia.

and we allowed ourselves to be guided. We were entering Ibagué, our next stop. The noise came from thousands of wild parrots that perched in the trees of the public square every afternoon looking for refuge and left town every day at dawn, looking for safety.

Their song summed up the tragedy of Colombia: each one of them represented a lost soul, a disappeared person, a kidnapping victim; each one represented the desperate cry of the dead at the hand of violence, someone tortured, a throat slit, a raped woman, a child thrown out into the street to beg or take up arms. Each parrot represented someone whose destiny had been walled in, those who had been despoiled of their dreams, the remains of a lost generation; they were the wretched of the Colombian earth, shouting their final cry for help into the air.

Rise up, brother, be born with me, they invited me.

I closed my eyes and looked for my parrot and my song.

I took off flying.

"Where to?"

"Straight ahead," I replied, "even if we have to go through La Línea and Medellín again."

The parrots showed me that the time of great decisions had arrived.

"La Línea or Medellín?"

"No, people always go through there; we have to find the door leading out of the labyrinth. On one side is Venezuela; we were invited."

"Venezuela?"

"No, the International Theater Institute; there are protective gloves over the talons of the little gray bureaucrats. There are stages that escape envy and rules; there are boards that beg to be trodden with love and to be possessed unconditionally, savage loves, the kind I like, the kind I've fought for all my life."

"Not for principles?"

"That makes up part of my principles; because I'm a lover, remember? Because I'm a lover, I grew close to my people and their desires; because I'm a lover I loved unconditionally; because I'm a lover and because of a need to be loved. Because I'm a lover I survived."

To the north, Costa Rica. Well, not exactly Costa Rica: the Chileans who lived in Costa Rica had gotten us a two-week gig at the Teatro Nacional de San José, the largest in that small country.

Our cry for help had pierced walls, flown over borders, both geographical and political, had watched from on high, looking for a place to land and restore functionality to the word, set songs free, offer a cracked mirror so that the actors could once again make up their faces, so as to reveal the true face concealed behind a question, behind a scream, behind a martyred body, behind an increasingly decrepit set, a stage where joy would be reborn at the hour of truth. That magical instant when one emerges from the shadows to die in the mind.

"Outta my way," said the truck. "We're going to Cúcuta," it said, turning toward Pescadero. "On the other side of the border is San Cristóbal, and I've been told he's the patron saint of travelers."

We changed direction and habits: the car with the actors in

it led the way, while the truck went from being a "divo" to just another cast member. In Colombia it was essential to watch your back.

"Don't get too far away," I said, perhaps thinking of the unspoken lines from the first time I saw her appear at the *L'Humanité* party.

How many undelivered lines occupy my life; how many speeches have escaped my lips and destroyed my life; how many ignored stage directions fill my sets; how many silences came to life when it was too late.

"Don't get too far away," I repeated, and La Bella entre las Bellas smiled.

We entrusted ourselves to the guerrillas, in memory of the sacks of coffee of yesteryear; we entrusted ourselves to Eduardo and the government, in memory of a cockscomb-and-chicken-foot soup; we entrusted ourselves to Pablo, in memory of the dreams of those who were unable to dream; we entrusted ourselves to the army, in memory of our hunger-ridden bodies; we entrusted ourselves to corruption, in memory of our empty pockets; we entrusted ourselves to our bad luck as miserable sons-of-bitches, in memory of the Second Prostitute – and we left.

She didn't go far, and it wasn't because she had listened to me. In this world you can hear everything, even thoughts, if you learn how to read the expression of the body, the face, the fluttering of eyelashes, of hands, of feet that slip under the table, the whisper of air caused by a voluptuous thigh, the intensity of a gaze that pierces desire, even thought itself, if in fact you have learned the secret of the symbols that allow the word to come through without fear of emitting a fatal sound.

"It must have been because a car isn't the same thing as a truck," said an eavesdropper whose opinion nobody had asked for, and as a punishment its windshield wipers stopped working and it had to submit to the humiliation of being covered with urine and tobacco to allow its tears to roll down its cheeks.

La Bella entre las Bellas appeared in the mist, at a curve in the road. She was waiting, sitting on a bumper of the car. A mini-skirt revealed her lovely legs; two laces from her red shoes twisted up her thighs like snakes. She was smiling just as she once had smiled at me, sitting on the railing of the Pont Neuf, waiting for me, quivering, in the Quartier Latin, that day when she wound her way into my life forever.

She was the same, only slimmer; her flirty red shoes re-placed by worn-out sneakers; of the miniskirt all that remained were holes in her pants, revealing her lovely legs. Her smile was the same, her 'take me with you' spirit was the same. The Seine had been replaced by the water of a spring that ran down the mountain; her gorgeous breasts had matured, and from one of them hung our daughter, drinking the liquid that would save her life.

The car had refused to go on. That piece of crap got over-heated, I thought in a fit of jealousy. From that moment on, it be-came a lover, overheating on every hill, and Colombia is a country of hills, of contradictions expressed in the shape of hills. I laid a towel on La Bella's seat; as with spiders, you never know with European cars.

We opened the hood so the car could cool off.

"With urine the engine cools down faster," said the truck, in a display of obvious bad faith.

With obviously bad faith that car did not cool off, which forced us to go back, bit by bit, to the natural order, truck first.

I took down the forklift that had caused such awe and delight for the children of the Bolivian *altiplano.* Pushing the car – please let it be downhill next time, we thought aloud – we forced it up the slope, tied it with the projector cables, and used diapers to muffle the blows against the doors of the truck.

We looked like a cross between one of those barges that plow the European canals with their cargo, a car parked on the stern for visiting cities and castles at various stops, and a poor Latin American traveling circus caravan.

La Bella, the truck, and the car took offense at this last bit; I don't know why, because to tell the truth . . .

At the peak we stopped of our own accord, an unusual thing in Colombia. A rest stop commanded the landscape, its open walls providing a view of the valley. For sure the gods had stopped there. A good man, just one would be enough to justify the journey, and it wasn't *The Good Person of Szechuan,* let alone the Second Prostitute.

Us? Forget it! For the gods, wretches like us didn't count.

We ordered a cup of *agua de panela*[44] for each of us. At the only table that had a back to support one's shoulders, a man wearing a broad-brimmed hat to conceal his face was watching us. I trembled: the rest stop must be on a steep slope, I thought, but I didn't dare look down to see if scavenger birds were circling around at the bottom of the ditch. I had grown accustomed to looking without seeing and seeing without looking. This time, apparently, my instinct had failed me; I had forgotten the principle that in Colombia not everything is what it appears to be.

I moved my chair to shield La Bella and my daughter with my body. The man stood up, crossed over to the other side of the place, passed us by without a glance, walked over to the counter, muttered something quietly, and left.

They'll riddle us with bullets when we leave, I though, slowly drinking my cup of *agua de panela*. In my lifetime I've been prepared to die many ways, but of hunger isn't one of them.

"Slowly," so that every hand movement is precise, so that the importance of every step is emphasized, so that lips separate to absorb the spectator's gaze, so that while imagining the golden liquid flowing from the container into his mouth, the spectator gets up to demand his share, so that, together with the dispossessed of the entire world he will demand: A sip of *agua de panela* to help us face death! "Slowly," I repeated to La Bella, my daughter, and the group.

Fifteen minutes went by. The empty cups were waiting to

---

[44] Hot water with unrefined whole cane sugar.

be collected from the table; clouds covered the valley. I asked for the check.

The door to the kitchen opened. Hit men: the guy in the hat wasn't alone. Three others came with him; three were enough. One of them carried some dented frying pans with scrambled eggs swimming in oil; another, *pan de bono*[45] and *almojábanas*[46]; the third, a bandeja *Paisa*[47] for us to share. Behind him came the waiter with a glass of milk.

"This is for the little one. Don't worry – it's all paid for. El Patrón" – he pointed to the empty table – "paid for everything."

The gods had been looking for a single good man, and they didn't find him. Just one, and we found him.

He saved my daughter, and I'm no ingrate.

You don't look for a good soul in areas protected by walls. You look for a good soul wherever shelter is offered, where blood runs through the labyrinth, where ideas set off sparks or are extinguished like damp gunpowder. And we found one there; the gods clearly hadn't known where to look.

Nothing and no one would stop us.

We stopped suddenly: Pescadero.

The truck, hero of so many battles, survivor of the struggle, in an unusual act of cowardice said:

"You go first," and got behind the car.

---

[45] A type of Colombian bread containing corn flour, cassava starch, cheese, and eggs.
[46] Colombian cheese bread.
[47] A typical meal popular in Colombia with red beans, pork, white rice, chicharrón, fried egg, plantain, chorizo, arepa, and avocado served in a platter.

396

Nobody wanted to look at the serpent with four nostrils. We were stepping on her tail, and she was fierce.

You should never step on an actress' tail, the director reminded himself. They turn around and dig their poisonous fangs into you in a flash.

Pescadero was no exception to the rule: we massaged its back, admired its beauty. The serpent coiled and uncoiled herself, hypnotizing us; there, down below, far from our sight, its head: Piedecuesta. On all sides of the beast, stripped and rusting, remains of those who were bold enough to defy her: cars, trucks, carts that missed a turn or forgot to pay tribute before starting the descent, slipping along the serpent's skin and her sensual curves.

In the distance, El Llano and the leafcutter ants that lay in wait to devour us.

As this was ELN territory, I asked one of them to take care of scheduling; that way I could count on other gods to clear our way.

"You're nobody's fool," said the truck, as it pushed the car to begin the descent.

I let 33 minutes go by before beginning ours, time enough for La Bella to move out of the way so the truck wouldn't run her over in case something malfunctioned, despite the fact that I had tested the snugness of the diapers wrapped around the brake tubes to be sure no air would escape, all the while knowing I wouldn't escape my destiny.

I shifted gears.

In Cúcuta three events awaited us: two performances and the Venezuelan government's refusal to grant us visas, using the most ridiculous and vile excuse:

"And where are you going afterwards?"

They wouldn't accept the logical reply, "Straight ahead."

They consulted a map, and apparently the country of Straightahead didn't exist.

The first performance took place at the Municipal Theater, in front of the plaza, on the other side of the church, beside the Government Palace. On the fourth side: the police station. We took refuge in the theater.

The manager had arranged for the show to be sponsored by the supreme civil authority: the area's military governor. He missed the premiere and sent his regrets. In any case we held the royal box in reserve; with those people you never know.

The house lights went out. I came out of the shadows to remain in shadow; I coughed discreetly to let everyone know I was in my place, ready to begin the play. Nothing. I closed my eyes in order to see. In the royal box, the head of the area ELN forces stood up; in the doorways, out of nowhere, guerrillas with their weapons slung across their chests appeared, prepared to defend their commander if anything went wrong.

There's nothing more painful for a theatrical director than to want to remain in the shadows.

That night I wanted to remain anonymous. With all the strength I had left, I begged that it wouldn't occur to the tech to turn on the lights. There are times when lights don't illuminate; there are times when they unleash a massacre.

In the darkness I heard Allende's name, the word "*compañeros*" repeated many times . . . Ooof, they were paying homage to us . . . a "they didn't take up arms" . . . *ayyyy,* they were criticizing us . . . to the usual "*patria o muerte*" that concluded a speech, I mechanically responded with a tremulous "*venceremos.*" I felt like I was in Bulgaria, but I didn't raise my fist, lest they take potshots at a moving shadow.

The side doors opened up. Prague, the Black Theater; the shadows came to life; they came to attention before their leader, raised their fists, and disappeared into the night.

Light flooded the scene, light, not the word. The Black Theater was followed by Bip. I hadn't frozen onstage in years. Columbus went from being Nureyev to being lame. The play just wouldn't take off.

The whores saved us; thank God there are whores to cure fear.

The next day we started mounting our set at Universidad Francisco de Padua Santander. I rejected the amphitheater.

"Out in the open; I don't want doors or walls."

The military governor summoned me.

"I heard about last night."

Silence.

"I didn't give the order to attack because there might've been a massacre."

(Grateful) silence.

"Now you understand why I didn't go to see the play."

"Because Your Honor isn't stupid." (It just slipped out).

Silence from the other side.

"I'm sorry, but I'm going to have to finish setting up," I said, leaving the office.

"Fuck!" echoed throughout the office.

After the show, the ELN commander summoned me.

"*Compañero!*"

"*Compañero!*"

"Well?"

The *compañero* was a man of few words.

"Well, what?" I replied, echoing his speech.

"The revolutionary tax."

The *compañero* was direct.

In a few words I explained that we hadn't seen even one cent, that the *compañero* manager had cashed the checks and taken off, and that the last time he'd been seen around these parts, he was crossing the bridge leading to San Cristóbal.

Embarrassed, I stopped talking. What I hadn't done in Rancagua, I did in Cúcuta. Unwittingly I had denounced him, one *compañero* to another, but the result would have been the same.

"We'll get him and make him pay."

That door of the labyrinth had closed. We left quickly for Santa Marta; there we would take the ferry to Panama, and from there to the Costa Rican Municipal Theater.

"I swear to you, last week I took the ferry. Go on a

Wednesday, it's cheaper," a newly- arrived Paisa advised us.

With all those details, it had to be true.

We needed to hurry; our legal visiting time was running out, and, dressed as illegals, we left so that we could arrive on a Wednesday.

The university students escorted us to the border, not the Venezuelan border – the other one, the one that led to the Magda-lena River and its ships. The jungle opened its belly to swallow us up. The mosquitoes started marking their territory on our bodies.

Between Cúcuta and Santa Marta there was no sky; every turn of the labyrinth ended in not two, but three spirals. I, the dream-maker, was acquainted with that of life and that of death. But the spiral of hope was brand new, and therefore more danger-ous.

"There's no ferry in Santa Marta," they said. "There's one in Cartagena." Cartagena, the city that erected its walls to protect itself from Sir Francis Drake, the city which, to earn forgiveness, had lent its walls to dreams and its brothels to dreamers, a friendly city like Sète, cities that give birth to poets and confer musicality on words, cities of refuge for beggars and homeless people, cities of refuge for lost souls.

"There's a ferry in Cartagena," said another Paisa, the ferry that would rescue us from the worst storm, the storm of newly-unleashed violence, uncontrolled violence that would last for seven years, violence that was born in the midst of the violence that de-stroyed Colombia and us wretches who were passing through, in anticipation of the six million wretches who were to follow in our footsteps.

"How is it possible that in the most violent country of all they dared to call it violence, and don't exaggerate, it wasn't six million, only five million seven hundred twelve thousand five hundred six. And for your information, those six were you guys."

"Seven, there were seven of us. You forgot one."

"Six: the seventh one's mark is on a different list."

The only ferry to be found in Cartagena left years ago from a curtain in a movie theater and disappeared in the distance, there where the sea and the sky come together in a kiss; and the beautiful Russian woman who came on board as a stowaway betrayed it; she works there as a singer, practicing her profession in a cabaret. The maestro of silent film gave her life, speech, and nobility; he called her "countess."

Once more, I arrived too late.

"You didn't arrive too late. You made another mistake: you arrived the first year, the decisive one, the one that determines whether or not the baby will survive, the one that marks its path and its destiny, the one which, because it was unexpected, opens up the infinite limits of horror; and if there's no ferry, there are barges. They're the only things that will get you across the Gulf of Urabá. They leave from Turbo, and if you think this is violence, you need to know that they call that mess the red zone, and not even the brave risk going there, and if I remember correctly, you don't belong to that category."

402

He was talking about the torrid zone of Colombia, an area where drug traffickers, paramilitary units, guerrillas, and the army clash, where one bullet is worth ten times as much as a human life, and an actor is worth less than that.

How devalued we must have been!

How desperate I must have been to exclaim, "Tickets to Turbo!"

"Careful, it's nighttime."

"Day, night, it's the same thing."

It wasn't the same thing. I was losing my mind; even my daughter understood that much, and after passing the last checkpoint, before the road disappeared in the shadows, she threw one hell of a tantrum. We stopped so that La Bella could nurse her, but no luck – she kept on squalling. A bus came by; the driver waved to us, and disappeared into the distance. Thirty minutes later he returned; the driver was bathed in blood. His assistant was draped across the door. Inside there were three dead men.

"They stopped us; they ambushed us; they were waiting. The dead guys were military in civilian clothes who were on the bus to protect us, and they killed my assistant for being a moron – he tried to collect their fares."

My daughter stopped crying.

"You can go ahead," the people at the checkpoint told us. "The road is clear. Whoever they were, they must have already headed toward the jungle."

At the wall a soldier asked, "Should I put a mark on the target list or on the others?"

"Don't be an idiot, soldier – the ones on the target list we kill ourselves. For this group add one mark to the civilian list – one hundred seventy seven thousand three hundred seven marks covered the walls of Colombia – and put three on the list of combatants." Forty thousand seven hundred eighty-seven marks were added, not counting the ones erased by the rain.

"But, let's be fair: we, too, added our little grain of sand to the target list," the drug traffickers, guerrillas, and paramilitaries admonished me.

"You all know it's the same thing," I explained.

We continued on our way. To protect us and just in case, I hung a small eraser from the steering wheel.

From there, headfirst into the labyrinth – no spiral of life, no spiral of death, just the maelstrom of limitless violence. The paths didn't fork in different directions; they forked into life and death. The big shots traveled by helicopter, slipping through like snakes, and like snakes they leaped three times in the same direction before biting. That was their undoing: the helicopters separated the clouds with their rotors; that was their undoing; all the uniforms were the same. That was what made them lose count when they were counting those who had fallen in combat, in ambushes, in treacherous sneak attacks from behind. Borders disappeared; drug corridors were born, and they were well-protected.

No one would emerge unscathed; it was a war without winners. On our way to the Gulf of Urabá we all lost.

At kilometer zero, the military; at kilometer 7, a plane loaded with drugs; at kilometer 9, guerrillas; at kilometer 13, paramilitary units; between kilometer zero and 13 a truck with the sign "Nuevo Teatro Los Comediantes" and a car containing La Bella, a baby girl, and some actors.

A lightning bolt shot through the first year of blind violence, the most terrible year ever to strike Colombia, a caravan navigating in the midst of war, without a compass, without allies, without even being worth the cost of a few bullets. That's why we survived, because on the stage of a war between brothers, a war of petty interests, a war of revenge, a war of the lust for power, the blind, the mute, and the mad are respected: the blind, because they see without seeing; the mute, because they don't speak; the mad, because, innocents that they are, they will serve as witnesses, extending the lives and honoring the memory of the fallen on all sides.

I turned off my lantern just in case; it wasn't the right time to seek a just man among the dead; besides, the destruction was so great that recreating a just man from the pieces would have been a titanic feat.

Modestly, the car lowered its eyes and went to work illuminating the *caimanes* that crossed its path. The truck had recovered its Latin American appearance and, like a fearful Cyclops, tried to find a way out of the labyrinth to save us and the golden car, with which it had secretly fallen in love.

Shadows fell on shadows, and in the middle of the road, at

the bottom of a descent and the start of a new rise, a van awaited us, blocking the road, its lights extinguished, a man sleeping at the wheel with a hat over his face.

I braked, even though nobody brakes at night in Colombia.

"Why would you brake at night when you don't even brake in the daytime anymore? Don't you remember?"

At Carrera Séptima, underneath the bridges at the hour of ghosts – don't you remember, you mustn't brake there; just the opposite, you speed up – the ghosts, their tattered bodies, bounced against the sides of the cars before being replaced by the still-intact bodies of other street urchins, those poor devils who populate the streets of Colombian cities, those who receive even the blows from the cars that run them over as if they were the caresses they were always denied.

"I'll stop – maybe that way I'll earn a caress."

We couldn't retreat. La Bella blocked our way. When we tried to go backwards, it got stuck in the mud. We climbed out of the vehicles with our hands in the air – we're actors, after all – and the barely audible lines vanished among the vegetation. Just like in Rancagua, the terrible moment of anticipation had arrived; it was impossible to guess what was coming. There was no time to talk to him of international festivals, even though I tried, earning me a brutal kick from La Bella. The driver raised his hat, studied us, turned on the engine, and moved to the shoulder to let us through.

I looked without looking: his hat and half-hidden face looked familiar to me. Mentally I thanked him. He gave us permission to go as far as Arboletes, which was the distance allowed by the safe-conduct given to us by the area commander in chief in San José de Apartadó. They didn't let us in; night had not yet lifted, and they forced us to sleep on the other side of the trench where they were held prisoner and with which they thought they were protected.

They finally let us in at noon, when the sun was beastly; they took a look at the safe-conduct. It had expired; they had gotten rid of the military chief of the Army's 17th Brigade and chief of the paramilitary brigade Héroes de Tolova. He had been bumped off in an ambush between a slope and the rise of another hill.

It was in revenge for the death of eight peasants from San José de Apartadó, accused of supporting FARC: five adults and three children. The kids were thrown in by the paramilitaries for good measure.

"Did you guys see anything?"

All of us looked at one another, repeating a long-rehearsed scene, one of us with a quizzical expression; the other, Rodin, sort of pensive; the one over there scratching his head, broad gestures from the Grand Guignol, grotesqueries that hid the word in silence, allowing the spectator to form his own opinion, ideally the most obvious and mistaken one.

"Anyway, in the hall there's always someone who doesn't know how to see."

It started to rain; it rained for a week, keeping us stuck in Arboletes. That gave us a chance to wash our bodies and our clothes. Memory, though, didn't allow itself to be washed; someday it would peel off, making way for recollections. We drank, we drank our fill of rainwater that the children of Arboletes sold in plastic baggies, little bags that my daughter sucked on with delight. La Bella rested.

Together with the poorest inhabitants, in the huts farthest from the center and the trenches, we devoured a fried beef lung, black, elastic, still possessing hollows containing a bag of air that escaped when liberated by our teeth, adding a festive note to the banquet.

My daughter cut her first teeth on a strip of fried lung, like all the other children of the lost town of Arboletes.

The sea had eaten away the edge of town, and some of the houses teetered between suicide by being carried off by the waves and a collective death by fire.

A traveling photographer, one of those with a box camera, took our picture in the town square, sitting in front of a sign that proudly read "From Arboletes, with love." He gave it to us as a gift.

Every morning at daybreak, a van or a jeep would try to leave in order to break the siege; for six days they returned defeated.

"There's no way out."

On the seventh day, one of the jeeps didn't return.

It ran into a roadblock, fell into an ambush, fell off a cliff. By the walls of a church, someone asked, "Where should I mark this one down?"

Was he a drug trafficker? A guerrilla fighter? From which

group? FARC? ELN? Quintín Lame?[48] Was he with M19? EPL? [49] Was he a paramilitary? Was he from the army? Was he a smuggler? An estate owner? A combination of drug trafficker and something else? Was he part of a movement? A peasant? A peasant with a jeep? Friend or enemy?

At first we didn't ask what he was; we asked what he was at the end, because happily in the sway of drugs, they jumped from one band to another to justify their existence.

"We'd need to label their feet in order to avoid any mistake when we mark them down," said the guy who was wielding the pencil beside the walls of the church.

We all took off our shoes; I wrote, "director." La Bella took off our daughter's shoes and asked:

"Does it matter if it's the left foot or the right?"

The Second Prostitute, from far away, said:

"I want the left one for the sake of my people."

What a principled woman our *compañera* was!

A donkey passing by wanted to ask a question, but everyone made him keep his mouth shut.

"You don't screw around with principles."

It was the only time there was any unity in Arboletes.

"It must be on account of what they call political syncretism."

"Huh?"

"The right wing's speeches, declaring itself part of the so-

---

[48] Armed indigenous guerrilla movement, named for Manuel Quintín Lame Chantre (1889-1967), a freedom fighter who tried to establish an independent indigenous republic in Colombia.
[49] Ejército Popular de Liberación, or Popular Liberation Army, created in 1967.

cial vanguard, and the left a bunch of religious fanatics."

In the distance we could hear the sound of a motor approaching; it was a motor, not a power saw. It was the jeep – it hadn't fallen into an ambush, and already they were making it disappear! The driver emerged, soaked to the marrow in mud, smiled, proudly puffed up his chest, and said:

"The road is open."

We all ran to our vehicles and lined up. They checked us, not to see what we were carrying – that didn't matter one bit – but to see if we could make it through, lest we got stuck in the mud and blocked the way. Then the armed shadows could really fall on us, and there'd be no one left alive.

The guy who had been standing at the church started to sharpen his pencil.

They stopped in front of the car; using a ruler they measured the distance between the body of the car and the mud:

"This one won't get through."

"I'll carry it," said the truck."

"You already weigh too much."

Panicking, La Bella muttered, "But I've already written the baby's name on her foot."

They took pity on us; a trucker who was traveling empty offered to carry it. They brought two planks and we all pushed. Once it was mounted, they tied it down – the road is uneven, they explained – and what lay behind us was child's play.

"Quick, let's get going; the road under the white truck is eroding."

410

I hit the gas.

I delved into my memory to bid farewell to Arboletes with love.

Behind us, to one side of the volcano, was the lake of boiling mud that emerged from the belly of the earth; it was the fountain of eternal youth, the coveted one, the one that Ponce de León had been looking for and for which he gave his life; the one I ignored and would never return to, which made me mortal.

"At last we can rest," said the truck, rolling into Turbo on the tips of its wheels so as not to disturb anyone's sleep.

By way of welcome, empty streets awaited us; not even a cop to ask directions to an open store. We parked and got out in search of a place to buy a glass of warm milk for the baby and a cup of *agua de panela* for us.

Once again shadows cloaked the city; once again other shadows slinked along the walls, gray, frightened, devoid of personality, and there's nothing more dangerous than a frightened shadow, powerful and lurking in the crowd.

"They were those, they were the other ones, and in the end they were all the same, and what something *is* doesn't matter if in the end it's all the same: victim and assassin die locked in an embrace; today's torture victim and tomorrow's torturer both find themselves involved in the pleasure of making others suffer; the honest and the corrupt exchange I.D.'s so as to confuse us; roadblocks that are lifted to defend themselves from others or to kill others point in both directions.

"And what about human rights, the rights of the destitute,

the rights of the dispossessed of the earth?"

"Those are like traffic lights in Bogotá; after nine o'clock nobody pays attention to them."

A mantle of darkness blotted out the sun during the violence in Colombia. Nine death knells had tolled in Urabá.

The doors of a parking structure opened halfway. Rosi, two enormous dark eyes shining in the darkness, called out to us, "Come in."

I showed her my hole-riddled pockets.

"Quick, before they start shooting."

We drove in.

We spend the night huddled under the truck for protection.

"Cowards," the truck said in a noticeable French accent.

"Hey, quit screwing around," Rosi countered, in a noticeable *costeño* accent. To calm our fears we told one another stories. Rosi had only left Turbo once, to go to Medellín. She had been told that her sister worked there someplace, but she didn't find her. She never left town again. We told her that we came from the other side of the sea, that La Bella and I had met in Paris. She didn't say, "How romantic!" like everyone else; she didn't give a damn.

La Bella told her she was an actress. Her eyes twinkled in the darkness.

"Like the ones in the *telenovela*?"

"Like them, but live, in the theater. In one scene there's a brothel; I play a hooker."

A necklace of sparkling fireflies sparkling in her mouth joined her beautiful eyes.

412

"A loose woman?" she said, laughing, and, in a very soft voice (Rosi understands men's reactions), "But doesn't he get mad?"

"No, he put me to work there."

"Like my sister," pronounced the good Rosi.

I was about to talk to her about the violence in Chile, but I kept my mouth shut. I was embarrassed.

In Paris you'd say "Chile," and everybody knew all about it; you'd say "Pinochet" and everybody knew about it all too well. There was no need to talk about the brutality of the dictatorship, and the people were aligned against the dictator. In Paris you'd say "Colombia" and they'd reply "coffee"; you'd try to explain about the violence that rocked the country, and at most they'd get to the massacre on the banana plantations; that was clear, the army slaughtering the peasants who were striking against the United Fruit Company, two clearly established factions, and they knew about that massacre thanks to Gabo.[50]

Apparently, I reflected, in order to get through the night and the gunfire, people need familiar parameters so they can react in the face of violence. If you say "dictator" there, everybody reacts.

"Ah, the violence!"

Violence, in order to be recognized as such, needs to establish definite parameters: who the perpetrators are and who the victims. That's how one can identify oneself.

---

[50] Gabriel García Márquez, author of *One Hundred Years of Solitude,* a novel in which the massacre of the striking banana workers is vividly portrayed.

"Choose, milord, choose between the good guys and the bad guys."

"Please, give me a victim to make me feel less alone!" I begged.

On the other hand, when the factions aren't defined and there is generalized violence and everyone forms part of a single faction, all the parameters get confused. When it isn't clear who's who and one is both torturer and torture victim, kidnapper and hostage, mass murderer and one of the nameless dead, con man and con man, what varies are the numbers, and not by much: If I am you and you are me, no one understands a thing, and since what isn't understandable implies danger, people avoid talking about it; and in Paris you'll keep on saying "Colombia" and they'll reply "coffee," and if in Amsterdam you say "Colombian coffee," they'll bring you cocaine.

In Paris Colombians sang to Chile, "L'Amérique latine chante au Chilli," remember? In Paris when we Chileans sang to Colombia, we sang "La Piragua." It was less incriminating.

I promised to put El Gran Burumbún, the universal dictator, onstage, in order to explain the inexplicable: the violence in Colombia, our mirror image, whether we like it or not.

Rosi tapped me on the shoulder, "Have a *tintico*. It's time to go collect the dead."

XXVII. Of how Wang made him understand that the solution to his problems was in the hands of men, but that in order to reach them he had to call upon the gods

The sea was before me again; I approached it with respect. It had always represented a way out, perhaps because each wave represented a road; as each wave was born, it wrapped around me, dragged me, and delivered me to another wave, opening new horizons, new stages, infinite roads that allowed me to plunge into the maelstrom, my destiny.

I wet my body in the sea. I dipped my daughter in to wash away the mud from the volcano and open up her path toward death.

"O gods! I don't wish anyone eternal life; I don't wish any-one the straight, insipid path, the rail that imprisons the mind. I don't want anyone to be unable to see, to be unable to possess the word; I don't want anyone to pass through this world without pain, without mirrors, or without searching for a good soul.

"I don't want anyone to live in a circle with no way out, in the spiral of life, with no opportunity to walk through the spiral of death, without being able to slip between the spirals in order to create their own and drag their loved ones along in it.

"I don't want anyone to hate themselves," I said, filling my hungry mouth with sand so as to rediscover the lost flavors of my land.

I opened my eyes: there were the barges. Not all of them:

some of them were on the high seas, waiting their turn to dock for unloading and loading merchandise. They smuggled in cartons of cigarettes that they would sell individually in the poorest neighbor-hoods or to thieves who waited for customers on Carrera Séptima in Bogotá. In Chile they would sell handfuls of loose pasta, but in order not to humiliate anyone, they would offer them with the elegant query:

"Would you like some noodles in bulk, dear lady?"

"Let Don Pepe measure them," my mother used to say, "his fist is bigger than Doña Margarita's, but most important, never let la Chechi measure them – her hand is tiny."

However, I liked it best when Don Pepe's daughter meas-ured them; when she did, they had flavor, they gave life to the stiff spaghetti and made them curl around my sex, breaking down the flavorless barriers of hunger.

"And don't let them give you the broken ones."

Even in my memory she keeps bugging me, I thought.

"The thing is, you people can't sell them one at a time like everybody else; you're a consumer society," pronounced the Second Prostitute.

All that harassment made feel like hiring a hit man.

The barges carried away the cheap drugs: marijuana, crack and base; the expensive stuff was transported on fast launches, light aircraft, cargo planes, and in diplomatic suitcases.

"Are women's bodies and sex organs considered diplomat-ic suitcases?"

"More like wrapping papers. We live in a world where the most sacred things are thrown away, like broken spaghetti, poor spaghetti that wanders the earth, never finding a pot or an empty stomach, their destiny."

Everything went out on the surface of the sea or through the air. They still hadn't considered moving merchandise out beneath the sea: the cost was greater, and besides, they didn't need to hide. In Turbo everything was what it appeared to be, a giant trading center where everything was up for sale, everything could be bought, and if people killed one another, it was for business reasons and nothing else.

In Turbo it was all business, just like in the rest of Colombia.

The trip to the other side of the gulf wasn't long, about four nautical miles. When it was official business, they docked at Coco Solo; when it wasn't, at any inlet; the important thing was to get through the checkpoints.

"As you see, it's not very far, and the launches can handle it. What are you carrying?"

They consulted among themselves.

"Theater stuff's for Coco Solo; if it was anything else we'd drop it off at Punta Tiburón. We'll have to get our hands on some firm planks, load them up between two barges, wait for low tide, get the truck on there, balance the weight with the car, and that's it. You guys know how to swim, right?"

I asked if we could get through anywhere other than Punta

Tiburón. "It's just that I'm not a very fast swimmer," I explained.

"If you want to go as far as Costa Rica, talk to your countryman over there; he's got fast launches and connections. You'll find him in his office, on the second floor," one of them said, pointing to the bar across the way."

"Who do I ask for?"

"The Chilean."

The Chilean transported something else. He rigged his outboard motor launches so they'd be the fastest around. He knew how to balance the cargo so that if he had any problems he could toss it overboard in a flash. They were tricks of the trade. In his office he played poker; he never won, but he still played religiously. That's what brought him luck. One time he won, but he lost two launches and their cargo.

He got the message.

In Colombia, as in life, you've got to know how to lose in order to win.

That business with the barges was suicidal: we were going to become shark food. They'd never let us through – and they might not even let you on board – he told me *sotto voce*. "Go this way and they'll be able to help you."

In Colombia you have to know how to listen and follow advice.

How desperate I must have been, I the rebel, the anti-establishment one, the navigator of history, the derailed one: I took the advice.

418

"Some people never learn."

When I found myself in quicksand, I secured the rear guard: the truck and the actors stayed behind with Rosi. As I was about to sally forth on a road I hadn't chosen, I secured the vanguard: La Bella and my daughter accompanied me.

I crossed the border at Turbo: sea and jungle took turns blocking my path, not ropes, not roadblocks, not ambushes. The sea and the jungle, my allies, were abandoning me.

"We tried to protect you; what happened was that because you were so desperate, you wouldn't listen. You weren't able to read the signs of destiny and you took the wrong turn."

"That's something I took long ago."

A barrier! Armed guards! I was back in civilization.

I slammed on the brakes.

"Don't put on airs – they *made* you stop, which is something else altogether."

I found myself at the gates of an airport; I had seen light aircraft like monuments, DC 3's carrying drugs, but . . . an airport? A fleet of planes in the middle of the jungle? Since we were in Urabá, it was what it was: an airport with a flotilla of light aircraft.

A wire fence marked off the territory; above the main door was the motto, "Dreams make you free." Very nice, and below that, in small letters, "No Entry." The rest of the warning was delivered in the flesh: the guards' faces, plus a finger on the trigger.

"Six million, there were six million."

What could be worse for a theatrical director than to be aware that he's putting his loved ones in danger and to know it; to feel threatened and to know it; and not to understand how the guards managed, in one second, to transmit a message that combined life and death, or how they mix inert, brutal ink with throbbing flesh.

What a terrible thing it is to have to wonder enviously how they manage to control the audience with a single finger. *Svoboda*, my ass, to hell with cardboard props or the Black Theater; stop screwing around, brother – this was perfect. Maybe at last I'd found what I had been seeking for so long.

I asked to talk to the director.

Calls made, calls received, eyes staring at us, stares that we returned with more stares. Since we were blind, we won.

"You never learn!"

They opened the doors. An ATV escorted us to the main house.

At the entrance, a guy with a wooden expression was smiling. Pure Brecht – you have to keep the character at a distance, add a smile to his coolness so that the spectator can see beyond the wooden face and behind the smile.

That must be the Chilean, I thought.

Something wasn't quite right about the character: he had strength, but he didn't exhibit any signs of power; he stood tall, but his shadow reflected the servile posture of gray characters; he was one character, and yet he was an aggregate. The stage swallowed him up. This was the heart of the banana region, in the Gulf of Urabá, the zone where indiscriminate violence was our daily bread.

I opened my mouth.

"The Chilean, the guy who runs the launches, sent me. He told me you could help us."

After hearing us out, he said, "Come in, I'll ask the boss. He's not here, but we're expecting him today."

He wasn't the boss. His shadow didn't lie; he was a pencil pusher.

"Aside from being a moocher, is the gentleman an elitist?"

"The *compañero*," I corrected. Any traces of gentleman I had, I'd consumed along with the alpaca scarf.

He went off to contact him by radio, turned his head, and said:

"You can walk around. What you can't do is leave the camp."

The wires seemed to grow taller around the perimeter, from San José de Apartadó to the airport.

"You can't see the forest for the trees. The perimeter was just a tad bigger, brother."

I felt the way I did when they used to let us out on the patio from our cells, half prisoners and half free. The jailhouse two-step had expanded from six meters to a hundred.

Hours later they offered us a tray. The pencil pusher asked:

"You there, you know where you are, right?"

I didn't know.

"You know who he is, right?"

"No. The owner of the business, I imagine."

"The colonel is General Pinochet's honorary consul in Medellín. I think you came here to kidnap him and that the guerrillas are waiting on the other side of the wire fence."

Shadows began to creep up the wire fences and advance toward the airport. They were shadows of shadows, not of guerrillas, but ... how could I convince him!

"It's getting late. We have to go. My actors are waiting for me."

"We're protecting the colonel. You're not leaving here; you're the colonel's guests."

That was the first time my daughter slept in a big bed and not in the car, her willow basket, or a projector box, and the little scamp was happy.

The planes took off at dawn with their precious cargo. In a gesture of farewell, they flew by at low altitude. The maid of the house brought a glass of papaya juice – for the mother – and one of milk – for the little girl.

The pencil pusher allowed us to leave; the colonel was now safe. When we reached the main exit, we could hear over the loudspeakers:

"Tell the Chilean that the colonel sends him a message: don't be a fool."

Two weeks later the guerrillas emerged from the shadows

and jumped the fence. I swear I had nothing to do with that. I don't get involved in that kind of stuff.

In the parking lot in Turbo, my actors were waiting. In the municipal theater in San José, Costa Rica, where our season was to begin that very night, a poster announced:

"Performance canceled."

As I got out of the car, I was seized with a terrible doubt: Which of the two Chileans had the colonel been referring to?

A new circle formed around me, silently. Seven, plus the car and the truck.

"Six – you weren't in the circle."

"Seven. Rosi was there."

There's nothing more terrible for an actor than that accursed moment, feared by all, when he finds himself at center stage – spotlights on him to capture his expressions – and when the music disappears to make way for the word, his mind goes blank, he can't figure out what to say, he attempts a hand gesture in order to buy time, even worse, lost time, and even worse, the tension mounts.

And what's more beautiful for an actor than that moment when he finds himself at center stage, spotlights on him, the music disappearing to give way to the word, and the lines flowing, stripped of all artifice, to give way to tragedy.

But that wasn't my case.

In my memory I reviewed the paths of the labyrinth, the curves in the road. I imagined what was there at the end of the turns I didn't take; in the distance the doors of a hall slammed

shut; the barges had already left; the Darién jungle grew threaten-
ingly denser; outside my circle silence fell; inside the circle of
death they stopped for a minute. A voice inquired:

"Does anyone remember why we're fighting?"

The word returned to my lips.

"To Bogotá, even if we have to cross La Línea and pass
through Medellín again. I'm going on a hunger strike."

Even the truck laughed.

"Against whom? Strikes are always against someone."

"Against the devil, if necessary. We've got to find a way
out."

I sped up. My daughter was about to turn one year old.

As we were ready to cross the threshold, Rosi appeared.
She was all spiffed up, tottering in her high-heeled shoes. "They
say tall girls are the most in demand." She had painted her face
and covered her fingers with trinkets.

"You guys convinced me; give me a lift to Medellín. I'm going to work with my sister."

In time she became the most sought-after madam in the
region; her realm extended from Buenaventura to Turbo, passing
through Cali and Medellín; from Turbo to Barranquilla, Cartagena,
and Santa Marta. As Rosi knew their secrets and the drug routes,
all the *narcos* bowed down to her. People even say that she set up
a branch in Cuba. She was some businesswoman, that Rosi.

We dropped her off in Medellín and at the same time hid
the truck; it wouldn't have endured a second Palace of Justice.

One of the Colombian actors, the doctor, came out beforehand to alert the press. Napito came out beforehand as well, to

alert those who were disparagingly called "las locas,"[51] beings pursued by all the perpetrators of violence, decimated by an unknown disease, a new Egyptian plague, beaten by their own people, and who nevertheless survived by hiding even from the gods. How terrified they must have been!

In Bogotá, looking for a place to carry out my hunger strike, I went to a church in a shantytown. "Sanctuary!" I cried.

"My son, this isn't Notre Dame," the priest replied, closing the doors in my face.

I left a cross on the stairs leading to the church and walked away humming: *I come from Chiquinquirá, to keep a promise* . . .

I went to a friendly theater; they denied me a stage.

Once again I was in conflict: I preferred an open set to a closed one, questioning to declaring, the individual over the masses; I chose the human factor, hiding myself from the gods, and therefore they condemned me to exile and death.

I didn't go to the Government Palace where Eduardo was; you don't go to a friend's house to carry out a hunger strike against the world.

I didn't announce it in the street because I would've been taken for one of those poor wretches who wander through Colombia and throughout the world.

I passed by the Museum of Gold; I didn't begin my strike there because the splendor of all that appropriated wealth would have hidden my wounds.

---

[51] Slang term for queens, or flamboyant gays.

I passed by the place where Gaitán[52] was assassinated; I didn't strike there out of respect for the dead, lest hunger and need eclipse his memory.

From each of the steps of my staircases the road ahead of me was opened and closed again. Invisible walls appeared relentlessly, and my knotted stomach cried out:

"O gods! Give me a place where I can deposit my pain."

Santa Fe de Bogotá, the heart of Colombia, kilometer zero, City Hall.

I was on Carrera Séptima; all I had to do was run to Octava and continue on to Décima. Besides, I had a name there.

"Of course, City Hall," said the car, morphing into the truck.

"If this one keeps bugging me, I'm gonna put a diaper in the carburetor to seal it up."

At the end of the hall, to the left, on a heavy wooden door was the name of the councilman. I had met Fidel, his father, in Medellín while presenting *The Good Person of Szechuan*, and his sister in Sofia, not during the time of the forest of red banners, but at the time of no-one-moves, as decreed by the Teatinos. Which is to say, I had a pedigree worthy of my knocking at his door.

I briefly explained the situation to him: I need a place where I can go on a hunger strike. The press is waiting to cover the announcement.

---

[52] Jorge Eliécer Gaitán (1903-1948), prominent Populist leader and mayor of Bogotá. His assassination while campaigning for the Colombian presidency in 1948, led to El Bogotazo, a period of widespread riots.

It was true.

"Is the Second Prostitute in on this?" he asked.

"She knows everything."

It was true; she knew everything. Nothing moved in the Colombian theater scene without her knowing it. I had the impression he interpreted this as meaning she gave her approval.

"What time?"

"At exactly five in the afternoon, in homage to Federico."[53]

We had an agreement: we had to hurry. In Colombia agreements are in effect for as long as a life lasts.

At exactly five o'clock, passing among the journalists, the Second Prostitute and the Teatinos holed up in his office and shut the door, leaving us out in the hall.

Horrors! Where had they come from? And I thought I had gotten rid of the last of them in Buenos Aires.

I began my strike and the press conference in the hall, requesting a lamp under whose light I could create, a circle for moving my thoughts, for giving life to the characters, where there would be a gap between the actor and the watchdog, and a sigh between the actor and the spectator; where complicity would serve to give and preserve life, and death would disappear behind a mask; where the only wall would be a *svoboda* that could be crossed in a single step to emerge from the shadows. They had denied me a chicken coop to deliver myself to the world; now that they were denying me the world, I asked for a chicken coop.

Immediately after that, La Bella entre las Bellas took the

---

[53] An allusion to *Lamento por Ignacio Sánchez Mejías* by Federico García Lorca.

floor, telling of the ambushes, of the planes carrying drugs alongside the route, the roadblocks, the corruption, the *caimanes* crossing the muddy road, the man in the hat, the glass of milk for the baby, the lake of boiling mud bubbling up from the earth on the slope of the volcano in Arboletes, the . . .

"In Arboletes? You were in Arboletes? That's not possible," said the journalist.

From that moment on nobody believed that we had spent months traveling in the midst of violence, in the red zone, the same one that had been off-limits even to journalists.

Reactions are measured; envy is measured; incredulous silence is measured and can be felt; it penetrates bones, assails memory, creates doubt even in oneself.

La Bella felt it. She was an actress; she knew when speech was born of silence and when she needed to plunge into it so as to disappear from the stage. Slowly she looked at them and started to unbutton her blouse.

"I knew it," Rosi exploded in a burst of joy in a Medellín brothel. "I knew she was a loose woman."

And from between her breasts, she pulled out . . .

"A tit!" the incorrigible Rosi interrupted once more.

. . . a photo, which she circulated among the journalists.

Silence spread throughout the hall. They took the photo, looked at it, looked at us, lowered their eyes and passed it on. In it our faces were still visible, as well as a sign that read, "From Arboletes with love." They returned the photo to us almost reverently.

From that moment on we were able to say what we wanted and they would believe it, except for the doubting Thomases of the entire world, whose numbers included Fidel's son, the Second Prostitute, and the Teatinos, barricaded behind the heavy wooden door that separated us from the office.

"Before thanking you for your gracious presence, I'll take one final question – anyone?"

The heavy wooden door opened up; I separated my legs to offer greater resistance, tensed my mind, closed my eyes to see where the attack would come from, and opened my ears to recognize the voice.

"They're calling you from the Caracol chain, *caballero.*"

Caballero isn't the same thing as *compañero*. *Caballero* indicates distance; *compañero* indicates belonging. If the Second Prostitute says it, it implies sadomasochism; if the Teatinos say it, it implies a box with broken glass. If Fidel's son says it, it means they can send you off in a box.

I prefer distance. I, the indomitable, had to give up my title of *compañero* until the day when the word regained its meaning.

The last question from the Caracol journalist had a double meaning, not a malicious one. It was double; let's not forget I was in Colombia; I had to search for its real meaning:

"Why do you think I'm interviewing you over the phone, maestro?"

My mind started to gallop: with that "maestro," he was sending a sign of friendship; the telephone bit was more complicated. Someone, and I have my suspicions who, might have insinuated that he shouldn't cover the strike – but then he wouldn't have phoned, and he was talking to me live, on the air; that he might have been kidnapped for seeing what he shouldn't have seen, for saying what he shouldn't say, for being honest, which was probably a blunder, for wanting to find out what everybody knows that everybody knows but doesn't say, or simply for making trouble; after all, he was a journalist.

I took a deep breath, leaving the audience in suspense.

The answer came from that same journalist:

"The army has surrounded City Hall. No one can get closer than a hundred meters in any direction. The colonel in charge of the operation says that you desecrated the flag and the Colombian fatherland."

This business was becoming thicker than a Santander hot chocolate. For a military officer to say that the sacred symbols of the fatherland were desecrated was almost as serious as referring to a lieutenant as "sergeant" when one is a political prisoner.

I had been surrounded without realizing it.

You, Nedjma, woman-poem arisen from the earth, you, daughter of the union between desert and sea, for the second time you failed to warn me and took refuge in the shadows.

This time the wall enclosing me was very close at hand, and I kept on trying to break through more distant walls. The labyrinth closed in over my corpse.

The heavy door blocking the office opened wide. "Sanctuary!" I managed to exclaim before the Second Prostitute briskly walked by, followed by the Teatinos and Fidel's son, who, on leaving the hallway, said:

"I was tricked."

I never found out whom he was referring to. As I'm no uncouth slob, I replied, "Me too."

I doubt he wondered whom I was referring to; Fidel's son belongs to that group of men who don't wonder about anything.

"It's dangerous to wonder, my friend. You might find yourself looking into a mirror."

The journalists camouflaged us among themselves and spirited us out of City Hall, the second time in my life that journalists allowed me to get around a border.

As we were saying our goodbyes, they – journalists, after all – asked, "Where are you going to continue the strike?" I looked at the closed doors around me and replied, "In the street, which I never should have left."

For seven days I wandered through the streets of Santa Fe de Bogotá. Every two days, supported by Napito's circle, I sent a press release together with a nurse's report documenting the progress of the hunger strike: the subject's oral mucus is beginning to dry up; skin is losing elasticity; his eyes are growing dimmer. There was no mention of the rumbling in my guts; it might have called their attention to our presence.

On the seventh day I was handed a note from the President's cultural director; the President had joined him to find a solution.

"It's not easy, you know; there are many strings to pull."

Eduardo would act as mediator.

Two days later we suspended the hunger strike. A way out of the labyrinth had been found; all that was necessary was to clear the path to reach that exit. Nothing is easy in Colombia; "yes" means "no," or in the best-case scenario, "maybe"; silence is a scream, and those were the parameters in which we were allowed to move. We were returning to age-old customs, to the first civilizations: madmen and troubadours are to be respected, brother. We are a part of them; in them our memory resides.

"You broke down the borders; the director isn't talking about Colombia."

"And we're not talking about our dead; our massacres are your massacres; our labyrinths have no way out."

Once more the sea offered me a way out.

"A way in, not out. Some people never learn."

The manager of the Gran Colombiana merchant fleet had been an actor, and his destiny had always been linked to water, and therefore to mine.

"I'm the official water carrier for this province. My work is tiring: giving drink to the thirsty. Everyone says that only the gods can help them," said Wang the water carrier, smiling at me.

"My good Wang, I am the Third God. Only men can help me."

"He's not following the script," the Second Prostitute said.

"None of the three were gods, just actors, and for your information, I'm not the water carrier, and if it's a good person you're after, you have to know how to find one."

At which curve did I take the road to barbarity?

At what moment was I taken prisoner for going from darkness to light, only to hide myself in darkness again?

At what moment did the red banners lose their color and their meaning?

At what moment did the mask point toward my insides, leaving my face exposed?

At what moment did actor and spectator merge into one?

At what moment did my spirals crash together, with one changing the other and its destiny?

At what moment, my dear Wang, did you discover that we weren't gods?

"From the beginning. You can tell that the gods don't work, but they eat well, and as for you, well, to be honest, you were a pathetic sight."

"It's just that I finished eating the alpaca scarf long ago; I gave the last little piece to our daughter so she could dip it in the glass of milk."

I had 21 days left to organize my departure from Colombia.

"Discreetly, please."

There's nothing more unrealistic than asking a theatrical director to be discreet.

"Within 21 days one of the ships from the Gran Colombiana line will make a stop in Santa Marta and take you all on board."

"Where to?" I asked, adopting my actors' line.

"Le Havre, with a stopover in Rotterdam. It's the first one to leave, and it'll give us time to organize the loading of the truck and the group. From there you can continue overland to Paris, but you're familiar with that."

Paris! Once again in my journey, La Bella's image that first time crossed my mind; how different it was from the scarecrow that stood beside me now!

"O gods, how could I have gotten my loved ones involved in this madness!"

In my mind I asked forgiveness, I, the one who never begs or relents, the one incapable of taking the wrong turn and yet who never took the right one, I, the maker of words, remained speechless with pain. La Bella, with our daughter in her arms, looked at me.

I,
the actor who begged for an audience,
asked them not to look at me, please,
not with those eyes.

I,
the one who defied the rules,
asked them to show me one that would justify me.

I,
The one who dies in order to be reborn,
Asked them to deny me a second chance.

I,
the dispossessed
the actor

the witness
invoked the void that precedes the word,

I,
who loves light,
invoked the shadows
to hide from the gaze
of La Bella and my daughter.
I,
the nonbeliever,
invoked Neptune
so he would allow us to cross
the great waters.

I,
the merciless,
forgave myself,
because I am unforgivable,
I had to end my wanderings.

Since I had forgiven myself, I had to continue my mental journey without remorse. I wondered what had become of the Black Hand, if he would remain in the shadows or if he had been rehabilitated. I wondered about the destiny of the little gray men, regulators of dreams, tireless builders of walls. I wondered why they had erased me from history just as they erased yesterday's idols from official photos or destroyed solitary monuments built with marble that was stolen from graves, just so they would die again.

O gods!
I exist and have a right to the word,
I have a right to possess it,
to love it,
to sully it,
to devour it,
to spit it out onto a stage,
or deposit it gently on other lips, in a kiss.
O gods, I exist,
without wanting to, I exist!
O gods, give me back my past; without it I have no future.

My present does not exist, but that doesn't matter to me;
it died imprisoned between the past and the future.

"By the way, the baby is another problem; according to international agreements we can't take her on board; we'll have to find a way to get her out with her mother."

Things were beginning to get stirred up, as if they'd ever been calm . . .

They gave us a safe-conduct valid up until the time of our departure. They sent me to see the person in charge of controlling imports and exports in Colombia, securing me an appointment in Tequendama and not at his office. Too many precautions, I thought.

"What an evil mind," said the truck from its hiding place in

Medellín.

An evil mind, true: walking into his private office was like walking into the Thousand and One Nights, Aladdin's lamp, the stories that filled my childhood, but all mixed together: Ali Baba's cave seemed small in comparison. It was the largest, but safest, contraband center in Colombia.

He gave me the papers for getting the car out; he showed me the two tickets for La Bella and the baby, but those he handed over later. He's got to want something in exchange, I thought, sensibly.

"The car registration papers are missing," I said.

"My wife has always dreamed of a gold car, and next week is her birthday."

"But, just like us, the car has no papers."

"It does, as well as Bucaramanga plates."

"What?"

"The tickets in exchange for the keys."

I handed him the keys and even thanked him.

Leaving his office, La Bella said to me, "We're free. At least he had the decency not to ask us to sing her Happy Birthday."

"True – as singers we'd die of hunger."

"Just as singers?" said the truck.

"How did it go?" asked the cultural chargé d'affaires.

"Perfectly, this time it's all in the bag," I replied.

The only piece missing was the guy from Medellín. For some reason the local customs boss didn't want to let me go, and I had to pass through La Línea and Medellín. Surely it would all end there.

I went over to a friend of the Second Prostitute's, thinking he would know if she was the one pulling the strings behind the scenes.

"No, what an evil mind."

A clever mind: the friend knew someone important, an old schoolmate whom he'd known since they were street urchins; later they went their separate ways, found themselves on different sides, one of them a general, the other, well, the other . . . For propriety's sake I'll just say he wasn't exactly a general. But, just like on roads, at night there's a certain magic that breaks the rules, and the fact that they'd played soccer together, had gone after the same girls, had gotten drunk together on their first *aguardienticos*, was worth more than any rank on either side.

The general wished me a safe trip, "And remember, theater people will always be welcome in Medellín; I'll take care of the guy from Medellín."

And so he did.

With time flying toward exactly five o'clock in the afternoon, I stopped.

One: to celebrate our daughter's first birthday. A year-and-a-half had passed since La Bella left Paris, a year and nine months since we created her in the City of Light; a year and six months since I told her, at Charles de Gaulle Airport, that I'd see her in a couple of weeks; a year since she was born in Cali, Colombia; nine months since she was stolen from me at the Manizales Festival.

After blowing out her first candle, I gave her a kiss and said, "See you in . . ."

Her mother shot me a lethal look.

Two: to bid farewell to Eduardo. In the hallway I bumped into the Second Prostitute, who was coming out of his office.

I trembled.

"I told you so, even the bravest of the brave tremble at La Línea, and the Second Prostitute is its reincarnation," said the truck.

"What are you people doing here?" she asked. "Did you come to see the doctor?"

"Eduardo," we replied, with no subtlety in our accent to emphasize the difference.

"Do you know him?"

"He's a friend." The triumph of the word needs to be short so it can be a triumph. And we walked into the office.

When he saw our faces, Eduardo said, "Don't worry, as Peace Commissioner I've gotten her a gig in Florence. That'll keep her away for however long you need."

We said our goodbyes. As we reached the door, Eduardo added, "Don't say goodbye to Napito; it's like saying goodbye to the Second Prostitute. Remember, in Colombia not everything is what it appears to be."

"Good luck!" he cried, when in fact he was the one who needed it most.

I took the bus to the outskirts of Medellín, descending another step on my staircases. At dawn I entered the parking lot to pick up the truck. It was in a corner, sad, crushed, its back doors wide open.

"They raped me," it said miserably.

"Don't worry, brother, it wasn't your fault. We left you alone too long." And before it could ask me anything, I added:

"She's in Bogotá." I didn't have the heart to tell him that the car was now in other hands and there it would remain.

Like old acquaintances trying to relive the past, we crossed jungle and mountains, skirting frozen ambushes, and smiling whenever people from both sides called out to us:

"You guys are still screeching around here."

We rolled down the windows to let in the light and drive away the shadows; we let in the sound of the *tiple* and the drums; we climbed steps, dizzily sliding onto the next one; we joyfully took the wrong turns. I think once we even took the right one, approaching the port: the boat on the high seas in the mist, us on land, from the shadows.

In Santa Marta we headed for the foothills of the Sierra Nevada, to an Arawak refuge run by a former ELN member, a woman who had demobilized.

Safe harbor.

The next morning we went to the port. The boat was at the dock; between the boat and us, a double circle of military.

"We have orders to inspect your cargo."

They removed everything from the truck. Behind every soldier, a professor or student from the Universidad de Santa Marta.

"We're here to make sure they don't plant anything on you."

They dismantled everything, even the projectors. A little tin soldier asked for a souvenir. I opened a box, took out a book, and gave it to him. It was *Eternal Curse on the Reader of These Pages.*

When it was time to embark, the truck looked around and said to me:

"The car's not here."

I explained what had happened, that they didn't want to let me leave, and that it was either the car or my daughter. I asked him to forgive me.

He forgave me, or at least he said he did, but something in him had broken; his heart was mortally wounded.

The former ELN member and demobilized commander was caught in an ambush as she climbed the Sierra Nevada to rescue some Arawaks who were trapped in gunfire between the drug traffickers and the narcoguerrillas. She survived, but was confined to a wheelchair.

"Then you're the one who brings bad luck?" said the truck.

"No, it's the times; the times and those who tried to set down history."

The boat took me away from the continent. Once again solitude, disguised as immensity, the labyrinth, threw me into another labyrinth with three cabins. In the first, the director; in the second, the Colombian actress going into exile for the third time – the first had been in Salamina, Caldas, during the violence; -- in the third, a mysterious figure who came up on deck only at night; by day he remained enclosed in his cabin. Nobody knew his name.

"Nobody? In Colombia?"

It was the former Minister of Justice. He had seen his shadow during that business at the Palace of Justice. From Nariño Palace he asked for dialogue and a ceasefire. He was a friend of Gaitán, a friend of Bonilla, who had been Minister of Justice and whom he succeeded in that post when Bonilla was assassinated.

He fought drug traffic; extradited criminals, and openly, revealing his identity, tried to return dignity to Colombia.

Today he was traveling in the third cabin, never showing his face, emerging only at night to converse with the stars.

The *narcos* had promised he'd get what was coming to him.

For his own safety, he was being taken out of the country; they sent him to the other side of the Iron Curtain, supposedly out of the reach of corruption and the *narcos.* He was to occupy the post of ambassador in Hungary.

Safe harbor.

They nabbed him in Budapest on January 13, seven months later.

The Colombian *narcos* were people of their word; they kept their promise.

It was 11:30 in the morning; they pumped six bullets into him, destroying his face, his hands. Six.

And Enrique Parejo, the ex-Minister of Justice, remained alive.

"Maybe the gods changed the trajectory of the bullets; after all, he was a candidate for being a good person."

"Then it's true you were hanging out in the center of the action, a real hot potato."

"Not just any hot potato, brother – a hot *Criollo* potato. They're smaller, but they burn hotter. They come from the red zone."

Dock of Mist

Are you sure, o stranger, that you have not taken a wrong turn? And since you are noble, or so it appears despite your misfortune, wait where you are while I consult the dwellers of this place. No need to go as far as the city.

They will decide if you are to remain here or continue on your way.

Sophocles, *Oedipus in Colonus*

XXVIII. Of what he discovered at the end of the day

Dawn was breaking.

The mist began to lift over the dock at Le Havre.

From the window of my cabin I hoped to spy a bar, one of my refuges, the bustling bars of the port, and inside them, sailors, rogues, and prostitutes. Among them, Jean, with a cigarette dangling from the left corner of his mouth, and Nelly, young and fragile, seeking protection and love. In the distance, among the shadows of the cranes, you could see the Casa de la Cultura, and on its roof a video camera indiscreetly recording the scene.

A shadow blocked my view; it was the truck, which as it descended, announced:

"I'm French; drop me off at Le Havre."

We were in Rotterdam! Someone didn't read the script.

Through the window I noticed three circles on the dock: the police, the customs office, and in the third, La Bella, together with representatives of the United Nations refugee office; that was what the sign said.

The police, the circle of security, carried off the former minister in a flash.

I took a deep breath.

Those from the customs office checked the truck; it was coming from Colombia. They removed everything, even its shoes.

The third circle was there to protect me from the other two;

447

since I had spent more than a year-and-a-half outside Europe, I had to start again from scratch and tell my story.

I remained silent.

They took us to The Hague, to a factory that had been taken over by the Okupas.[54] They received us with open arms; they, the link between the streets and a roof; they, who cracked locks to give meaning to the city; they, the wretched of The Hague, harbored life before the tribunal of history.

The truck slept in the cobblestone street in front of the factory, at the edge of a canal. Just like in Arboletes, rain began to fall and flood the street.

The next day it wasn't there. I saw it sailing along the canal, Columbus' sail fluttering on its roof. They say it was on its way back to look for the car.

The Trappist monks of Emmaus took us away to dress us in a semi-ruined church. La Bella and I held hands as we walked in, our son beginning to walk in her womb, our daughter walking close beside us, lest anyone steal her from me.

The benches languished in the main nave. Light filtered through the broken stained-glass windows, tracing circles and reflections on the altar, which, devoid of crucifixes, cried out for life. At the back of the church an old organ bellowed three notes to call attention to itself.

---

[54] A social movement that reached its peak in the 1960s and '70s, dedicated to the appropriation of unoccupied land and housing and their conversion into public spaces for social, cultural, and political objectives.

Along one side of the altar, beggars would enter; along the other side, a prostitute, not the Second one, but the First, Rosi. In the tabernacle she would deposit a pot full of food . . .

"And now what?" La Bella interrupted me.

I closed my eyes, looked toward the altar, climbed the final step.

And I smiled . . .

About the Author

Gustavo Gac-Artigas, writer, playwright, actor, theater director, and publisher, was born in Santiago, Chile, "but raised in Temuco," as he would immediately add. Since 1995, after living by mounting and disassembling pyramids, operating rooms, temples, and magical tenement rooms in France, the GDR, Bulgaria, Holland, Puerto Rico, Argentina, Peru, Bolivia, Ecuador, Colombia, Switzerland, Denmark, Tunisia, Belgium, and various other countries that fragile memory stores in oblivion, he resides in New Jersey, United States.

"Chile? Chile in my heart, as Pablo would say."

He is a contributing member of the Academia Norteamericana de la Lengua Española (ANLE).

About the translator

Andrea G. Labinger, professor emerita of Spanish at the University of La Verne, holds a PhD in Latin American Literature from Harvard. Labinger has published numerous translations of Latin American fiction and is a three-time finalist in the PEN USA competition. Among her translated titles are Ángela Pradelli's *Friends of Mine* (Latin American Literary Review Press, 2012) and Ana María Shua's *The Weight of Temptation* (University of Nebraska Press, 2012). She received a PEN/Heim Translation Award for her work on Guillermo Saccomanno's *Gesell Dome* (Open Letter, 2016).

Praise for Gac-Artigas' works:

And All of Us Were Actors

"Gac-Artigas engages in dialogue with diverse literary voices that . . . reflect on the meta-reality of literature, whether in theatrical, narrative, or poetic form: Shakespeare, Neruda, Brecht, Dante, Cervantes, Joyce, Homer . . . We readers rise and are born with him, as the narrator invokes Neruda, who in turn invoked the vigorous Incan people in *Heights of Machu Picchu*." Moisés Park, *Revista de la Academia Norteamericana de la Lengua Española,* Vol. V, 20 September 2016).

"... the lyricism and different levels of interpretation found in this marvelous journey to the interior of the American continent . . . of the theater . . . [and] of the mind of this actor and witness throughout his journey across the century . . . capture the reader's desire to immerse himself in the story so as to discover, along with the protagonist, the brutality and beauty of a century that cannot leave us unmoved."
(*Resonancias.org,* 3 January 2016).

Tiempo de soñar (*It Was a Time to Dream*, 1992): "Imaginative writing of extreme theatricality and fiction (based on occasionally recognizable history facts) that results in a halogenic, personal, and unique text" Severo Sarduy, Paris.

¡E il orbo era rondo! (*And the World Was Round*, 1993): "I was greatly impressed by the playful treatment of time and the interplay of the historical, the mythological, and the surreal. A difficult, but

worthwhile, book, more like an epic poem than a novel", Edith Grossman, New York.

Other titles by Gustavo Gac-Artigas

Narrative:

Y la tierra era redonda (And the World Was Round). 2nd edition; 1st edition in digital format.

Tiempo de soñar (*It Was a Time to Dream*), 2nd edition; 1st edition in digital format.

El solar de Ado, 2nd edition; 1st edition in digital format.

Ado's Plot of Land, 2nd edition; 1st edition in digital format.

Dalibá, la brujita del Caribe (Dalibá, the Caribbean Witch)

Un asesinato corriente (An Ordinary Murder)

Theater:

Cinco suspiros de eternidad (Five Sighs of Eternity)

Gonzalito o ayer supe que puedo volver (Gonzalito, or Yesterday I Learned I Can Return)

El huevo de Colón o Coca-Cola les ofrece un viaje de ensueños por América Latina (Columbus' Egg or Coca-Cola Offers You a Dream Voyage to Latin America)

Te llamamos Pablo-Pueblo (We Call You the People's Pablo)

El país de las lágrimas de sangre (The Land of Bloody Tears)

Made in the USA
Middletown, DE
21 September 2022

10931385R00272